THE BEAST OF
BABYLON

Rise and Fall of the Last Dictator

a novel

J WAYNE ANDERSON

ISBN 978-1-0980-0308-1 (paperback)
ISBN 978-1-0980-0309-8 (digital)

Christian Faith Publishing, Inc.
832 Park Avenue
Meadville, PA 16335
www.christianfaithpublishing.com

Printed in the United States of America

ABSTRACT

Steven Alexander, being raised in a Christian home with loving parents, falls victim to Satan's influence, not quite accepting the salvation of Jesus Christ, believing that being a good person, treating others fairly, honestly, and with kindness and a degree of holiness is good enough. He quickly finds the folly of this belief when he's not taken when Christ returns at the rapture.

This is the story of the world of the Antichrist and Steven's personal survival of enduring the Tribulation without taking the mark of the beast. He knew God's wrath upon those who do. All prophecies of Scripture of the "after the rapture" is remarkable in the details of what events will happen but does not tell us the how they will take place. This story fills in the how with imagination and conjecture based upon today's technology, weaponry, and cyberpsychological possibilities.

CONTENTS

INTRODUCTION

The Beast of Babylon is unlike traditionally written novels. Authors of novels create their plots, the content, and the endings. I could not. The script of this story is already set by Scripture. The outcomes, heaven or hell, are known as well as much of the prophecies (that make up the content and plot) are predetermined.

So much of the prophetic Scriptures are the foretelling of the what of various events to take place in the days of the Lord. And in some cases, when. *But* very little is told of the how they are to happen. Some of the events are specifically described as to when they're to occur relative to each other; however, most of the when is vague. This leaves that the chronology of all the events prophesied cannot be factually known or told. All of us must concede there are many mysteries in Scripture that can never be unfolded until after the Lord's return! This is particularly true with the content of Revelation and the many prophetic Scriptures.

The story of *The Beast of Babylon* is portrayed with humble imagination filling in the details of the unknown and a hint of human nature when man's heart is voided from the influence of the Holy Spirit. I have taken the approach that everyone who had knowledge of these times who are left behind at the rapture will, in vivid detail, recall what they had known about the Scriptural foretelling before that event.

Then is the Scripture "It is appointed for man once to die and after that the judgment" (Heb. 9:27), which indicates that there remains a chance for someone who is living at the time of the rapture but left behind to still find salvation during the Tribulation, though nearly impossible (Rev. 7:14).

Part 1 of the story are glimpses into some of the more significant events taking place in the world indicating the last days in which we are surely living at the time of this book's publication. Not any of the events must be fulfilled before the rapture can take place—the rapture (called the Event in this story) can take place at any time. Next week? Tomorrow? Yet today—or yes, tonight? And that brings us all to one question: Where will you be in the morning if you die tonight?

Read the book to know your possibilities in the future.

About those who think they do not need to concern themselves about what happens on earth after the rapture because they won't be here when the Tribulation occurs. I can see your point. But consider this. Please.

"For we must all appear before the judgment seat of Christ that each one may receive what is due him for the things he has done, whether for good or bad" (2 Corinthians 5:10). Let me ask you this. Knowing what you know about what the Book of Revelation describes of what takes place after the rapture, do you actually believe you can do nothing about telling others about what the Bible teaches about this and not be held accountable on that judgment day? There has to be a reason that God uses 80 percent of Revelation (seventeen chapters) about a seven-year space of time out of all history! Don't you think it's important? God does.

One of the most fundamental reasons God called me to write this is for the believers to purchase copies of this story for the purpose of distributing them to unbelievers who they know.

PREFACE

The beginning of this Scriptural interpretation of prophecies for this book was 1962.

My parents owned a novel entitled *The Mark of the Beast* (1933). We lived in the basement of a nine-bedroom house in which rooms were rented to University of Oregon students in Eugene, Oregon.

The house manager, Barry, seemed to me was enrolled at the university more for partying than getting an education.

My folks gave the book to Barry with the encouragement to read the story, hoping it would do some good.

It certainly did. One morning we heard a frantic knocking on the door just after 2:00 a.m. When the door was opened, he was standing there in his pajamas and blurted out, "How can I avoid this?" He was literally scared to salvation, accepting the Lord on bended knee with my folks that morning.

He changed his courses of study and three years later became the Youth for Christ director in Eugene, then went to seminary, and entered the ministry.

Over many years, I have tried to find a copy of this book. No luck. Then one day, quite many years ago, I knew God instructed me to write it. (At the time, I had no clue I could write.) He would guide me when the time to write it would be in his timing. But what I discovered, the Lord was waiting for me to have my heart where it should be. He wanted fertile ground to work with. He had a lot of work to do in my life!

And one day, as in a conversational voice, I heard him tell me to get started. I guess he thought I was ready to write what he called me to do. It was 2006. Study, listen, write, study, listen, write; it has been quite the journey learning from the Lord. I only pray that I got it right!

Some had told me I better get it done quickly because the Lord could come before it gets published! That could be, so the timing couldn't be more apt.

The advent of today's hundreds of technologies has made Christ's return in the clouds, the rapture, to be more realistically possible to occur in this generation than any other generation of history! So I wrote what God had inspired in my mind's eye and imagination by asking hundreds of times, how? How can *that* happen?

My finite mind cannot wrap around the how of most of the Book of Revelation. Maybe we're not meant to know how. One thing I got though: While man tries to explain stuff, God just does it. If we can explain something, then we're satisfied in some way. Sometimes, why can't we just accept the fact that God created this earth, and so, being the Creator, he can instantly make the things happen as prophesied? Does it take too much faith?

This book is relevant for today. It's vital to anyone who needs to understand the results of not accepting Christ as their personal savior.

This book was written for two reasons: Primarily, to warn those who have never accepted Christ as their savior; and then, if you have accepted him, I pray this book, *The Beast of Babylon*, will inspire you, ignite you to warn as many as you are able to while they have a chance! Those are the only two reasons this book has found its way into your hands.

Relevant to all of history and compared to eternity, God has to have some reason John's vision consumes seventeen out of twenty-one chapters of the Book of Revelation to tell us of only seven years! He must consider those seven years as really important. Important enough for us to get it!

The Book of Revelation is not one to get dogmatic about. What is important is that what John saw is that we understand those things will indeed happen.

Through John's visions, as guided by the angels, God has provided a map of events we know to occur. God will direct, allow, and make his final judgment just as he says he will.

Referencing the writings of authors of books, as listed in "Alphabetical List of References," will provide you with some of the material I used to create *The Beast of Babylon* to provide interpretation and understanding of the Book of Revelation. I say *some*. Mostly, I spent unknown hours studying Scripture on my own while praying for understanding and preparing to write what God had laid on my heart.

I must admit the writings of those who have years of scriptural prophetic understanding has been of great assistance in my understandings to write this book. I am just a simple layperson, by no means a learned man. Nor do I consider myself to have any special knowledge of prophecy or the Book of Revelation than what anyone can learn. Let me warn you, however, that to put the pieces together and into a resemblance of order as prophecies indicate, while understanding the severity of the ending results, does not come easy.

It is, in my opinion, why there is a special blessing in store for every person who studies the Book of Revelation and with understanding to "take to heart" (Rev. 1:3).

May God bless you as you read of the prophetic truths as he has blessed me. So I ask you, how are you and Jesus, the savior of the world, getting along?

ACKNOWLEDGEMENTS

I must thank the following persons who contributed their input for the writing the Beast of Babylon; Johanna my wife for her supportive insight and patience; my pastor, Scott Lidbeck for providing countless hours of hia valuable time with me to share his discernment, consultation, and sharing of scriptural knowledge; Kristie Slette who offered valuable wisdom of storytelling connectivity; Jennifer McKay for her contributing a clear understanding of cohesive family relationships; Roland Joy for his hours of discussion and determined questioning of prophetic truths; and Darlene Day (now deceased) for her broad and accurate input to assure thought clarity. Without any of them this story could not have been written with such meaning and hopefully, desired impact. I thank each for the glory of our Savior, Jesus Christ.

PROLOGUE

I saw it all happen! What the Bible prophesied centuries before, I actually witnessed—me, a professor of philosophy in what I knew to be the last days. I should have known. I was brought up in an evangelical Christian home but chose to not follow what I thought was well-intended instruction by my mother.

In less than an hour after the sunrise of the mostly peaceful eastern America horizon, the event the world had been waiting for will strike without warning. Millions had waited with great anticipation, billions of other people, however, with equivalent fear. The Event, the rapture, happened.

This is the beginning of what I believe to be the most chaotic time man has ever known, to last possibly, for a few years! Maybe a decade God will allow Satan to have his way with those of us who are left behind, save for a few chosen to be protected. I, unfortunately, was not one of the protected. I am completely on my own. Every decision is mine alone. God is nowhere to be found. I have only the memory of what I had learned before that moment, an instant when everything changed in and of the world. I am extremely lonely and far worse off than merely being alone. There isn't a single person to turn to who I trust—no one.

Everyone feels the same as I. We're without hope anything would ever return to be the same. It quickly increased of lost morals than what the worst had ever been before.

Now, God's time of judgment has come! Over one-fifth of the living throughout the world disappeared as quickly as a blink of an eye. They simply vanished. And I definitely knew why and where to.[1]

I'll fall wholly short of words or thoughts to describe what had taken place as I lay some kind of an understanding for it all.

In cities, the most heartrending scream is the terrifying sound of mothers crying for their babies—missing, gone. Their chilling anguish heard in spite of the startling, eerie sounds of the crashing of cars, trucks, buses, and other vehicles suddenly without their drivers. It's the disappearance of the babies of what clued me in; in the baby's innocence, they were taken too.

Most people knew what has just taken place, millions did not, leaving them totally clueless.

But I knew.

A new sense overcame everyone, by total surprise, as a vacuum of an emptied space, an unpleasant force, overcame us. Somehow we felt different—became different.[3] Evil filled our hearts. No power of our own to shake it loose. We were left without conscience. No behavioral censoring; we were without moral restrictions. Thoughts of wickedness now reign with malicious results unchecked. No one escaped the new unlawfulness! Previously nice folks, the young, elderly, moms, and of all people, ministers—every human is an evil being. Those who lived good lives now have hardened hearts.

There's no responsibility imposed for any wrongdoing of one upon another. Or mayhem inflicted. Criminals are naturally more prone to their evil tendencies now that they're without accountability.

Committing atrocious acts upon one another, which we would have shunned before the rapture, takes place easily. I've found myself in a new, corrupt world order.

Within moments, chaos flared up; there's confusion, alarm, and anguish as the world slowly realizes persistently what has taken place and that we're all imprisoned into it.

Churches are being broken into as answers are sought with honest explanations. No one, it seems to me, was told it would be *this* bad! They're all asking, "Why were we not warned of this?" *But we were warned.* I for one heard about it—often, in fact, but didn't *listen*. Just as most wouldn't listen when we had the chance!

Within hours, police stations are too overcome to continue their purpose, that is, keeping peace. Police forces are rapidly dismantling as a substantial number of their officers disappeared. All forms of laws, ordinances, and enforcement now useless.

The same has taken place too of fire departments. Their number is drastically depleted too. Fires everywhere have broken out triggered by looters and open malice.

Hospitals and health clinics are quickly being vacated by large numbers of physicians and nurses. Bedlam triggering accidents and critical injuries are rapidly increasing moment by moment so severe they can no longer be cared for.

Businesses, schools, and government offices are shut down; there's too many missing executives, staff, teachers and administrators, and government workers to carry on any slightest resemblance of *before*. The wheels of commerce and government have fallen off.

Banks have not escaped the disarray. Worse than the 1930s crash, there are thousands of patrons waiting for banks to open, but they won't, no matter how desperately the mobs want their money. They're frenzied, ready to break down doors without thought beyond what they would do once inside; the money is put away, secure, in the bank's vault protected by the latest security technology.

Store owners, like the rioters and looters, are in a panic mode, having a sordid resolve—not in the least hesitant to open fire at trespassers or looters. They are willing to be at risk to be shot or seriously maimed as they protect their store from being pilfered. More often than not, spouses are forced to watch their mate killed, battered, or sexually attacked.

People, who being away from home when the world is being turned upside-down, if they could drive a car or get their hands on any vehicle, sped home beyond safe speeds as possible. But roadways however have become obstacle courses by many broken-down or out-of-gas cars and trucks blocking passage. At times, adding to this disarray, drivers in their panic mode collided into the stalled vehicles. Some died in those collisions, their bodies left unattended for days.

Food has become the primary target during this spell of panic and pandemonium. Everywhere, pilferage of grocery stores, quick markets, supermarkets, and even restaurants is rampant. Quickly shelves are emptied by looters who had no hesitation to harm or even kill owners attempting to safeguard their merchandise to get what they want. Even employees turned against their employers. The looters are not just typical opportunistic thieves. Now the looters are moms, young kids, old people, parents, and everyday otherwise honest people. Within three days, the shelves became bare and destroyed.

Knives and guns along with ammunition are gone from the sport shops. Everyone seems to possess a gun. It's safer to assume that others do than to assume they don't, what with the new evil mind-set of one and all.

Before *the Event*, every single item we bought was at some time transported by truck. Food, water, clothes, batteries, etc. of all the things needed in a catastrophe formally came by way of trucks and trains. Now those trucks and trains are not running. Some trucks departed from their docks only to be prevented to negotiate around the stalled or broken-down vehicles on roadways and streets. Slow-moving or stopped trucks are immediately vandalized. The drivers are fatally shot or beaten beyond recognition.

Former places of distribution where supplies, merchandise, food, and medicines could be bought now cease to be open. Factories, of course, have shut down too. All for the same reasons that commerce had stopped: too many missing employees and an acute shortage of inventories. UPS, the US Postal Service, and FedEx cease to function; thousands of drivers and support personnel have vanished or, if not, have not reported for work.

Nursing homes, convalescent and health centers, and clinics, even though there are overwhelmed physicians, they're without replacement of medicine; once what is on shelves is gone. Hundreds of thousands of patients will soon be forced to endure the agonies of pain and repercussions of diseases and infirmities. There is no relief. An incalculable number face death and die for the lack of needed medicine.

Sports, recreation, entertainment, and leisure time is cancelled and replaced by mere survival of the new violent, rampant behavior.

The reason for all of this, I know, is that the restraining power that once held evil in check by the mass number of born-again Christians is gone;[3] the function of goodness in the world, by the Holy Spirit, is also removed from the earth. Satan now has full reign to do with man as he wishes. And he's succeeding quickly. It is this evil causing unspeakable atrocities of one person upon another for no reason other than that they can. I should have known it would be this way. Me, of all people!

It has quickly become the jungle where the fittest live. It is of no consequence of what one thinks of their selves; a bigger, stronger, smarter, or more violent aggressor comes along. The stronger men and women fear nothing. They kill for the enjoyment of killing. When death had been caused by another aggressor, the conquered is marked by a diagonal slit across the throat, cutting the jugular artery of the vanquished; the bodies are left for others to bury.

The insane and already criminal people are the most feared. For no reason, without any provocation, they will just as well stab anyone in the back as not, feeling no remorse. In fact, they celebrate the event with a display of enjoyment as did athletes after a conquest of an opponent football for instance.

Women with older children are most susceptible. Many are beaten within a breath from death, sometimes while they or their children watch the brutality. Elders are targeted by yet others who prey on the defenseless who know escape is impossible. Victims are too slow or too weak to take any avoidance action.

Only days had passed from *the Event* before courtrooms across the world shut down; enforcement became nonexistent. Courts no longer provide a purpose. Rioting over the world in prisons has led to uncontrollable breakouts, which, gaining their unimpeded freedom, has become too violent to yield to any authority.

Every known vice, sin, cruelty, debauchery, immoral act, or offense of one against another has become the new normal—everywhere throughout the world. Satan now has his way. The world is truly his. He has begun his exploitation of it and all who is in it. Few will come out of this alive as eventually they will learn how to have a spiritual meaning, but at a cost.[4]

The beginning of the world's final annihilation has arrived.

I now vividly recall Avril Harrington, a fellow colleague at Westbrook College, a world affairs professor, introduced a revealing thought not often, if ever, voiced aloud. He told me of his modern discovery because he knew of my spiritual and scriptural knowledge. He correctly assumed I knew the meanings and prophecies of the Book of Revelation.

"Steven," he announced, "are you aware of whom the army from the north bent on the annihilation of Israel will be as prophesied in Revelation?"

I had to admit I was taught it would be Russia.

"Wrong," he declared. "That's because of the symbolism of the bear, right?"

I conceded it was.

"Let me interject a possibility. Russia will be amongst those from the north—granted. But it will be Turkey who leads the pack of ten nations of the north who attack Israel. It will be Muslims who attempt to bring the fate of Israel, namely Turkey being the leading force."

"And how did you arrive at the conclusion it would be Turkey?" I responded with surprise.

"Listen to me," he demanded, "if a straight line is drawn from Jerusalem to the North Pole, that line crosses over Ankara, the capital. Furthermore, the crescent and star is on the Turkey flag, which was also on the forehead of the golden calf Israel worshipped when Moses was on Sinai they thought too long."

"So?"

"Muslims have declared Israel their number one enemy in the world."

"And so?"

"Though, I believe, Turkey today is not so forceful, it will lead the ten nations into the Gog and Magog war to annihilate Israel, and it will be the Muslim faith that challenges Christ to be the savior of men's souls in the last days. This will unite Turkey with all other factions and nations who are Muslim because of a common enemy. It is said that ideology, politics, comradeship, and friendship has no binding ability greater than sharing a common hatred for the same enemy."

How could I refute his logic? But a serious question remained. "How does this Muslim faith become a challenge to Christ so emphatically as you put it?"

"It's their belief of the pilgrimage."

"What's so threatening about millions a year going to Mecca and worshipping at their mosque?"

"That's just it," he countered. "It's not the pilgrimage of itself. There's more. Have you ever seen a photograph of the swarming mass of Muslim believers around the Kaaba? The Scripture refers to the mass of people as water circling about. At the end of a pilgrimage, Muslims are drawn to the ritual of surrounding the Kaaba seven times. The pilgrimage is complete only when one kisses the Black Stone, what is believed to be the cornerstone of the Kaaba. Why do you think that is, Steven?"

I didn't have a clue.

"When one kisses the stone, their sins are forgiven them, they believe. You know what that means?"

"It's a substitution by Satan of the death and resurrection of Christ to be the savior of sin," I answered assuredly.

"That's correct, Steven."

I can tell you of this incident because now that I am living at the beginning of life after the rapture, I wonder just how much of Harrington's prognostication will come about.

PART I

PROPHECIES OF
THE END-TIME

This prophecy *will not be understood until
the end times, when travel and education
(knowledge) shall be vastly increased!*

—Daniel 12:4
(Living Bible, paraphrased)

1

LAST MONTHS BEFORE THE RAPTURE

I have to remind you that 2,700-plus years ago, the world in which Daniel the Prophet lived considered the moon not much more than a close star of earth, which enticed some to be what was called stargazers. We though in modern times have traveled there: a space station and a spy craft, Voyager, scouting faraway planets, sending back photos of worlds we never knew existed.

We both know and hardly go without saying that travel is far, far beyond the wildest of imagination of those using horse-drawn chariots and coaches centuries ago.

Computers and the Internet, medicine and the healing arts, transportation of the masses, and the millions upon millions of products making our lives easier while we live longer! How readily we know how rampant and exponentially expanding knowledge is! Daniel was told by heavenly means that when, by travel and the increase of knowledge can we understand that the last days are upon mankind.

This fact is the reason of my pursuit of what I know to be my calling, including my tenure at Westbrook College of over eleven thousand students. It's located in the Midwest USA. I'm Steven Alexander, a professor of philosophy, middle-aged.

We consider health as a most important activity to keep our mind fertile and coherent in these times when there's so much to learn, so much to sift through!

Though the pursuits outside the classrooms of current world events are a strong magnetic pull in my life, my family is stronger. I refuse to let those interests affect the quality of my relationships with Demi and our three children, all teenagers, as did my mother's interests neglect her attention with my brother and me when we were kids.

Yeah, can you detect I'm still hurting about that? Mom was gung ho to save the world with her overbearing commitment to the church that we all had to attend. It seemed to me we were less important, that getting people to church was her calling. My brother Raymond weathered it okay with a musical interest he shared with her.

Unintended I'm sure, she let me flounder. And that was paradoxical; a paradox because ever since a tiny tad to this day, the Scriptures have held a peculiar fascination in my life. This fascination was robust enough to entice me to pursue my career in theology, even to teach it. But Mom would much rather I would have chosen the ministry. But to be a minister in the manner she envisioned, I would have to be born again. Sorry, but that's taking the Scriptures a bit too far. I am content living a life free from malice and evil activities and one of one love for one another, especially family.

There is one subject of Scripture though that I cannot ignore in my life.

That is, what does Scripture say about the end-time? There is simply too much evidence to construe what is prophesied to be anything else but that we are living in that period of time. This is the magnetic pull that coincides with my philosophical points of view of which my teaching in the classroom is based. Conditions of the world and positions the world leaders are taking certainly point to a conclusion that a great catastrophic event is looming over us to occur very, very soon.

This is what has a powerful force compelling me out of the classroom and into strict observance in areas of politics and government powers, the world environments, world finance, and cultural intermingling—which all relate to my slant on world philosophy. Especially here in the United States.

One observation of current world affairs is the Americanized version of Christianity mixed in with democracy. Americans overwhelmingly think that the nation's form of being a Christian is enough for the rest of the world to adopt or it isn't Christian. If an Americanized version of democracy is not adopted by a nation of rigid, ancient laws and creeds, that nation is a prime candidate for change. I say this arrogance causes more problems than solutions. Look at Iraq, for instance.

It is why I am so compelled to study, research, and track the backstories of the world's state of affairs. I believe there is a strong influence upon one's personal or political persuasion founded by their core philosophies. Take Israel for instance. It's their core values causing their national position in the world, whether considered by outsiders good or bad.

My tenure and conditions with Westbrook allow me to immerse into the learning and absorbing all that is possible about the intricacies making the world work as it does. An invitation to the White House verifies, at least to me, that I must be getting somewhat where I wish to be in this pursuit. For some reason, this conference with the president of the United States gained a degree of national notoriety, at the pleasure of the Westbrook College's board of trustees.

But I never allowed my schedules to distract from parental responsibilities; being home Friday through Sunday mornings is a paramount importance. I never want to hear from my daughter and two sons I was never there for them or that I missed most of their participation in sports. I must say that this got more and more difficult as they aged from junior high to high school, and at the same time, I became increasingly involved with my pursuits. It is puzzling to many VIPs when, frequently, I turndown opportunities to be a keynote speaker when scheduled for weekends—which most are. And at the loss of a significant income!

What really amazes me are the frequent occurrences when I turn down an invitation, a crew would come to wherever I happened to be, to professionally videotape my presentation as a substitute, for playback to their audiences (I get royalties of course). I guess that's quite a validation that I'm making some kind of headway!

I suppose too that the importance of being a responsible parent is being respected. You think?

❧

There are notable conferences I have attended during the past year.

Dr. Don Gillium, a longtime friend and colleague, requested my attendance at a certain conference to be held in Minneapolis. He, being the keynote speaker.

"Sure, when?"

"In three weeks, Thursday, 2:00 p.m."

"I'll be there. How about lunch beforehand?"

"Of course. I'll call you later. Have to run. See ya."

Gilliam, an etiology professor at Williamsburg Valley Bible College, is a standout expert on the subject of philosophical influences of causes and origins. He's combined history with the goings-on today in a manner to make that relevance irrefutable. When he's engaged in debate, his demeanor and style makes him a worthy adversary; brimming with confidence, dressed in simple yet stylish attire, and a manly physique set him apart from a lot of men and desirous of many wannabes. I'm looking forward to his addressing the conference the Christian Alliance.

We met at Rosie's Diner, known for its huge tasty roast beef sandwiches and extraordinary crust pies. It's within walking distance to the convention center, being on Twelfth Avenue South. Our conversation was no match compared to the stimulating taste and enjoyment of the food and being with each other after more than five years. We had a lot of catching up to do that included our chat an hour later as we walked to the center.

Dr. Gillium spoke, "Both Israel's problem and solution are from the same origin: Israel is God's chosen people.

"When regarding Israel, we must understand a key cause for what is typically Israel's demise. In all of God's history of dealing with man, Israel has been the only people, the only nation, which he has chosen as his own. And as such, Israel is a natural enemy of Satan. Any government opposing God's chosen is his immediate adversary. If a country is not an ally of Israel, then it is inevitably an enemy—cause and effect.

"Israel is in one conflict after another, always being in a threat of war. It is challenging to distinguish who causes the greater threat of war. Is it Israel or its enemies? No matter which is thought to be the cause, Israel will always be in some kind of skirmish, if not in an all-out war. Since Israel came by exodus into the Holy Land, as their return to Canaan to establish their sovereignty in 1948 by supplanting the Palestinians, the Israelis will never be at peace: cause and effect.

"Nearly every day the news of the end-times contains stories of the hatred for Israel simply because of who they are. That Israel had overpowered dwellers of a land, Palestine, and then claim it as their own surely has caused the hatred experienced.

"Israel is in many ways a unique nation. It is the only nation during all of the world's history to have been exiled so completely throughout the world and yet remain to carry on their traditions, worship, and language—only to return and regroup as a nation. I repeat: the only nation to do so!

"Despite its small size, it is one of the most significant countries in the Middle East. Since its inception as a sovereign nation after WWII and has established itself as we now know it, the world has feared the day it would be financially independent. That day has come. Oil has been found within Israel's boundaries.[1] That event will allow Israel to be wholly financially independent, completely autonomous if it so chooses.

"Combined with its leadership in areas of technology, banking, and agriculture, Israel will become the target of every Islam and Arab regime or country in the Middle East—more fiercely than now or ever has been! The recent oil reserve discovery will only add to the severity of threatened war against her.

"But do not fear for Israel. During the past several years, they have launched satellites capable of numerous technological assets. Among the assets are surveillance, of course, and the advantage of a worldwide communication asset. They have a serious satellite expansion planned, defined with one word: readiness. Now they can afford it!"

---

[1]   Oil and gas discovery in Israel's Levant Basin, in eastern Mediterranean Sea by *Noble Energy Inc.* reported by *Oil and Gas Journal*, Dec. 12, 2013.

Same week, Washington DC

Janice Singleton, the office manager of a friend, Lester "Les" Thompson, senator (R) from Montana told me of this incident.

He inserted his digital passkey into the door slider of his office and entered. As he removed his overcoat and flicked the powdery snowfall off his shoulders, I entered. As you know, I had been his news gatherer all of the four terms he's been in office. I knew every detail down to the tiniest thought of what news interests him the most. For sure, it's Israel at the top of his list of over thirty subjects. Usually I place the news items in order of urgency without comment. Today is different.

"Les, have you heard? About Israel? Their natural gas and oil?"[1]

His interest now acute, and rather than hang up his coat, he put it over his arm as he strides to where I'm holding the printout from an e-mail. "Oil, huh?" He grabs the printed e-mail from me to read it. "That about covers it, doesn't it, Janice?"

"Covers what exactly?"

"Israel now has everything they need," he mused. "No dependence on anyone else! They are about as self-reliant as any country could hope to be. This oil and natural gas reserve discovered in Israel waters will cause them to be more independent."

"I'd assume this affects the US a great deal then."

"You're right."

⚜

Terry Beckerman, the White House news troll, who was a Westbrook student of mine over fifteen years ago, informed me of his paraphrased discussion with Rueben Goldstein, senior senator (D) from New York.

"He was swamped by news reporters as he bulldozed through the crowd to arrive at the safety of the elevators. Less impeding but sounding as urgent as the newsmen, five senators were already in the elevator. Each wanted Rueben's reaction to the newfound wealth discovery of his home country, Israel. They knew he spends a great amount of time every year in his country of personal heritage."

One of the senators, John Bixby (D) of Pennsylvania, a senior member of the Foreign Relations Committee, corners Goldstein for a short impromptu time together. He accepts.

After pleasantries, "Rueben, how long ago did you know of this oil discovery your country is enjoying?"

"About six months, John. Why?"

"Oh, no real reason. I'm curious. That's all. It wasn't too long ago the committee discussed how much of our budget should go to financing the F-16As Israel ordered and the Iron Dome. In fact we didn't know if any more than the last $680 billion can be financed. And if the truth be known, I doubt if we can be of any help to Israel at all especially with finally having your country's suspicion of oil becoming reality! The president has already mandated to cut funds earmarked for Israel."

"Mr. Bixby, it is estimated that it will require three to five years before any gain can be realized from the oil fields in the Mediterranean. In the meantime, we need to upgrade and to retool our military, especially the Iron Dome. Sorely too, I might add."

"Mr. Goldstein, let me remind you, without any attempt to belittle you, that the Israeli military and intelligence apparatus is already the finest in the world right along with our own without upgrading."

Startled that a small gathering had collected around them to catch every word, Bixby and Goldstein agreed to continue the conversation in private. Quietly the little get-together disbursed.

Moments later, Goldstein's phone alerted him of a text. It wasn't Bixby. It was Sunny, his appointment and scheduling secretary.

Suggest u use back door. Office crowded. Voice and e-mail boxes to capacity. U have 9 at Henderson office.

He followed her advice.

The camera in his office revealed the overcrowded waiting room. He felt sorry for Sunny, but she had become used to this during the past five terms New York had returned him to office. The time was 8:22 a.m. Just enough time to get to Henderson's office, the US vice president. He could not be late.

He wasn't. He was surprised, however. Jim Volkner, staff adviser of the vice president ushered him from the entrance to his boss's office door across the elaborate front office. He informed Goldstein the president had arrived moments before.

As he entered the private office, he motioned the president and vice president both to remain seated as he exchanged salutations and then sat at a sofa chair near them. "To what occasion are we blessed with your attendance, Mr. Jefferson?" He puts words into the answer, "Is it the oil? Or about Syria? Or Lebanon? Another matter?"

The president gets to the point quickly. "As a matter of fact, it is about the oil. Rueben, I know how close you are to the Israeli prime minister. I would like to utilize your relationship to better understand the Israeli mind-set as to how the oil and natural gas findings are going to be put to use."

"Sir, with all due respect, I do not know if I can."

"And that implies?"

"It implies I do not have the slightest idea outside of what is general knowledge."

"And that is?"

"Israel will construct more housing developments, irrigate more land, upgrade our health care for its citizenry, improve its educational system, and equip Israel's law enforcement with improved technology."

Henderson broke into the conversation. "You failed to mention military improvements."

"Yes, of course, that too."

"That too? You make it sound so casual, yet that is Israel's number one most funded agency. And it is the most problematic for the world!"

"Problematic because the rest of the world chooses to make it so, Mr. President. We do what we must do."

knew Mr. Michaels but had met him only one time in person. I think I have every one of his writings, including four books on advanced nuclear physics. As a profound and uniquely respected MIT professor, he's conducted hundreds of workshops, seminars, and keynoted conferences everywhere in the world because he speaks with such clarity about a sophisticated subject that even a novice can understand.

The significance of this particular hearing is a topic that will, or could, severely affect the world's future and is surely an indication of the end-time. I know it is the third time, as an authority, he has been invited to speak to congress on this same subject: threats of nuclear warfare. His invitation came about following a recent CNN interview that caught the attention of world leaders.

The day before his congressional appearance, we were in the hotel lobby, both of us waiting for parties to show up. I introduced myself, and he declared he knew who I am. He extended an invitation to discuss some things the next day that he thought would be of interest to me.

I must say, his appearance surprised me, this being the first time after more than fourteen years being face-to-face with the man. I had forgotten that he couldn't be more than 5'6", hair combed forward to hide baldness, extremely bushy eyebrows, flattened nose, and an oversized mouth that readily showed crooked teeth though gleaming white. His gray sport coat hung too loosely as did his black pants. Somehow though, the façade did not stop him from ready engagement. The negative first impression swiftly gives way to his warm and forthright manner. We've all experienced this with someone we know.

Confidently he sat in the hot seat before the congressional body to hear what he had to say.

They rapidly came to the point, asking, "Professor Michaels, can you explain the technologies you discussed with CNN that possesses an intense danger of devastation and consequences to the world as we now know it, particularly the United States?"

"I am quite sure you already know, and have known, of the technologies for which you have invited me to update your knowledge.

"Let me say that far removed from the past has the technological world brought us fast-forward. We're now into domains never thought of, let alone what we failed to know how or what to do about them. It is believed that knowledge increases four times every five years. Evolved from this knowledge are the four technologies which, if any are merged with another, will provide the owner a great deal of power. The kind of power an evil dictator would go to great lengths at enormous costs and endless sacrifices to possess."

The panel was deeply engaged to learn more of exactly what they were hearing.

"Those four are (1) GPS omniscience, (2) holography, (3) neurologic invasive control, and (4) electromagnetic pulse.

"First, GPS omniscience is the technology to create full knowledge of any person or event taking place by anyone who has a smartphone or smartwatch, whether the device is powered on or not. The USA's NSA has this technology, which I am sure you know. Congress probably approved it, in fact.

"The capability is always present wherever a smartphone or a smartwatch is located. And that location, as we all know, is a GPS triangulation showing precisely, within inches, where the wearer or owner is. We have the ability to convert such devices into a microphone, whether the devices are turned on or not, without the owner knowing the conversations (and background noises) are being heard. We have come much further in these days of course, when back in 2013, one could buy a spyware app for less than $180 and now much, much cheaper!

"Second, holography is so advanced that an image cannot be in the slightest way detected whether it is an actual object or merely a computer-generated simulation of an object when more than only three feet away. A three-dimensional holographic image of a person can have all of the human motions: walking, standing, sitting (in all the different postures), talking, singing, and facial expressions. It is as lifelike as it being real in a 'soft image' unlike that of a 'hard surface' mannequin. Such motions can be remotely directed through satellite technology, allowing replication control from anywhere in the world. The eyes of a 'human' holographic image are cameras allowing an operator immediate control to respond to situations and/or conversations in lifelike detail and timing, even blinking. This is a tremendously powerful spying apparatus.

"This ability could enable one to have an image of themselves at a locality where they would want to be witnessed when in reality they were not there at all.

"Imagine a deviously evil person to commit a capital crime, being 'seen' at another place—home with his wife and children. Or maybe an orator influencing a crowd's behavior without actually being at that location. Holography, as you can see, could be a powerfully effective tool for massive crowd deception.

"Third, neurologic invasive control technology was scientifically proven and introduced in 2013 at a major university in the NW and perfected through extensive research. This is a science where one human being, if they have perfected this technology, can 'mind control' another human being though not in the company of that person. It is proposed and considered possible that one could induce thoughts into the minds of a group of people which in turn would create mass response. Think of the possibilities such a person would have available to them if immoral, criminal, or unchecked acts were acted out! Or worse, if a sinister group of people utilized neurological invasive control to incite and control a sizeable crowd from a distance without them knowing why they're becoming violent protesters!

"Consider this. What if one was able to place neurologic invasive control into a holographic image of themselves? Is it possible? I do not doubt someone is working on that possibility. But how many advances have been made from merely asking, can this be possible? We've been proven many times over in the scientific community to never say *impossible*! So yes, NIC and holography will be combined, I imagine, soon.

"And fourth, there is EMP, electromagnetic pulse technology. You know what that is. Here's a briefing of what it will do. If the nuclear device is detonated more than fifteen thousand feet elevation of more than twenty tons, all electrical power would be lost within a twenty-five- to fifty-mile radius. Plus the devastation of the 150–200 mph wind from the heat of the blast. To my knowledge, there is absolutely no protection from this source of devastating power. I mean, how can our electrical grid system be protected as it now is in place in open air or railroad tracks?

"Consider how vulnerable the world will be when this technology is in the hands of terrorist organizations! And that day, I'm afraid, is not too far away. Let's look at that for a moment. Let's say that Iran has a couple of nuclear bombs to spare. One is in the hands of North Korea, the other in the hands of the Taliban. Do you think we'd be safe?

"A few months ago I was interviewed on CCN. You've seen the videotaping of that interview, the reason I'm here.

"Iran and two other bogus powers have acquired EMP since that time. The US is no longer safe. Any day and without provocation, I might add, any major city in the USA could be totally, without discretion, shut down and, within moments, later flattened by a second nuclear device, as like first knocking a victim out cold before killing them.

"While I am on the subject of the electrical grid, NSA has made public their knowledge of numerous attempts of cyber stimulus from foreign countries, namely Iran, to shut down the grid system. If there is a single most comprehensive way to literally immobilize this nation, it is the shutting down of the electrical grid. To think that this could be in simultaneous combination with EMP to destroy America is terrifying."

A loud silence overcame the audience as the seriousness of the consequences is chilling. After recovering, there were clarifying questions lasting a couple hours. By the day's end, they had heard enough—and then some, terminating the hearing scheduled for the next day.

We had our little meeting when he expounded to me more of the details, iterating that what was discussed the previous day is a real danger and that it is surely an indication that these are the last days as Christians claim them to be.

The hearing brought the attention again to CNN, but this time more by public demand for another interview to calm the intense fear felt nationally because of what he expressed. He received the call in my presence. Afterward he wondered how he could do that without marking down the reality of those technologies and what they could do when in the wrong hands that is happening.

⚜

A CNN Telecast: EMP

Professor Michaels is on air being interviewed by a three-person CNN panel: Cindy Parker, Hank Pattison, and Jill Remlar. Each of them has reported on the Scriptural Last Days taking an unbiased approach.

It is more than five minutes into the interview.

Pattison asked, "Threats of preemptive nuclear strikes have much of the world entangled in anxiety. Exactly how close are we to having a maverick nation, for instance North Korea, actually send a nuclear warhead-equipped missile into an unsuspecting nation?"

"We are living in times that a nation who feels slighted or is ridiculed, with or without a reason, could launch a first strike. Four nations, other than the US and Russia, have this capability, and to my knowledge, there are three others experiencing minor problems getting theirs on line.

"Second, you said the *unsuspecting*. There is no such thing in today's world, Mr. Pattison. There is no leader of any nation who ignores the chance their nation could be the victim of a first strike."

"Especially the US and Israel," Cindy chimed in.

"Yes, especially."

Cindy continues, "Granted, it is the US and Israel who has the best chance to be targets of a first strike. Let me ask you this. Which countries, in your opinion, are the most likely to launch a first strike?"

Michael leans forward in his chair as though he was about to quietly reveal a secret. "I cannot point specifically to any one nation for the position I am in regarding national security. I will say this however."

Now the three reporters lean forward as they might hear an exclusive comment.

"The country most likely to launch a first strike will be that country whose leader has a passion for gaining instant control or to make a statement to the world. That leader will have no regard even for his nation's people or the people who will be the victims of this massive, two-directional nuclear bombardment."

"Can you speculate who that might be, Professor?" quizzed Jill Remlar.

"As I said, I cannot. And will not," replied the professor forcefully.

Jill presses, "Then, Professor, can you speculate that if an attack, whether first strike or not, of a nuclear ready missile upon the US would occur, what will it be like as a result?"

"Within seconds, the US will launch four types of weaponry. First is the launching of a nuclear device more powerful what is launched toward us. Second, diversionary missiles are launched to steer the nuclear missile away from populated areas. Third, a battery of nonnuclear missiles will be launched upon all known military and weapon locations of the striking enemy or enemies. And fourth, SAC aircraft will be deployed to the offending country to cause havoc after the nuclear missile has detonated. We expect the diversionary missiles will also only do minimal damage to occur. If not, well, the US could very well be destroyed as we now know it in matter of minutes. A first strike would certainly include many nuclear missiles arriving simultaneously on known military locations and major cities."

Cindy thoughtfully interjects another question, "Professor Michaels, on the fringe of discussions about nuclear warfare we hear about EMP. What is that?"

He nervously shifts his posture, and an expression of uneasiness is clearly noticed. "Oh, electromagnetic pulse. Yes. This is a horrifying possibility when considering its effect."

"How so?" asks Jill, sensing the disquieting impact on Professor Michaels.

"First of all, there is little protection against this. If a UN-nonconforming country with a nuclear warhead were to utilize EMP disabling technology, the targeted locations and cities within a given country will certainly be rendered inoperable."

"What do you mean by that?" inquired Hank Patterson with cautious regard.

"This technology of nuclear detonation is meant to be ignited twenty thousand to sixty thousand feet in the atmosphere. If a fifty-ton warhead is detonated in this manner, an area of a fifty-mile radius per each twenty thousand feet of elevation would be impacted."

"What would happen?" Hank queried.

"All forms of electricity will be wiped out. All electrical power stopped. Gone. Purged from use. The grid system, if in the wake of this blast, is surely imminent, cease. The Internet would close down, no power. All forms of communication dependent upon electricity, electronics also, will be jettisoned. No phones, except, possibly, satellite phones."

The four of them remained in silence before Jill asks the professor, "How much damage will occur beyond the electricity elimination?"

"The nuclear blast creates an enormous heat wind at a very fast velocity, over one hundred mph. It would reach earth within thirty seconds or less. The heat will ignite anything of wood, causing immediate combustion. People will literally be fried in place."

Patterson probes further, "How is such a nuclear blast ignited? How does it get to that height?"

"It could be as simple as a shoulder missile launcher capable of hurling a missile to at least ten thousand feet."

Cindy introduces another notion, "Let me get this straight, Professor. If such a missile can be propelled into the atmosphere with such a lightweight launcher, then any of the major metropolitan areas of a major city is actually in danger of an EMP neutralizing nuclear blast. Right?"

"This is so. Yes."

She continues, "Is it possible for a foreign adversary, then, to launch such armed missiles simultaneously from, say, small freighters, or a private cabin cruiser even, for that matter, within harbors of cities?"

"Again, yes. It is more than possible. It is likely, in fact."

Cindy becomes curious, "Professor, I'm going to change the subject somewhat. Of course you know about the biblical prophecies of the last days and beyond, true?"

"True that I know about them? Or are they true?"

"Answer as you will," she clarifies.

"Yes, I am aware of the prophecies. Are they true, will they come about? Well, they are far-fetched. I think they're a stretch. I will say this: we are living in the last days, and I really don't know what that means. What I think is far-fetched is the coming of Christ."

"So I take it that you are not what is called a born-again believing Christian," Jill qualifies.

"I am not," concludes Professor Michaels.

The subject is dropped, as Hank Pattison restores the interview back to nuclear threat.

"Professor. Though North Korea, Iran, Pakistan, and China appear to dominate the issue of nuclear threat thinking, were does Israel stand in all of this?"

"A good question, Mr. Pattison. I will attempt to offer you the short description. Israel has quietly and steadily moved forward with nuclear power for military use. They do have nuclear capability. They have it as Russia and the US had nuclear bombs to protect them from each other during the Cold War. And now with their oil reserves, Israel can afford nuclear development.

"Now, however, in today's world, there are diplomatic concerns that were nonexistent a decade or two ago.

"For instance, back in 2013, we had Syrian internal warfare with genocides. The Syrian genocide issue reached the conference rooms all over the world as to what, if anything, to do about it. Iran waited in the wings, happily, I might add. The significance of Syria is that they could have ignited a nuclear war by a domino effect. Then also is the watchful eye of Putin to engage or not.

"We have hatred toward Israel by Arabs, Islam, and Palestine that has accelerated far beyond years past, to name one serious situation affecting the entire world.

"Now. Here's the problematic trouble for the US and Israel in the mix of those issues, and many more in the Mideast. You must understand that the Arabs and Arab nations maintain a position of nonengagement. Any such engagement would upset their economic balance.

"We must ask why this is so important. It is a vital concern because the Arab religion forbids the killing of another Arab. This then creates the need for a country to do the dirty work of annihilating Israel. If turmoil and unrest can be blamed on Israel, forcing Israel—by their own stated cause—to retaliate. Guess who. The United States! The US would be, and has been, inadvertently become the Heavy in the Middle East.

"Then there's ISIS. They're well-funded. They have the intelligence. And they certainly have the impetus. Though Islamic, they have no hesitation to annihilate any person or any influence against them as we all must surely know."

Ms. Parker joins into the assessment. "Let me get back to EMP: it is an important device to catch the attention of the world or to obliterate a diplomatically important city—by anyone."

"Yes, you have stated precisely a most important danger."

"Would you clarify for us how widespread the damage would be from an EMP blast?"

"The larger the size of the nuclear device and the higher in the atmosphere it is detonated would determine the distance its impact will be felt. If a seventy-megaton nuclear detonation occurs at forty thousand feet above Memphis, Tennessee, the entire eastern seaboard of the United States would be impacted to the fullest extent and westward all the way to Denver, Colorado.

"There is more to consider, however.

"Though no one knows for certain because there has been no opportunity to test this fear, the EMP technologists are quite sure that the bare high-tension wires and railroad tracks would carry the electromagnetic force outward from the targeted locale like tentacles. For what distance is anyone's guess.

"The danger lies that outlying towns or cities, the devastation would be carried to them causing havoc as EMP effects travel outward. For instance, with a forty-megaton blast at twenty-five thousand feet above Washington DC, cities within 150 to three hundred miles could conceivably experience EMP's impact.

"Because of its nature, there is no way to protect the wires or tracks from EMP's damage.

"There is another crucial phase that will occur after an EMP detonation. Because of the elimination of electrical power and electronic switching devices and control substations, all food processing, agricultural activities, distribution systems, cold storage, and water systems will also cease to function. One of the most important losses of the infrastructure is the enormous number of water pumping stations to deliver water to homes within the range of an EMP attack."

"Is there anything else we need to know about EMP, Professor?" asks Parker.

"Proportionately few people will be killed by this detonation. The impact of death upon an attacked region comes from starvation and dehydration. Those living in remote areas who have their own food-growing capability and continual water supply are those who stand the best chance to persevere beyond the effects of an EMP attack."

"Further, when such an attack occurs, it will take an estimated three or four decades, some project half a century, for such an affected locale to restore the destroyed infrastructure back to any resemblance of what it once was."

This was the last comment before closing his interview.

❦

Reactions to Michael's interview
Tehran, Iran

Al-Abib, Iran's minister of Military Preparedness, an Iranian cabinet member, has called a conference with his nuclear science team.

"Gentlemen and ladies, I suppose that all of you heard Professor Michael's interview on CNN last evening." Everyone nodded yes.

"I ask you. How far away are we to have such a device to disrupt EMP of the US?"

"In such a massive way that Cindy Parker indicated?" one of the women inquired.

"Yes. As massive as she suggested."

"Then we are years away," she responded. "But I do have an idea." She seeks permission to describe her idea.

"Let's hear your idea."

"First we must ask why we would do such a thing. Merely to cause devastation and wreckage? To gain respect from other Islam nations of our desire to rid of infidels? To prove to the world our resolve to advance Islam?" She continues while having complete attention, "I would like to think, and I suggest, that if we are to use this nuclear technology on America, we do it not on a major city, but on one that is not so important. We can accomplish two objectives. One: create a fear of Iran and Islam—praise be to Allah, and two: we can do this within the next six months." She sits among applause.

Al-Abib shows pleasure of such a suggestion, then expands upon it.

"Let me ask this team a question. I am not minimizing our colleague's comment to suggest that we do this upon Israel, rather than the USA. What do you think about this?"

They applaud this suggestion. The woman stands to speak.

"I endorse to proceed our efforts upon Israel rather than the United States. We will have much greater impact and respect among Arab nations and Islam too. And we can do this earlier with much less risk."

"I will present our desires to the premier tomorrow," declares Al-Abib.

The White House

At 6:30 a.m., William Jefferson, president, requests the immediate presence of two top aides, three cabinet members, and a foreign relations specialist adviser to the Oval Office. All are present within two hours.

He promptly commences discussion following a brief courteous greeting. "In 2007, Newt Grengrich conducted a special investigation by members of the National Security Office regarding EMP. Their findings were very sobering.

"I assume all in this room have read its report or know about it. If you have not, I highly suggest you do. This meeting will be short. The balance of your morning, however, will be taken up with further attention upon EMP.

"There are two items now on your top priority list: First, is there any protection from EMP now in place anywhere? And two, what can be done immediately in response to this specific report? Though I wish for the best, I doubt there is much at all. I need to know. Directly after this meeting, I request that you all meet together in the Diplomatic Conference Room to establish individual assignments of (1) what technology is already in place, if any; (2) how the United States can take measures to protect the effect of a nuclear attempt to neutralize EMP in this country, and (3) a projected budget to get done what we must do both in the short-term and long range.

"Following individual assignments, you have two weeks to assemble your responses and get back with me with the detailed report in hand. That is all, the meeting is concluded."

⚜

Moscow, Russia

The office of the Minister of Nuclear Research and Implementation is filled with scientists involved with EMP technology. They represent both sides of the issue: offensive deployment and protection of assault.

The minister, Dimitri Scholsen, conducts a meeting of the Russia's finest nuclear scientists rarely assembled. Of the fourteen in the room, eight are women.

"Comrades, the subject of this meeting is EMP. It has taken a high priority in diplomatic and political attention all across the world, compliments of CNN's interview of Professor Michaels."

"We all know Professor Michaels. We know him to be a reliable, most knowledgeable scientist of nuclear technologies." Everyone nods their head in agreement.

"Every person of importance in the world has now heard of EMP. There is fear everywhere, and the professor had only skimmed the surface of the bad things to occur with this nuclear provocation. He was quite careful to not tell the whole story.

"Be that as it is, we now have a formidable job ahead of us. We have the capability to launch such an attack. But the question is, do we have any strategy or protection from EMP in place to protect our motherland should another country irresponsibly launch such an attack upon us?

"This is our new agenda over the two months. It's at the top of our priorities.

⚜

Pyongyang, North Korea

Knoi Lau, Officer of Nuclear Development, conducts a meeting with his staff to redirect scientific research to EMP nuclear deployment.

"We have no fear another country would attack this state with EMP disruption. However, they need to fear us. We have four such nuclear devices only months away from testing. Only one will be tested, leaving three we can arm once the testing is positive." All heads are bowed forward as acceptance.

"Beginning today, by order of Kim Yang, our president, we are to channel all nuclear readiness upon deployment of EMP. Unlike other nations, we need not worry about being attacked during the next foreseeable months, or maybe years."

⚜

Hebron, Israel

General David Weinberg, Chief of Strategic Military Operations, summoned his department heads together for a preparedness meeting, as he called it.

"All of you saw the CNN interview last evening, right?" Everyone indicated they had. "If you're like me, people, it gave me the fear of hell. I can think of at least two countries who have nuclear EMP devices targeted on us right now."

A pall of uneasiness fell over them.

"We must expect at any moment such a launching will happen, and we have to be ready. That means some type of diversionary technology has to be created specifically for this occurrence. This is going to be difficult as the launching is not a sophisticated missile detected from hundreds of miles away.

"This can be launched from a small water craft in the Med Sea to be detonated over the Holy Land. Very little time is available. It isn't as simple as a missile coming down after its ascension after launch. This rises to ten thousand feet or more and is detonated at the predetermined apex of its climb.

"In fact, I doubt if there is any device that can be created to divert such a missile detonation. So what do we do? You are to discover what we can do."

❦

Current World Outlook Conference
McCormick Place, Chicago

Issik Lindell, author of *Israel, Islamic, and US Rule*, a professor at New York University, is the guest speaker at this conference.

"Israel continues its renowned arrogance and dominating force causing many Middle East nations impatience. They always refer to the disregard and aspiration of Israel to rid of Palestine on what Israel considers their land, not Palestine's. But after all, the entire Holy Land was Palestine during the Second World War. It is Israel who were the invaders, not Palestine! Winning the long, continuing war, as with all their other wars, Israel's military confidence is high.

"The Arab nations cannot and will not tolerate Israel's continued position.

"The USA is firmly, at this current time, encased with its diplomatic and military position with Israel. In the US halls of government, the Israel Lobby is second when regarding the amount of dollars being provided by the US Congress. Some of the funding are by loans in terms of military equipment and defense technology. Some is by out-and-out grants, never a repayment expected. All of the funding is without accountability as to how the funds are utilized. Israel is the only country being subsidized by the US who is not required to account for its spending. And now the discovery of Israeli oil reserves will allow Israel to become wholly independent.

"I am not taking a position of judging this circumstance, only revealing it. You can decide for yourselves which side of the balance of justice the US-Israel relationship you place it. My point? That this relationship will always cause disharmony among the Middle East countries and other countries involved with them, nearly all countries the world over.

"This causes immense strife in every nation considered to be in or neighbors of the Middle East, in particular, Israel. And merely because the US is so much an ally of Israel, tensions with other countries in this part of the world causes the ingredient of spontaneous wars between them.

"In point. The Turkistan to Pakistan oil pipeline traversing through Iran. On one hand it strengthens Arab nations against Israel and omits Russia from sharing the oil's riches. This further strains the relationship of the US with Russia. Why? The US has provided in 2013 an additional $1.7 billion to Pakistan to complete the pipeline feeding its refineries, also with the help of the US. The US, on the other hand, had to concede Iran's share of the oil by allowing the pipeline to be built through their soil! Iran is already a primary oil supplier to countries including the US. It is a way for Iran to control yet another oil source to balance power against Israel.

"Every Islamic country considers the US a nation of infidels: people without regard to Allah, their god. Iran is Islamic. It is part of their name in fact: the Islamic Republic of Iran.

"The ties of the US to Israel causes further animosity in the form of hatred of Christianity.

"Sitting along the sidelines are significant financial players in the advancement of Islam. Because of religious restraint, one Arab cannot kill another Arab without brutal consequences. Though most of the Islamic nations are not militant, they are waiting in the wings for the annihilation of Christianity and Jews, quietly in the background while others do their dirty work.

"As though the Islamic hatred of Christianity alone isn't enough!

"Maybe by the war that Russia is being pulled into, planned by Iran, a war involving several of previously southern Russian countries along with Turkey. A religious undertow is the pull of unity like a magnet drawing metal toward it becoming attached. That explains the other countries' desire to be a collaborative effort, but not Russia's. For some unexplainable reason other than the sharing of oil to be acquired, no one understands why Russia has been invited by Iran to join them.

"The collaborative planning comprises seven nations from the north of Israel, one from the east, and two from the south. Egypt is not invited, a mystery that remained to be."

⚜

Big Four Monetary Conference
Paris, France

Brenda Mitchell has also tracked the trends of both the Euro and Chinese yuan in their path to overtake and replace the US dollar as the world's currency as well as Japan's ongoing willingness to continue buying, almost worthless, US Treasury Bonds. Among other privileges, she has full clearance to attend meetings and conferences conducted at the International Monetary Fund (IMF) headquartered in Washington DC. She reported, "On a Thursday in May 2006,

Radolfo Amerinero, a rising upstart in the world finance arena, was the keynote speaker of a conference on concerns of the world's currency. The primary issue is the weakness of the US dollar. All of his comments of reproach were upon the frail condition of American decision of their own dollar's value. He produced no comment about a solution, only the problems.

"During the day after his dissertation, I followed him to a variety of discussion panels. By the time the first of four days were completed, he had violently rocked the boat with numerous effective points. The conference's agenda began slanting away from what was planned to the points he had so persuasively made. The US delegation walked out.

"One of the points was to take note of the US's real estate situation and mortgage loans, called derivatives. Before four years all of this came crashing down and to cause a serious collapse of the way business was conducted.

"It happened two years later, like falling dominoes.

"In 2009, Amerinero hired Ivar Hansen as his world monetary counselor with the objective to place the euro in contention as the world currency, replacing the dollar. At least that was my suspicion along with many of my colleagues. We were proven correct a year later.

"During February, representatives of world monetary experts from six nations held a secret conference to which the US was not invited. Ivar Hansen of Norway chaired the meeting.

"I quote, 'For such a situation we are now placed into, that being the tremendous weakness of the US dollar, we need to go back to a provision created in 1969 for just this situation! It is called the Special Drawing Rights, SDRs, that will enable countries to convert any currency without the use of dollar to purchase imports or sell exports. By creating SDR bonds, the central bank's dependence upon US Treasury Bonds is passé.'

"As I understood SDRs' impact, it would mean they could be used to purchase oil and gold, the two commodities that keep the world monetary system afloat.

"Then I wondered about China, Japan, Korea, and Pakistan. Pakistan? Yes, Pakistan. Surely it is one of the poorest nations intermingling with world powers, but they have an arsenal of nuclear weapons. Think about the impact SDRs will have on Pakistan!

"One of my colleagues at Reuters stated that China and Korea have recently signed an agreement to do cross-border use of their own currency, the yuan. He quoted a Beijing financial leader saying, 'Displacing the dollar will reduce the volatility in oil and commodity prices and belatedly erode the "exorbitant privilege" the USA enjoys as the issuer of the reserve currency that has become seriously and hopelessly outmoded.'

"Now with an IMF conference on the subject less than eighteen months away, a special, secret meeting again took place and again without the US knowing. As a backstory, China had signed agreements with Germany, Brazil, Russia, Australia, Japan, Chile, the United Arab Emirates, India, and South Africa in a currency pact. It was obvious Amerinero came to this covert meeting with his own loaded agenda.

"He pointed out that the first indication of the US is worrying about its dollar being removed as the world currency is the level of its denials such a thing could take place! That is what countries, governments, and people do when their world is about to collapse—they deny or ignore that a problem exists. The second indication is the increased velocity they are printing more money: And is going further and further into debt. It will take only a short time before the US is more than $24 trillion in debt, far beyond their ability to even pay the interest, which incidentally, they struggle to do now!

"Next he pointed out that two countries in attendance are massive creditors to the US. China and Japan. When looking at a balance sheet of China, the debt of the US subtracts from their assets, which weakens their ploy for the yuan to be the world's trade currency.

"Then he made 'the kill.' He continued, 'Since 2012, the euro has exceeded every forecast as to its strength of currency, coming out of a recession.'

"Opposite that, now after a few years, on a balance sheet, the euro is half again more valuable than the yuan because there is very little credit or debts owed against the euro's value. When the IMF meets in a few months, I will propose and work toward the euro to replace the dollar.

"I followed how he worked to achieve that objective. One by one, beginning with the least powerful, Ivan Jensen and Amerinero began influencing the members of the IMF, never making contact with the US. They work fastidiously and quick to recruit votes in favor of the euro. He knew each country's representative had only one vote, and they needed to get a two-third approval. This meant with all the force China and their cohorts might assemble, a new currency or form of currency will replace the US dollar.

"The day of the IMF world conference began, the keynote opening speech wasn't much more than that: an opening speech. Throughout the week, scores of meetings, panel forums, and debates took place. All of the subject matter revolved around how to replace the dollar and whose currency would do it. On the second day, the US representatives, knowing the doom of the dollar had already been decided, again, in protest, walked out of the deliberations.

"On the last day of the conference, Friday, at ten thirty a.m., a vote was taken. Of the thirty-seven members, twenty-eight voted for a new currency, to be decided within six months time to replace the dollar. Amerinero got his way. He was also able to put a ceiling on the number of yuan China could buy/sell without the use of a new currency to be determined, as well as any country who traded commerce with China.

"At the close of the vote, the delegates were reminded at the end of the keynote presentation, given by Radolfo Amerinero. A few chose to not attend the conference ending speech at one thirty p.m.

"They missed out on a gangbuster closing talk that lasted only twelve minutes of a thirty-minute time allotment. He cited a vast outlay of data to illustrate the enormous success of the data-based Internet form of currency that he had invested into heavily and that over the past twenty-one months, he acquired a 2,448 percent gain!

"His last comments drove his blockbuster concept home.

"The future world's economy will be propelled by this Internet technology regardless of what any of one of the world's financial system that might be adopted or what government's financial form of money we might approve. This e-money based databank will enable full tracking and accountability over the entire world without any bank's intervention.

"This comment alone caused gasps and kept them silent in their seats after he'd finished as they contemplated what their ears had just heard. As for that matter, so did I.

"What he implied is that with the introduction of a monetary system of this magnitude, it would bring into play new lords and masters who would have full and absolute control over every trans-action—business, government, and every individual—without any say-so. I wonder just how far he is planning to be involved with this concept himself!"

❦

The World Health Conference
Geneva, Switzerland

An international finance analyst considered to be an insider authority of world concerns, Brenda Mitchell, is the opening key-note speaker of the conference. Scores of the world's most influential philanthropists, business leaders, and authorities in world affairs are present in the audience of tens of thousands.

"It is an honor to discuss with all of you such an important issue facing us, facing the world, and each of you. Let me remind you why.

"There is no question the world's assets are disappearing before our eyes! I refer, in a shrouded description, the world's resources. Shrouded, because the earth provides us with only two resources, and one dubiously qualifying what we can rightfully call a resource. One is the forests. They can be reforested as we take the trees down. The other is rainfall. In a matter of speaking, it's a resource by its natural weather cycle. However, when the aquifers are deleted and used up faster than their replenishing ability, they cease to be a resource.

"Now, allow me to clarify.

"When we understand the difference between a source and a resource as it relates to the world's assets, maybe we can turn things around, but I for one highly doubt it. A source cannot be replenished. Once gone, always gone! A resource can be replenished. Fossil fuel, for instance. We know that once this source is gone, well, it is gone forever!

"Being that oil is a source of the earth's once bountiful supply, we must never refer to fossil fuel as a resource. As you can see, it is not a resource. As long as we call it a resource, there is little recognition of its consequences when it will be depleted. And at the rate we're heading into it, that is soon to occur.

"This leads me then to the core of my presentation. As the sources of this earth we live upon are dwindling at a faster pace than ever known by mankind, the world's population is exponentially multiplying.

"We can look at the many birth preventions going on today. China's one-child policy, condoms, abortions, sex education—all such has certainly not thwarted the increase of the world's population. In fact we have drugs, remedies, treatments, and medications to extend the years of life expectancy, doubling the 1700s, which was barely over forty."

Unrest hovered over the audience. She certainly had their attention. But what was she getting at? Definitely not to suggest all of the life-giving research and its findings be stopped! Or is she?

"I know what you're wondering. I can assure you, that is not it.

"What I am saying, the world is quickly arriving at a point of living beyond its means. Too many people, less and less sources of the earth to support its growth of people.

"It is time we have to consider our dilemma. Here are the facts: (1) It's required from creation to the mid-1800s for the world's population to reach one billion; (2) it only required a hundred years to double, to reach two billion in the 1920s; (3) then only fifty years to double yet again to four billion living on earth in the 1970s; and (4) with a quarter million added every day, the equivalent of Germany, the population will reach ten billion by midcentury of 2000.[4]

"And now, today, what are we to do? What action will we be required to have the guts to take to remedy the situation now confronting us?"

She stepped away from the podium and seated herself among her peers on the front row. Following her comments, moments of quiet contemplation filled the room before a standing ovation engulfed the auditorium. The emcee went to the microphone. The audience sat back down as the applause went away. Quietness returned. Very quiet, everyone in thought was posed by the seriousness of her question.

A distinguished man stood up in the middle of the seated audience. All eyes turned to him bewildered by the interruption. He waited for the emcee's attention and permission to speak. All was quiet when he spoke.

"My name is Clifford Hargrove. I am pastor of the Evangelical Free Church in Charlotte, North Carolina. Thank you for your allowing me a voice.

"Most assuredly we do have a problem. The lack of the earth's sources and resources are indeed a concern. But that is not our immediate dilemma however. Granted, population is a distinctive problem, I do not have a solution, but I do have a suggestion. A warning, actually, a warning you haven't anticipated."

While visibly anxious to hear what this preacher has to say about world population, they're suspicious he lacks credentials to act as an authority! What kind of warning could come from a minister who traveled to Switzerland representing a relatively unknown church near the eastern coast of the United States? That alone gained everyone's attention.

"I will be brief. We have all heard from our knowledgeable and respected speaker of the challenge that lies before us. That is all well and good. But let me tell you of another challenge I need to address.

"We are in absolute agreement that the world's demise is rapidly closing in upon us.

"What I must remind all of you in attendance that the End of Days upon this world, in God's time, is upon us."

Eyes rolling, shifts in seats, and quick murmurings break out, signifying upsetting responses among the audience, were easy to discern.

"I am attempting to have you include future discussions that God possesses the power to bring our dilemma to a close." Audience displeasure mounts as he continues, "In Scripture, there will be a massive taking away of the believers of the Gospel from this world. Many catastrophes, upheavals, pestilences, and disease will follow. I suggest at that time, with approximately twenty percent of the earth's population taken, earth's overpopulation will be resolved."

He was poised to say more.

Another in the audience stood up to successfully interrupt Hargrove.

"This man has no right to bring religion into what is a universal world issue. In this auditorium, I venture to say there are at least a couple dozen or more religions represented. Before we get caught up into each religion having a say, I maintain that no further remarks of any religion's beliefs be allowed. More, that if Mr. Hargrove expresses another comment reflecting his beliefs, he is to be escorted out and away from this forum."

Applause pronounced wholesale agreement. The conference continued without comment of Hargrove's dissertation. He knew an understanding of what he said pervaded throughout the audience, similar to a jury being swayed by a disallowed comment by a witness: once said, always remembered.

Global warming was debated. Diminishing water and fossil fuel was not debated. The discussions were not about the fact of their diminishment but what to do about it now. That is if any worthwhile action is possible in consideration of the earth's population growth. Various leaders of industries in use of the world's supplies provided considerations their individual companies had taken.

Hargrove's comment lingered in everyone's mind without verbalization. It just might be a race in time, after all!

And What About America?

Reverend Michael Newsome is speaking, the black pastor of the Missionary Baptist Church of the Last Days, Montgomery, Alabama. In just six years, it has nearly become a megachurch with a congregation of well over a thousand. Fourteen HDTV stations televise their Sunday morning services across the southeastern United States.

Reverend Newsome speaks out at every chance he can get about the harsh reality of the modern United States and how it has become a classic failure. He's authored two books gaining respect by the audience who care about their country, the good ol' US of A. *The Fall* and the second book, *Stopping the Fall*, are detailed and precise, deserving them to be a must-read status by government officials. But apparently few did.

"America was once the home of the strong, the brave, and the free is now perceived by world governments as a nation of the weak and restrained. Our once great nation was built on the freedom to worship the Lord without fear of government, to separate church and state. America has become a nation to separate itself from worshipping God altogether.

"We have abandoned the Christian principles this nation had formed at its founding. At every turn, it appears we are deciding to make our world and country as though to replicate the idea of the Tower of Babel.

"Why do we need God at all? America is contemplating.

"Even the Supreme Court is admonishing the idea that Christianity should lower its standards to accept lower morality! Such as same-sex marriage.

"Christianity has taken a major hit when the Supreme Court declared prayer in classrooms is prohibited. At every turn, it is our Christian faith that takes a hit when political or social issues are decided. Why should we compromise when no one else is directed to make social or political compromise?

"Christianity is what made America strong. America has become fearless by having God along its side. Sadly, it is turning away from God at an exponential rate during these last days."

❦

NATO's Dismantling
Paris, France

On Tuesday at 2:00 p.m., representatives of the Euro Union had begun their conference a few minutes ago. Major Ian Thomason of Bulgaria has the floor.

"I congratulate our president Turamali for his delicate and effective leadership in the dismantling of NATO. It should have taken place many years ago. Simply put, we certainly did not need the US to tell us what to do. The Cold War ended more than two decades ago! Now, we need to move forward as a unified body, the Euro Union, without the help of any country outside of our membership."

Thumping of the metal steins against the oakwood table signaled an endorsement of Major Thomason's statements.

John Andreason of Sweden stands.

"I have always been a staunch supporter of almost everything the US would do. Now? No. They have made fools of themselves. Over the past decade, the US has made blunder after blunder with their decisions affecting the world. And they have responded to problems and attacks upon the problems as frantic novices, often accelerating bad results rather than solving them."

He sits as all others stand to a long ovation and, in unison, shout three "Here, here!"

Radolfo Amerinero, the youngest representative from Italy, twenty-six, is given the floor as Andreason yields.

"The USA is a country that seemingly cannot help itself with its frailty. It has become a country that ceases to acknowledge how weak it has become as it pretends to be strong. It troubles me to know the US's fragile leadership, beyond whoever happens to be the president, remain to have under their control the largest and most up-to-date warships policing the world's seas, their Fifth and Sixth Fleets and their nuclear war bases on the western Gulf coastline. It scares me when thinking how much power is at their disposal, the arsenal and weaponry onboard those ships and military bases!"

He continues, "Then when we consider the USA is always flexing its weak muscles to strip other countries of developing nuclear war devices as it continues to advance its own, it is even scarier. What gives them this right to do this? If it would come down to a decision of who can possess nuclear capabilities, I for one would not allow the US to have that right or to possess any nuclear armament at all!"

He sits as he also receives cheers and applause of agreement.

⚜

Los Angeles, California
Western Banking Alliance (WBA)

Walter Benhousen, the newly elected CEO of the WBA, San Francisco, is the keynote speaker of the Alliance's annual meeting. It is the first time he has addressed the Alliance as its CEO. He's often referred to as the Silver Fox because of his likeness of Kenny Rogers, the popular singer of the '70s. He has a natural demeanor of confidence and ready forcefulness, surely what a leader of this financially healthy organization requires. Being a former NBA power forward, his size and posture is commanding. But once he begins to speak, his low voice and articulate panache causes all other observations of him to disappear.

"China—let's talk about China. Volumes could be said about what is going on in that country. But I choose to hit upon only the highlights as they affect the US generally and the Western Banking Alliance specifically.

"While the United States continues to print money without either silver or gold security, China prints its yuan backed up by gold. It is the most active buyer of gold in the world including two gold mining operations. They have a stated agenda to amass their vaults with gold equal to the money they print and place into circulation.

"China is a major stockholder in America's largest steel and copper manufacturing corporations. They have become a leading purchaser of significant US properties, which I shudder to think what they can do with that! All of this what China is doing has great impact upon the power or decline of America's wealth and its consequence in the world, let alone at home. It has become more of fact that China owns America. We are in their hip pocket, so to speak.

"The United States continues to borrow from China to keep its economy afloat. China is quite happy to do so. In the meantime, America continues to implode financially! This was once a great country because of its financial stability. That now cannot be said. So I ask you. What happens if and when China decides to stop buying Treasury Certificates and make demand to collect payment on this debt? Then what?

"And we must not neglect to consider Japan either. In any three-month span, a quarterly report establishes that Japan and China purchases US Treasury Bonds alternately more than the other. They are the world's two highest volume purchasers of the bonds.[2]

"The ramifications of the result if the two countries decide to cash in their holdings of the bonds within the same year would be an incalculably enormous hit on the United States. It would devastate America's economy far beyond any recession or even the 1930s depression.

"Not counting interest, in 2013, the US was $17-plus trillion in debt. Want to know how much a trillion is? There are 8,640 hours in a year. If you live to 80, you've lived 691,200 hours, give or take. How many lifetimes is a trillion hours? How about 1,446,760 lifetimes! This is only 1 trillion. Convert that to dollars. The US is 17 times that in debt. Think we can ever repay that debt?

"An economist noted the other day, 'When a child wants something, it is the parents who buys it for them; in our economy, it is the kids who will be paying for the whims of their parents…and grandparents!'

"Also in 2013, the government shut down until its legislation allowed a higher debt to remove the shutdown. When will this mentality stop?

"We continue to play into the hands of who could become our enemies when push comes to shove! As for me, I am distraught that our kids, their children, and their grandchildren are stuck with our bills. And more, they will have their own world to finance too.

"I do not think anyone has an answer to fight our way out of this one.

"What we do not realize is that America is engaged in a financial war."[1]

With that he stepped down and slumped in his chair at the head table, his posture being the final significant stamp of his dissertation.

❧

UC Berkeley, Berkeley, California

Jack Robbins, a news interviewer at the top of this profession in California, is conducting an interview with Harvey Walstrom, a leading and highly regarded national and international financial and political analyst.

JACK. Do you agree with the majority of US citizens that the US is in a position of never righting itself from its massive debt? And why.

HARVEY. Yes, of course. For whatever the reason. For whatever the rationale. Whatever the belief or whatever the cause, the government leaders have overcommitted the federally sponsored financial obligations.

JACK. Such as?

HARVEY. First of all, let me say that it isn't any one obligation. It is the accumulation of them. Especially when adding borrowed debt with interest to cover the obligations. Military and military retirement; VA health care costs; social security; health care; the national highway infrastructure—roads, freeways, bridges; flood, fire, and tornado recovery; foreign aid; long-term health care; federal prison expenses; and now support of illegal immigrants. It is simply too much to bear.

JACK. Couldn't we cut back or raise taxes? That seems logical enough.

HARVEY. Neither, it seems, will occur at least to create any significant difference. The problems are (1) too many people with wrong skill sets to satisfy the severely changed job market leaving millions without incomes;(2) lobbyists will prevent any favorite program to be cut back or noticeably altered; (3) politicians want to remain in office, so raising taxes is not very feasible; and (4) a few corporate leaders have powerful sway in the political arena, who in fact always persuade legislative decisions in their favor; (5) most politicians owe favors to each other. This assures passage of bills even though they may not be in favor because of their debt causing a loss of freedom to vote on bills that their very own constituents put them in office for.

JACK. What a mess! Even though it could take one generation after another to fix this mess, is it possible?

HARVEY. Oh, sure, but there is not enough time! And there is another appalling political decision coming into the horizon.

JACK. What do you mean, Harvey?

HARVEY. As for time, I believe we are living in the last days as Bible prophecy indicates. The most appalling decision on the horizon is the abolishment of the US Constitution to accept a world constitution for its own. Just a decade ago, such a voiced thought by one of our political leaders would be enough for treason.

JACK. That won't happen…will it?

HARVEY. According to four senators, it will, yes.

JACK. You alluded to Bible prophecy. Are you a Christian believer?

HARVEY. No. But I cannot ignore how events taking place in the world today—this very day, are taking shape as the prophecies of Scripture has foretold.

JACK. For not being a believer, you seem quite knowledgeable about prophecies of the last days. How did that come about?

HARVEY. Suffice to say I have a devout Christian grandmother who makes sure her family is well-informed about Scripture.

JACK. Is there anything else you feel you should warn us about?

HARVEY. Yes, one. That unless our congressmen and women make huge changes to correct our present government, the only strength we will have is the war armada on the seas and the nuclear-equipped military bases in the Gulf. All else simply won't matter in the world regard to diplomatic or military might or sway. We have, I might say, flushed our core strengths and founding beliefs down the toilet! And far beyond any degree of recovery.

The interview then goes on its station break. It does not return on air.

⚜

The Mind Sweep Corporation
Franklin, Virginia

Mind Sweep is a private corporation of mind-trusts dedicated to the possibilities of the future world.

"A troublesome perspective among nations surrounding Israel has come, more than ever, foreboding, especially Iran.

"Iran's arsenal including nuclear warheads on numerous missiles has clearly crossed a threshold dreaded by many countries. Even its allies are fearful. And well they should be.

"The most troubling concerns of Iran is its proxy terrorists. They are planted everywhere around the globe. Undetected, never identified. Not a clue who, what, or why. They could be living next door, teaching our children, conducting a viable business, attending our churches unaware, or being elected to political offices. They could be living aboard small water craft in our harbors. Or in upscale neighborhoods as upright citizens. Or managers and vice presidents in the corporate world. Then at a moment's notice from Iran, they would spring into action for which they are uniquely trained. They could act together simultaneously or separately in unison or sequentially and individually. No one would know who they are until their actions reveal their mission.

"North Korea is alongside Iran in regard to its ultimate goal: control of the masses. The two may even battle united together for a short while before becoming enemies. One thing is certain. North Korea is an independent power without one shred of censorship by another governing body, such as the United Nations charters.

"And they also have nuclear warheads. That's plural—*warheads*. According to surveillance by drones and graphic displays of digital war games, their missiles armed with nuclear devices are aimed at major world cities except cities in Asia or other locations not in their interest.

"China could be a winner-take-all kind of situation. They could own the Western world without firing a shot or launching any form of missile. Every Western country could be under China's control by either unrecoverable debt owed or property they are downright owners or corporations where they are major stockholders.

"Japan is again a threat. Only this time they're right up there with China in the buying of US Treasury Bonds! At any given time, they can outpurchase China of the US Bonds offered by the USA to satisfy their frenzied need of cash to avoid bankruptcy.

"Then there is the measurement of a nation's actual worth: gold. Though it wavers between $2,600 and a low of $2,100 an ounce, it will likely reach $4,000 within a few years—if not months, as the gold supply and mining of it becomes nearly nonexistent. China will own the larger portion of gold in the world.

"Has anyone looked at Psalm 83 in the Scripture lately? We should pay attention to it. For the first time in modern history, the Muslims in Arab countries have joined in with the Arab nations against Israel as prescribed in Psalm 83. War is brewing that some are referring to as the Middle East War.

"Not much can be said for the United States either! It long ago has sold itself to the devil by selling its assets to other world powers and making horrifically poor internal choices:(1) allowing China to become its master; (2) being a participating country of the forming of the world constitution; and (3) becoming a country without companionship with and derailing from God in its activities and principles. In these last days, the last days of the good ol' USA has come: much too late for any form of renewal or turnaround.

"Finally, a consideration never mentioned: the Internet. It was begun as an academic exchange of information between universities, the principal being UCLA. It soon became the method of relaying US military information between bases. We all know what it is now. All routing of e-mails, blogs, websites, and cloud communication is through only a few massive, secret computer locations in the United States. Maybe you knew that. But did you know that all, as of 2015, communication originating outside the borders of the USA passes through US's Internet computers? And further, did you know during 2016 to 2017, the Internet is now a function of multinational countries, outside the USA, of which America has only a small part?

"My question is this: could a country, or an empire of the future, construct its own system of computer databanks so massive it would overshadow that of the multinational Internet and transfer all of the routing to an improved version of Internet transmissions?

"Before we assume not, just consider how many countless of times during the course of computer technology we have come upon barriers to only discover ways to overcome those barriers in the creating of what we have today! There will always be barriers to further knowledge, seemingly impossible barriers. But we, mankind, always find solutions to overcome them. How can we be aloof enough to disregard the possibility that the Internet could be hosted by another country or empire in the future we now know nothing about? More on this later!

"The fluctuating status of the EU only needs a leader capable of taking it to a higher level of power and influence, and this is now transpiring.

"Since 2015, the European Union—Euro Union or EU—is rebounding at an accelerated pace following a financial and governmental slump reaching its lowest point in 2014. A young man has risen notably upon the political scene from Italy, Radolfo Amerinero. This voice has brought a fresh outlook into the parliament of the EU and effectively reminded it of its purpose.

"The EU consists of twenty-four countries after the withdrawal of England. A host of countries are seeking the advantages of being included in the EU and are actively seeking membership. The quiet control of Radolfo Amerinero, the young man from Italy, introduced to the ten representatives governing EU that the membership be expanded to thirty-two over the next eight years, allowing two during each of those years.

"Supplies of oil are rapidly diminishing in the countries which the EU membership is forced to depend upon. Israel does not want to share its recently discovered oil or natural gas reserves with the EU for fear they will use the asset against them.

"The reluctance is causing hard feelings toward Israel. War, again, is considered to force to change the minds of the Israeli leaders. Once again, Israel is the object of war threats but now from a whole, new, and different source. It is not Arabic. It isn't even Muslim. Within a short time, the Roman Empire of Amerinero's doing could be reestablished in size or even expand beyond boundaries of historic times with his guidance. Israel is being squeezed from all sides because of its being viewed as a prized spoil of war, now that it has the oil reserve and other natural amenities in abundance.

"Rumor has it that Israel and Iraq is building, supported by funding from their oil and gas sales, satellites having the capability to detonate an EMP blast upon command from a control center on ground. Iraq's technological mind source is from the EU scientific community believed to be led by a political upcoming force, Radolfo Amerinero.

"All of the Middle East countries are in fear that this rumor could actually be true! No region, no city on earth can be warned quickly enough of the detonating of this device. It is impossible. After ignition of an EMP from a satellite, the instantaneous blast and its force will take place within seconds.

"And now, as promised, here's more about the Internet and global finance.

"A financial phenomenon is occurring on the Internet right now—today. A single, digital, open-source based technology allows a separate economy generated only on the Internet to exist. This new and burgeoning economy sidesteps any government-sponsored form of money and eliminates the need for a central banking system throughout the entire world.[1] At the present time, it's unstable. But its premise deserves a long, hard look at this technology. Sooner or later, the public at large will recognize its significant advantages when adequate safeguards are implemented to prevent sabotage. Predictably there will be the typical break-in factors, hacking, and other challenges of this monetary system until one day it or another improved nontraditional banking system will come upon the scene. When that transpires, the entire banking system as we know it, and which the world depends, will be replaced.

"The question is then: who will own the new financial system? China? Certainly not the USA! Japan? Iran? Russia? A single individual? A clandestine group of financiers? A few warmongers? A collection of foreign isolationists?

"In 1834, the United States made gold their single monetary standard, a currency backed by precious metal. Thomas Paine wrote, 'Gold and silver are the emissions of nature, the quantity of which is determined the earth's limited source; paper, too plentiful and too easily obtained, is the emission of art. Paper currency not backed by precious metal will undoubtedly remove freedom.'[2]

"So how is a paper bill that states its worth, say ten dollars, is actually worth ten dollars? Or more than ten dollars? Or less? Who determines its worth? Let's ask ourselves this: Can a village in a remote area, totally self-sufficient, create a financial system based upon rocks weighing between such and such ounces or pounds where the surface of their ground is all sand? Who or what determines the rocks' value? So it is with establishing the value of the dollar or any form of currency.

"When all is said and done about only a few determine the new financial concept and worth,[2] the real danger is that a single entity—whether it be a government, a dictatorship, a conglomerate, or for that matter, a single dictatorial, powerful individual—could gain full rule of the world's economy and the movement of money merely by a declaration when he or she is that powerful that they could!

"Incidentally, the Scripture foretells us that such an individual[3] will so dominate the world, and he will do exactly what we fear."

Skirmish or War on Israel?

"It's apparent that a great war upon Israel is within a few days," voiced the Middle East news analyst Jolene Jacobsen. "The horizon of war has given in to a boiling point with Arabs. They are fed up with all the Israeli rhetoric and power ruses. It is more than my mere opinion that they are doing this knowing full well that the Israeli military strength is second to none in the region.

"No matter," she continues, "the sheer power of those nations' resolve will drive them ahead.

"With great success, Iran is adding fuel to the flame while it is leading nations of the north to bring about its own war on Israel in the very near future. There is every indication Iran is forming a coalition army of countries to swarm upon Israel. The strategic planning has begun. It has been discovered to be so immense that it will be the first and final in modern history to completely annihilate Israel. So of course, to fan the flame of war by others upon Israel before their attack will soften the resistance.

"I might add that numerous Bible prophecy scholars of renowned respect have concluded that what Iran is amassing is the coming battle of Gog and Magog. They could be right."

Jacobsen continues, "Last week I had an interview with the Reverend Anthony Delano and asked him questions on the subject.

"Israel continues to be a target, especially with the newly discovered oil reserves. When combined with its established wealth, its highly regarded prized geographic location, who, by the way they took from Palestine after World War II, is certainly in envy of other surrounding countries. This is my lead to my first question: Is this the Gog and Magog battle?"

"No, because this is of the Arab countries taking arms against Israel, not Muslim."

"And that means?"

"First, it is interesting that Scripture says that God will put a hook in Russia's mouth to draw them into an immense war with Israel.[1] But Russia is not involved with the planning by the Arabs of this war on the horizon. Though the battle of Gog and Magog is forming,[2] I believe that what Iran is putting into place, as we speak, cannot be avoided by Russia. This is thought so with many of my colleagues."

"Could this be referred to as the Battle of the Middle East?"

"Some believe it's the prophecy of Psalm 83. It is possible. I'm not sure, though likely, I believe."[3]

"Is there a possibility for the US becoming militarily engaged when a significant attack on Israel would occur?"

"The US would engage, I suspect, hopefully not. This could lead into a war the world does not want."

"Next I asked about another concern: What about the Islam Caliphate in Iran? How do they figure into the planning of the destruction of Israel?"

"They'll have a significant role in the formulation of Gog and Magog."

"So you believe we are living in the last days?"

"Oh yes."

"I have to ask. Are you a born-again believer? His answer was the last of the interview."

"Yes, certainly."

"That was refreshing. I find it difficult to believe a person with any intimate knowledge of Bible prophecies would not be a Christian in the most basic sense, born-again. Even nonbelievers seem to know we are living in the last days as Scripture warns us."

Jolene continues her report a few weeks later.

"Armies of an Arab coalition are now in position to attack. To avoid detection of significance by Israeli guard posts, the troops are in small numbers at many locations surrounding Israel's borders. They had begun their assembling over weeks each day, an hour after dark slowly and quietly into the wee hours of morning.

"Iran and the Euro Union, with Amerinero heading a delegation to call off their war, is conferring from sunrise to sunset with the

Arab war strategists. All to no avail, they are determined to conduct war on Israel, a war to end all wars against Israelis.

"Weapons and plastic explosives are hidden in their robes, large artillery skillfully camouflaged, no mechanized combat weaponry.

"Camels, horses, and donkeys number in the hundreds are the way of advancing through Israel's checkpoints once they're open. In less than two hours, the Arab militants are within Israel's borders.

"At a predetermined predefined moment, the Arab militants begin their killing as a swarm of bees sting people at a picnic—swiftly, effectively, and during panic of its subjects. The locations of the killing grounds are so many that Israeli soldiers are initially dysfunctional and disorganized at the onslaught.

"Soon though, the Israeli military responds with killings of their own in like manner, effectively eliminating the Arab attackers unwilling of taking prisoners. The war is over before midday.

"Iranian leaders, Saudi sheiks, and the United Arab Emeritus strategists are unhappy with the result. They had hoped for far more damage to Israel.

"In the aftermath, Israel maintained tighter checkpoint control, causing hours upon hours of delay to gain entrance into Israel. Soldiers' presence on roads, in cities and villages, and places of gatherings are doubled. Searching of every individual is mandatory, including women and children.

"The world's response was newsworthy, for a short time. The news of The Middle East[1] war had become so common that its news value waned. Foreign country interventions were limited as usual as in the past, creating little alarm. The Arab Middle East war had miserably failed its mission to annihilate Israel.

"As most wars engaged with Israel, the hatred continued toward them while Israel kept its vigil and resolve intact. The media quieted quickly. What was called the Middle East War by the media withered away after a few weeks."

2

THE ALEXANDERS

The Alexanders are an uncomplicated family of a laid-back rural, small city in mid-America. Leo and Connie, parents of Raymond and Steven, would not stand out in a crowd the same as most families don't. Leo works in a small company to support his family, having a beer with his buddies after work on Fridays. Connie is a stay-at-home mom and is quite comfortable, thank you, in her role.

Raymond and Steven are gregarious young teens having excelled in junior high through high school. Raymond became a musician and locally popular country Western singer. Steven is a serious book-worm with particular fascination with Bible stories and the New Testament Scriptures.

Steven's mom wonders why his interest is so enthusiastic. She avails herself frequently to Steven's pursuit of learning the passages, realizing there are far worse things he could be enticed to be doing.

Connie, once being a lead singer in a regional popular rock band, encourages Raymond with his guitar to being a player rather than a mere strummer. As it turns out, she is an adept guitar teacher for Raymond. Leo gave in to Connie's pleading one Christmas and bought a Fender Stratovaris guitar when Raymond was just twelve years old. Having such a fine instrument began his storied music career early on.

Because of Steven's influence by his studying Scripture, Connie insisted that the family begin attending church—the whole family. Leo balked. Raymond suggested that she and Steven attend. But she was insistent for them to all attend together; after all, how could it not help her family?

"What's wrong with our family?" Leo insisted.

"Nothing, really. Ah, come on, Leo. Be a sport. Tell you what. Let's all attend for a month every Sunday. I'll pick the church. A

Protestant one. We go there four Sundays in a row. If you don't like it, I'll concede, not letting it become an issue." Connie's deal held up. She selected North Shore Bible Church in Grand Lake, Ohio. They all attended the four Sundays of April.

Leo liked the pastor. He was inspiring, polite, a straight shooter, and knowledgeable. Leo and Steven immediately hit it off with him. Raymond was undecided but went along. Soon the family chose to continue attending every Sunday, including Raymond.

Connie became increasingly interested in the messages that Pastor Ben, as he preferred to be addressed, delivered. They rang with truth and meaning. Leo continued his Fridays with the guys; Raymond diligently practiced his music, as Steven grew in scriptural knowledge. In fact, two or three times a month, Steven would drop in at Pastor Ben's office after school for discussions.

Betty Jean Tercel, pastor Ben's wife, and Connie hit it off as though they had known each other since childhood. Like sisters. Soon after, the Alexander family began to steadily attend church, and Connie began being involved with a number of activities.

Only a few months had passed when Betty Jean took it upon herself to confront Connie about salvation and where she stood concerning it. They had completed a planning meeting and the others who attended were gone when Betty Jean had decided to talk to Connie. They got coffee and sat at the table. Connie was puzzled at Betty Jean's change of demeanor from gaiety to seriousness.

Betty Jean came to the point without ado.

"Connie, have you ever accepted Christ as your personal savior?"

"What do you mean, Bet?"

"Well, you know, invite him into your heart to be the lord and master of your life. That is why he died on the cross and was resurrected, so that we may live a life of holiness before God. Have you ever done that, Connie?"

"No, I guess not," answered Connie thoughtfully.

"Would you like to? Right here? Right now?"

"Yes."

They prayed together. Afterward they embraced. Both had tears on their cheeks. As Connie wiped them away with the back of her hand, she declared, "I feel so clean inside! Never have I felt like this."

They chatted about what had just transpired on the way to their cars. The drive home for Connie had a new thrill in her heart. She could barely wait to tell her family about it. She even thought of driving to Leo's workplace to share her excitement with him. But instead she went straight home.

Neither of the boys were there. She would have to wait though she was at wit's end to share her new love for Christ with her family.

A few hours later, she did.

Leo wondered what his "new" wife would now be like as did the boys wonder about how their lives would be affected with a "new mom."

Almost instantly, the Alexander home had changed. Connie's love had taken hold beyond what she could have ever imagined. Everyone, in as well as outside their home, readily recognized a new Connie. It didn't take much time before she became interested in the last days as the Bible has prophesied.

After numerous discussions with Pastor Ben on the subject of the last days, Connie became sensitized to its meaning and what she needed to do about it, if anything at all. She prayed.

Not long afterward, she felt compelled to approach Pastor Ben with an idea she believed came from her prayers of what to do about what she could recognize were the last days. She set an appointment with him, not informing him what the meeting would be about.

At the appointed time, she presented her notion.

After a few minutes of soft talk, she began.

"Pastor Ben, I have lately engrossed myself with studying the lives of the old-time preachers of American history. There were many. I am also paying attention to whatever I can to some of the Bible prophecy. There, one thing stands out to me. It admonishes us that in the last days we should be telling the world more about Christ as these days approach! We are here, in the last days, right?"

"Why yes, we are, Connie."

"Uh-huh, well. I've put the two together. Why can't we have an old-time revival campaign as in the old days for these last days?"

"I don't really know why we can't," he casually replied, much too casually for Connie, in fact.

"Tell me, Pastor Ben, can we do this right here in your church?"

"Well... I—"

"I detect a big hesitation with the idea."

"When is the last time you heard of such a meeting?"

"By my reading only, quite a few years ago. As far as my own experience, never. So what are you getting at?" inquired Connie.

"Connie, I admire your enthusiasm. But there's a reason. No one would attend. Times are different. People have too many commitments to find the time or have the interest to attend a revival meeting compared to back then."

"I don't believe that is altogether true, Pastor Ben."

"Oh?"

"Yes. I believe in these last days, that is, believed by more people than just the born-again Christians, such meetings should be conducted, and further, I believe God will bless the efforts beyond our remotest expectations!"

"Maybe you're right."

"So you'll do it?"

"I didn't say that. Slow down, Connie. There's the church board to deal with. They have to approve such an undertaking. I sincerely do not believe they'll support such an idea."

"Then I have no choice, Pastor Ben, but to keep trying until I find a church that will." She stood as a signal her time with Pastor Ben was over. He stood following her lead. They parted friendly enough. He realized she was on a mission and meant what she said.

Acting on her own, Connie continued to follow the call in her heart. Only one pastor of the eleven churches in town could grasp onto her vision. Every one turned her down without even a moment of consideration. Nearly all had the same response as did Pastor Ben.

Fearlessly and undaunted, she kept trying.

Her efforts finally paid off.

"Connie, the board has been noticing and hearing from people of other churches throughout the area what you are trying to do. Cecil Watson, our board chairman, called a special meeting last evening. Let me be the first to tell you that they unanimously approved your plan on one condition."

Overjoyed she managed to ask of the one condition.

"You must be the one to cause it to happen. The board has also approved three thousand dollars to fund your efforts. There is another stipulation: every significant decision you're to make must be approved by the board in advance. Okay with you?"

"It certainly is," she responded with excitement and tears forming. There remained one possible snag however.

Leo.

Stretching her patience, she waited for Leo to return home from work. Hours crept so slowly. Though the boys had come home from school, she chose to tell Leo first.

From as far up the road as she could see, Leo was finally arriving home from his drive from Columbus. Her excitement grew as he turned onto the long driveway. *What is taking him so long to get out of the truck when I have this important news?* she thought. And finally she could, at last, tell him.

He sensed her eagerness to inform him of something vitally important, something positively good.

She threw her arms around his neck as she declared in his ear (a little too loud), "The church is endorsing the revival meetings that I have an idea to do. Isn't that just so outstanding, so awesome!"

He immediately realized his "Yes, it is, honey" fell far short of the mark of congratulating her. She pulled back and looked into his eyes.

"It is, isn't it?"

"Let's go inside. You can tell me all about it. When were you informed?" Arm in arm they went into the kitchen and sat at the table, the table where important conversations usually took place. To Connie, this was probably the most important of all their meetings. Leo knew enough about his wife this was one of those moments.

She told him every detail. "So what do you think?"

"About what, dear? About what?" he repeats to stall a moment in time to make sure he answers without dampening her enthusiasm. He knew he could never live this one down if he answered too casually or too confrontationally.

"First that comes to mind, it's a lot of effort required and a whole bunch of time too, I'm sure you appreciate that fact. You know how much effort and thought it takes to make any worthwhile production to happen successfully. And you have your family to take care of too."

She gives him a look he knew all too well when he's close to stepping out-of-bounds, so he softened his response. "Oh sure, we'll pick up the slack with you being busy on this. And just to make the record straight, I am with you one hundred percent for whatever you need to do."

She relaxes as he continues.

"Second, what if in spite of all your efforts, it's a flop?"

"A flop?" she responds incredibly.

"Well…yes. People have hordes of stuff to do during a week, so what makes you think they'll attend a weeklong religious campaign or whatever you call it?"

"Prayer and God," she confidently replies, "God will inspire attendance."

"Yeah, well, I hope you're right. Again, honey, let me say that I am fully supportive of you with this." He gets up and walks around the table to the other end and kisses her on her forehead. She reaches up and touches his face to show her appreciation. They understand each other.

❧

As it turned out, Steven Alexander was what he thought, the satisfaction of his career after college knowing that he'd made the right choice in engineering. He appreciated and liked the challenge of mathematics and the infinite sciences that creative algorithms can achieve. His employer, Shuttle Technologies Inc., assigned him to join the new developmental design crew. He was soon nearly over his head. But he was a survivor and quickly became a contributor.

Steven's interactions with his family gradually slipped after he moved away from home to becoming somewhat distant. His study of Scripture did not diminish however. But his interest in the Bible somehow did not make its way from his head to his heart. It was all an intellectual exercise bearing only some resemblance of the scriptural message. Satan had deceived him by being satisfied to his living a good, moral life. He lived with this belief to his satisfaction.

❦

Raymond in the meantime became an accomplished locally popular musician with his band. The money rolled in while his spiritual life dwindled in an equal, opposite direction.

Connie and Leo were hurt of course, but continued to believe God would intervene in both of their sons' lives. Leo depended upon Connie's prayers while he continued to be supportive of her project.

Connie stayed the course—very diligently. The date was set. She had ten months to pull it all together for the revival meeting's opening Saturday afternoon. This included obtaining the speaker having a highly regarded gift of persuasive preaching to obtain a high degree of spiritual awakening. Once she had the speaker in place, the rest seemed to her would be easy.

Prayer for success consumed much of her time. It seemed like prayer dominated her every thought.

She often considered hiring an advertising firm to publicize the weeklong event. But each time she had that consideration, an inner voice told her no—plain and simple no. As the date drew nearer, the more she had to depend upon the Lord about the matter of attendance. It was, by itself, a proof of disciplined faith and trust.

Three weeks into the planning, she received a return phone call from a Taylor Benjamin, an evangelist out of Missouri. He was the fourth who called in response to her list of nine potential speakers. There was no witness to her heart with the first three. Within minutes, Taylor won her heart with his forthright and straight approach of the Gospel and its message meant for the last days. She recommended him to the board through Pastor Ben.

As they had never heard of him, they approved only after checking out his references. They received high marks from many pastors where he had held meetings such as was being planned by Connie.

But the real test of Connie's resolve to see the revival meeting's success came two weeks before the date was arriving. Leo had fallen off a ladder and shattered his hip, broke some ribs, fractured his forearm at multiple places, and hyperextended his wrist, causing separated bones. Her attention upon Leo took first place as she barely kept her heart and attention upon her duties of the upcoming meetings. But she's undaunted and focused, keeping herself prioritized. And Leo insisted she stay with it; he could manage.

God blessed her efforts.

3

RADOLFO AMERINERO

That man, born near Milan, Italy, in the countryside of rolling hills covered with vineyards, Radolfo, was born into the Amerinero family. Except in the eyes of his parents, he wasn't particularly a special baby. That opinion changed dramatically within weeks of his birth when it was realized his development was far advanced beyond what is that of even gifted children.

Before he was three years old, he had acquired interests of equal abilities with a wide range of skills and curiosities. Most noticeable was his physical dexterity and mental associative aptitudes. By five years old, because of his parents' awareness of the powers of their son and their encouragement, he displayed competence with soccer, mathematics, deductive logic, and strategic planning learned during his extraordinary skill on the chessboard.

With special tutoring, he had completed college prep studies before his eleventh birthday, a multiple of BA of science degrees from Berlin University and three master's degrees from Oxford, including international finance, world diplomacy, and domestic politics prior to his turning eighteen. He acquired his divinity doctorate from the Vienna School of Divinity the following year after which he studied Shia law of the Muslim faith. Secretly from close acquaintances, he converted from Catholicism to Islam taking on the name of Amid Baker Mohammed.

Private tutoring as a teenager kept him from undesired notoriety and recognition. Every single professor or tutor signed a contract to never divulge his age, courses of study, or his faith except when legally required to do so only with his authority. No one thought of scouring public records to reveal his age.

During his youthful studies, he found that he could compile international political wisdom, most of all, to assemble them into single, useful conclusions. Over a short time, this aptitude yielded unusual financial gains. The world seemed to build his platform for him as an authority. Soon his website blogs achieved fast acceptance because his shared knowledge became a legendary trust factor. The massive monthly income from the website enabled Radolfo to buy a Greek Isle villa when he was just sixteen, a gift to his parents and his frequent retreat. His age was never disclosed. The world assumed he could not be a day younger than forty. No one could be so wise in so many aspects to endure unscathed by the scrutiny he seemed to embrace! No one younger could have either the maturity or insight. So it is not surprising how totally amazed the world was when he released his age—on his twenty-first birthday, accompanied with a photo.

Two years later, he sold his twelve-year-old Internet website having over 900 thousand subscribers worldwide paying $350 for yearly subscriptions for $145,000,000. Then, to learn more about the Internet's Bitcoin,[1] he made a $17 million investment realizing such a significant amount would have an invaluable schooling effect in what he knew a continuing prolific career was awaiting him.

Soon after his twenty-first birthday, with special interests in the EU, he entered Italian politics. Though his peers knew of his online expert opinions—some were subscribers—they surely wanted to know how he would hold up, being so young, in the halls of parliament when under fire as an honorary, guest orator, or panelist. Not only did he hold up, he excelled. It took less than a year and a half before his leadership skills took hold. Many of his adversaries—his age thought to be to their advantage—were taken by surprise by his oratory skill combined with his depth of wisdom. When a debater learned they'd be one-on-one with Amerinero, their eyes rolled in devastating reluctance: they knew the forcefulness of his presentations has overwhelmed every previous adversary.

Mysteriously he disappeared from public life, taking a year's sabbatical. This is when he was drawn to Turkey for Shia training and became a Muslim. As a Mohammed convert, he did the pilgrimage incognito to Mecca, followed the ritual of circling the Kaaba in the mosque seven times, and fought others to kiss the Black Stone, believing all his sins were forgiven by doing so. He returned resolving to be a faithful, ardent believer and engaged his daily prayers as all Muslim devotees.

Before two years after his return into public life, he was chosen to be Italy's representative at EU conferences. There, he was as successful as in Italy's parliament. More often than not, he won the majority of votes usually handily. So much so that he was often requested to present EU's strategic global plans at many diplomatic conferences. His persuasive skills were then extended to the UN General Assembly frequently when the EU determined to increase their recognition in a program bringing an increased positive posture. The UN never refused to schedule him as a knowledgeable expositor of timely world issues when that need arose.

Studying the various religions of the past and present is what gave him the most pleasure in spite of his new Muslim faith. He particularly studied archeology, anthropology, and studies of the Roman Empire in relationship to their religious beliefs. And of particular interest, how Christianity could have played fundamental roles in history. He studies this as though drawn to it and that he would have a future part in its unfolding! This is something he often explained to others in confidentiality.

A close friend, a major general in the Italian Army, often discussed notable military leaders of the world. Whether in the past or present, it didn't matter. Radolfo was most interested in military strategies and logistics, especially when engaged in war.

All during his educational experience and travels, his mentor of finance during his youth was always at his side or near him, at least, when in public or at home. He paid him a hefty salary to offer financial advice when areas of his expertise were required. Radolfo's attention was always quickly absorbed in the complexities of international finance.

At every opportunity that came in his path, to excel, he always hired the best knowledgeable, experienced, and proven supernaturally wise people. Money was of no object to have the best all-around counsel in law and subjects he thought would assist in his career goals.

He is keen to craft and utilize the leading edge of psychological/technological controls of the masses, it becoming his foremost obsession.

During his formidable years as a young man not yet turned thirty, he realized he needed a second-in-command skilled assistant who could make strong and intelligent decisions and who, like himself, possessed a wide range of abilities—all excellent and equally skilled in their deployment. And who had the same viewpoints of world dominance, if not Muslim as himself.

4

ALEXIS WERNER

At sixteen, Werner had become a gifted magician and witty entertainer. The two combined skills welded together so perfectly his performances are packed out. This income during his high school and college paid for his engineering degree, his master's in communication, and doctorate of international finance.

Prior to receiving his degrees, numerous companies recruited him offering low six-figure salaries. The best position that he accepted is senior manager of Robotics with the World Techniques Development Corporation based in Silicon Valley.

The company was in the middle stages of creating its first simulated human holograph complete with comprehensive word enunciation with facial expressions with precise synced lip-and-mouth movement. This was Werner's first assignment. His easiness in applying his skills set soon caught the attention of his coworkers, amazing them. Within a few weeks, he excelled with minimal assistance or instruction. That awareness by his colleagues developed into management's desire to include him into the senior management echelon.

He rapidly moved his department up in the company's respect. His team began producing quality images with such clarity the lifelike simulation would be, well, as life itself! This holographic plateau had never been reached, astounding everyone.

Two months or more passed by when he was called into the office of the vice president of New Development, Mr. McGregor, for a meeting at 1:00 p.m. He was not informed why.

He arrived on time, and McGregor's secretary walked him into the office and introduced him to the vice president. She asked him if he'd like tea. He did not; she turned and exited as she closed the door behind her.

"Please take a seat, Mr. Werner." Alexis sat at the chair across the desk from his host, curious. "Don't think for a moment we haven't observed not only your technical skills but your observational skill and technical leadership ability as well. Those are the attributes we require of the candidates from which we select executives."

Alexis's heart skipped a beat in anticipation picked up from the introduction.

"Thank you, Mr. McGregor."

"Oh, not at all. You caused us to realize that what you are doing is highly marketable. We're changing the name of your department into a completely new, autonomous profit center, apart from our other profit centers. We're calling it the Human Holographic Simulation Group. You are now a new vice president and the head of HHSC as its lead engineer. Sound good?"

"It certainly does, and I do accept. I trust that I will not disappoint the selection committee."

McGregor stood, and Alex followed his lead, then they shook hands. At that point, he thought the meeting had ended.

"By the way, Mr. Werner. I understand you're a practicing magician, true?"

"Yes, that's true."

"I bring this up because next month, we're having our twentieth anniversary and a companywide celebration for the CEO since its inception. Will you be a part of the program? We'd love to have you give a performance. I'm told you're quite good!"

He accepted with delight, knowing it will help his career.

It did.

Outside the fact that his little company within the company was the leading new categorical revenue generator of the company's sales, for which his salary reflected that success, the magic performance enhanced this lucrative avocation for him.

After gaining authorization to use a holographic model for his magic shows, he also became a local celebrity. He had gained the attention of Italy's Radolfo Amerinero.

A meeting was arranged.

They met, both having great mutual admiration for each other.

Following their exchange of respects, Amerinero came to the point of his desire to meet the young Werner.

"Mr. Werner."

"Please, call me Alex."

"I could have merely e-mailed you or otherwise introduced myself. But being in a nearby city, I decided it best to meet with you in person. I want you to give a presentation of your newest magic act at my villa in Greece. My staff of about forty would love to see it. You will be paid handsomely. But more than that, I have something more important to discuss with you in private. Suffice to tell you that what I have in mind is of worldwide impact. By now, Alex, you likely assumed I have thoroughly studied your file. Yes?"

"Yes."

"I need to discuss an important subject with you."

Radolfo moves to the edge of the overstuffed chair to communicate significance. Realizing it, Alex mimics Radolfo's posture. Radolfo appreciates the response of the young man.

"During the past few years, your career with holography has surpassed anything anyone has accomplished before you or even now."

"Well, I—"

Radolfo raises a hand to delay comment and continues, "I have engaged many conversations with your superior, Mr. McGregor, concerning your ability and possible interest to pursue another leading technology necessary for the safety and security of life as we know it on this planet. This is a discussion of another subject.

"But first. Do you accept to do your magic performance at my villa?"

Upon acceptance, Amerinero handed him a $70,000 check.

Radolfo had expected Alex to be taken by surprise as he was. His jaw dropped, his eyes opened wider, his hands disappeared between his knees delicately holding the check. An expression of amazement caused a speechless response. This, before he could ask Radolfo to inform him of what technology he had in mind. It had to wait until later, as Radolfo quickly excused himself with a "See you then" after standing.

Two weeks later, Alex, with two assistants, presented his magic show at Amerinero's villa. The response was genuinely overwhelming. Minutes afterward, Alex and Radolfo met in a lavish side room to have their planned discussion.

"Alex, I'm talking about EMP. The world knows how detrimental an EMP event can affect an intended target."

"Sure. I know about that. What has that got to do with me?"

"Plenty, I would hope."

Alex is ready and eager to listen what this charismatic man has to say.

"I need a science researcher like you to discover effective, comprehensive, and sure protection against an EMP attack. Such as how to harden present devices and new devices being manufactured against the injurious result of EMP. I do not wish to look further for that individual beyond you, Mr. Werner."

A significant silence ensues, much longer than Radolfo desires, but he waits as Alex absorbs and connects the new information to result in a choice. Finally.

"I've spent nearly my entire career on holography and human neurology. What you are asking of me is wholly, completely a new field for me. EMP has been around since the 1960s. There must be many you can choose from who've been in the EMP tech science better than I!"

"Yes, there are. And as you say, many. Hundreds in fact. None are like you, Alex. You think outside the box for new approaches and new methods to solve old problems. Surely way more than most. And certainly beyond the top in their fields. We have considered a few."

"How many is a few?"

"Eight."

"Eight? That's all? It's a short list."

"Of the best, Alex, for what we need. You always came up on top."

"If I accept, will I be able to continue my work with holography and neurology? They are not in any way similar to EMP technology."

"We have made accommodations with your job description to allow your continuation of your work in your chosen fields. All we ask is for meaningful progress in your work for us."

"Who, by the way, is *us*?"

"My company, of course."

"Do I have some time to decide upon your offer? I assume my compensation will be quite worthwhile?"

"Well worthwhile. Far more than now. Is two days enough time?

"Tomorrow's fine."

"Tomorrow it is, then."

Another hour is consumed in discussion of other mutual interests before they disband. They like each other and know they can work in harmony together. Both strangely feel their lives are pulled together as a magnetic force.

Alex Werner eagerly accepts Mr. Amerinero's offer before boarding the yacht to return him to the mainland the following day.

5

DAMIAN KALENCO

Like most six-year-olds, Damian could teach his grandparents a thing or two about computers, the Internet, smartphone devices, and cyberspace. In fact, a great deal! Unlike most kids his age, he not only quickly mastered video games to their highest level but began learning how the programming of them was structured.

Having parents whose lives are built around technology sciences certainly helped. But not any more than a cat will become a dog by sleeping in a doghouse. To become the whiz kid Damian has become takes hours upon hours of practice to develop demanding skills at the peak level where he performs every day. Half a million gamers spend four hours a day playing video games. Not Damian. Six to eight hours is his norm; Brenda, his mom, home-teaches to make time for him to spend in front of the screen. Doc Kalenco, his father, encouraged Brenda this routine because he understood the potential of what Damian's interest could achieve. He didn't look at video game playing as a waste of time like most parents.

And most parents are correct; for most kids, it is a waste of time. Most that is. For many, however, it becomes a foundation during early year development of the math sciences required to write the programming of video games. It is not unusual for high math classrooms in colleges to be filled with avid game players.

The Kalencos lived in an overcrowded suburbia town east of Seattle. Microsoft is only a few miles away. There's an abundance of children in Damian's neighborhood. One day when he was nine years old, he decided to have an online video player's club whose members are required to live within a two-mile radius of his address. He made this a rule for the purpose of conducting a monthly live club meeting.

Four months after the first meeting (forty-three kids attended), the attendance was mounting quickly beyond seventy. Not expected! Over a hundred kids were turned away. The fifth month was held in the local library where there's room for two hundred. Doors were open at 6:00 p.m. for the meeting to begin at 7:00. They didn't wait for 7:00 p.m. to arrive; serious discussion began far before. Within fifteen minutes, capacity was reached! The fire code forced an estimated sixty to seventy kids to be turned away.

Much to the surprise of the kids' parents, who were the children's taxi drivers, the majority of kids had the self-taught skills to write the programming for simple but multifaceted video games. The majority of discussions involved line programming shortcuts and algorithms. To do this in the real world of video game production requires advanced calculus and trigonometry, which the kids had little, if any, formal training. Shortcutting to the open-source codes, they simply learned how! While nearly all the kids were older than twelve and thirteen years, Damian was ten and had skills far advanced over the others.

By the time he and his fellow students were sophomores in high school, they were all practicing high calculus at the college level.

Along with this knowledge, they developed a few of their own renditions of video games. Some of the games reached the commercial market. A few of the students, including Damian, were offered serious retainers by video game manufacturers. Unwittingly he had become the leader of high demand sourcing of superstar video game developers.

One day, when seventeen, Damian read a report on cyberpsychology, a theory to obtain psychological powers to control actions of people by use of cyberspace technology, a form of subliminal persuasion discovered in the 1950s used for marketing purposes.[1] It was then he decided to pursue the study of psychology in college. He had become intrigued by the concept of combining neurological science with psychology and cyber-persuasion. With the help of a career guidance counselor at Stanford, he devised a fast-track master's degree plan. At twenty-two, he had his doctorate in neurology from Stanford University.

Soon after, he began his professional services: cyberpsychoneurological consulting. He thought that if a client could enunciate the name of his service, then he would have more of an open ear toward those clients rather than who could not. Plainly put, he specialized in the adaption of the psychoneurology science into cyberspace marketing of products and services with a video game. In effect, after playing the video, a person could not explain why they would buy a product they didn't care for, or accept a philosophy they never believed, or take sides of a debated issue contrary to their own values, or accept a perceived premise opposite from their beliefs, or to join forces with a cause they disagreed with by being subjected to Damian's approach of mind conditioning and manipulation. Because of the extraordinary success, he is paid excessively high fees for his commercialization integration.

The patented video game is always included whenever a prospective buyer comes online to review a client's offer. It is irresistible to play because of significant discounts offered according to the level of victory over an adversary in the game. What the player/prospect does not know is that a subliminal message is not apparent as they play the video, all the while convincing them they need the product or service at any cost!

Damian's customers report that sales increased between 465 percent to over 600 percent directly attributed to use of the video game in their reworked website featuring the video. What caused Damian's fast wealth are the 132 patents he held that comprehensively limited any competition. If a video producer wanted the benefits of this new manipulation science, they were forced to come to Damian and pay him fees in the millions of dollars for licensing the use the patented techniques.

⚜

"Have you heard about Damian Kalenco, twenty-four years old? He's the one whose making a ton of money from what he calls cyberpsychoneurology?" asks Werner of Radolfo.

"Cyberpsycho—what?" replies Radolfo.

"Cyberpsychoneurology."

"No. No, I haven't. Why?"

"I bring him to your attention because he has hit on a really valuable, unique science that I highly regard as something we need to take a serious look."

"Sounds like you're quite adamant about it. Why?"

"It seems as though by satellite utilizing virtual reality with the Internet, this new science technology can literally cause people to do things, think of things, and act upon things merely by suggestive powers they hear from his techniques in a video game!"

"You have my undivided attention," responds Radolfo as he leans forward and clasps his hands on the desk. "What is his background? Any special training?"

"Yes, he has very special training that actually includes his work experience. The combination of the two makes for a special fellow. According to our research, he was instrumental in bringing multithreading architecture into his knowledge of program language design which he used for complex computer graphics and technology engineering management. As a result, he's created a software graphics program of virtual reality for lifelike video games with imbedded mental manipulation instructions that is totally subliminal."

"Sounds like we should make an offer he would consider foolish to refuse: including buying the hundred-plus patents he owns."

"Then what? Send him on his merry way? Take residuals from his efforts?"

"Oh no. We envelop his company into ours and continue him as CEO with freedom to carry on with unceasing perfection and development. We'll pay him an enormous salary of course."

"Of course," agrees Radolfo, "do it. Report back at important steps of progress."

By a plan set out, a staff member of Werner's became a customer of Damien's. They bought a successful Chevrolet/Buick dealer to use the video game that they played on a series of sixty-inch flat screens in the waiting areas where there's comfortable, separate viewing rooms a customer could have control of a video game in which they were the main heroic character. However, they were totally unaware of a subliminal message being repeated over and over again while they played the video: convincing them that buying a new car is better than repairing the car now being serviced.

Within a month, sixty-seven service customers bought autos as a direct response to the video game. In the third month, new car sales jumped another 154 percent. Profit on the trade-ins went off the charts because of the high-quality autos being traded in.

Werner was convinced it is mandatory to bring Damian aboard. During the fourth month of using the video game, Werner had Damian sitting across from him at his desk in Brussels after his flight from LAX.

"You probably do not know that we bought an auto dealership solely for the purpose of using your video game on service customers to convince them to purchase a new car."

"Did you now? Did it work well for you?"

"It exceeded our expectations, I assure you," replied Werner.

"Is this why you brought me here, to tell me how well it worked for you? You could have texted me that."

"Okay. We'll get to the point."

"We want to buy your consulting service, including the video game patents, and full licensing rights from you."

"Can't be done. Not for sale," he said as he stood up and extended his hand to signify the meeting was over with a handshake. "Thank you for my trip to Brussels. According to my return ticket, I have tomorrow to tour your city."

"Please, at least hear my offer. You can do that, right? On balance, we paid for all your expenses to get you here and your return. You can give us the benefit of doubt, am I not right, Damian?"

Damian slowly sat down. "Yeah, I'll give you that."

"How's $750 million sound to you?"

"It's a start. You have my attention."

"A start? That's all?" A long silence before, "Okay, five hundred million dollars, you keep the patents, sell the licensing rights to us without restriction, just as you're doing now. But we own your business and pay you a salary."

"That's closer. Any other ideas?" Another long silence as the two stare each other without a blink of the eyes.

"All right. You continue with the same clients currently in your stable. We pay you a three-million-dollar salary to work for us toward our agenda."

"Are you talking about the car dealership? You've got to be kidding me!"

"Oh no. A whole lot more than that. Much more."

"Are you aware who Radolfo Amerinero is, Damian?"

"Yes, of course. He's a prominent world leader. Who wouldn't know about him? Why?"

"He is the one who wants to hire you. All you have to do is name your price. Your skills to produce such a powerful video game are the precise skill set we need to accomplish our goals."

"I'm still listening."

"So. Are you in? Or out? Need time to think about it? If you do, how long before you decide? And feel free to make a counteroffer. You can e-mail your response through our secure website."

Werner hands him the address.

Damian returned to his beachfront, hillside Malibu mansion overlooking the Pacific Ocean. The following day, Werner received an e-mail:

> *Save ur money. No need to hire me. For 500k will produce a video. Can do five times a year: each a masterpiece of subliminal manipulation. Will not sell company or patents. This does not deflect from my serving you with the best possible results. I'm out if not acceptable; in, if you accept.*

Werner returned his text:

> *Accept. one mil deposited directly for first two vids.*

Werner returned the e-mail to Amerinero:

> *Damien contracted to produce 5 vids a year for 500k each. Says each will be masterpieces of mentally subversive content. We made the right choice. He has been paid for first two; to begin 1ˢᵗ vid immediately. We should have vid within 3 mos: Will not sell company or any of its patents.*

After his return to his production office, Damien conducts a meeting with four of his most skilled video technologists to explain the new contract. He fills them in with the peripheral data before making the challenge.

"We need the first of three to be an example of our capabilities. Pull out the stops, let your every imaginative innovation to trip up viewer's subconscious to accept, by manipulation, the strongest subliminal influence we are capable of producing."

They ask a few questions, and get satisfying answers. During the same day, they divide up the task according to skill sets and subsequently select a team to work on the assigned segments. A target date of two months is set.

After seventy days had passed, Damien arrived in Brussels for the first video's showing. He is introduced to Radolfo Amerinero, they having mutual admiration, both thanking each other for their opportunities.

Finding out that Radolfo shuns cauliflower whenever it's served, Damien made sure that cauliflower was available and brought into the viewing theater at the appointed time. Along with water.

Damien provides an opening narrative of how the video content can be changed with snippets available from a separate, accessible segment of the video and inserted at will by a trained techie. "You will be aware of certain influences by the time the video is over, not known by you while viewing," he asserts.

The video game plays forty-seven minutes. A Werner staff member played the game with a wireless console. Fourteen people are watching. A total of sixteen scenarios with each having separate subliminal messages are included in the video.

At the close of the showing, everyone in the room went to the rear of the theater knowing there would be cauliflower to munch on. Including Amerinero, who hated cauliflower; but even he could not resist.

The realization of how powerful Damien's video struck Radolfo full force, while he was actually enjoying his snacking on cauliflower, the only available finger food. And only water to drink, normally totally unsatisfying with the vegetable, he actually thought it tasted very good, he realized to his absolute surprise.

PART II

PROPHETIC WARNINGS

There's a lot of folks in the world today who think they'll change their ways at the eleventh hour...but God will either return or end their days at 10:59!

—Anonymous

6

REVEREND ANTHONY DELANO

The pastor of the Phoenix Church of the Open Door, Reverend Anthony Delano, is as much an activist as a preacher, or teacher, or minister for that matter. The easygoing countenance of Tony is disarming as he sets his audience up. For the unsuspecting, he takes them by surprise. For the familiar, he continually astounds them with his understanding of human nature and the wisdom to guide them into deeper meaning. He's a master orator.

Not once that anyone can remember did he neglect to look over his audience for an extended time to seemingly size it up before beginning to speak. Always a smile, posture straight, his head moving left to right as he surveys. Other than those attributes, he was quite ordinary in height, build, stature, and attire. Only his slightly graying, thinning hair gave a hint of his being fifty-four.

His message is always fixed on salvation through Christ. But what sets him apart from other ministers is his zeal for his parishioners to be involved in the community in as many ways possible, as he is himself and his family of Janice, wife, and three teen daughters and an elder son.

Rarely the theme of his sermons lacked the subject of preparation: preparation of spiritual, mental, financial, and physical resources and assets. He maintained that only when a person or family has more than what they need will they be able to be effective in helping others. To give from abundance is the highest calling one can have is his constant message.

Tony maintains the system of God in everyone's life is a network of simple, yet complex, activities from obedience of his will and a faith that God knows what he's doing when trusting him.

"Wisdom," he says, "comes from paying attention to what's going on all around us, in the world, in our nation, and in our communities, to know what to do and how to conduct our affairs in the light of eternity with God leading the way.

"In the news lately, we've been hearing a lot about EMP. Essentially we can do little, if anything, about it. However, there are certain minimum preparations we should be undertaking regarding EMP.[1] (1) Stock your home with two months' supply of canned food; rotate every sixty days. (2) Stock ten gallons of water per person in your family; be prepared to ration. (3) Equip with a high-output generator and an ample supply of gasoline, if allowable by city codes. (4) install a high-capacity, solar powered battery system.

"Unless of course if you live in an apartment. If you do, move out! In the event of an EMP attack, you're toast. Few apartment complexes are equipped with emergency generators and, if so, only for a few days. An EMP effect will last years—at the very least, months. You could be dead by then. If you live in the city, you should move too. Relocate into the country outside of the suburbs. Only in the country where you have opportunity to raise your own vegetables and have water by hand pumping will you and your family have any chance at all to make it through. Sorry to say you may have to move out of Arizona to avoid this disaster. In any event, there's a few other things you must do to prepare for this or any other disaster: (4) maintain an adequate inventory of personal supplies—batteries, toilet paper, etc.; (5) portable lighting; (6) lots of reading, researching, and materials for sharing—books and such; (7) extra Bibles, Scripture workbooks and study guides; (8) have extra beds and bedding; (9) extra clothing; (10) if your morality allows, acquire a firearm for your protection; which you'll surely need to defend yourself against violence.

"We need to make sure that each of us tells our circle of friends this disaster is to be taken seriously because not only is it possible but highly likely, particularly if they live within two hundred miles of a major city that is more than likely expected to be targeted by an enemy of the USA.

"Learned authorities tell us that the results of an EMP attack will most likely set America back to before the industrial age. A lesser powerful EMP nuclear blast could set America back thirty to forty years. By stocking up, you and your family will have the capability to live through the totally unstable living conditions and into the new days. That is, unless Christ comes before then in the air to claim his church—you and I who are believers in him!

"While you're at it, warn them, most likely again, that the last days are upon us. All they have to do is look at the conflicts of the Middle East, the world's connection to that region, the astronomical growth of Muslims, and Israel conflicts—to know your warning is warranted."

Tony's admonitions also carry a solemn message: that during all of the joyous worship and praise of all the believers of all ages in heaven, there remains to be a danger of disappointment after the rapture. There's another clock ticking: the White Throne Judgment of all believers will happen before the end of the Tribulation and before the Second Return of Christ to earth, a span of approximately twenty years.

"This is when the rewards are given by Christ according to the works, thoughts, and actions you've taken between the time of your salvation to the time of the rapture, or your death. Millions upon millions of saints, the bride of Christ, will be judged. And there's more. According to what you have done for Christ in that time allotted you will determine what level you'll serve in his future world government during the millennium.

"I warn you of the possibility of shame you will suffer when it is brought out that you fell far short of opportunities God had given you, but you squandered them. Or how about the instances when reading the accounting of John in Revelation of the Tribulation only for you to ignore or discount the chronicle by your saying, 'I'm not concerned, I won't be there because I'm *saved* from it.' Let me point out a fact of the Book of Revelation: Seventeen chapters of twenty-two (eighty-six percent) is devoted to just fifteen-plus years space in all the time of history. Doesn't that imply how important God places on these years?

"Let me ask you. How will you answer the Lord when he probes into your thoughts and actions of your failure to warn others of this impending nightmare they will face while you sat contentedly and smug about escaping it? I encourage you to warn other of this to "snatch them from the fire of hell"

"And now a greater question: now that you've been brought face-to-face with your responsibility to warn others of this terrible plight, what are you going to do about it?

"When I encounter other ministers and Bible scholars about the new normal of worship throughout this great land of ours, they don't seem to understand what I'm talking about. The new norm I explain is the absence of Sunday evening services, no midweek prayer meetings, no sustained revivals, and no sidewalk Gospel services.

"'Oh,' they reply. 'Things aren't the same as they were when we were kids brought up during the old days.'

"Since when, in Scripture, does that make a difference? Granted, the world we now live in has changed indeed. It seems to me that since the late 1960s and early '70s, the Christian, evangelical church has given way to the social changes forced by new ideals and inert concession of the once-strong fellowship. Over the past forty years or more, the church has compromised to the way of the world rather than stay the course so vividly taught by the Scriptures.

"Here's a thought. When did TV make its greatest onslaught into the homes of America? Like instant news reports from all over the world, sports events, movies, and special documentaries. I'll answer that: during the '60s and '70s. And when is the biggest prime-time for TV? I'll answer that too: Sunday evening. Coincidence? In the light of Scripture and what we know about Satan, I doubt if it's coincidence!

"Then there is busyness. Family, jobs, both parents working bringing in a new definition of kids, latchkey kids. The pressure of debt strangling many Christian households makes cause for preparations of the coming week necessary on Sunday evenings, if not engrossed in the TV programming.

"When the Great White Throne Judgment comes upon you, how will you explain the hours you spent entertaining yourself rather than worshipping, praising God, and in prayer, giving into to the social expectations of *today*?

"I can only pray you'll get it."

7

CONNIE'S REVIVAL MEETINGS

Six more days until the special meetings are to begin. Connie has worked hard putting all the fragments in order to pull this off! Not that there weren't tense moments at times. But it's all come together. The revival service preparations now only need the speaker to arrive. That happens at 2:30 p.m. when the *Citation* four-seater single-engine aircraft lands at the county's tiny airport. It is 2:16 p.m., and Connie's all knots inside. The plane is sighted as it makes its approach.

A distinguished-looking, tall, gray-haired, middle-aged man exited from the craft as he straightened out his ruffled topcoat. He's followed by what looks might be his wife. She is, as they are introduced. Connie is immediately impressed with their meticulous style and presence. Both are extraordinarily blessed with a pleasant persona.

Taylor Benjamin's voice commands spontaneous respect—perfect for an evangelist, Connie concluded. She was later to find her deduction to be right on. She would also discover his thorough knowledge of prophecy and how to relate it to this end-of-time days.

Before they had arrived at the church, Benjamin requested to have all people involved in the production of the meetings to be present the next morning at 8:30 in the church's sanctuary. For this he was hard-nosed. Only those who were serious about this were being allowed to participate. He would explain this then.

Twenty-eight people had helped Connie with the preparation thus far with nineteen committed to whatever was required of them. At eight thirty, only fourteen showed up. Those not there were dropped from the list of folks who would be counted upon. Taylor, again, explained he wanted only dedicated assistants.

He gave a quick introduction of he and his wife, Sandy. Then he requested everyone to kneel at their chairs, and each were to offer an out loud prayer for the coming revival services. And that's what followed.

After returning to their sitting position, he asked Connie if any promotion, advertising, or other marketing activities had been put out for this campaign. When she answered no, everyone was surprised of Taylor's response, "Good."

Quizzically they looked upon him standing in the front of the two rows of chairs making up the pews. He explained, "God is our director of marketing. We will leave it up to him. If we have just the fifteen of us in attendance, that is what he wants. If we have overflowing audiences, that is what he wants. But let's pray for an overflowing. Right? Let's pray." He prayed for an overflow audience at each meeting.

During the next two hours, he conducted a training session of how to be of assistance during the revival meetings, focusing on counseling, for those who respond to altar calls. Some had never heard of an altar call. He described what that meant, to their surprise. It made them doubt they could go through with this. But they did anyway. He was too overpowering to decline being there when needed.

At the close, he requested to have another session the next day at the same time. Only this time they would pray on their knees longer tomorrow. They did too.

After prayer, they were provided with the outline of the eight meetings to be held, which Benjamin would preach and what results he would be expecting. Everyone considered his expectations to be quite aggressively positive. The reason they were given the outline is to know what they would be inviting others to hear. The key to the success of this revival meeting is word of mouth by those who attended. That is how God works. By word of our mouths and testimony of our lives!

Finally, he admonished everyone to pray in earnest at least three times a day consisting of not less than a half hour each session. Many in the group balked at how they could pray that long on one, single subject. He told them simply, "God will teach you how to pray as you pray. If you don't pray much, God cannot teach you much."

Apparently they did pray as instructed. God used their prayers as marketing fuel along with their evangelistic charge given them by Taylor. He formed five groups of four people to go out into the community with flyers to promote attendance at the meetings. The two activities worked. Action borne of prayer seems to always work.

On the third of the eight evenings, the auditorium was jammed. This caused the rental of the Junior High auditorium for the meetings, which the school board authorized with some debate before permission was granted. By the fifth evening, it too was packed.

People from neighboring towns began to attend. God was at work! It all started with willing hearts. One willing heart, Connie, someone to hear the voice of God to be led to do something. She heard. She took action. Some had never heard the Gospel like what was being spoken. In part, the message they heard was as follows:

"All of you hearing my voice know who Lucifer is. Of course you do. He is Satan. Heaven's outcast. Now the world's master deceiver. He would have you think all this Jesus stuff is malarkey. Well, I am here to tell he is wrong. Dead wrong. If you believe him, you'll be just as dead wrong for that belief.

"On the other hand, there is Jesus. He is your answer. He is your savior. But saved from what, you might ask. First, to be saved from your sinful nature. Christ died on the cross for you. Each one of us can now have a life free from the consequences of sin. Second, you can be saved from his judgment of spending eternity in hell. There is such a place, you know. God didn't create hell for those who reject Christ. Hell is created for Lucifer and all his host of fallen angels to cause him to cease from his deceiving the world, to stop his influence against God.

"By rejecting Christ, even today, you're actually announcing you'd rather follow Satan and the plight he offers you rather than the freedom from your sin nature offered by Jesus. Do you want to be free? Accept Christ tonight." Many did.

8

A LOOK INTO THE LIVES OF COMMON FOLKS

Success drove Daryl further away from a reckoning with God. By now his twin daughters in their sophomore high school years are excelling in volleyball, already gaining attention from college recruiters.

He's become a senior partner in the law firm, leading his clients into enormous tax savings they would've not known about without his counsel.

He moved his family into the city's most prestigious gated community, having every amenity available. His girls attend a prestigious coed private school that outrivals any other high school in academics, sports, and science in the state.

His wife is a successful social climber making contacts with wives of other successful husbands, affluent women, and female politicians. She has become a graceful, adept conversationalist with a quiet but forceful manner. The mayor, a woman, had requested her to serve as her campaign manager and spokesperson for the past two terms of which she was a great success.

"Why, tell me, would I need God?" he would reply whenever he was confronted by the issue, "I have everything because of how good I am at what I do. Look at my life, my home, my family, and my work."

Little did he know there were only a few more months before it would all come thundering down.

❧

April's great-uncle Charles passed away at 101, making his life more than a centurion. Harold and April Dunsmuir became owners of the thirty-five-acre organic veggie farm. Harold had become Charles's highlight. He had learned much from him. Not only farming but about life itself. He taught much from his wealth of essential, practical knowledge.

Harold also became more appreciative of April's allegiance to growing vegetables and fruit and protecting the water environment. It impacted his life too.

What made the most difference though was April's steadfast belief in Christ. He slowly began to have a softer heart and listen to her without becoming antsy. Her emphasis on these being the last days began to grow roots, no pun intended.

April's prayers were working. She could tell it. She prayed more earnestly. She knew the days were getting close. Would he accept Christ before the end of days occurred?

❧

Though Reverend Wendell Wallace's secret remained intact from knowledge by his church, the addiction to porn burrowed deeper into his mind, causing his heart to be blackened with sin. The slightest incitement required satisfaction. Trips to Los Angeles where sex shops abound became often. His regression further and deeper into his fixation kept dragging him downward. No amount of preparation for his Sunday sermons made any difference. He had become a preaching reprobate, and he knew it.

Never could he preach about sin or living in sin; he would condemn himself! His sermons were soft. They were weak, nearly meaningless. Impotent and certainly not inspirational; yet deceptively charismatic, he held his own from an entertainment sense. But his church board seemed to not notice or ignore the shallow delivery every Sunday morning. Other than his internal torment, he was happy to be the pastor of a church—any church. His ego was being served. Some kind of value was being realized, he supposed.

What he was unaware of, a lot of the congregation sensed something was amiss. Some had begun asking why his sermons were punchless, without impact. The board was not, apparently, listening.

There are two ministerial associations in the town of Cerritos. One is the Evangelical Ministerial Association and the other is Brotherhood Alliance Ministerial Association. Wallace's church is a member of the latter. Prompted by his alluring nature, the member ministers voted him their president of the association for two years, adding to his stature in the community but had no bearing whatsoever on his addiction.

The trips to Los Angeles increased their frequency; now at least three times a week. After all, he rationalized, it takes only four hours for the round-trip to engage his activities. No one would care even if he was noticed not being in the church office as he should be. So he went.

⁂

The curly, dark-haired Maji Steinman decided to obtain his college education in the United States. He made the decision a couple of months before his graduation from high school in Israel. His father was visibly upset when he heard the announcement from Maji. He hung onto the idea his only son of four children would be educated at the nearby university while helping in the family's business. Then with a degree in business, they would be partners after his two-year military obligation. All of those ambitions for them working together were destroyed in a matter of minutes with the announcement.

His father gave little credence when Maji promised he'd return to Israel in six years—four getting his degree and two experiencing life in the US of A.

During the first week after registering and determining his credit hours Maji, sat in an overstuffed chair next to Steven Alexander, a stranger to him who looked about the same age. They struck up a conversation that lasted for more than a few hours and over half a dozen cups of coffee and a dozen machine-dispensed donuts. Before the discussion ended, they decided to share an apartment. Little did they know they would be roommates during all the four years of college and, in the process, become lifelong friends. Of course in each correspondence Maji wrote to his father, it was cemented more into his head that Maji would never keep his promise to return home.

The intriguing thing about Maji for Steven is that he is an orthodox Jew having beliefs based upon the Old Testament. Steven created countless numbers of conversations revolved around Maji's faith. In return, Maji learned much about the New Testament and had taken interest in prophecy as Steven attempted to decipher its meaning. Some of the discussions would last through the night, usually on Fridays because neither of them had Saturday morning obligations; they could sleep in.

After graduation, both with honors, having their BAs in hand, Steven started a consulting business. Because of Maji having unique computer technology skills, he hired him and made him a noninvesting partner. For some reason unknown to them, the business did very well. All the while, Maji studied for his master's.

Maji had completed his master's of political science and continued working for Steven three years. He then returned to Israel and joined up with his father to learn the business as he had promised. He had at least done that. But it was not a good match. Both he and his father came to realize it soon enough. Maji was far too anxious to put his education to use for his country. But he also discovered he was far too impatient to do so compared to opportunities available as he had thought possible.

When Magi's life failed to produce the results he had expected, Steven received a text message.

> *Please advise. U know me. Cannot fit in as prepared. What do I do? Thoughts?*

After he pondered how he should respond, Steven sent back:

> *Think u should not decide now. Wait. Work for father. Something will come ur way.*

Maji did as Steven suggested.

This time it worked well with his father, who was much more understanding. And something did come his way seven months later. He became a member of the advisory team of a prominent Israeli diplomat, who in turn advised the prime minister. Maji's father was proud of his son.

⚜

Sara Gasten is a name revered by Knight's High School in north Seattle. Any student within fifteen years of the date of Sara's graduation from high school knows of her. Her feats are legendary. She made the school proud as she continues to do so. Her parents, missionaries in the Congo, sent her to Knight's and lived with her mother's sister on Queen Anne Hill, just north of downtown Seattle.

As a 6'3", senior, she excelled in volleyball, basketball, and track (high jump), receiving state recognition along with the basketball team taking first in the state playoffs. Academically her skills in the classroom stood out more than athletics, thanks to the robotics team taking national honors. That was her first love.

In college she was the captain of the medical robotics research lab at the U of Washington. It was then she entered premed studies before moving on to her medical degree. Over this seven-year period, she continued living with her aunt a couple of miles from the U of W hospital.

This led to her calling into providing remote hospitals with the technology of robotic medicine and assisting in the necessary fund-raising to facilitate the purchase or take possession of proven equipment.

After nearly three years working tirelessly, she had to be ordered to take time off from what seemed to be an obsession for her. She also was reminded to not visit her parents as that would not offer her sufficient rest; she would probably not resist the temptation to get involved with their work. She followed the advice giving them extended phone calls often all the while they understood how it would be if she did visit them.

She went home to her aunt's on Queen Anne Hill. During the first week, she visited the Knight's campus and attended a 6:15 girls' basketball game. Word got around quickly among the Knight's fans. Between the girls' game and the boys' game, she was given recognition and asked to say a few words before offering a prayer before the start of the boys' game.

In the ten-minute talk, she had most everyone in tears as she told a couple of stories how her life affected others in the mission field before giving credit to the robotics endeavor of the Knight's. The following day she spoke in the combined student bodies' chapel. It was her turn to tear up as she recalled how valuable her time at Knight's High School played such an integral part of her serving Christ.

At two in the afternoon, she met her aunt for a late lunch at Ivar's on the Seattle waterfront. Surprise! Her folks and siblings (two sisters and a brother) had a lot of catching up to do during this memorable lunch.

⚜

Walter Belkins inherited his father's farm given over to him by preferences made by his three brothers and a sister; they wanted nothing to do with dairy work and its responsibilities. As property, all the siblings remained equal landowners. For his siblings, they knew he would know what to do to make the operation of the farm worthwhile.

He did. The farm of five hundred acres with over nine hundred milking cows kept he and his family—a wife, three sons, and two daughters—busy enough. His kids ranged from fourteen down to six, including a pair of twins.

He saw to the management of the farm with dexterity when weather or other uncontrollable outside influences affected the success of the operation. This included modern milking, fieldwork, and harvesting equipment needed for this size of undertaking. Eight employees as milkers tending to the two-a-day milking of the cows and their handling seemed to work out just fine.

He and his family lived a good life. It even included going to church on Sunday mornings. Since the trip was over twenty miles, they also did most of their shopping after church. During which time they would occasionally eat dinner at a favorite chicken specialty restaurant. For the most part, this time away from the farm as a family is looked forward to by everyone.

Church was meaningful as that is what the Belkins families did every Sunday morning. Mostly it was neighbors who knew each other forever who attended. Seldom did strangers or new folk attend. The worship service is traditional; singing established songs and mostly an inspiring sermon of living a good, decent life in the community and wherever you go or whoever you come into contact to be a good Christian. That is it. Sunday in and Sunday out.

❧

If Travis Olsen had heard it once, he heard it a million times over, "You own too many businesses, man!" and maybe they were right, he thought many times. Be it suffice to say he owned nine different profitable businesses and only frequently felt the pressure of so many. He made sure he hired extremely well-qualified people to manage the day-to-day operations of each one, who in turn hired capable people in responsible position.

As a child, he lived in poverty, swearing one day he would be rich!

His dad had simply taken off, disappearing without a word to him, to his mom, or his two older sisters when he was seven. Travis thought his dad was a success at whatever it was that paid the bills. He had no reason to think otherwise. Up to then, he had known his mother never had a job. His absence forced her to go to work for a very meager income. Their quality of life dwindled to only just enough to get by if everyone scrimped. When he was sixteen, both sisters left home to better lives, so he was told.

He determined to do the same, whether or not his mom needed him to stay home and find some kind of job. Working for low wages at some quick-food restaurant was not for him.

Every day after school, he walked different routes home to observe various types of businesses and gauged within his head which would be best to think about for him to pursue. He even read a career book once in a while.

Taking somewhat a lead by the girls in his high school classes, he considered himself good-looking. He was that. He carried a countenance of friendliness and a walk of confidence, which caused engagement even when he did not initiate it.

One day he visited a used-car lot to look at a nice Chevy that caught his eye. The salesman was, what Travis thought, quite rude. So he walked away. What if, he thought, the salesman was polite, willing to answer questions, and portrayed care for the potential customer?

He was a week away from graduating and a month away from turning eighteen. He decided to return on his birthday to talk to the owner to hire him as a salesman. The owner was reluctant. Travis expected it and asked if he could demonstrate what he could do. Of course the owner agreed. Why wouldn't he? A potential customer stopped in looking at numerous cars. Travis went to him with the owner following within hearing distance. He practiced what he knew how he would like to be treated if he were the customer looking at cars. Within a short time, the would-be customer is signing the contract to buy the first car he looked at. It taught the young man an indelible lesson.

From that day, fourteen years later, his successes became routine. All of his dealings with employees, the customers, suppliers, and associates of all kinds were on the up and up, honest in every way, including his taxes and other such liabilities. He had become, in his estimation, rich.

One item was missing. He depended upon Travis. God never entered his mind as something he needed. Though accepting Christ had been presented to him numerous of times, he simply dismissed those times as inconsequential.

The twenty-seven-year-old Heather Fording and her husband, Darrell, have been married and childless six years, both wanting to be parents. They tried all kinds of advice from doctors and counselors, to no avail. Both were tested for reasons why not; prognosis? Nothing wrong, nothing at all.

Finally Heather gave in to Darrell's suggestion: they adopt a baby.

Both have well-paying jobs with futures, their home with low interest and a comfortable mortgage payment, two cars and Darrell's Dodge 3500 diesel pickup truck, their credit excellent, and both of them as well as together possess savings and investment accounts doing quite well. Stability and finances are not problematic for adoption.

Neither is their church life holding them back. They attend a megachurch regularly and subscribe to the weekly newsletter that includes daily devotion Scripture, which they actually read every morning. Both were raised in churches where the Gospel of Christ was seldom taught or preached, that Confirmation and baby Baptism is enough to get to heaven. What was good for them then is quite good and well for now too. Living a life of holiness and good is the truth what they thought to be quite enough, failing to understand that Christ is the only way to holiness.

"It will take five months to process the paperwork and conduct mandatory interviews with you," they're told by the adoption agency. "Then it will be another two months before the process to locate and provide the baby." They started the process by filling out the seven-page questionnaire, a component of their application.

Anyone visiting the Fordings felt the electric karma permeating their home. Excitement of anticipation filled the air. Happiness is constant.

Four months after beginning the adoption process, Heather began having spells of vomiting and craving strange combinations of food and snacks. She felt nausea most of the time. Darrell suggested she could be pregnant, which she thought to be such a crazy idea. "At least go to a doctor, okay? See what it is," he prompted. She went; she was.

She wanted to notify the adoption agency immediately. Darrel requested she wait a month when she'd be showing more. They waited and glad they did. It was worth the expression on the face of the agent handling their case when Heather walked into her office.

The pregnancy went well and as each day blended into the next, soon toward the delivery date. Heather was astounded at the emotional level a woman can reach with the birth of her child being at hand. Darrell seemed to be joyously along for the ride, a fantastic father-to-be she felt.

Three days beyond the expected date, she gave birth to an 8.5 lb. son having a lot of hair as his father and a face with features of his mother—already.

Their happiness when the adoption was anticipated is nothing—nothing at all—compared to having a child of their own. Samuel did well.

9

CONNIE'S FOLLOW-UP

Chris Holman, a board member of the North Shore Bible Church in Ohio, recalls Connie Alexander's follow-up.

"Soon after Connie's eventful success of the community's spiritual revival meetings, she approached me about something else she felt the call of God about. She said she had come to me because I would have the most supportive ear to hear her out.

"She called the project she had in mind as the Six O'Clock Good News Hour. She explained it before I had a chance to ask what it was. She was so pumped up about it!

"Chris," she said, "I have taken serious notice that all but very few churches have more than one service in any given week. That is deplorable. In these last days, every evangelical church should have its doors open with meaningful purposes every day of the week."

"I can see you have an idea toward this end?" I asked her.

"I do. Because there are so many churches in our area who have their doors closed on Sunday evening, there needs to be a spiritual outreach at that time, don't you think so?"

"Well… I," was about all she let me respond with.

"Don't you see this opportunity? We would have the ol' evangelistic services as we had years and years ago!"

"Well… Connie—" she shut me off again.

"This would be a joint church effort for the sole purpose of having some place to invite or bring someone to introduce them to the Lord. Anyone, no matter which church they attend, would be welcome to participate in the worship and evangelistic outreach. Since their church is more than likely to be closed anyway, this church would be available."

"Please," I said, "Let me talk."

"Oh, sorry," she acknowledged she had not allowed me to get a word in edgewise.

"Connie, I can think of a few reasons why this will not work. First, there are too many things that most everyone is doing that what you are proposing would simply not be well attended. Second, it would take a tremendous effort to publicize this to acquire the number of people to make it worthwhile, and three, the biggest challenge is who would be the preacher?

"Preacher?" she queried.

"Yes, a preacher. He would have to be extremely dedicated and be an exceptionally influential speaker—like evangelist Taylor Benjamen was, only permanent. This preacher's persona and message would have to be strong enough to overcome the TV, family plans, and preweek preparations people do these days."

"Yeah, I see what you mean."

"Besides, it will take money. The financial support must be reliable over a period of time. And the preacher would only be preacher, not as a minister of a church as churches."

She grew solemn before her eyes lit up. "If God gave me this vision, he can see it through. And I know he did make me responsible to make this happen. So I am moving forward."

She certainly did. She recruited two other local pastors who shared the project's worthwhileness. Together they hammered out a plan. It was designed from the start to be a small outreach innumerous communities as an evangelical mission to bring the Gospel to many people in the last days, as the apostle Paul had written, "So much more should you spread the Word as you see the last days approaching."

An anonymous wealthy Christian in California gave over $80,000 to fund the ministry's startup with very few caveats. He said he felt as Connie for a number of years. He had been on a church board when he was overvoted to keep the Sunday evening evangelistic services intact. If the project failed before the funds were used up, the balance was to be returned to his lawyer with a full accounting. Otherwise, no accounting for the money was necessary.

Over three hundred Six O'Clock Good News Hour locations had been opened within two years, none closed—all without any harmful encumbrances. Thousands had accepted the Lord.

But Satan is at work too.

During this same time, Chris Holman had taken a business trip to Los Angeles and stumbled upon an article in the *LA Times*.

London—Torrey Mendenaul, multimillionaire of Westchester who became wealthy by creating apps for the social media industry is now quite popular in another mission.

He began the Atheist Worship Association. Membership is not required. He did not expect his association to amount to what it has become: hundreds of multihundreds and some multithousand congregations throughout the world. He only meant it to be a neighborhood thing. But a friend put the idea on the social media. That is all it took.

Chris found such a congregation in Los Angeles. Fearful of attending himself, he paid a stranger, Lonnie, to attend and report what went on.

"It was like attending a traditional church," he reported.

"How do you know? Have you attended a church service before?"

"Oh, sure. Once in a while, I go to the Lutheran Church just up the street."

"Okay. So what went on?"

"First, they sang a bunch of songs. Rock, pop, and Western. Five or six of 'em."

"And then?"

"An offering, to defray expenses, they said. After that, a woman got up, went to the platform, and sang another song, solo, it was a ballad kinda song."

"And?"

"A speaker was introduced, a businessman, who talked for nearly a half hour on the power each of us have to make others happy or not, depending upon God to tell us who we think we are. He admonished everyone to worship mankind as a whole and themselves, individually."

"No mention about God?"

"Nope. Other than what I said."

"Anything about Satan or the devil?"

"Nope. But I have something for you."

Lonnie then handed a brochure to Chris. In it, he read the Articles of Beliefs.

We believe there is no God. We are not against those who believe otherwise. We are not against God either. We believe, simply, he does not exist.

Therefore, our worship services consist of worshipping freedom from the plague of rules, traditional scriptural laws and traditions, and commandments to regulate our behavior.

Conversely, because we believe there is no God, neither is there Satan or the devil. We do evil upon ourselves and others only because we will to do it. There is no other cause, instinct, or behavioral influence.

He read it again. Thanked and paid Lonnie. They parted as Chris could not believe such a movement had grown so rampantly. On his way to home through Cleveland, he inquired about the atheist movement. Indeed, there were two, much to his surprise. He had never heard of them.

10

STEVEN'S UPDATE

I had grown to 6'3" by the time basketball arrived in my senior year. The coach convinced me to at least try out though I had only played in makeup games with buddies. I did surprisingly well, good enough to earn a place on the varsity bench. When a starter was injured in the third game, my name was called to replace him. My play was good enough to be selected on the state's second team and winning a scholarship at the local Division II college team.

College Days

There, I began studies majoring in marketing with a minor in theology, though my theology professor Dr. Dwight H. Tymon suggested I make theology a central course of study to obtain a master's and possibly a doctorate because of my keen extraordinary enthusiastic knowledge of Scripture. He said he had never encountered a student with such scriptural depth. I often considered following Professor's counsel before caving in, as he saw it, to pursue a career other than theology or philosophy. The professor's advice was based upon how well-regarded I had become in the professor's circle of esteemed philosophy professors, as he frequently invited me to attend their get-togethers.

Two students in Professor Tymon's classes became close friends: Maji and Spider.

Maji, Jewish, and I hit it off really well from the first time we met. Girls considered him cute. I thought of him being charming and a delight to be in his company. He was also brilliant as he questioned everything—my kind of man. It is this insatiable curiosity that kept our friendship vibrant. I feared the day that I knew distance would separate us although I knew we'd stay in contact with social media.

One day he told me the circumstances how he came here for his education. In my dorm room, I was seated on my bed and he at my desk, as is often the case. A random discussion, also as often, led to a serious moment.

"Have you ever wondered how I ended up here in this small college?"

"I have. How did you?"

"Because of my uncle. I live with him. He came to this town without any particular reason over twenty years ago and stayed simply because he liked it and reminded him of Israel he has mentioned often." Thoughtfully he continued, "My father was brokenhearted when I informed him I would like to go live with Bernard, my uncle."

"Why? What's so bad about that?"

"You don't understand. My father has been dead set on my being a partner with him in his produce distributorship. So when I told him I wanted to live with Bernard, he thought for sure I wouldn't return either."

"Are you?"

"Am I what?"

"Going to return to Israel?

"Of course. It's the reason why I'm pursuing my master's in business. I know I can contribute a lot in my father's distributorship. Yeah, I'm going back."

"It will be a sad day when you return. You can't possibly know how much I will miss you," I informed him.

"Me too. We'll stay in touch with Facebook. Okay?"

"Sure, but it's not the same, Maji."

Many times he reminded me how much he looked forward to return to Israel and to his father after college graduation.

During the remaining five years of obtaining his master's in business finance, our relationship became more interesting as he kept questioning me about the various beliefs of Christianity and the New Testament writings. Just as he questioned me, I questioned the deeper points of the Jewish faith. These discussions dominated most times over any other subjects combined. As we both began to understand the other's religious position and why, our friendship jelled into what we would experience as extremely valuable.

What we did not know—could not know—was just how valuable our friendship would become in the future!

❧

A tall lanky student with an unruly chunk of coal-black hair, nicknamed Spider, is the other student I formed a friendship. Spider fit his thin, lanky, long legs and arms, and thin neck supporting a narrow-shaped head with a long, pointed jaw—always the first physical impression of Jason Franks. Our friendship developed into quite something different than that with Magi. There seemed to be no correlation at all with his interest in law enforcement and mine of business. We met in the cafeteria in the Student Union building. For some strange reason, we found ourselves sitting across from each other to eat our lunches. It didn't take long for a casual acquaintance to become a somewhat aloof friendship that grew into something more substantial. It started when we decided to meet one afternoon in the student lounge outside the library.

As time went on during the college days, Spider and I got to know each other nearly as well as Magi and I. It was a mixture of common and divergent interests that held our attention enough to develop into more than a mere close acquaintance.

He had also formed a relationship with one of his professors, as I had with Dr. Tymon. He mentioned often that his adviser was a retired CIA investigator and continues to be a sometime agent. This influenced Spider to change emphasis from domestic law to international espionage technologies.

Observing his emotional transformation as a student from that of ho-hum to excitement readily gave reason he had found his niche. His new exhilaration certainly caught my attention as to what caused such a change.

"What's goin' on, Spider? Why the excitement?"

"You don't know?"

"Should I?"

"Of course!" he replied with surety.

"Why?"

"Steven, you're knowledgeable about the end-times, right?"

"Yeah, so what?"

"You should know how all the unrest in the Middle East points directly to Israel and, because of this intensified emphasis by Islamic countries to annihilate Israel, that the last days as Scripture tells us are upon us."

"I do know…but how do you know what Scripture says about this? That surprises me. We've never discussed it much—some other things in Scripture, sure, but not prophecy!"

"I know a little. The thing is, Steven, I might have the opportunity to be in the middle of all that as a representative for the United States."

"How so?" I asked.

"Mr. Davisson—I've told you about him—feels I have the personal abilities and qualifications in foreign services with the CIA, and he's willing to recommend me."

"Spider, you're only a sophomore. You're telling me this Davisson agent is going to recommend you so early in college and without you having an inkling of knowing that you'd even like this kind of work?"

"Yes, I will like it, and yes, he's going to recommend me."

Three weeks later, Spider conducted an interview and completed an aptitude test administered by the staff of the CIA. So far he was right about himself. A week later, he received notice about half a scholarship for the balance of his sophomore year and half of his junior year, and a full scholarship in his senior year only if he passes certain criteria before then. His excitement made it nearly impossible to be around him; it's all he could talk about. Who could blame him?

It all worked out as he had thought.

Little did I know how complete it *would* work out for him and in the world to be!

After completion of obtaining a master's in business, my life had become quite comfortable and more than well-off financially with both lucky and knowledgeable investments. I am, in fact, living a carefree life as much as can be expected as a husband and father of three children, who are doing well in every way with the partnership of a loving wife.

Nearing thirty-five years old, I had made—what Jim Weismann, my financial adviser, told me—unusually sound decisions with money. Their investments have paid well, and the cash reserve ratio to earnings is far better than even the upper echelon of the wealthy.

One Wednesday afternoon, Jim Weismann sent a text message to me:

Need to talk with u. important but not urgent
tho sooner is better. 10 am Friday good for u?

At ten on Friday, we met.

"What's up, Jim?"

"There are situations of national financial concerns, which you may know about, going on that I, as a financial adviser, see as warnings."

"They affect me?" I asked curiously.

"Steven, let me tell you that I think it would behoove you, as well as most if not all of my clients, to exchange at least three-fourths of your entire assets into gold bullion."

Astonished, I declared, "Are you kidding me? Why would you make this suggestion?"

Jim's arms are resting on the desk with his hands clasped together; his face twisted into a serious expression as he hears my tirade before offering an explanation.

"Bear with me, Steven. I want you to have a firm knowledge of the basis why I am suggesting this action. Okay?"

I leaned forward as I pulled my chair closer as he gathered his thoughts.

"I was informed by a colleague the seriousness of the US debt and the government's method of coping with it. Basically, it simply prints more money. It is the only nation in the world who can do that because the dollar is currently the world's monetary standard.

"The fact is, by taking that action, Congress has allowed the dollar to be greatly devalued outside the US in an exponentially accelerating woe-some worldwide financial crisis. This will drastically affect every US citizen, company, and municipal government by placing everyone on the brink of bankruptcy. None of us will own our own properties. It could come to that if we continue to depend on the almighty American dollar."

My jaw dropped in awe, speechless.

Jim continued, "Only a few months ago, China instigated a secret meeting with seven countries of which the United States knew nothing about. Know what they discussed?" He answered his own question while all I could do was shake my head no. "To eliminate the dollar as the world's new monetary measurement as money exchanges hands between them."

He continued, "A financially renowned authority in international finance and capitalization was a representative of the World Monetary Fund, present to guide them in complex matters to make the transition away from the dollar an easy process.

"There's more, Steven," he warns me. "In the meantime, China is backing all of their currency with gold reserves.[1] In the near future, gold reserves will be the guarantee of the money a nation prints. I ask you, Steven, do you know what this means?"

I pondered the question before answering, "That the debt cannot be hidden by merely printing money because sooner or later the money would be worthless. Therefore, it places the United States in a disgraceful bias, if not weak, everywhere in the world as well as domestically?"

"You are absolutely correct, Steven. You got it."

I added, "The United States could then be subjugated to China, which is possible but highly unlikely."

"No, Steven. It is not highly unlikely. If this would—and can—happen, the dollar will most certainly be replaced by another form of currency backed by gold. To do the same is the only thing an individual can do to assure their wealth," he thoughtfully says out loud. "Got it?"

"Yeah, sure. But I detect there's something else you want me to get!"

"There is. On the Internet, there's a whole new form of commerce—only on the Internet." Jim grabbed a Post-it, scribbled a website address, and slid it over to me. "Look this up. It just could be the answer to the dilemma we've just discussed."

"What is it?"

"Look it up and tell me what you think," requested Jim.

"Will do."

Before I left Jim's office building, I was already on my mobile device taking care of business we had just discussed. As soon as I sat in the car with my laptop, I continued research on the info Jim had advised. I was stunned by what I read; it created an immeasurable excitement.

Jim's note read, "bitcoin dot com."

At just over $635, I bought ten. That transaction gave me a newfound peace knowing he had taken another step to assure my family's happiness. Within the next two months, Bitcoin's price went over the $900 threshold. I turned the profit over into buying more Bitcoins.[2]

About the same time, I also began attending a local Bible study group our neighbor had invited my wife and me to join in. Everyone was so friendly and accommodating whenever I commented. My wife seemed surprised at how thoroughly her husband repeatedly demonstrated how well I knew the Scriptures, leading to many discussions continuing after arriving home. Even with all his knowledge, none of the salvation story seemed to penetrate into any consideration. Being an honest and just man, husband, and father is certainly good enough. It has served me well so far, so why would the future be any different? All the while, the group began its study on the Book of Revelation, as encouraged by one in the group who had a thorough knowledge of the End of Times, as he put it.

They readily agreed, but not knowing it was also one of my favorite Bible topics. This led to in-depth discussion and new awareness few else in the group had any knowledge. For the most part, the two of us nearly saw eye to eye on the interpretations, which caused deeper interest of the group to seek out more of Revelation's truths.

After nearly a year in my business profession, Dr. Tymon contacted me with news he thought important enough for us to meet. It surely was that important! He wanted to coauthor a book on the subject of symbolism in the Book of Revelation. He divulged to me that he could not write the book on his own without me because of the in-depth knowledge he knew I had. Six months later, the University's Press published our book intended for other philosophy and theology professors. It was well received by its intended market but not so well outside in the public realm. My name became well-known in the broadest sense within his circle of professors.

In spite of the book's success, one unanswered concern mattered in my mother's life I knew remained unresolved: that was me! I had become such a success in my chosen field I never contemplated to accept God in the manner as she believes. I tell her the same thing: "I just don't need to believe the same as others," every time we discuss this issue. When she asks why I believed what I believe, I answer that I don't believe her religion is the only way to God; and I thoughtlessly disregard her feelings by reminding her that my life is going quite well without becoming a believer and that I don't need God at this time. I could tell she grieved every time as though I twisted a dagger in her heart.

I know Mom is thankful for her life and how it's going except for this one thing. She is happy all else is going good for me and our family. She worries that it might require some catastrophe to happen to cause my change of heart. She often tells me I'm a smart kid, just not spiritually wise. She continues to earnestly pray for me; she once confided, while looking at her own life, "Could I have been at fault as your mother?" To that I told her she did all that a son could ask, and that's the way it is.

Life *is* good to me, the result of having rooted parents who loved me as parents should. And still do. Although I understood this, my success stemmed from choosing the right career path and marrying the right woman.

Not long after my last conversation with Mom, I received a letter from Dr. Tymon. The first thing noticed was a sizeable check from book royalties. Next was a shocking but pleasant request: Would I consider being an assistant dean of the Theology Department? I had to read this three or four times! Then I shared it with Demi. She was elated. "Yes," she replied uncontrollably as she wrapped her arms around my neck, "accept the offer."

"Honey, I have to give this serious thought. My position at Technologies pays an outstanding salary that the college would have a problem matching, so we'd have to take a lesser pay. Dr. Tymon went through a lot of trouble elevating me above other professors' tenure to be able to make possible this offer!"

"He did it because he wants you there, Steven," she admonished as her eyes sparkled with pride for me and an excitement she cannot keep within her as our embrace continued. I could feel a comingling of emotional enjoyment of the moment and sheer anticipation of what it meant. For a few moments, I could feel the pressure of business deadlines, quotas, burdensome responsibilities, and the daily challenges to seemingly slip away. Then I compared it to what it could be like as an assistant dean, which of course I had no idea except it couldn't be any worse pressure than at Tech.

"You're right. What do you say I accept?"

"Really? You'll do it?"

"Sure. Why not?"

"Well, honey, why would you turn it down, is the better question."

"You're right again. I cannot turn it down." She embraced me tighter as a way to extend her increased delight. I squeezed back. The thrill of the moment was guarded for a few minutes before breaking apart. I wrote an e-mail to document our decision before making the phone call of acceptance.

Disappointment filled the office of my vice president at Tech when I officially gave my month's notice. He understood and wished me well as he thanked me for such a value I had contributed to the company. That was nice.

On that day in particular, I remember being unusually excited in the anticipation of the meeting with Dr. Tymon in a few days. I knew only something good would come out of it. But I'm getting ahead of myself—way ahead! An unexpected event would occur in a few days.

Standing in the hallway outside the conference room following the meeting, I called home. "Honey, it happened. I gave the notice. We move to college town next month."

"That's so awesome, dear. It'll be good for us. I know we made the right decision."

"For us is right, Demi! It frees me up to engage my research even more than in the past! And, Demi, since the kids are nearly adults not needing you to stay home on my trips, from now on, you'll come with me." She produced that little squeal of delight that drives me nuts.

In a moment of contemplation, I slowly clicked off the mobile device and refocused my attention. I noticed it was Tuesday when I went offline.

I then stepped into the doorway of my assistant's office. "Julie, do you have a minute?"

In apprehension, she responded, "Sure, what's up?" As she sat across from me, she added, "I hate those words. In my experience 'do you have a minute?' only means bad news. Like being fired."

"Not this time, Julie."

Nervously she repositioned and crossed her legs, the left knee balanced over the right knee as she leaned forward, as though not wanting to miss a single word.

"Dean Johnston at my college alma mater chose me to be his assistant dean. I gave notice less than five minutes ago." I could see a letdown. "Wait, Julie. There is more. I would like you to go with me—to be my secretary. It was discussed, and the college has the budget for your salary the same as here at Tech. Okay?"

She offered only a smile. "Thanks. But no thanks. I would have to move, and I have two children to uproot from their school and friends. Being a single mom, I can't do that." She stood, extended her hand as she completed this discussion. "I would like to go because you're such a good, decent man and an exceptional boss. But I think you understand. You do, don't you?"

I told her I did understand, and we wished each other the best.

But it was the last Tuesday I would be in Julie's company, though four more remained in the month as I worked out my resignation.

Even before making it to Friday, my world changed. Whatever my normal activities were before Thursday, they would not ever return; and I am not talking about the job change!

On Thursday, two days later, a little after 1:00 p.m., right before my eyes, midsentence, in an instant, she vanished. Just like that. I felt incredibly alone. The many varied street sounds of the world turned really goofy, terrible, reached my fourth-floor office window clearly. When I looked outside, sheer panic and pandemonium, like what's occurring inside the building. Instantly I called home. No answer. Called again. And again. Then I called Demi's device number. No answer after numerous attempts. It was then I realized she was a Christian in Mom's sense, though not as devout. And I realized there would never be an answer.

I knew what had happened. Feelings about my children were mixed: I hoped I would see them again while wanting them to be wherever their mother had gone. I had no way of knowing.

11

A WAR BEING PLANNED?

Joe Hastings possessed valuable information and data on the events about to take place in the continuum of prophecy taking place in Turkey. He filed the following report to Langley, Virginia, headquarters of the CIA.

> At approximately 9 am on Thursday, July 23 I video recorded representatives of Iran and countries of the former Soviet Bloc south of Russia meeting in Izmir, Turkey taking place in a defunct warehouse.
>
> Repeatedly four times a week for three weeks the same representatives met for more than six hours. Most arrived by private yacht behind nearby islands then transported by smaller crafts more than 4,000 meters to Izmir as though not wanting to be detected. Each time they were quick to enter the building but slow to depart.
>
> The names of the representatives were forwarded ten days ago; all have been present at each meeting described without anyone else attending. I emphasize that it is my opinion a major coup has taken the final steps of preparation to subject a war in the Middle East, presumably against Israel. It is assumed Israel has been made aware of this series of meetings as a precaution.

Hastings's observation and comments have taken pathways to those who must know. The Fifth Fleet has been put on alert along with Israel. He has completed the first phase of his job. Now is the waiting for the second phase.

The wait is not long; just weeks later, another meeting takes place in Izmir comprised of the same representatives of countries. There is an exception: Russia's president is added from the last occurrence. This meeting, unlike the first, is wired without their knowing. Hastings records the proceedings.

"Gentlemen," it's the voice of the Iranian, "we welcome Sergi Molanski of Russia." A courtesy applause is heard as Molanski bows with his acknowledgement, it is presumed.

The Iranian continues, "We have many decisions to consider including exactly what we aim to achieve with the war effort and how we are going to be successful. After those decisions are made, we must determine the date and the necessary preparations to make those decisions wise. One of the considerations is the element of how the enemy will respond against our attack."

Another voice is raised, "We should not initiate the attack with advanced technology or weaponry. Why not, you might ask. My answer is that Israel has a reliable defense strategy, having the ability to annihilate any offensive force in response. I think we do not wish that upon ourselves!"

A third voice, a female, responds, "I agree with our comrade. Maybe I have a suggestion that could work for us." If there was a lingering aloofness among those in attendance, she now has their undivided attention before she carried on. "We use wooden weaponry."

Loud multiple voices respond, the gist being dominantly a silly idea. It seems unanimous. She has a lot of persuasion to do.

The Iranian's voice calls the meeting back to order and offers the floor to another. It's the voice of yet another. I agree with our colleague that military power should be deferred unless another mode is decided. Further, I do not consider wood weaponry should be included in our decisions. Murmurings of agreement are heard.

A new voice is heard, saying, "Before we dismiss wood weaponry"—disparate comments are heard from the attendees before the speaker continues—"we should at least look at the advantages."

"There are any?" an opinion is uttered from the audience.

"Yes, certainly. First, our northern countries' plenteous forests is ample beyond our needs. Second, the weaponry's production of wood would not raise an eyebrow. After all, what could be so important about a significant increase of wood product production? This can be accomplished without suspicion. Third, the costs are nothing compared to any other form of weaponry. And fourth, I do not think the Israeli's radar and detection systems will pick up an advancement of an army equipped with wooden gear."

"And the downside?" inquires another voice.

"The downside is the logistics to stage tens of thousands of troops before the attack without causing alarm. Israel has one of the best recon schemes in the world. We must account for that."

"Yet another deliberation is necessary: the neighboring countries of Israel. It is imperative we have their cooperation and their swearing of secrecy. These are Arab nation countries. We must trust them for our success. We know their aspiration to rid of Israel is a strong resolve as our own! Their cooperation should not present a problem…if one exists at all."

Again, the Iranian's voice is noted. "It seems we need to consider wood weaponry after all. This method of attack brings new issues to the table for evaluation before we decide determinations before we bring other concerns to the table. We will take a lunch break and reconvene at two thirty."

Hastings's team makes a copy of the recorded meeting and attaches the sound bites to an e-mail sent to Virginia.

A half hour later in the warehouse meeting room, one of the attendees grabs what looks like a vase but is a cigarette lighter and lights up a cigar. As he replaces the vase, he notices a plastic twig with a leaf attached that is near to the location of the vase. His curiosity forces him to pick the twig off from the hall table. It is then he discovers a tiny microphone on the underside of the leaf. Realizing their meeting has been bugged, he reveals the fact to the Iranian who is alone at the moment. The Iranian takes it in hand and retreats to the men's restroom to immerse it in a stream of water from the faucet. It's shorted out before he tosses it into the trash bin. Four other bugs are discovered and subjected to the same result.

Hastings and his crew return after their brief lunch, only to listen to a deadened sound, a muffled buzz when switching to the four channels. They switched to the fifth, which remains to be active. It had not been discovered.

When the meeting began at 2:30 p.m., the Iranian informs those in attendance of the findings with a note obviously written hastily and placed in front of each chair on the conference table. He instructs them to read the note in front of them:

> *Our meeting this morning has been taped. In case there remains another mike, we will act as though we do not know we're being taped and carry out the rest of the meeting with totally false information. We will adlib as we go; all of us will become convincing actors. Understand?*

Everyone looks up after reading the note and nod their heads yes.

During the next two-plus hours, nothing said is true.

One microphone imbedded in a shelf's edge against the wall picked up all of the comments. Those in Langley, after recording the e-mail attachment, immediately acted upon the new intel and warned Israel. The coup had turned down the idea of attacking with an army supplied with wooden armament. A date had been given. The locations of staging the infantry was discussed and decided upon. Israel and her allies will not be taken by surprise! Or so they thought.

Future meetings are to be held elsewhere, not in Turkey to his knowledge. Hastings has no clue or does he have much time to gather any additional intel before the war is scheduled to commence. From Hastings, Langley is left in the dark.

12

AMERINERO'S BABYLON

At age twenty-two, Radolfo Amerinero hired a genealogy firm to trace his ancestry. They found his lineage led straight to a successful Roman Empire governor before its fall. Prior to this investigation, he seemed to be drawn with immense interest to the Babylonian Empire. With equal verve, he wondered what a replication of the Roman Empire in modern times would look like. One thing for certain, he thought, is a new city for its capital would have to be built.

It became his permanent preoccupation. He also realized he had the funds to hire the best city planners the world had to offer to rebuild the ancient Babylon as the capital of the new empire. He waited for the right time, not knowing when that would be.

He correspondingly needed to rise politically, to make a name for himself in the government arena outside of his financial and world affairs expertise. Italy had become a weak voice in worldwide politics—much too quiet for Radolfo. Looking upon France's political persuasiveness gave him a model to exceed. He set out to make the change by using his infamous website abilities to engage blogs and social media to make Italy's position known throughout the entire world.

A few months later, he overwhelmingly defeated the incumbent legislative representative of his province. He rapidly moved forward in this new audience, being a key member of two major committees and chairman of another. After two years, he became speaker chairman of the ruling party before elected to senior speaker a year later, the second most powerful man in Italy.

His Greek isle villa became more important as a recluse from the demands of his political office. It became his single location where he could find much needed rest and relaxation. It also is where he could play out his obsession with Babylon without the usual distractions.

Understanding this fixation on Babylon continually haunted him. He could not pull himself from it, mercilessly drawn to what now has become a focused project. His visits to the villa became more and more frequent.

Finally, at age twenty-eight, he could take it no longer without doing something significant about this Babylon Project. Just thinking about it got him too intoxicated about the whole idea. He had to do something more meaningful about it.[1]

He hired a team of engineers and designers to create the concept of Babylon, an entirely new city. They would be accommodated in his Greek villa, free to come and go as they wished. But all the work is to be performed only at the villa. He provided them with a design studio equipped with the latest technology they requested.

He continued to wonder why he was so enamored with Babylon as he composed a list of criteria for the designers to include:[1]

- A city of 5 square miles
- A large port adequately equipped to process no less than 30 container vessels a day with ample container staging space[2]
- A canal carved out of the terrain from the Red Sea to Babylon that is straight, deep, and wide enough for cargo tankers to easily navigate,[3] utilizing as much as possible of the existing Euphrates River
- No high-rises; structures less than 45 ft high
- No less than 50 theaters for the performing arts—lewd and otherwise
- Numerous religious worshipping auditoriums
- Scores of pleasure rooms
- 30 hotels of 5,000 guest rooms
- Luxurious restaurants with exotic entertainment ambiance
- A residential community of 250,000 for employees in one area; long-term guests in another; separated by a park such as Central Park in New York
- One stadium
- Airport; 60 passenger limitation of aircraft; no commercial airlines

- A small light-rail system; no vehicle traffic in core city areas; wide promenades rather than streets; an abundance of trees, shrubs, and vines as in ancient Babylon
- Spacious shops and modern warehouses for worldwide commerce
- Underground storage facilities accessible for numerous delivery trucks of supplies arriving daily
- Underground facilities to have capacity for the largest computer system in the world, including financial databases to control world economics
- Underground utilities: sewage treatment, water desalination, electrical power, and maintenance supplies and equipment storage

Many other details for a city to function as Babylon are designed in. After two and a half years, the finalized design is approved, and construction could begin without delay.

Everyone involved in the city's planning, design, and specification writing rapidly became impatient for the word to begin from Amerinero. They believed he had the funds at his command to achieve the enormous undertaking. They were right: he did, including the Iraq oil reserve discovered back in 2012 will pay for it—somehow. He will find a way.

Word got out, of course, of the enormous project to begin in the unknown future in the Red Sea coast Saudi Arabia, a city to be named Babylon! He was bombarded without reprieve by newsmen wanting something really significant to write about. But he stayed mum. It required colossal discipline to not tell anything of which he was so proud. Just as he could not understand his obsession, neither could he understand why he felt so strongly to keep tight-lipped about it.

Not a day goes by without his receiving notices from kings, rulers, prime ministers; corporate officers, big-box store executives, and franchise owners of their serious intentions to occupy space in Babylon when he builds such a city.[4] From what they knew, it's a perfect commerce environment combined with all of humanity's extravagances. Many significant players in both the commercial and entertainment industries are adamant about it.

Deep down inside him, he knew there will come the right time to announce to the world the construction of the Babylon Project. How he would know that time remained a puzzle to him.

PART III

Four-Year Pre-Tribulation

Diabolical forces are formidable and eternal.
Satan exists. God exists. And for us, as people, our
very destiny hinges upon which one we follow.

—Ed Warren, a credibly known
paranormal investigator (Maine 1976)

13

THE RAPTURE

Moments Before

Amos Cantrell is a hardworking gravedigger in a rural town in the Midwest, Bethany, of less than a population of 3,500. He is one of five who work in the maintenance department of Bethany. Amos and Jeb are assigned to the two cemeteries; one is a Catholic and the other a Protestant.

Amos always complains about his job, but does it anyway—glad he has one at all! Many of his friends don't have an income, being as broke as broke can be except for government assistance. His incentive to do as he's told is clear-cut. His biggest complaint is the boredom and disassociation of what he does. Dig a hole in the ground and later cover it up. Only a few months later, his work has no telltale signs as the grass has morphed into the surrounding lawn.

On this particular day, there were two funerals requiring graves—both in the Protestant cemetery, Peaceful Haven. This meant the other maintenance worker, Jeb, is needed to assist Amos as many times before. He knew Jeb was a believer.

The graves were dug, the graveside services completed, mourners returned to wherever they had come from, and the task of shoveling the dirt over the caskets finished. They went home, though the reseeding of the grass was yet required. It would be done the following morning by both of them.

As scheduled, at 9:15 a.m. the following day, Amos and Jeb were busy reseeding the two graves before continuing onto other work their supervisor had laid out. But only Amos returned.

Now!

My secretary vanished. Right into thin air! She as did hundreds of the thousands of students, a few staff and administrative personnel, a couple of professors and some others in the offices; they all abruptly disappeared—gone. At least a third of the people around me or on campus disappeared.

Only a second or two after grasping what I had studied in the Scripture.[1] I was left behind. But I also knew there still remained a slight chance I could make it. I hadn't died before the rapture. That sounds silly to mention it now, but the Scripture says, I recall, "It is appointed once for a man to die, and after that the judgment."[2] Though if left behind, if I can endure over the next twelve years or more, I could still make it to heaven though it would be rough, I know.

As those thoughts flashed through my mind, I also thought of my family. The kids! Demi! I quickly called home. "All lines are full to capacity" continued to be the message every time I tried to get through during the next few days before the system went out altogether. In the meantime, panic surrounded me. Most likely I will not see my kids again. Or Demi. I wanted so desperately to cry but could not; my heart was changing into something I didn't like as pandemonium kept up an accelerated pace. All seven floors of student services and classrooms are in chaos. Elevators are crammed and soon to fail working at all from the overloading of them. The stairways are filled with swarming bodies frenzied trying to get to the ground floor. Many are trampled by the scurrying mass.

I managed to look again out the window near my desk. The streets were a mess. Vehicles had collided, smashed into poles and over sidewalks into buildings, signs, and signposts. Cracking, snapping high-powered electric wires were writhing wildly, occasionally electrocuting any one pushed toward them or carelessly getting too close. People are running in all directions and treading on others who've fallen in their paths.

It required more than a half hour before arriving on the ground floor to join the throng to head home, just two miles away. I knew to drive the car for mere convenience would be futile and not worth the trouble. I walked, more like being shoved into a trot, frequently harshly pushed or knocked sideways by uncaring persons in their hurry to go wherever. I knew that if I somehow lost my balance, I could be killed by the stampede of people behind me in their fit of panic.

It surprised me how quickly I was shoulder to shoulder with looters who began their work as instantly as they took advantage of the opportunity presented to them. The smarter ones took food and supplies from the Quik Markets. Others stole clothes and items having any trading value. Not a bad idea, I thought.

I began to observe other consequences of *the Event.*

Traffic lights stopped working. No longer were sidewalks adequate for the mobs of people everywhere. By droves, people exited the buildings on campus and in the neighboring community.

Vehicles attempting to leave the underground parking spaces were refused entry onto the streets and were soon left abandoned. Some remained running until they ran out of fuel. Carbon monoxide began filling the deeper underground levels.

Public transportation out of the city, both buses and trains, is stymied before ceasing altogether.

News reporters are seen everywhere, futilely filing their reports of this historic, phenomenal event—most not actually airing. They had reported that all major airports were closed down and that scheduled flights had been cancelled all over the world. Also that many aircraft in flight had crashed, but they were not sure about that. Hundreds of small city airports were still operating however.

Police are ineffective. The fire departments are unseen as fires, though small at first, had begun all over the city. They're busy with providing first aid to the infirm and injured. Stalled traffic renders paramedic vehicles useless except for the supplies stashed inside them. Traffic jams of bumper-to-bumper; standing and inoperable vehicles are in addition to the overflow of the mass of people on foot on sidewalks, flooding the streets that prohibit vehicle movement of any type anywhere in the city.

The three hospitals near downtown began filling up. They are sorely shorthanded as many doctors, nurses, and staff had disappeared too. Only a few qualified nurses remain and fewer doctors. The number of staff capable to admit patients is wholly deficiently shorthanded.

Weapons of all sorts begin to be seen among the masses. An abundant number of AK assault rifles are held ready. Armed people are taking control. Unarmed people are in total panic packed with sheer fear. Protection from each other has become their foremost priority.

Outside, churches, cathedrals, mosques, and synagogues of every religion, sect, or denomination are teeming with anxious people ready to riot in their quest to know what had happened and why they were not told of this; no one seemed to understand it would be *this* horrendous.

No one dares to look another in the eye for fear of being seen as vulnerable. Speaking of being vulnerable, it's the young children of all, especially girls, who are in the worst jeopardy.

The hydroelectric plants at the dams have been, for the most part, left unattended. Many generators had shut down by their auto-control mechanism. The grid system is near to being shut down as a result. Soon cities will be in a total blackout. Without lighted streets, night crime will become more rampant than it is already.

As though all of this isn't enough, any inward power in anyone to hold evil in check has been removed. Every person alive—men, women, businessperson, etc.—now function with barely a trace of morality and as though knowledge between good and evil is evaporated. All of us remaining on earth have become evil beings. Greed, envy, malicious acts, debauchery, and deceit have become the norm.

Including me!

The love I once had for my family is a memory, and what's amazing? It's only been a short time had passed before the change took place. Now, no one but me matters. I also am deeply aware that no one cares about me either. We're now all drained of love, filled with subtle hatred for anyone without reason and rapidly growing into something more desperately callous. It saddened me deeply to

been vacated by those who disappeared! From apartments to bungalows, from simple homes to mansions, from small-acre plots to corporate-sized farms—now vacant, unoccupied, waiting for anyone to take over what was left behind. It's the same across every continent and country in the world, only fewer. Raiders of the vacant homes remain as long as the food and water last. Some stay longer when shelter from the elements is offered. There is no honor among thieves, it's been said—never like this! Seldom does much time pass when shelter is not the issue: always food and water supply. The fittest always wins. It never matters even if an occupier is a woman with babies to feed and protect; she's nothing more than just another adversary.

Though it's fast becoming a rarity, some of who occupy these homes are homeowners left behind, just as anyone else in this world, who are willing to slay anyone who's a trespasser. Protecting what is theirs is a necessary consumption of every minute day and night. Loss of life is common among those trying to defend their home and family.

Once what were peaceful towns in remote areas are, within a few days, now being invaded by nomadic masses of people bent on possessing what is not theirs. A few prepared landowners with weaponry meant for hunting game have turned their attention to the waves of invaders threatening to take their land, rob them of survival preparations, and quite possible do serious harm to his or her family. That will last only as long as their ammunition holds before overtaken and killed. Death comes after a tormenting beating of body and soul.

In the country, it has become a common sight to see large farming equipment on the highways and roads until the machine being driven runs out of fuel, subjecting the operators to be savagely beaten before slaughtered and mutilated like an animal.

There is no remorse, no restraint. Evil acts follow evil ambitions of completely uncontrolled evil hearts.

At the town's graveyard, less than a moment later, sixty-four-year-old Amos was startled by a gruff, grinding-like noise he had never heard before. It lasted only two or three seconds, if that. Somehow, as though by a mystic power, the grave he was preparing opened up; the dirt was shoved aside by a force from below, covering Amos's shoe tops. The casket's top lay to the side. The body gone.[2] In near shock, he looked around.

Jeb *was* there and had vanished. Only a moment before, he could've reached out and touched him, but now Amos could not detect where Jeb went, only that he was no longer there.

Hundreds of graves opened exactly as the one he is standing near.[3] He is transfixed. He cannot move, he cannot speak, he is locked as still as the headstones, fear has reduced his mind to a feebleness, he felt his heart beating doubly its normal pulse, and his spiritual heart had withered to a void.

A moment later, he realized what this was all about. Conversations with Jeb had something to do with it, but it was all of those "laid at rest" eulogies he had overheard by preachers who had explained in shortened thoughts what had just taken place! He knew where Jeb had gone to, and those who were buried in the ground, now gone. Heaven, Jeb had told him more than just a few times.

In that instant, Amos knew he had been left behind. And knew he had changed somehow. Once a quiet "live and let live" kind of guy, he felt his heart being filled with vile evil and horrific thoughts he had once thought disgusting.

Before leaving the cemetery where the empty graves lay opened, he haltingly made his way to where he knew his deceased wife had been laid. Her grave was open as well. She was gone.

In a depressed, heavy-hearted, and bewildered state, he returned to the maintenance shed three miles away, driving the Toyota pickup in a daze. Many cars and trucks seemed stalled on or at the side of the roadway. He passed many folks he knew with injuries pleading for help and others walking along the side with their thumbs out for a ride. He ignored them all. *Before*, he would have helped them; but not now, surely not now!

Upon his arrival, frantic workers welcomed Amos to seek answers. He had none to give. Their supervisor had disappeared. "Where is he?" they asked. "What happened?" they inquired. Then, "What do we do?" To all of this, Amos had no clue what to tell them, except for his counsel, "Go home."

He remained seated in the outdated Toyota belonging to the city of Bethany. He had to make sense of all this. The last question settled in his mind, "What do I do?" He restarted the engine, noticing the gas tank was nearly full. That was good. He thought his advice to go home was wise enough for him too.

The little town of Bethany is being torn apart. Only less than an hour earlier, it had begun as any day before. But now the town's main street had become a war zone, at least as Amos assessed it. Particularly when he saw, at the far end of the street, Officer Pettibone being beaten with a crowbar by a twenty-something. Amos wanted to help but knew he couldn't. Obviously Pettibone was paying the price of trying to stop looting.

The Toyota's windshield suddenly shattered, splaying large granules of safety glass filling his lap and the seat beside him. He responded as quickly as his age would allow to rid himself of further danger. He saw that it was a kid not more than thirteen years old who had destroyed the windshield with a baseball bat. Then as Amos headed the small truck in the opposite direction, a band of kids of the same age chased him until his speed outdistanced them.

Just as quickly as the windshield had shattered, a woman with a child somehow walked into the path of his speeding Toyota. It was too late to avoid running over them as he skidded to a stop. They were trapped underneath. As he pulled her and the child out from under the truck, he saw unspeakable injuries to both, knowing they would be dead within moments. His heart no longer cared about anyone else. He left them there to die.

Strange, he thought, *I feel no remorse*, as he left the scene.

Few seconds after

Millions witnessed the taken disappear from sight; it is all that anyone had witnessed. Gone as quick as a split second.

Those left behind who knew me recalled my significantly vast Scriptural knowledge. I am surrounded by coworkers seeking answers. "What happened? Where did all those people go to anyway? What are we to do now?"

Of course I knew where they had gone. I also knew what those who were taken were now experiencing. I also knew the hopelessness of any action anyone could take. It was too late.

"I'll tell you what I know. Don't get angry with me. I am only telling you what I know has happened. Agreed?"

"Yeah. We understand," they responded in unison.

"All right then."

The number in audience grew quickly as more clamored over each other to get a grasp on their present condition.

"First, it does not matter what you believe or how you regard Christians or whether or not you believe the Bible. That is a moot point. Your belief will get you nowhere. We have experienced the rapture as had been foretold in the Scriptures. Believers, the people who are Christians, have been taken away to heaven."

Fidgeting revealed dissatisfaction and fear.

"We have been left behind. It is obvious we are not in heaven, but in a chaotic world. If you examine yourself, you will discover a whole change of heart. Feel the evilness you never felt before? The uncaring? Your amplified selfishness? And a new loneliness? There's absolutely nothing you can do to change those feelings."

Everyone glanced at each other, nodding while disliking what they had now come to be. Steven had struck a chord, and they knew all that he said was true.

Uneasy, incontrollable anger suddenly filled everyone. A well-muscled, tall male began destroying anything destructible in sight; others joined, obliterating anything within their reach out of raw anger.

14

THE COMMON FOLK:
TAKEN FLIGHT OR LEFT BEHIND?

Of course, it's true. Daryl Wessen, being senior partner in the Whitmore, Wessen, and Walton law firm, would seem he has little need for God in his life! His twin daughters gained national attention when being teammates of the US Olympic volleyball team, winning gold. His wife had become Mayor Christiansen's personal assistant and confidant. And now one of his daughters is a successful business-woman in her own right as her sister continues toward her doctorate in international politics while an adviser for the Brazilian Consulate of developmental computer technologies.

During the years of his daughters' education, Daryl and his wife had traveled extensively in Europe and purchased a sixty-nine-foot Freeman yacht to cruise the Greek Isles.

Numerous cases of wealthy clients in trouble with the IRS, which he successfully negotiated or acquired dismissals, brought him and his firm monetary windfalls rarely achieved. In fact, the mayor herself inadvertently got caught in the middle of a financial situation that without fast resolve could mean her political ruination. At a great financial reward, he kept her out of the news and made clan-destine settlements with parties involved.

He could say he was on the fast track of financial prowess. So busy was he that he was not aware of Julia, the business daughter, had become a born-again Christian. She told him so. But it had no meaning as all he could say was, "That's nice, dear."

Daryl and his wife were in the back seat with Julia driving from the five-star restaurant toward their home; Julia disappeared from behind the driver's wheel. Gone. The car without a driver caromed off the street and crashed through the large plate glass of an antique shop after barely missing a head-on collision with another car out of control, sending displayed artifacts everywhere as the owners of the shop stood as a deer in headlights.

They got out of the AMD 550 Mercedes, now mostly mangled, and themselves with minor cuts bleeding as they panicked in bewilderment of what happened to Julia. At the moment, they knew nothing of where Julia is or the condition of their own lives.

❦

April Dunsmuir's prayers turned out worthy of her concern. He accepted Christ as she had prayed he would. And in time. The rapture had not yet occurred.

God blessed their every endeavor with the farm. Crops exceeded expectations in matters of both great yields and exceptional taste. Friends and neighbors alike held April and Harold in high regard. Their lives are exemplary and joyous, the kind of people everyone wishes to be. He once was asked why they seem so fulfilled.

He replied, "Oh, I suppose it's because, other than the love we share, we are about as close to God as one can get."

"You mean as in worship or something like that?"

"Well, yes. But what I'm thinking is that we are on our knees with our hands acutely involved in the soil. Man's first command was to take care of the earth. What with all the buildings, roads, highways, parking lots, and general neglect of the earth sources, we have gotten far away from one of the most important reasons God placed us on this planet: to take care of it." He smiled his all-consuming contented smile of fulfillment. April is standing near him as they answer questions by the numerous guests admiring the Dunsmuir farm's bounty.

"What is your yield of crops compared to other farms in the area?"

"We've discussed this very subject with neighbors, and we—" April and Harold vanished into thin air; they along with three of their guests.

⚜

Rumbling along the road extending what seemed endless miles over a parched terrain of sun-bleached desert grass is Sara Gaston driving an older Overland Datsun. With her riding in the passenger seat is Watanda, who just a year ago was the village witch doctor, now the village's leading Christian. In the back seat is Juan Marcels, a handyman. They're pulling a worn-out trailer loaded with wooden crates too large for safety of the old truck. Cautiously she refused to drive over 45 mph even when the road would allow a higher speed.

After avoiding the thousands of potholes in the roadway and deep ruts remaining from cars traveling in mud during heavy rainfall, she arrived at the remote hospital. The gruesome trip of eighty-five miles seemed three times that, ending. They are met with excited hospital staff and a throng of villagers, all very happy.

Bunched together like too many people to carry a small container, they slowly maneuvered the largest of the four crates out of the trailer and somehow managed to lug it into the hospital, along a hallway, turned a corner, and finally placed it on the floor nearby where the installation would take place. Sara then supervised the uncrating of the medical equipment.

Within the week, the laser surgical device is fully operational including the electrical connection to the diesel-powered generator. Sara had designed an elevated 1,000-gallon diesel fuel tank that by gravity feeds the engine. (She has to make the 85-plus-mile trip five times to fill the tank, toting a 200-gallon tank in both directions.)

Gunnysacks filled with sand lying on the surgery table to simulate a body are used to test and calibrate over a hundred settings necessary to assure safety. She worked on this from early mornings into the evenings until she could no longer concentrate. Her attendants made sure she ate something, or she would no doubt faint from exhaustion. But it is vital to her to get the equipment ready for the trained physician to schedule surgeries impossible to perform without the device. Overcoming physical comfort to achieve her objectives had never bothered her, and it won't now, either, she maintained.

After almost a week, the physician took over the controls of the machine to gain full familiarity before the first patient until he was satisfied.

He and his staff along with Sara are in one of the many meetings of preparation when suddenly all but three in attendance disappear along with Sara; they were there among them all and then gone. Just like that—gone!

⁂

Walter Belkins was in the early spring with only so many hours needed to prepare the fields for crops and to feed the over 1,500 head of cattle. Though four large eight-wheeled GPS-guided powered tractors are doing various functions, it is a rush to get the seeds planted in case poor weather keeps them from the work. And that is what is happening on the Belkins farm from dawn to dusk as the cows are being milked on schedule day after day.

All during the fall and winter months, maintenance and upkeep activities are completed to assure to the best of their abilities that the farm equipment, including the tractors, is ready when springtime arrives. A major breakdown could cripple a farm's financial picture for the year.

Walter has been accused many times of taking better care of the farm equipment than his family, unfounded of course, but that is how he's perceived. Not all the farmers are given that much praise. He's proud of how he treats both his family and his farm. By looking at the results of his children in school, it is a mirror of how well (or badly) their home life is. At PTA meetings, the principal and teachers are welcome windows into the success or failure of the children, and all the Belkins are doing very well.

Seated at the supper table one evening are all the children and their parents, as usual. Their conversation is sprite also as usual. A guest at their table would be totally confused as they all seem to talk at once to each other, a menagerie of topics between them. Oddly enough, it works.

Imagine this: In the middle of these tangled conversations, the two youngest children vanish from the table. Everyone else remained seated and outright shocked at the disappearance of the two who were there. A moment later, everyone quickly got away from the table and began searching all about the house, outside, upstairs, every room, nook, and cranny, and all of the farm's outbuildings. Nothing, not a single trace of their being was anywhere close by. No one seemed to realize what had taken place.

⚜

As with Mr. Wesson, Travis Olsen is spiritually floundering and caught up in the travesties of being wealthy. They do not know of each other though having the same choice concerning their destiny.

Olsen's lifestyle is much different than that of Wesson's. Wesson is driven by wealth and prestige. On the other hand, Olsen is driven by acquiring for each company an obscene profitability and equally obscene bankroll, which is the ultimate measurement of success. Wesson is driven by what money can do by proving it with his collections of evident wealth. Olsen is satisfied with just having the money to do what Wesson does with his wealth.

Like continually keeping watch with scores and win/loss records of a favorite sports team during finals, Olsen monitors the profit margins and surplus cash of every one of his businesses and the overall totals every week. He is wise enough to allow his chosen managers to have enough rope to either pull as a team member or hang himself so to speak. He knows the dangers of micromanaging. For him it continues to bring atrocious dividends.

Oh, yes, by the way, he is married and has two sons: one a senior in high school and the other in college. Neither wants to follow in their father's footsteps or want to be wealthy. They have experienced a distant father wrapped up in his own world of business. All but

Travis realizes Dawn, their mother, has been the shaper of her two boys.

Sundays, claimed Travis, is one of the more important days of the week regarding the success of the businesses. He preferred to attend to whatever it was in his office a half hour away, leaving around 8:00 a.m. after reading the financial and community page of the newspaper. He would not return home until after 4:00 p.m.

Dawn and her two boys attended both Sunday Bible classes and the morning worship service at the Riverside Community Bible Church around the corner from their home. When the boys were small, Dawn had accepted the Lord and encouraged Travis to do the same many times since. She was always turned down. Both sons did as she led them to the savior. And over the years, they attempted to have their father do the same. They met with the same result as did their mother.

On this particular Sunday, all was well with Travis when he left for the office. All was not well by noon. From the office window, people were heard wailing. He witnessed cars crashing into objects lining the streets if not into parked cars. Some uncontrolled autos and pickup trucks slammed into pedestrians, inflicting serious injuries; and he thought one or two unsuspecting people were killed.

He called home. No answer. Hurriedly he ran to his Audi and barely manipulated the street of his short drive home. His house is deadly quiet after calling out his family's names. Then he remembered they would be at church. It was close enough to run from home. Panic had enveloped the church. Asking what happened, all he could get was, "Nearly all the congregation, the pastor and his wife and the youth director too have disappeared. One second, there, another second gone, just like that!" Travis searched through the crowd attempting to find his wife and sons. He did not find them.

In a moment, all of his business concerns disintegrated to unimportance. There was no way he could have planned for this. Then he remembered the many times Dawn and both his sons pleaded with him to accept the Lord. Not only did he refuse, he recalled, but thought it totally unnecessary. Now, of course, he thought much differently about that. Soon his concern for his family was overtaken by merely staying alive. And his money meant nothing at all now.

❦

Samuel, their son, is now eight months old. Talk about doting parents! Daryl and Heather Fording could conduct a clinic on the subject. He's one lucky kid. Nothing is too much for him. Even the toy box is a cabinet with raised panel doors built in under a settee. At even a whimper, Heather came to him in a run to solve whatever the cause. His diaper is changed every thirty minutes though not needed; it used to be every quarter hour!

At every chance, Daryl brags about his new son to the point of being avoided; his repeated stories became overbearing.

Visits to their doctor were more frequent than necessary as Heather had a great fear they could lose Samuel to some unknown disease; although each time, the doctor assured her he was just fine, that she had nothing to worry about.

But she did have something to worry about.

Attending a church that makes you feel good including having God in your consciousness and the reading of daily Scriptures is all well and good, but is it enough? That question never entered the minds of Daryl and Heather. The sermons they heard nearly every Sunday in their lives did little to cause much questioning about spiritual things. Both however were challenged to live better and more meaningful lives as each day becomes the past.

And so they did. Oftentimes it was the subject of their conversations in their more serious moments. In general, they were quite happy with this area of their lives and each time concluded that they would be involved in something with spiritual benefits. They obeyed their leanings by once a month for the majority of a day assisting with a homeless program the church sponsors. A deep satisfaction in their hearts seemed rewarding enough each time.

Then Samuel's birth entered the picture. He influenced a change in most of that previous commitment. Heather was more than happy to rearrange her life for the benefit of her son. Not even a "thank you,

God" entered her mind because she assumed having a baby is a rite of marriage. And now after all the troubles she and Daryl had gone through to have Samuel, God became less in her consciousness, as she felt she deserved to have a child. Maybe more.

The Fordings are absorbed in their getting ready to attend church. They're both in their robes after showers as they attend to the matters of having Samuel all decked out and snuggled into the baby blanket, lying him in his crib as they get ready. His nursery/bedroom is the room adjacent to theirs, where he is cooing as contented babies do, playing with his toes. Daryl and Heather are side by side in the master bath tending to their grooming details before getting dressed. Ten minutes later, they're ready to go out the door.

Heather goes into Samuel's room to fetch him.

In a loud, chilling scream, she manages to declare to Daryl that Samuel is gone. His blanket remains in the crib as a vacated cocoon. Daryl scurries to look at what she's screaming about. Samuel is missing. To where could he have gone? Or how? The side of the crib is up. He is too tiny to crawl up and over it. Plus, if he would have fallen, they would have heard that! He checked the window for indications—any indication of use, in or out: a kidnapper possibly? There is no evidence. None.

After a few minutes in total disbelief, they search all around inside the house. Heather can barely see through the heavy tears in her eyes not accepting the possibility Samuel could just simply be gone! Daryl wondered if some demonic power took him away. If not that, what? Or who? Where is his son? The question continually resonated in his brain. Frantically they searched the house many times over, calling 9-1-1 more than a few times. Every time no answer. It was down or overloaded. Daryl inspected every inch of property immediately surrounding the house for footprints or any trace of anything or anyone who could have snatched up their baby. Not a clue.

In shock they sat on the sofa being still and quiet. It was then Heather heard tormented cries of women's voices. She ran to the door with Daryl behind her, fiddled with the lock before opening it to listen. It is true what she had moments before thought she heard.

Other mothers are weeping and crying out to find their missing babies. Daryl is convinced it's demonic. Heather has no idea of anything. She is like the other mothers—too absorbed in their grief to seize any sensible thought.

Within the hour, they will know where Samuel had been taken. And that they had been left behind to face the torment of Satan or the wrath of God, dependent upon whom they will follow. In the process, eventually their mindfulness toward each other will be torn away when they choose Satan. The memory of Samuel will always haunt them even in their death—soon to come.

15

HALF HOUR AFTER

The US Senate and House of Representatives, various US agencies, governors of every state, and mayors of every town called emergency conferences. Most had to settle for quorums due to many had been taken and others stymied in traffic or caught in traffic of the closed-down roadways, freeways, and in inoperable taxis and airports.

US Senator Joel LeCosta of Maryland describes the Senate floor when asked by a *Washington Post* reporter.

"Not one senator had remained calm. Every one of us was near hysteria, mentally blinded by what had taken place. I included. The devastation had overwhelmed any common sense.

"And not only in this country. On the way here, I discussed what was happening with a CIA official. He told me the same had occurred on every continent and in every nation and city in the world!

"I also talked with our Senate administrator who contacts us in emergencies as this. He told me twenty-six senators are anticipated to be missing as they cannot be reached. He added that over thirty other senators had stated it is impossible to arrive at the senate today, and they didn't know when. Among them was the Senate speaker. The first on the agenda was to declare the speaker from the list of protocol. We did that quickly as an interim.

"That in itself is a wonder. The commotion and upheaval was one I'll never forget!

"Because the commotion was so disrupting, it required the full day to calmly, logically discuss illogical circumstances of what had happened and the first priorities to adopt. No decisions have been made yet. This will be an all-nighter. Never in the history of the world has mankind been forced to deal with such a ruinous event.

"In this pandemonium, I understand all forms of government, including the UN, have called their membership and diplomats to determine, like we, what needs to be done. The needs, of course, are unimaginable both physically and financially.

"I have to go." With that, he ran up the Senate's front steps.

He didn't have a clue of how evil man had become. He could only think of the great destruction of assets, not realizing the desolation of the human heart being overcome by the whims of Satan and how that would further cripple his efforts. He and all officials now have the same evil heart as the rest of the world!

The first order of business in the halls of the barely functional congress is the announcement the president is on Air Force One to the Rocky Mountain caverns.

Two hours later
The president of the United States,
from the presidential cavern

"Men and women who hear my voice, this is the president of the United States. We have a clue as what has taken place all over the world. It has been prophecy centuries old told by the Scriptures. I am sorry that we had not taken its warnings of this event as seriously as we should have.

"We are doing all we can that is possible, but limited resources at hand make any effort to make an impact on our condition impossible. What little intel we could muster, it is the same ordeal in most countries.

"I plead with each American to regard each other with kindness and responsibility as best you can."

With that, the screens and audio went blank. For days, it is all that came from the president.

Israel's premier

"The best scholars in Israel, after much deliberation, have determined that what has taken place is explained in the Christian Bible. We believe this because the disappearances of the people now gone are of the Christian faith.

"This forces us to take a deeper look into their Scripture to make our nation more prepared for our future and the infliction we can expect from other nations surrounding us. I suspect it is not good.

"The scholars are immersed in this very ordeal as I speak. We fear Islam the most, Iran in particular. Both we and the Palestinians are doomed if Iran chooses to take advantage of the world chaos and activate a preemptive nuclear strike and follow-up bombardment.

"I caution every civilian to keep indoors and allow our trained military to deal with the local as well as the national circumstances. They are doing what they can amongst the chaos in the streets of our country and limited resources."

✦

Brussels, a message by satellite

"God has finally done it. He caused more than *three billion people* to disappear off the face of the earth. You can blame God for your new distresses and anxieties by doing this."

"As president of the Euro Union, I will reverse your dilemma and bring peace to the world to the best of my ability. This includes all individuals and governments of the world alike. But I need your undivided obedience to the edicts I pronounce for the betterment of the world.

"We have resources which any government in the world do not have access. Not that those resources are endlessly deep, we can only say we have prepared for this very event that God gave us warning. We just did not know when.

"At this present time, we are sifting through the world's problems and making the necessary decisions on your behalf to cause everyone's life to be easier.

"When I say *world*, I mean it—from China, the USA, the Middle East, Russia, Australia, and all of Asian descent. I will see to it that at least your problems will be less than at present."

⁂

Peking, China
The emperor's palace

"People of the Republic of China, this is Hou Sing. Catastrophic events have taken place over the entire world. Hundreds of millions of people have vanished. Gone. There are no reasonable explanations.

"Some of the American teachers and hired consultants—but not all of them, and many of international prisoners have also disappeared at the same, precise moment as others in many parts of the world."

"Even many of our nationals have also disappeared.

"Our best scientists are working to make an understanding of what has taken place. We assure you there is nothing to harm you in the present or in the future. To make certain, we have set in motion to amass an army of over one hundred fifty million men or more in case an event would materialize, leaving our country vulnerable. We will not let that happen unaware."

⁂

Tal-Tamir, Syria

Al-Sumad, a twenty-eight-year-old rising star with the ISIS, has one responsibility: to keep an eye on the captives in their detainment cells that they do not escape. He assumes recognition for such a remedial task and more responsibility in the service of Allah. He felt the slight tremor, thought to be an earthquake as often occurs in

Tal-Tamir. A few minutes later, he walked from the entry room to the room behind the desk where the cells and the captives are. His chest heaves with horror upon the sight that all but two of the Christians are gone! "But how?" as he looks around.

He ponders what he should do—tell his superior right away? Or wait. Or just leave and forget his ambition. Or kill himself. He feared the threat of his head being lopped off for letting the infidels escape. He knew he didn't, but that wouldn't matter to his superior. Maybe if he told him straightaway that at best he would not face decapitation.

Only fifty-six meters away is the alley entrance to the local ISIS hideout. Before the next ten minutes expired, he'd have told what happened—nothing that he could've avoided. He thought that that is the best plan. Before sunset, Al-Sumad's body was headless.

Even before the daylight succumbed to darkness, four other containment jails reported they experienced the same thing. All four jailers met with the same fate as Al-Sumad. Then another three jailers met of the same fate during the next morning. Bewilderment prevailed as to what and where of the Christians. Then news came that other Christians being watched and considered to be captured also disappeared. A young American who joined the ISIS in rebellion made a suggestion of what he remembered what his mother had told him before he was a teenager.

"The Christian's Bible talks about this—called the rapture."

"Yes, the kid is right," an elder volunteered, interrupting the discussion. "Based on what happened here, this must be true. I investigated this last night on the Internet. Then I discovered not only here, but all over the world, everywhere. We killed nearly a dozen of our own people needlessly," he added as a mere observation without remorse.

16

MINISTERS LEFT BEHIND

Three Hours Later

According to a report by the only satellite TV remaining in operation, I saw that the Reverend Wendell Wallace, a minister, was not taken as were the believers. He was left behind. The news reporter thought it peculiar, that a minister of the Gospel would be left behind. I too was bewildered until he heard the remainder of the report.

It was then I knew it would be more peculiar if the minister would have been taken!

"By five p.m., only a little more than six hours after *the Event* took place, Reverend Wallace's church in Cerritos, California, was the object of an angry mob who insisted upon him telling them why it happened to them and why he didn't tell them about it. There were many other churches in the area, but it was his church they had targeted. They didn't stop at breaking down the doors and swarming inside. They dragged him out of his office, out of the church, onto the lawn, and stripped off his clothes leaving him shamefully naked. I noticed other ministers were alongside Wallace being treated the same way."

The reporter filled in some backstory.

"We had researched a small amount of this minister's past before arriving on the scene. He had been fired from numerous congregations by their boards for continued sexual indiscretions. We assumed by the crowd's violent activity they probably knew more about him than our brief research revealed.

"As we watched and recorded the vicious activity, there were even more ministers forcibly brought onto the lawn, joining Wallace and the others. They too were stripped. Word got around to us that these ministers had never made it a subject they preached anything about. In fact, the ministers had verbally renounced the epics of the rapture, God's judgment, and the existence of hell. They believed and knew that God would never do such a thing, being a god of love. By this they had discredited the Scripture altogether. For that, they're now paying the price for their negligence."

On video, Steven watched the remaining activity, the reporter not narrating, being speechless.

Without warning, Wallace was hoisted up to the crossarm of the ornamental cross in front of the church. While that was going on, the other ministers are being roped in a cluster around the base of the cross. From many directions, their wives have come upon the unimaginable setting displaying horror, bewilderment, and concern that their husbands were being so disgracefully displayed.

The crowd quickly cleared a pathway between them as three or four of the leaders of this brutal display of anger shot the wives—first their body parts before shooting them in the forehead, as the traumatized husbands watched them suffer before death occurred. The pain of watching the malicious act was purposefully and mercilessly held back for nearly a full ten minutes before they were shot to death.

We all saw that they left Wallace hanging there in a shocked, stunned numbness as the screen we had been watching went blank.

17

TWENTY-FOUR HOURS AFTER

Radolfo Amerinero is requested to immediately return to his office in Brussels from his Greek Island villa.

Upon his arrival, nine of the 27 EU countries are represented and seated at the conference table, including the EU president, General Thornton Sholtsen, of Germany. Most of them are excitedly in an uproar, verbalizing their anxieties all at once. None could be heard specifically, though a common theme seemed to be aired. Amerinero quieted them merely by raising a hand.

"Gentlemen, why do you want to meet with me? How can I help you?"

"Our senior council has decided to have you be our president. That decision was taken to the Tribunal Council. They agreed. All that is necessary is for you to accept the position."

Radolfo trained his eyes on Sholtsen. "What about it, General?"

"I will graciously step down from the presidency if you accept. In fact, it was my idea because the EU requires the best leadership available. That leader is you."

Radolfo scanned the expressions of the representatives. They seemed to be of one accord. "Well then, I accept on one condition."

They exchanged questioning glances among one another. The general responded, "Of course. Anything."

"I need an oath from all of you that neither the senior nor the Tribunal Council, of which all of the members of both bodies are present, will not refute or disagree any declaration, order, or action I may take while being the EU president. That they will, of one accord, willingly accept any of those actions. Agreed?"

A few moments of pondering the request between them took place before accepting the condition. "We agree. But are you not eliminating the need for them?"

"No, I am not. They will be needed from time to time for counsel. They will be valuable to me as the EU moves along through all the turmoil that exists all over the world.

"I shall have my secretary write up the terms and conditions contract of which each one of you are to sign. I have already initiated the first draft of this document in anticipation. It will be ready within an hour or two. In the meantime, I request you all discuss what we must do in view of what has taken place the world over. Want tea or a drink?" No one wanted to reply. They were already too occupied.

Not quite the two hours had passed before the secretary presented the contract and just over two hours with all signatures attached.

⚜

Unrest and threats of war had accelerated everywhere. Nowhere peace could exist—whether it was nation against nation, governments against governments, agencies against agencies, businesses against businesses, or individuals against individuals. God's restraining influence of peaceful coexistence had been removed. But God did have a plan.

God permitted Satan to take control over the earth. He allowed Satan to try his hand at peace.

⚜

The Antichrist's calling

The first priority for Radolfo Amerinero is to create a peaceful world, having no idea how he could accomplish this until one evening.

Lounging quietly in an overstuffed sofa chair, Radolfo was studying a large file, one of many in a massive pile beside him. The laptop on a small table near him was off. A number of assistants had vacated the large office only moments before he delved into his vague preparation of what to do, looking for a key to unlock the secret to formulate a successful global peace plan. He is especially focused upon the Holy Land with Israel and other Middle East Islam warmongers.

Without warning, the laptop whirred on. The buzz of the boot-up brought his attention to it. Being closed is supposed to prevent it from coming on. But there it is, now on with the screen fully loaded. He opened the laptop to the usual dark-blue screen but without any icons to choose from. He feared all the files to be lost. That, though, was not correct.

A scrawl began to occur.

> *I am Lucifer. The world is now mine. God has vacated. By the releasing of millions of people from the earth a few days ago, I now rule all peoples in the world: kings, lords, presidents, government leaders are now under my control. I need a physical presence walking about being my protégé.*
>
> *I have been preparing you, Radolfo Amerinero, to be that man. Do you think it was an accident, fate, or whatever that you have become the EU president only yesterday in spite of your being a Muslim? And the burning desire to rebuild Babylon? There is not one person like you with so many skills and with a mind-set I can trust. I need someone as powerful as Jesus Christ was when he was on earth. You will be like him—an Antichrist. For this I have tutored and prepared you.*
>
> *God has opened the door for me to make you into the man of my will and choosing. You will represent me. The world will be drawn to you like a magnet. You will solve the mystery of peace in the world that you're puzzled about at this very moment: How to craft that peace. I tell you now that you will be successful. I will see to it that you are. You will be respected as the savior of the world; first by acquiring peace throughout the world and building the*

best of all cities ever built, Babylon. You are chosen to spearhead the rebuilding of the Temple.

There is another step I want you to take. Alexis Werner is in your employ. He has the skill and technological know-how as any man. More. I have chosen him to be your forerunner and prophet.

As with you, he will have enormous power to deceive even the highly educated, sophisticated, and world influencers to worship me, which begins by worshipping you established by the leadership of Mr. Werner. He, especially, will be able to perform great signs, wonders, and miracles. He has also received from me the power to perform prevailing deceit—including to perform resurrections from the dead!

He is waiting for your call. Your quest and his recruitment shall begin immediately to fulfill my destiny on earth.

The laptop is once again silent. Only for a quick split-second Radolfo was overtaken by astonishment. Supernaturally he comprehended all of what Lucifer had said—everything, present and future, especially Babylon.

Quickly he and Alex conversed about their new union together. They were on track immediately to what Satan had requested. Both felt Lucifer's power overcome them in a special harmony of creed and purpose.

World peace became his first and only focus. The rest of his work would be known—some in short order, others in due time. He understood clearly the entire world would soon be his footstool.

For this to transpire, other events he must cause to happen, most importantly to establish peace.

His First Act

Peace—the world over, thought Radolfo. The problem starts in the Middle East; Israel against the rest of those nations. Or maybe, more likely, the Middle Eastern countries against Israel. The key to peace is to somehow neutralize the aggression of all nations, including Palestine, against Israel.

What would happen if a promise was made that Israel will remain protected with peace guaranteed? he questioned himself.

The Antichrist, Mr. Amerinero, will provide the resolve of others to go along. All he needs is the instrument to bring the various factions together. But what?

Food! That's it! Food. And water. Israel has both. All of the surrounding nations do not. A famine in tandem with the continued wind-blown sands of the wilderness and deserts are wreaking havoc and desolation while Israel basks in the sunshine of plenteous food and water. Strike a deal between them, and alas! I am worthy of worship. All without a shot fired or a missile launched!

18

FOUR DAYS AFTER

Mr. Werner summoned Jolene Gillespie to his office, all expenses paid with full use of any of Amerinero's fleets of aircraft and vehicles. She was not told why she had been invited. Her e-mail was written with quite forcible verbiage. Her curiosity wielded more incentive than the way the e-mail was stated. At every stage during her flight and transporting, she was treated royally.

Ms. Gillespie had worked hard to get where her career as a news reporter has taken her. She has yet to have her fortieth birthday but has interviewed many powerful world leaders, as like had Barbara Walters considered the very best in her profession.

She was led to Amerinero's office. No one walked behind her or at her side. She was merely requested to follow the gracious man. She could sense he was well armed.

Guards attired in dark-brown suits, tan shirts, striped matching ties, and meticulously shined brown shoes opened the huge ornate door to provide her entrance into an office, Mr. Werner's. He is seated nearby. She had never seen such a huge ornate desk as the one Amerinero was seated in front of. Both stood as she entered. Werner extended a hand to shake hers then indicated with a sweeping motion for her to sit. Showing respect, they sat when she sat as she nodded acknowledgement to Amerinero.

"Ms. Gillespie, I shall come to the point straightaway," began Werner.

"Please, gentlemen, call me Jolene."

"Jolene," he continued as he nodded to accept her graciousness, "we would be honored if you accept the position of being our news spokesman—spokeswoman."

"Ours...meaning who, exactly?"

"Trident Technologies International, of course."

"Excuse me... Trident what?"

Amerinero broke in, "We design and produce aggressive new technologies for governments."

"Such as?" inquired Jolene.

"Leading-edge products of surveillance, spyware, security, and neurologically based technologies," stated Werner in a manner that indicated she should have already been well-versed with the company and its products.

"I wish you had told me in the e-mail of my summons what the subject of this meeting would be about. We could have saved all of us a lot of time."

"How would that have mattered? We need to have you tour our facilities before you make a decision to accept," inferred Radolfo.

"Mr. Amerinero. Mr. Werner. I cannot accept your offer as wonderful as I assume it to be."

Mortified with surprise, they look at each other; they're visibly astonished that she would turn them without knowing not only her duties, but even the salary being offered her!

They clamored over each other to entice her to reconsider her response. "You haven't heard the offer of salary! You don't know of your function. We didn't have the chance to tell you of the freedom you'll have. The power you'll be given for all the world to see."

"Sorry, I'm not interested."

Silence. A loud silence. Both parties knowing the next to speak wins. She outlasted them. They spoke first. "But why?"

"Call it a woman's intuition. Call it whatever you like." They knew her decision, though made immaturely, would stand.

"If you're not accepting this offer, can you recommend someone on the same professional level as yourself?" Werner sounded distressed, anxious.

"Yes, I can. Emile Dowdson of MSN. He would be perfect. He has an inside track of understanding your products and accompanying technologies."

For days after, Jolene studied the profiles of the two men she had met, although she knew some about them both. But what she did learn of them astounded her. She had met with very, very strong and influential people! That they were together declared by many publications to be the most powerful duo in the world on many simultaneous fronts ranging from military strategy to theology, from finance to neurology. She was duly impressed and contemplated that maybe she had made the wrong call for her career, but this is now what it is.

19

BABYLON'S REIGN
BY AARON CARLISLE

Aaron's two-part book was more than an accounting of world trade and how that fit into Biblical prophecy but also how the elements of the Middle East's continuous crisis became central to the prophecy of Babylon. It does not surprise me how his insight was so adept. A student in my philosophy classes at college, we had what one could call a common interest: Biblical prophecy. In fact it was I who encouraged his writing this book because of his enthusiastic, nearly continual studying over a few years of the two powerful influences in the world. He wrote it three years before the rapture.

Part 1 exposed and explored the vulnerability the world had been subjected by the enormous international trade and commerce every country then depended upon for its monetary wealth and stability. If there was one commonality among nations, trade was it.

Along with the dependence of import-export commerce between countries, there arose a need for common currency, an internationally approved currency to replace the weak American dollar. This is the trend Carlisle saw to occur. The EU in particular in partnership with China, India, and Russia were strong advocates to achieve a new currency. A strong supporter of this was a world-renowned authority of international current affairs, Radolfo Amerinero of Italy.

Amerinero had yet to turn thirty-five years old when he already had established himself with an uncanny wisdom on many issues that caused a ten-plus million following on Facebook. His opinions were well respected and gained the unwavering alliance of many country leaders. He has certainly gained Carlisle's attention.

Amerinero was the leader in the unification of an international trade agreement, a single trade agreement's language common to all participants, which has as a purpose to bring wealth equality to all nations through their trading. This of course led to a single banking system, already being utilized to a much smaller degree then when created. Carlisle presented this ideology as dangerous.

According to Carlisle, this unification, while sounding solid at the onset, would actually be very dangerous to the world and in fact could be the demise of the United States. He made an issue, rightly, that an international unification falls into the genre of Bible prophecy in that a unity of financial sources and trade worldwide is completely exposed to the takeover of an Antichrist, setting up his control as Lucifer has ordained.

For the Antichrist to be in control, there had to be a centralized power originating from a single location, with a single agenda, having a singular authority, and possess a singular control over the populations-at-large. That is what Scripture prophecies declared to occur according to Aaron Carlisle's convincing book; then there's the second part.

Part 2 disentangles what was going on in the Middle East as has been for many centuries. It is all about prominence, power, and possession of land. One country stood alone as the instigator in 1947—in particular, Israel.

Israel merely doused a fire with fuel already in flames. They possessed a land promised to them by God, as God's chosen people.

This alone infuriated the countries in the Middle East region who responded with avengement by annihilating Israel.

It became much deeper though, according to Aaron.

He stated in *Babylon's Reign* the initial cause for disharmony stems back to the days of Abraham, in the Book of Genesis. Chapter 11, in fact, a son was born to Abraham. His name was Ishmael. God cursed Ishmael by declaring that all of Ishmael's twelve brothers and his and their descendants could never get along with each other. All of Arab descent is those of Ishmael's lineage.

In AD 650, Mohammed added an enduringly substantial ingredient into the mix of world beliefs. Today's Islam was born.

Islam is now a worldwide population of over 1.5 billion Muslims and gaining over Christianity, now becoming more than a passive religion in these last days as Mr. Carlisle states. He challenged traditional interpretations of prophecy taught and believed during the past in modern decades; feeling strongly that a new possibilities of prophecies fulfill a new application of what could occur.

Carlisle's position was that a possibility exists in God's plan in the last days for a prominent religion to be where the creation of the Antichrist originates. He claimed he knew that Radolfo Amerinero had converted to Islam a few years previous and that the Islamic leaders listened to every word he utters. At the present time, even Baghdad, the ISIS Caliph give Amerinero honor with reverence to Radolfo's opinions.

There are then other events, by virtue of happenstance or planning, that quite naturally fell into place.

First, it was not only possible for Mecca to be Babylon, but it did! It makes more sense than to be in Iraq along the Euphrates River as was believed by Christians. The Red Sea already supported millions upon millions of tons of mariner trade beyond that of oil. Combined, the response by mariners as prophesied in the Book of Revelation when the destruction of Babylon occurs can only happen clearly with Babylon in Saudi Arabia, certainly not that of the plentiful valley of Baghdad, Iraq. Being a major trade route since modern times, the harlot—Babylon—as prophesied in Revelation 18 and 19, can easily be what the angel told the apostle John it would be but only on the coast of the Red Sea. All that was needed? Someone to build it! Amerinero maybe?

Secondly, masses of people by the millions every year make their pilgrimage to Mecca. These people are Muslims who are ardent believers of the Islam faith. So according to research by Carlisle, what do the Muslims do after prayers in their most prominently significant mosque? They circle the Haaba in the mosque's courtyard—seven times. Then, if they can get near the Black Stone of cornerstone importance to kiss it, all their sins are forgiven. A faith this strong, contends Carlisle, in the last days that offers forgiveness of sins is a plain and simple substitution of Christ's taking upon himself the forgiving of sin. Satan could not have devised a plainer deception than this! If Radolfo Amerinero is Lucifer's appointed Antichrist, then the conclusions Aaron Carlisle have drawn are more than 90 percent accurate. By the way, he informed me that he would welcome anyone to provide him proof his conclusions cannot happen. No one did because it was too much of a likelihood he was right.

These facts substantiated for Carlisle that the position he took with *Babylon's Reign* were right on.

Many scholars, whether Christian believers or no, considered Carlisle's essay on the last days as accurately interpreted and relevant as any book published on the subject. Most, though, questioned Mecca being Babylon or that the Antichrist will come from Islam. As for me, Steven Alexander, I must consider the possibility as the Book of Revelation is not a book of the Bible to get dogmatic. There are simply too many chances for wrongful conclusions and too much left unsaid by Scripture's prophecies. Therefore I could not at that time refute his conclusions any more than I could accept them. That is until the discovery was made that Mecca is 666 nautical miles from Jerusalem. Let me tell you, this fact alone changed my well-substantiated idea of where Babylon's location would be!

We witnessed Carlisle's conjectures of *Babylon's Reign* to be true. Amerinero had converted to Islam with the name of Amid Baker Mohammed. Lucifer did indeed choose Amid Baker to be the Antichrist! Also is that Amid Baker followed through with the development of the new city Babylon near Mecca on the shoreline of the Red Sea, just as Carlisle had believed would happen. The nautical miles from Jerusalem of 666 coincided with the mark of the beast to come later in all of our lives exactly what the prophecy in the Book of Revelation told us would happen.

Now when it's too late to be transported to heaven, as what occurred for those who had accepted Christ as their savior, it puzzles me why these truths were not told us or discovered when I could have done something about it. If nothing else than to save my own skin! For real, I am trapped to live in this world to be wholly controlled by the Antichrist, Amid Baker Mohammed. I know enough about what scriptural prophecy has to say about what I can expect. It ain't going to be pleasant over the next twenty years or so... I hope less! I have this last chance. The Bible says that one can die only once and after that the judgment. Well, I am still alive; only I'm on the wrong side of the rapture! Oh how I wish I had listened to my mother! I remember every discussion with her that I refused her invitation to accept Christ as my Lord.

As the saying goes, that was then, this is now. I am living in a world that my only concern is my survival, and I could care less about anyone else. The significant part of that? I have no remorse, no regret, no apology—absolutely none for anyone but me for any action I choose!

20

BABYLON

Four months later, Dowdson is the news spokesman for Trident Technologies International'. He had no idea his real job would be the media contact for the Antichrist and Mr. Werner, the False Prophet, in months to come.

His first news conference after being introduced to the media is being held in Warner's largest of three conference rooms located on the twenty-fifth floor in the Amerinero Plaza Building, Brussels. Over a hundred invited guests are seated in attendance representing the few major news companies in the world still operating. Most of them are in the employ of Antichrist, but few realize it.

On the podium at one side is a gigantic display hidden by a forty-five foot wide curtain. Curiosity of what's veiled dominates conversations while guests mill about waiting to be seated.

Dowdson taps a water glass, gaining attention.

"Welcome to the first of many announcements which the Euro Union president wishes for each of you to attend. There are two events he has already inaugurated. They are for the benefits of the world to enjoy. Please gather round the veiled display before taking your seats."

Slowly the curtain is drawn from left to right revealing a highly detailed gigantic model of a city, measuring an estimated ninety feet wide and thirty-five feet front to back. A large brass plate identifies the model as Babylon, the Great City. The model is displayed at an approximate ten degrees, angled to optimize its viewing. Also included of this exhibition is the detailing of a proportionate gigantic cargo depot for the unloading of supercargo vessels of goods, the model ships having identification of countries from all over the world.

Everyone is awestruck, without conversation, absorbing the concepts for the new city's design. They're transfixed so deeply they nearly missed Dowdson's request for them to be seated. Slowly they break away before conceding. The curtain remains open as the conference continues with all eyes remaining to comprehend Babylon's magnitude as Dowdson begins his words of acknowledgement and the future this city will bring to the world.

"The finest, most innovative architects and construction engineers in the world—some from Dubai—have completed the design of the new Babylon City in Saudi Arabia. As you can see, it is designed to be in Jeddah, not far from Mecca on the coast of the Red Sea. For decades upon decades, it has been believed ancient Babylon's location lying in ruins near the Euphrates River will be rebuilt to its splendor of centuries ago. Saddam Hussein had begun this rebuilding even before the Gulf War took place. The USA and Canada have already donated seventeen million dollars for repairs inflicted upon Hussein's project during the war. He was wrong. They were wrong too.

"Mr. Amerinero's objective is to make Babylon the world's center of finance, data, world trade, education, and entertainment to match the desires of kings and rulers no matter their religion.[1] He has selected Mecca to be the location of what the Protestant Scriptures refer to as the Mystery Babylon. Antichrist is quite familiar with this, as Christianity believes a Scriptural account of what they also believe is prophecy.

"It is not his plan to have the largest, most innovative city with the tallest buildings, he wants it to be the world's most profuse commerce center of the world teeming with riches and innumerable pleasures. He expects this Babylon City to surpass New York, London, Hong Kong, Singapore, Shanghai, Seattle, and Los Angeles' capacity of shipping and commerce as world-class ports."

Dowdson enjoys the responses of enthusiastic kudos of such a project. But he's surprised by Amid taking the staged display and announcement. A new display is wheeled into view with its curtain drawn to hide its content.

Among "oohs and aahs" from the audience and breath taken from Dowdson, the curtain of a new display is drawn open. Gasps occur when they see the splendor and beauty of interiors of buildings, lavish theaters, promenades, private clubs, parks, and opulent open-air markets that he's enjoying to display.

Following a series of many questions and answers lasting more than an hour, Amerinero closes the news conference by informing them, "Site work of the infrastructure of this spectacular city has already begun. Completion of Babylon is scheduled by the end of twenty months from today, hopefully less, ready for preliminary tours."

21

STEVEN NOW

Plus Five Weeks

Jolene Jacobsen discovered me, she said, from someone who thought I am an expert of Scripture knowledge. She told me more. She arrived in the city to specifically find me. After chasing records and files, she found my address, hoping against hope she'd find me home among all the havoc going on. I soon knew she has knowledge of more details of what on earth is going on and what is to be done about it than I, actually. She knew from experience that her chances finding me home would increase as the evening wore on. It was 2:00 p.m. when she began her wait as every minute carried the heft of danger as it seemed to intensify. My photo she had obtained made it easy to ID me as I rounded the corner and proceeded into the gated entry of a large apartment building, one of the fourteen-building apartment complex, which is mostly vacated, that I call home for now.

She ascended the eleven floors of stairs (the elevator ceasing to operate), stopping to vomit because of the overpowering stench of corpses before she knocked on my door, at 1107E.

Before she could identify herself, I had shouted through the door to warn whoever it is to stand clear; for if they did not, I will shoot through the door. She stood clear as she informed me who she was. I knew her only by name.

"What do you want from me?" I demanded.

"There's a lot you know what's going on. I have been told your knowledge of the Scriptures is as thorough as anyone, and I believe that the Scripture has answers. I would like to ask you some questions about what is happening. Can you do that for me?

"Only if you do not divulge where I live."

"Done, I won't tell a soul."

"No one has a soul anymore," I quipped as I begin to unlock the five deadbolts and two security locks to open the door. "Everyone's soul seems to belong to the devil now."

She stepped in as I grab her arm and, with a yank, hastened her entrance and hurriedly reconnected all the locks. I motioned to her to sit on a closed, double-walled cardboard carton box. I sat on another close enough that our knees are nearly touching, our feet plying to make space. It's the only noticeable place to sit. "How did you find me?"

"From government records. Your last tax return actually."

"I thought the IRS filings are confidential."

"Not now they're not. Not since that Event happened."

"No, I suppose not."

She paused while observing me, the man in front of her. My unshaven face with a disheveled beard and shaggy hair did not hide a small glimmer of kindness in my eyes, she said, hidden behind my cynical countenance.

"And this brings us to why I am here. I do know enough that what had happened was the rapture. Right?"

"That's right. All the Christians, the born-again believers, that is."[1]

"Then my question is this: where did they all go?" She thinks through her question further, "When they disappeared?"

"Some say they saw them vanish from out of and beyond the clouds."[2]

"But where did they go to then, Steven?"

"To a form of heaven, a literal place.[2] There is a little room for interpretation on that point. A massive throng of worshippers of the Lord will be in that place, where friends and loved ones will welcome each other."

"They will recognize and know each other?" she asks.

"Sure. Certainly."

"Can you clarify?"

"The welcoming parties are those who have passed away on earth prior to the rapture and have been waiting for the reunion—all the time being in God's presence.[3] Those being welcomed are those who were caught up in the event of what is called the rapture."

"Wait! You're telling me that while the bodies were in the graves, which were opened during the rapture, they joined the souls of them to become the welcoming party of those who were alive during the rapture?"

"You've got it. That is what happened. That is what Scripture says."[4]

"And then what?"

"I cannot even imagine what I am going to tell you what happened next. There is no way you, I, anyone, or those even who were taken could have known—really know the impact of the next event! And I might add, though you and I and all who were left behind will never know it, those who were taken will experience it."

"Tell me. What?"

"Millions upon millions, everyone who had died on the earth who God had been redeemed from both the Old and New Testaments of Scripture, will be worshipping God together, singing. It says in Scripture the number of people worshipping is too enormous to count![5] I can't imagine that. Can you?"

"No, I can't. Tell me this, Steven, at this particular time, will those in wherever they are have any knowledge of what is going on in the world today, what and who they had left behind?"

"Again, Jolene, Scripture is interpretive vague on that issue, so I can only tell you what I, personally, believe to be true."

"All right. What is that?

"Yes, I do think they know. At this time there will be concern they experience for their loved ones. I would like to think that my parents and brother are up there, somewhere, rooting for me and shedding a tear in prayer for me that I will join them sometime. Do you have such people?"

"I have no idea, Steven. I hope I do if what you believe is true. What about you, are you going to make it?" she inquires.

"I hope so. But, Jolene, what I believe is now a mystery yet to be known. I don't—whether it is true or not. What I do know for sure is that my chances to make it are nil to none!"

"Why would you say such a thing with the Bible knowledge you have?"

"That is just it. Because I have this 'extensive' knowledge, as you put it, I am being held more accountable. I had failed. That is why I am here and not up there with my family. As far as how I feel about others left behind, I could care less about them. You too, Jolene."

"Should I be scared of you, Steven?"

"No, not at this moment as you're not threatening to me. But I cannot know how I would treat you if we happen to meet on the street in the future. Our hearts are so totally evil that we can say at this moment we're controlling ourselves to some degree. If you look inside yourself, I suspect you have the same thoughts."

She pauses to evaluate, then observes the time. Darkness has come about. "It's true. Can we keep in touch? I would like to have further talks with you."

"Sure. But it has to be soon. My supplies to keep me alive will be gone soon—enough to keep me here for three or four weeks. We can talk before then but not after because I have no idea, other than to get out of the city, where I will be trying to survive."

Jolene stood up and walked to the door amid the carelessly stacked empty cartons. I started to unlock the secure door. We looked at each other as though still strangers having inordinate doubts concerning themselves before she turned toward the door.

"I'll look you up before then," she reassured herself as much as for me.

"Okay," I replied without interest one way or another. I stopped midway unlocking the locks. "Jolene, it is dark and not safe for anyone at night. Even if you have a place to stay though even a block away, you cannot be alone, and I am not about to leave from here myself, even to protect you. Not."

"You're proposing what?"

"Sleep here. You're safe from the hoodlums."

"And you? Am I safe from you?"

"More than out there," I reacted with a sweep of my arm.

She concedes realizing I am right. She is safer with me than walking alone in the unlit, very dark streets the ten blocks to the shanty excuse of a hotel of her room. She had to trust me for her safety—easier to do than at that hotel!

We arranged the cartons, most partially empty, to provide her privacy in the only room available. The space is at the opposite side from my corner. The only bedroom of my apartment is chock-full of supplies and gear for safety in the future when I leave.

She woke safe as the sky began to lose its blightful darkness. I was looking down at her and had placed a blanket over her during the night, she noticed. Hot coffee and a half piece of toast is thankfully accepted. Minutes later, she left my apartment as she heard my locking the door behind her. I was already looking forward to when we agreed she would be returning within a few days.

The streaked blood now stained into the carpet made her sick, though she is trying to get used to seeing such aftermath of death.

I knew that she wondered if she would actually ever see me again as I wondered the same thing.

I heard her throw up her small breakfast as she passed yet another corpse on the stairway combined with the stench from hallways on the many other stairways.

22

THE GOG AND MAGOG WAR: FOUR MONTHS LATER

Jolene reports:

Five years in planning. All down to the finest of details: Then to last only a few hours.

Israel had to clean up the mess, requiring four months to bury the dead plus more time to mark and bury the bones remaining on the ground,[1] the six years and some months more to clear the battlefield of wood weapons and war gear.[2]

A combined army of twelve countries swarmed upon Israel like a thick blanket of clouds[3] from the northern and eastern wilderness and mountains. Israel seemed doomed by an overwhelmingly outnumbered contingent of soldiers.

None of the high-priced, know-all, see-all, and defend-all technologies succeeded to detect the invading army, failing to detect wooden armament. Israel was caught by surprise.

But God was not.

That is all it took.

First the earthquake disarmed the attacking soldiers of any confidence among their rank and file causing both death and destruction. The eastern Israel mountain range collapsed into the valleys as a strong, swirling wind began. The resultant dust storm was so blinding they could not see beyond an arm's length. In a ravaging folly, they fought what they thought intruders so intently they mistakenly began killing each other with arrows, spears, and swords; many were brutally injured beyond saving. Nearly half of all the assaulting soldiers were rendered incapable of fighting if not dead already. Then to add more sorrow upon them caused by a source they knew nothing about, an infestation of painful boil-like, cancerous sores began breaking out all over their bodies, adding more to the death count. How they longed to be back home, safe from all of this! And finally the fourth pestilence: a heavy rain that turned into large hailstones that ignited into fire upon landing upon the ground killing more. The constant torment of inflicting bodily and property damage decimated the enemy of Israel so completely only a very few, if any, remained alive.

No one living during this time could remain oblivious to what had occurred. Even on the other side of the globe. First, it was too well-known in prophecy. Second, the warfare was too uniquely shaped and so devastating by Israeli's attackers, this war could not be ignored or fail to have meaning!

23

THE TEMPLE MOUNT

Another event also took place. The earthquake,[4] with its epicenter near Jerusalem, had flattened Islam's third most sacred place, the Dome of the Rock. It is now only rubble. Islamic leaders and people immediately blame Israel for its destruction.

Geologists contemplate that two activities occurring at the turn of the century to the time of the earthquake superseded the ruin of the Dome. The tunneling under the Temple Mount by the Jews to find the Ark of the Covenant and the excavating north of the Mount by the Muslims to find the Arc before the Jews so that they could destroy it are the two events allowing the earthquake to do its prophetic work. Both of the tunneling activities were given permission by the property owners of the Temple Mount: the family of the King of Jordan.

As a courtesy by gaining permission from the Jordan Royal family, Amerinero acted quickly to post select guardsmen at the Temple Mount where the Dome of the Rock had stood only hours before.

The Antichrist's overall plan for the world had just become easier to implement! Now he could rebuild the Temple *and* appropriate the Saudi Arabia land to construct Babylon near Mecca, he being Muslim, of course.

Soon after the revealing of Babylon's model city, Dowdson is provided at his request an assistant to help him with details of research when necessary. After much deliberation over applicants, he selects Dimitri Senchini from Italy, having an array of references from top news services including McClatchy Syndicated News. The reviewing of his reports on record thoroughly convinced Dowdson that Dimitri is the finalist. After a scrutinizing background check, Werner approved his coming aboard. Hidden deep to a level scarcely detectable in his resume is his connection with Israel four contacts removed. This fact was kept so hidden that even the McClatchy News Service had no idea of this, though if they did, it wouldn't have mattered. As a mole, it certainly would have mattered to Werner!

"I see that your nickname is the Spider. Why is that?" inquired Werner. Almost immediately he checked himself as he realized why.

Dimitri stood over 6'4", and Werner guessed he weighed less than 185 lbs.; his arms, fingers, and legs were as spindly in appearance as a spider. Black stringy, thick hair fell loosely past his ears around a narrow face with eyes sunken more than normal. His broad smile with pronounced pearly white teeth had a certain charm to overshadow what some might consider his otherwise bold facial appearance. His deep voice and articulate enunciation of every syllable and letters of words caused the hanging on of his every expressed thought. Few failed to recall what he had said nor did he theirs. His memory shocked people when he'd recall what they'd said even months before no matter how slight they meant the words at the time!

Dimitri offers this information: "Iran and Syria were still in the throes of a severe famine. Harsh winds continue to blow their soil worth having to anywhere and everywhere and places unknown. A low supply of water counted on heavily for survival is adding to their catastrophic lives, causing destitution and decimation of everyone regardless of wealth or position. Only the dishonest bureaucrats, now a few, in higher government are escaping the suffering that their own people are forced to endure."

Israel has plenty of both: food (bountiful agriculture) and water (from the mountains above the Golan Heights). Because of nuclear threats, Israel has placed an embargo against food or water to the two countries and any other neighboring countries that assist them.

It is time for the Antichrist to begin his plan. He started with the idea of peace by creating a pact with Israel to help Iran and Syria during this natural hardship, in exchange for dismantling their nuclear capability. This would be a true "peace for food" mission.

"Have a trusted, high-ranking staff member take this to Tel Aviv," Amerinero instructed Werner. "Then if Israel agrees go to Tehran and tell them what we hope is good news. Keep me informed."

It was hesitantly received and agreed by Israel with minor caveats. Iran and Syria also agreed. He went to other adjoining countries under the same duress of nature. They also agreed to the treaty only if Israel would share its resources. Representative of each country agreed to meet in Brussels within days.

Upon signing, Dowdson made the announcement to the world. Nearly overnight, Radolfo Amerinero became a peacemaking hero.

The premier of Israel soon hosted a closed-door meeting with himself and Amerinero, which Dowdson and I were also invited to attend. The conversation, in part, was as follows:

"Well, Premier. The problematic Dome of the Rock is gone, and as you know, I have twenty-four-seven postings of my elite guardsmen protecting the site."

"You're protecting it for what purpose? To my knowledge, you are not Christian, Muslim, Islamic, or anything, for that matter. What is your interest? As a matter of fact, we do not like that you stationed your people there so quickly. It is very puzzling why. This rock has a tremendous amount of meaning to a whole lot of people—both living and dead, Christian, Muslim, and Jew alike. As for you, well—"

"Are you finished, sir?"

"Yes."

"Then let me tell you. As I understand it, you Jews have all kinds of components ready to rebuild your temple. Am I not correct?"

"You are."

"And there are old parchments indicating the temple will be restored in the latter days of history, whatever that means. Right again?"

"Yes."

"I am authorized and prepared to offer your country the ability to rebuild your temple without any disturbance from any country. The Euro Union will see to it that it happens."

Israel's premier is visibly grateful and shaken at this momentous news. The traditional handshake quickly became an unusual hug and backslapping. The deal is set.

Israel began shipping food and water of their bountiful reserves to the hurting countries. The disarming of nuclear warheads is verified by Werner in person. Israel is at peace—long-term peace. Conflicts with the Palestinians are placed on hold, assured by Werner. Israel can now concentrate on the rebuilding of their temple while cleaning up the remainder of weapons of the Gog and Magog (short) war.

24

MUSLIM TURBULENCE

Amid Bakker Mohammed is conducting a meeting with ten of his frontline military strategists, according to the Spider.

"Forty-nine countries are significantly Muslim of more than forty-seven percent comprising three point six billion people, twenty-three percent of the world's population.[1] They're mostly in the Middle East, North Africa, Indonesia, and over thirty-five percent of Euro Union countries are Muslim. The last Israeli war with the northern countries and the earthquake that ended it has toppled the Dome of the Rock. It was the third most important mosque of the Muslims. I am known by Islamic leaders as Amid Baker Mohammed, not Radolfo Amerinero because I am Muslim though I have not made it an issue until the appropriate time.

"So we can obviously blame Israel for Dome's collapse to ruins." He continues, "Because of laying that blame, we've instigated rioting. A war outbreak has passed mere possibility but can be expected. However the scale of war, we must not let that distract the Muslims' goal of world dominance—by ISIS or by popular majority and power. My question is, how can we handle this riotous blame on Israel to best serve our needs?"

The room is pensively silent before a suggestion from the floor is made. "We have many choices. One of course is the selective use of EMP on key cities, simultaneously as a demonstration of power."

Werner responds, "If we do this, we must first make an assumption that collateral damage would result. How many will be killed outright? What would be the toll of the seriously maimed? And hardships imposed as an aftermath. No, I consider EMP a last resort."

Amid injects, "We must do what we must do to achieve our objective, regardless of the means toward achieving world control."

"Are you telling us that we can do anything we want and that the end does not require an accounting?" another asks.

"No, that is not what I am saying. I am saying we have reason to give an accounting to anyone. We are in control of our own destiny. The sooner the world leaders, the kings, rulers of other countries, and people of various religions realize it, the better! World control leads our war against God, Allah as I believe," Amerinero replies in a tone of ire mixed with resolve.

"Are you saying we use EMP or not? Do we discuss any other alternative?" Werner requests a response for action.

"I suppose I am," as he sweeps an arm as an indication the meeting has concluded.

"Wait," interjects Werner, "let me suggest, Amid, that we do not act upon this situation so radically so quickly. We need not kill or harm the Muslims in this fashion, or in any manner in fact. I think we have the resources in this room to decide an effective way to quell the riots before using such drastic deployment as EMP!"

The others nod and voice approval of Werner's suggestion.

"Noting the adverse consensus, we will determine a plan of alternatives, their strategies, and tactical deployment we desire. In my office, gentlemen, in half an hour."

EMP logistics planning and deployment is completed within the week while Muslim rioting mounts at Amid's consternation. Millions over the world are gathering in all the key cities over the world. By satellite they are warned by Amid Bakker of an impending devastation if their uprisings are not stopped, including an announced deadline and a date and time of when this damage will occur. The warnings seem to work in reverse as greater crowds respond to the threat. That is all it meant to them, just a threat, placing Amid in a precarious position: being Muslim and the person Lucifer designated as the Antichrist.

Precisely at the announced time stated on the warning, flashes of nuclear detonations appeared over two minor cities mostly populated by Muslims. Few were killed, tens of thousands injured, and all forms of electricity and electrical currents ceased to exist. Lighting, vehicles, computers, the Internet, telephone including iPhones, trains, trucks, and all forms of transportation, including air travel closed down within a seventy- to ninety-mile radius of each of the affected cities.

By satellite transmissions, Amerinero announced as the Antichrist taking credit for the destruction inflicted upon them. He promised a second barrage of the same if rioting does not stop immediately. There will be no peace discussions. "Your hope is to stop rioting. It will not be tolerated."

Pakistan with over 156 million Muslims responded with promises of their own. As well did Turkey and Iran, each having nearly 70 million Muslims. Another attack will bring nuclear bombardments on Brussels and the new Babylon-Mecca alike.

"Will you look at this," declared Amid to Werner. "They're threatening nuclear war! What they fail to realize is that they do not have electrical energy to launch such weaponry, except by shoulder rocketry. I say, call their bluff. We will show them who is in control," responded Werner.

Major-General Abdul Rashaan, who's responsible for the attacks, speaks up. "What size of impact do you wish for? And where do we show this power? There is a thin line between all-out war or gaining control that can be expected being determined by the size of devastation we inflict upon our target areas."

"Would a nuclear warhead of say, fifteen megatons at fifteen thousand feet do the trick we want to result?"

"Rashaan contends that this size is too small and not high enough in the atmosphere."

"What do you suggest, Major-General, and what can be expected?"

"I suggest the blast should be a thirty-ton ignition at twenty-five to thirty thousand feet."

"It will take out all electrical power as what happened before at other locations, up to a hundred-thirty-mile radius and an increase of sixty to eighty degrees Fahrenheit and an over a hundred and twenty mph wind lasting five minutes or so. Much more damage will occur. Significantly, the tall spires of mosques and city towers surely will crumble. Some of the weaker constructed buildings will collapse.

The heat wave will cause some million people bodily burns, and falling debris will cause an innumerable amount of serious injuries of course."

Before three days expire, two special op soldiers in nomadic attire are sent on their missions—one to Jeddah South Beach, the other to Yanbu, both in Saudi Arabia. Their artillery and munitions are picked up at prearranged locations from team members who also provide backup and protection.

Colonel Jacob McAllister in the Jeddah region on a fishing boat in the Gulf Sea is readying his shoulder missile launcher armed with a thirty-megaton nuclear warhead set to detonate at twenty-eight thousand feet elevation at precisely 12:00 noon, during prayers. The target is Mecca, fifty miles inland.

Colonel William Bozeman has turned off the Ulthman Highway and driven ten miles into a wilderness area just over thirty miles from Medina, the location of his launch site hidden by mountainous hills.

He will be ready to launch his nuclear missile to detonate at the same time in the same manner as McAllister's. They both wait for the go from their general, as their primary wish is to not be ordered to fire. An unbearable ten hours pass at the ready before told to "Stand down, return to base."

❦

6:30 p.m., EMP stood down

The two soldiers with their fingers on the trigger realized what would happen if they got the go command. Most of those praying would charge out of the grossly damaged mosque, promising violent revenge on the infidels. The spires and towers would fall into ruins as expected and many building stumbling and disintegrated into mere debris. Those who would remain inside would have been killed.

Injuries would be more severe and of a higher count than predicted as the fear of radiation and fallout would mount in panic causing expected mayhem.

In rebuke, but fearful to retaliate, millions of Muslims would engage shouting their displeasure and threats of violence over the globe.

In spite of risks of Amid's objectives, his quest seems to remain intact, though hatred by many of the Muslims remains just for his considering this plight upon his own people.

All the while, the Jewish nation continues to rebuild the temple, undisturbed and as has been planned.

25

INTERVIEW: FIVE DAYS AFTER GOG AND MAGOG WAR

Jolene

I had been assigned three months ago to Tel Aviv to interview General Gorge Walenski, a Turkmenistan commander-general believed to be the master planner of the most recent war against Israel. The war had been five years in preparation but lasting less than a few hours.

I was in Spain, en route to Tel Aviv with my husband, Jack, vacationing. It is when the Believers disappeared. I knew what had taken place the very moment it happened. Jack was a Believer, but I considered his beliefs as mere religion, that the Bible was not an inspiration of God as he had tried desperately to convince me otherwise. He vanished as so did many, many others in Spain.

I was transformed from a pleasant, knowledgeable, endearing woman on air into a resolute pragmatist, intent, and forceful woman. It had become inadvertently my new manner of surviving in the new world of constant endangerment.

Impossible could easily describe the task ahead of me to obtain the interview of the general. The world had gone into a state of chaos as never before so quickly. Every nation—from the United States to the EU, Arabs, Islam, Israel—hastily shrouded their diplomatic communications with distrust, animosity, and caution. Every nation felt that all others were corrupt to their core. Many were. Many had become so. And many others will be soon. Trust is an ideology of the past, now only a memory.

But first, I'm instructed to return to the United States by way of private planes and multiple transferring between numerous small airports. Two weeks after my debriefing and provided with new orders,

I was flown out by military aircraft to a desert airport outside Tel Aviv. Prior to the flight, I was given permission to interview Steven Alexander before returning to the Middle East.

My orders are given at the CNN's Foreign Correspondence HQ. In the halls of the NSA, the war on Israel that had lasted in such short order, curiosity as well as its meaning had to be known by the USA leaders. The CIA is at my call should I determine that I need them. The White House, from deep inside the Rocky Mountain caverns carved out for the safety of the president, has declared the importance of this interview. They all pulled strings for my task. Few worked, but enough. CNN was my cover.

The commander-general is the lone survivor of the military leaders who planned what's referred to in Scripture as the Gog and Magog war.[1] This is his accounting of events. Though the war was highly touted, it had woefully failed against Israel.

I arrived at the Israeli prison somewhere in a remote wilderness far south of Jerusalem. I was blindfolded from the moment that I was politely taken aboard a small aircraft to the room where the interview of the general took place. There wasn't a guard present.

The room was comfortable, well appointed, as though the turmoil all around the world was volatile at best didn't matter. He was brought into the room without any restraints. I noticed his beard was trimmed, and he looked well taken care of; I didn't expect that. We sat across from each other at a finely crafted table. Snacks, sandwiches, coffee on a Bunsen, orange juice, and pastry had been set out for our enjoyment. I noticed surveillance cameras in the four corners against the twelve-foot-high ceiling, so it could be assumed the interview was monitored.

I began as I turned on my camcorder.

Jolene: "Why this war? How is it different than the Middle East Arab War against Israel just a few months ago?"

"All of our nations involved had decided that with a little ingenuity that Israel could be had for the taking. We need to have its newly discovered oil and gas reserves, water, technology, and industrial assets. Our attack was intended to completely annihilate Israel once and for all time. The Arab nations were forceful to have our planning a war on Israel to be shelved. We soon discovered why. They wanted to have their own war, so then we tried our best to talk the Arab nations involved in the Middle East Arab War[2] out of attacking Israel because it would not be thorough enough. Based on results, it was not."

"All but Russia are Islamic. How did Russia get involved with your war?"

"Russia's czar at the time. During the few years before we began planning *our* war, as you put it, he cultivated Russia's relationships with Islamic nations, particularly Iran. At first Russia had no business being part of our war, but it seemed as though it was compelled by some influence to muscle its way into our group.[3] I suppose they watched the Middle East War's failure and chose which side to join. It was us. Iran fully endorsed Russia's involvement, though many of the nations were once in Russia's dominance, and we didn't get along very well after sovereignty was gained apart from Russia."

"How much of a role did Russia have during the planning of this war?"

"Not much, actually. Russia offered six battalions, 5,100 men. This brought them to a somewhat significant role in the planning in that they had charge of integration of their people into the larger scheme of things."

"What do you believe was the compelling factor of why they were drawn into this war?"

"Russia needs more backup oil reserves. Accepting Iran's invitation to join would cause a formidable pact with Iran and thus be able to share in the spoils of Israel's defeat."

"What influence, do you think, did the US have on Russia's place in the world affect their decision?"

"It had very little influence. All of its attention had now deflected to Iran and being cohesive with the Islamic nations away from ties with the US. The US had become a near nonentity except for the Fifth and Sixth Fleets. Plus the fact Russia had an innate hatred for Israel that was exploited by Iran."

"My sources tell me your war was three years, or more, in planning. Why so long?"

"Because of the ingenuity that had to be deployed. That requires details not commonly confronted by today's military minds. The first of which is the method of attack. Then the weaponry, logistics, surveillance, staging locations, and to overcome the difficulties of being detected. Not to say how problematic it is to do intricate planning when an army consisting of ten nations' armies are involved! We considered every detail thoroughly as none had ever been done before."

"Of course there's the timing."

"Especially, yes. The timing was carefully considered. Skirmish after skirmish, war after war since their sovereignty as a nation, Israel got pretty much what they went out to get. And now after more than a couple of years free of suicide bombings and shelling of short-range missiles, and after successfully defending against the Middle Eastern War, the Israelis were now quiet, confident, and somewhat arrogant. Even our quiet assembly of armies was not being taken too seriously, that word of it was considered as only a rumor of an approaching war."

"Was their disbelief a surprise?"

"Quite so, yes."

"How did the use of wooden weaponry, of all things, come to mind?"

"One of the generals had remembered a Biblical prophecy in Ezekiel that a war would be waged against Israel using all manner of weapons made of wood.[4] In an effort to consider any kind of deployment, wood seemed extraordinarily unique. At first we dismissed the idea. But after debating other styles of mounting a war, we returned to consider wood. After a short debate, we decided to use weapons of ancient battles made of wood."

"What tipped the scale to use wood weaponry?"

"There is no amassing of mechanized weaponry, no buildup of warplanes, and certainly no assembling of an equipped army of today's technology. Israel could not detect any modern warfare apparatus, even though the Israeli military minds were on alert, but not equipped to defend an attack by nonmetallic weaponry. All of their billions of dollars of defense apparatus is against modern warfare tactics—not wooden."

"What actions did you take to prepare for this attack, albeit bordering on absurdity?"

"Looking back, it was absurd, wasn't it? But it worked. Almost.

"We planned to deploy large cavalries at six spread-out locations in Lebanon, Syria, and mostly Jordan, just beyond the eastern cities nearest Israel, in the plenteous wastelands.[5] When the time came, over a few weeks, the number of cavalries was enormous and foot soldiers by the tens of thousands.

"Our preparation involved desert camouflage techniques. This took place during the two years left of planning in our respective countries. You could say we were highly skilled with camouflage by the time we arrived in staging areas. This enabled us to load up the selected areas during the night and remain undetected during the daylight hours. Even the hundreds of horse corrals remained hidden from view of drones or satellites. The campsites were in crevasses, gullies, deserted castles, and the many dried-up riverbeds in Lebanon, Syria, and Jordan—mostly in the Jordanian mountains. We stayed miles away from the paved highways that laced through those wilderness areas of wasteland and desert sands.

"We were well received by the three countries. Our presence was held confidential to an amazing degree as for the hatred of Israel. I heard that severe punishment would come to the families of anyone who would reveal our being there."

"What was your greatest concern?"

"To march upon Israel, we counted on the element of complete surprise. We were certain the use of wood weaponry, though as limited as it was, could not be detected except motion detectors. We knew this detection technology had not been updated for decades, spending their resources on US-supplied sophisticated weapons and other detection modern apparatus, drones, and satellites.

"Even if they would discover our strategy within a week or two before the date of our attack, we depended upon the possibility that it would be too late to prepare for such a battle. A massive cavalry assault backed up by foot soldiers protected with transportable wooden barriers would be difficult! We were convinced that by the time they could bring together an arsenal to deal with the few minutes of an onslaught, we would have accomplished what we had intended: the killing of Israeli men, women, and children."

"Surely you knew the news media would be stirring things up a bit, if not a lot, for you to deal with."

"Yes, we anticipated that. Of course we had our spies. It was easy to infiltrate the Israel checkpoints at their border. And, of course, there were reporters from all over the world who attempted to discover what we were up to. They were disallowed to know anything from any of our military, including soldiers. But the reporters' imagination went rampant. There was nothing we could do about it except to move the date of attack up two weeks to avoid too much discussion.

"But the winds of our war against Israel began stirring."

"Getting back to what you briefly mentioned. How much relevancy did you place on that Scripture in Ezekiel…chapter 38, I believe?"

"Although we knew the Christians' Scriptures predicted what might be the battle we've planned, the actual believing of it caught us by complete surprise. Every news analyst in the Middle East, most of the world's leaders and business advisers, and certainly the religious authorities recognized and pieced together how this war is actually prophesied in the Scriptures."[6]

"How did this affect your planning and execution?"

"We then moved the date up two more weeks. Surprise was still king, but was rapidly being diluted. We simply could not wait any longer. Only four days before the day of our attack was there any sense of urgency by Israel. But for them, it was too late."

"Then what happened?"

"Most of the army was moved at night to within twenty miles from Israel's border. Fortunately it was raining with a low, dark cover of clouds. Waves of thousands of soldiers were behind them. We had determined to be on Israel soil during the early morning twilight and sunrise. It was thought this to be the best time to catch Israel in an hour of natural, habitual disorder. We swept across Israel from the east to the sea on the west, through the Palestinian West, only sixty miles across. It had worked as planned. By a little after noon, we were nearly in position to wreak havoc and cause death all at once, all over Israel, like a thick cloud hovering over them."

"Do you know you have just described your blanketing Israel in the same terms as Scriptural prophecy?"[7]

"No. Did I?"

"Yes, you did. I have another observation. I gather your army did not engage or initiate your objective as they progressed through Israel. Why?"

"It was designed as an element of deception to create surprise. No weapons were drawn or shown. To the Israelis, it appeared the army was merely displaying some sort of exhibition. We had printed numerous signs in Hebrew to divert their attention away from our lethal purpose. All of the protective gear we were wearing was hidden under nomadic outer garments to deflect any detection once we were in place."

"That must have been impressive to the citizens of Israel and confusing to Israel's military! So how did you fare, then, at that time?"

"I cannot explain what occurred next no other way than an act of God decimated our armies without warning. First an earthquake[8] spoiled our detailed plans. Moments before the command was given to accomplish our mission of death and destruction, an earthquake took place so strong the movement broke many horses' legs causing soldiers to fall to the ground. The foot soldiers could not stand or walk for the shaking of earth underneath. I could not avoid seeing mountains breaking apart and walls being reduced to rubble before a ruthless wind came up!

"I cannot say the wind was caused by the earthquake or act of God, but it stirred dust so thick we could not see what we were doing. At any noise, from whichever direction, we threw spears, shot arrows, and slung weapons to kill whoever or whatever caused the sounds. But instead we were killing each other![9] It lasted like that for what seemed hours.

"It wasn't long after, while the sandstorm dwindled, we began having sores all over our bodies,[10] especially where exposed skin was then spread from there. The pain of them was unbearable. Thousands died from this. It was all we could then think about, and we had no answer.

"Suddenly a heavy rain began to fall,[11] causing streets to be flooded and large pools of water gathered. The worst of all was to come. Hailstones, the size of which I had never seen. Huge. And when they landed, having caused great damage and killing many of our soldiers upon impact, they became fireballs on the ground in spite of all the accumulated rainwater.

"Death cries of my soldiers was deafening to me. All around they and other officers were being slaughtered in every direction! Our army was completely disarmed, in hysteria, and in total confusion of how all this could happen to us. It didn't take the rest of the day before all the soldiers of my army were killed, not by Israelis but by these events of God."[12]

"It seems as though God accomplished something else with the earthquake, General, that is beyond your army's destruction."

"What is that?"

"The Dome of the Rock, located in Jerusalem on the Temple Mount, was reduced to ruins, flat as the ground it had stood upon."

The general merely shook his head in disbelief but not realizing the impact this would have in the immediate, coming events.

"Ever since Islamic rulers built the Dome on the Temple Mount, it has been a bewilderment of Christian scholars of how the temple could be rebuilt as is prophesied on the exact same location. Few realized the possibility that the Dome's demise would occur at the time of Gog and Magog's short-lived battle!" She changed the tone of conversation back to the general.

"So why is it you were not killed?"

"Maybe to tell my story. I dunno.

"All through this, I was caught under my horse trying to free myself. The harder I tried, the tighter my leg became, but I maneuvered what little I could to be more protected by the horse. As the animal went through the trauma of dying, its writhing caused excruciating pain.

"After some time I managed to locate and fire my pistol to kill the animal. But to be freed from the weight of the horse, I had to cut the hide between his ribs to relieve the pressure keeping my leg steadfast, then pulled my leg free. It was broken, as was my ankle.

I was bleeding profusely. I think the weight of the horse was like a tourniquet, and that saved me. Somehow I crawled into a darkened alley, shed my military gear, and put on civilian garments we had with us just in case this event would happen. A youngster thinking I was an Israeli helped me, or I would have bled to death in that alley.

"As a pair of Israeli soldiers dragged me to their jeep, I was able to take a hard look at what had happened. My army's soldiers lay dead everywhere in every direction. All our weapons seemed many more than what I could remember. There were thousands upon thousands of them strewn about everywhere."

"Was that when you became a war criminal, according to the Israel Tribunal Court?"

"Yes, that's correct."

"Do you know what the outcome was of your Gog and Magog War?"

"Did the war actually get that name? The Gog and Magog War?"

Jolene nodded yes.

"As a prisoner of Israel, I learned that it was projected to take a few years to completely clean up the mess my armies had created.[11] I was told it took four months to bury my dead.[12]

"A few weeks before our assault on Israel, I heard about the disappearance of millions of people all across the world. I heard the 'gone were Christians.' Heavy conversation about it was then rampant of what happened. I do know my thoughts regarding God had become hateful, and my heart had become full of evil desires, including against my cellmates and them about me. Here in prison, each of us has to be on guard for our safety more than ever before. And by the way, some of the guards had disappeared too. I guess they were Jewish Christians."

"There is more you should know."

"More?"

"Yes, and you won't like it. I think it's better you hear it gently from me rather than from a revengeful Israeli interrogator."

Though he appeared that he couldn't take any more disheartening news, he ventured, "What is that?" looking more broken than just a moment before."

"I suppose you do not know what the Scripture describing the Gog and Magog War has to say about its ending. Well, whether or not you do, what it prophesied has become true."

"Maybe I do not want to hear it."

"Let me remind you: it's best you hear it from me," declared Jolene.

"Okay."

"The Israeli military did not immediately bury the corpses, they were left for the birds of the air and wild animals, as Scripture says, to feast upon. That is what's found in Ezekiel,[13] and that is precisely what happened."

The general could only sob, his head turned from me, buried in what was an excuse for a pillow. He no longer wished to live but could not end his own life because of the chains, now fastened on him after the interview, restraining him from doing it. His hanging would be his liberation.

26

THE STREETS: REPORTED BY STEVEN ALEXANDER

While peace between nations is gradually being gained because of actions by the Antichrist, all the while, street crime, violence, and all manner of carnal activities remain to saturate every city, town, and village, including byways and properties in rural areas. It is the same everywhere in the world on every continent from the smallest island to the largest country.

"No one is safe. Period. Constant looking over one's shoulder is not enough. The weak, frail, children, and the elderly have no chance to avoid malice done to them, with death a usual result.

Within two weeks' time, usually in less time, food and supplies have disappeared off store's shelves. No water either. Neither are there any water or water-based bottled drinks. Gone. Only the lucky can find just a morsel of food or smidgen of water. Usually, discovered food is stale and moldy and water is stagnant. Money has now lost any value. Only food and water matters, certain supplies along with clothing, and having a weapon with a sufficient amount of ammo. Soap had become an unnecessary pleasure; it requires water to be effective. Clothes are ultraimportant—for modesty if nothing else, but mostly to provide weather protection and staying warm in the night air.

It didn't take long for gangs to discover that office buildings and skyscrapers held an enormous volume of water in the sprinkler systems and water pipes for drinking fountains, toilet flushing, and hygiene. (For every fifteen stories, a building has an asset of over fifty thousand gallons of water.) The plumbing systems were soon drained by hundreds who bought the water at very high sacrifices from thugs demanding payment including clothes, weapons, and ammunition and food until the depletion of a building's water occurred.

Defecation and urine odors became the shrouded over by the stench of the corpses alongside dead corpses lying in the streets, curbs, and alleys. Few cared. Some of them who did care took it upon themselves to dispose of bodies by burning them in piles like cordwood. It was necessary to lessen disease. The fear of rats or their fleas carrying the Bubonic Plague is a continual consideration.

Women, notably, were always in danger from beatings, rape, and killings. Husbands, wives, and older children no longer had regard—let alone love—for each other. The evil in their hearts had long left behind any feelings of caring of one another. Only themselves mattered.

Other than food and water, weaponry and ammunition had become the major difference of the haves and the have-nots. Weapons are the guarantee of safety, or at least kept from being in harm's way until rounds of ammunition were gone. Gangs, thugs, and those bent to their malicious, brutal acts of intimidation and domination hoarded supplies, though scant, of ammunition.

I was fortunate. I knew what had happened early on. I stocked up on food, water, supplies, weapons and ammunition quickly from as many of the apartments in the huge complex that was quickly left vacant by its frenzied occupants. Very few had their wits about them other than to quickly flee and failing to lock their doors. After more than a week of days of eighteen to twenty hours, I had filled every nook and cranny in the rooms of my three-bedroom residence. Every inch of space stacked to the ceiling, wall to wall, was filled by the pilfered stuff, leaving only very narrow lanes to maneuver remained. I had managed to change the locks, reenforced with three additional bolt-locks of two neighboring apartments provided additional space for more supplies.

My apartment was up eleven stories in a rather nice building. Numerous tenants returned when they realized how valuable what they had left behind in their panic became. I had already raided the apartments left open on the ninth to twelfth floors providing me with food, cases of bottled water, clothes, and other life-support items. Resolute anger consumed those who returned to their emptied apartments of those previous possessions that I had taken, not knowing of course I was their culprit.

It proved out that I was able to be holed up a few months.

There isn't refrigeration to keep food fresh and no electricity to cook with. Survival is nearly impossible with even the simple things no more!

I could care less about other people. It is me—only me—I care about now had to for…any degree of surviving. Only a few times I was hassled, having shot and killed one would-be looter. A streak of blood down the hall and two landings and stairs below to where I had removed the corpse seemed to be enough warning for future attempts upon me. No one cared to go beyond the stench of the rotting body.

What will I do after the stuff is gone? I don't have a clue other than knowing I cannot stay in the city.

Like thousands of others traipsing toward the outer regions beyond, I had to join in or die of dysentery or other unsanitary conditions. So I bid my time until only enough food, water, and supplies remained that I could carry with me in my two overstuffed backpacks as I headed out into exile any overstuffed backpacks became an immediate interest of those who had very little—an invitation to being pilfered.

A treasured time are any extended moments when I remember the days I experienced the luxury of relaxation and minimal stress. Every day and every night of every waking second is chock-full of trauma to keep me alive! Very seldom a day or even a short time do conditions come together that allow me a tiny measure of quiet or sleep from the tensions of survival. It is during these quiet spells that it's apparent birds no longer sing or they no longer want to exist where people are. Only during the few moments before *finally* falling asleep do I clearly hear the anguish of pain and torment of others. The distinct sounds of the young children crying out for someone to love them, care for them, is disturbing. Also in this relative calm, I cannot help but to take notice of the old and the feeble groaning in their subdued strength wishing for death to take them. It is then in these moments that my memory of what it was like before the rapture is sharper than ever, tantalizing my thoughts of my acute awareness of aloneness becoming greater with each time. My sadness soon returns me to struggles of survival and once again comes into sharp focus. This cycle occurs daily and often disallows sleep.

I know Scripture. Each day my recall of Scripture intensifies. Though I can't imagine things getting worse, I know it will, based upon prophecy. Plus, I will not make the same mistake twice! I have made the decision to make sure this time around that I do right: I accepted Jesus as my savior and that he is, for sure, my savior! It's hard. It is very difficult as the witness of the Holy Spirit as once on this earth has vacated my life. Accepting Christ is barely felt as a heartfelt thing. But I must add that a significant change in my awareness had taken place almost immediately after. It's impossible to describe the change, like a new awareness had taken place.

In those days before what is now after the rapture, there were a lot of people who considered the days we were living in as the Tribulation. Even I considered that maybe we were. I would be amiss to tell you how naïve we were to think it, let alone actually believe it! Unless you're here, there's no way you could be close of realizing how terrible the people on this earth have become. To those who thought that God is love and would not create such an event as the Tribulation, I can tell them how very wrong they were. In fact, I would think they are now here in this world realizing just that.

❦

On another front, I cannot help but to believe there will be organizers to make some kind of sense through all of this, especially business and economic leaders along with people who do the part of the political process.

They'll attempt to bring back what they can. I for one cannot possibly fathom how to go about making the world we live in better. By *the world*, I mean the tens of thousands of local townships and suburbs. Attempting this in larger cities seems to be a futile effort.

The first attention has to be the infrastructure, beginning with roadways and highways.

At the present time, the Antichrist is focused upon world countries mostly in the Middle East, vowing peace in that region. He certainly has not made individual people his priority concern. However, Bible prophecy says he will. He needs the masses to honor him, but as Scripture says, the masses will *worship* him. It is only a matter of when!

27

SANCTUARIES

Spider

Werner texted Amid Bakker:

> *Have U heard about the sanctuaries? They're*
> *sprouting up all over the world.*

He had not and requested more information. Werner e-mailed the gist of the files to Amid that his people had collected on the sanctuaries.

"Sanctuaries are a place where individuals trusted by each other can live with relative safety in numbers. At first, within days of the Event, everyone alone became targets of criminals and malicious people without scruples having no sense of decency. It did not take long for people to realize that safety in numbers is better than alone—by far!

"Typically sanctuaries have no leader, no founder, or any memberships, etc. They spring up more or less on their own anywhere that people collect. They're an extended communal group crowded together as production cattle. The refugee camps of Iraq and Syria during the ISIS wars come close, but conditions in sanctuaries are far worse.

"We needn't be concerned. At this time they pose no problem to anyone. There is no creed or belief system established or heard of being required. They are wholly devised for safety. A few of them are nomadic, going from town to town or where new sources of food or water might be possible for a family's survival.

"According to my spies who have participated in many of the discussions, the constant and usual subject is about why they weren't taken during the Event. And then plans for the immediate future discussed and shaped such as what's to be expected the next day."

❧

Steven

Sanctuaries gained in sophistication as their numbers flourished, collectively or individually. Each differed from another. They typically sprung up farther than a hundred or more miles beyond the suburbs of cities quite far from arterial highways, most often in farmlands. The sanctuaries were either takeovers of vacated farms or invited by owners who hoped that the presence of the occupiers would prevent hostile thieves. Sizes of the sanctuaries depended upon availability of water and the capability to grow crops.

Sanctuaries usually conducted simple elections to create a resemblance of governance; the concept of sanctuaries has proliferated.

It is typical for them to limit the number of transients in their commune for more than two days, and limitations because the concept was born in the perception of safety. Anyone even slightly unruly is ordered to leave. Often it became necessary to have an appointed sergeant at arms to supervise a sanctuary's overall safety. Preferably he is tall and muscular, well acquainted with firearms, gets along with people most of the time, and has a self-worth view of personal territory.

For the time, Amid and Werner relax regarding the sanctuaries. He has other things more important needing his attention.

28

PLANS OF THE ANTICHRIST

Nine months after the rapture

I am Assad Hussien, nicknamed The Spider. My boss, Dowdson, has been assigned, as a secondary function, to monitor and report on the progress and status of the Antichrist's projects. Dodson, in turn, has a liaison at each of the ongoing projects who file weekly reports to me. These are the reports of the eighth week since the start of this practice.

From Jerusalem:

> EU soldiers have a gigantic, nearly impossible order: That is to keep Muslim enthusiasts from harming the Jewish workmen as they clear the rubble of the Muslim's Dome from the Temple Mount and constructing the new temple. Every day there are harmless forms of rioting, but danger is real and present. Workmen arrive in armored personnel carriers.
>
> A great fear is that from a maverick group of fringe Muslims would launch a missile to land on the exact location, thinking they would be heroes. Israel refuses to concede allowance for the Muslims to erect even a small monument in recognition of the destroyed Dome. Israel will not allow a trace of what once was there, gaining assurances they would be backed by the Jordan royal family in case of a row over that.
>
> The engineers and architects had built luxury offices and living quarters nearby to enable

their continual presence on site. The work never stops, every day, 24/7.

All the while, the soldiers of the Antichrist are keeping peace intact.

Within days after the site was cleared of any indication the Dome ever existed, excavation of rock to allow deep footings of the temple were completed. The tunnels below mostly filled in.

Werner has promised heavy retaliation if not annihilation of any government or an organization who dares to endanger the temple's rebuilding, promising to utilize EMP as enforcement if needed.

Amid, from Babylon:

The massive site work stretches miles in all direction southwest of Mecca, extending to the Red Sea coast just south of Jeddah. The entire city's elaborately designed efficiency for its suitability has all the building trades frenzied with activity. The coastal cargo facilities feature the best loading/unloading equipment and transportation terminals the world has ever seen. Its designed to accommodate twenty to thirty freighters, large and small, on both sides of a dredged waterway are possible to be attended simultaneously with ease and safety.

Streets are designed excessively wide to give an illusion of splendor and vastness. Traditional vehicular traffic will not be allowed because of the plenteous promenades. Leisure foot traffic is protected with strict regulations rule the streets, and transporting is enabled by a light-rail subway providing fast travel between destinations in and around Babylon, to Mecca (thirty miles), and Medina (seventy miles) away. A connecting fast, light-rail system is planned to Tel Aviv and Jerusalem. A specially tunneled rail line is built from the seaport to all of the sensual "pleasure palaces" for extraordinary guests of power and world influence.

A freight subway system in companion to auto traffic is routed with special underground tunnels to provide small transfer trucks access to service elevators of stores, shops, pleasure palaces of offices aboveground.

Commercial buildings are limited to ten stories high, their footprint cannot consume more than forty thousand square feet of land. A sprawling city is the aim, rather than emphasizing height. Street-level signage is encouraged to be ostentatious and majestic, at the high elevations even more grandeur.

Hundreds, if not thousands, of heavy construction equipment are continually in motion allowing only for refueling and change of operators.

Work remains ahead of schedule. Amid and Werner are extremely pleased with the progress.

29

DISMANTLING OF THE UNITED NATIONS

Spider

Werner is in Antichrist's office. They're discussing the United Nations.

"I've been thinking," states Radolfo, "that the UN is basically of nonessential importance in our new world. We need to do something about it. If not, the UN would certainly be a formidable problem for us."

"I agree something must be done and that it's having little bearing on global issues. What do you have in mind?"

"We could relocate it to Babylon," suggests the Antichrist.

"No," responds Werner, "why physically relocate the UN at all? It can only cause us more, unwanted, and needless problems down the road!"

"What suggestion do you have?"

"Well, we simply demand that a majority of member countries cease their representation at the UN. I recommend we target those countries who actively participate in finance, trade, and commerce committees."

"Yes, of course."

Werner continues, "I'll have the Spider to do the research with the intent to make up such a list of nations. Between the two of us, I have no doubt we can pull this off rather quickly."

"Quickly?" asks Radolfo.

"Yes. What with the altered satellites and the Loniancoin-based commerce all through the world, yes, quickly by utilizing what we have control over."

A week later, I presented my list of eighty countries as the result of detailed research, focusing on subcommittee involvements of finance.

Werner examined the list with full approval and set about the task to convince representative countries to leave the UN. Amerinero assigned the objective to members of a task force of seventy-five skilled, multilingual communicators. We are proven correct. Seventy of the eighty countries committed to vacate during the first two weeks. In fact, fourteen other countries inquired about the strategy and why; twelve of them were convinced to join flight from the UN.

We were armed for the next general assembly of the UN.

Radolfo Amerinero, a.k.a., the Antichrist, Amid Baker Mohammed, texted a message to every EU member country's president.

All Euro Union member nations are required to withdraw their memberships from the United Nations, World Bank, and other organizations having world peace or environment objectives at the May 23 general assembly. "If not, you shall be dropped from the EU membership on June first and fend for yourselves."

The date is April 5. Next he telephoned the administrator of the United Nation's speaker's scheduling.

He announced himself to four levels of authority before he was able to introduce himself to James Lateil.

"Mr. Amerinero calling."

"Yes, Mr. Amerinero, how can I help you?"

"I need to take the podium precisely at eleven a.m. on May twenty-three, the date of the next general assembly. Is this possible?"

"It sounds important. Is it?"

"Very."

"I can shift the schedule around somewhat, but I can clear you for the date you desire. May 23?"

"Correct, Mr. Lateil."

"And how much time do you need?"

"Less than half an hour."

"Will discussion follow?"

"Some I imagine, but not a lot of time will be granted for discussion."

"Done," Lateil declared.

"Thank you."

Eleven a.m. on May 23 arrived. Amerinero walked to the podium while being welcomed by a polite, standing ovation. He looked about the audience for a few moments before beginning his address to the UN General Assembly, skipping the formalities, getting direct to the point while showing a confident smile.

"As of today, the following countries of the EU and others who have joined with us in this announcement no longer are considered members of the irrelevant United Nations. Our seats of representation will be vacated. As each country's name is called, they will also cease to be involved, immediately, in any of the numerous organizations sponsored by the United Nations."

Slowly he names each nation involved in the absconding of their seats. The representatives stand, place their earphones onto the desk in front of them, turn reverently, and quietly, professionally leave the floor as their country's name is called. A total of eighty-seven countries leave their seats, permanently vacated. Not expected, thirty-four additional represented countries in response vacate their seats as well. Before the week ends, a total of 129 countries of the 196 members have vacated their posts, 65 percent.

Amerinero's greatest accomplishment in this swift action is with the IMF; only three UN members of the twenty-nine who set policies and administered the IMF remain. It opened the door for the Loniancoin to flood the world's economy and to determine who has money and who does not!

He made sure the organizations that Amerinero considers a future threat to the establishing of the New Roman Territories, one of many Amerinero's goals of dominance, remain on the outskirts of commerce. The Loniancoin assured it.

30

ANTICHRIST'S EXTENSION OF POWER

Spider

A few weeks later, I was taken by total surprise at what the Antichrist did next!

He declared that with great penalty, Germany is restricted from selling or to ship any production machines or assist with any technology to China. This is intended to disrupt China's economy severely as their production machinery wears out, thereby shutting down China to a trickle. Sales and exporting to the United States has long ago ceased as has sales to many other previous highly regarded customer nations of China. Incoming shipments of coal and oil to China are also ordered to be stopped. The same embargo is to apply to Japan, the Philippines, and Indonesia as well. Even with all their gold in China's possession, its impact upon international influence has now dwindled a level of significant unimportance.

As with the rest of the world, the aftermath of *the Event* certainly was not favorable to China or any of the Far Eastern countries.

They soon knew of the power wielded by Amid Baker Mohammed. They also now understood the reason the Euro was so forcibly demanded by Mohammed a few months ago. He had successfully made it the world's currency standard, headquartered, for now, in Brussels. They fear he has plans to have world trade and currency control under Babylon's rule rather than through New York, Tokyo, Berlin, or Hong Kong—all of which would then be gutted and powerless from any financial, diplomatic, or commerce substance.

Over the past three and four decades, the databanks of the world were progressively and covertly channeled through Brussels in harmony with the USA's databank including redundancy with the data center in Utah. A body of less than a dozen prominent money magnates of the United States had orchestrated this endeavor, paid huge bonuses for their cooperation and guidance.

Since Amid Bakker had become the EU president, the transferring of large financial data bases and personnel and corporate records of the United States, Central and South America, Australia, and Canada to Brussels had accelerated exponentially. Because of the interrelated connections in cooperation with the various countries he had with Asia nations, it was simple to, technologically, combine their data bases by streaming them into the Brussels database along with Internet data. One factor, however, has been kept away from common knowledge; the databanks are written to enable all the various data sources to be easily downloaded faster than ever thought possible to the data center being built two hundred feet below Babylon extending under the Red Sea.

At his fingertips, the Antichrist has knowledge of every person's file and whereabouts (if they own a smartphone) in every significant country via the vast satellite network he soon will control. Mr. Werner orchestrated that advantage.

Three miles outside Brussels, Mohammed had built a sprawling office complex to conduct his work while his underground Babylon control office building is being completed.

During this time, he directed scores, if not hundreds, of secured emails with Mr. Werner to provide him with all the activities of business for which they were called to do.

"Today had become a lynchpin. On this day, this is their conversation—"

"Mr. Werner, we begin today what we have been chosen to do."

"Yes, sir. I am ready. Anxious, in fact, to get started. What is it?"

"First, I want you to put as many qualified people as you need to create a fully remotely controlled simulated likeness of myself in a holographic image. It must talk, walk, stand, sit, and maybe even run. It must be of such high quality that it cannot be detected as a holograph as close as two feet away."

"That's easy."

"Is it. Wait, there's more. I want you to create three of me. I want them all to be ready for my use within the next six months. Can you do that?"

"Sure. When you approve the first rendition, we merely copy the construction data, and we can replicate as many of your image as you want in a matter of hours."

"Put as many people on it as you need."

"Done," Werner states as he turns to leave Radolfo's office. "Good luck."

"All right. I'll see to it. Anything else?"

"Yes, as a matter of fact."

Werner traces his steps back to his boss. "And that is?"

"Please. This might take a few minutes, Alex."

"First, I want to know if what I am about to request is possible. Then a time frame if it's possible to do, and finally, it must be remotely controlled."

A silence permeates the room as Radolfo forms his thoughts.

"Can, from a satellite, a giant holographic message be placed in the open sky, the message to be clearly read by a fairly large town or small city? The message would be a frameless screen, if you will."

"The first thing that comes to mind is to assure that the message will be clear no matter the background the sky and its clouds provide, which do change rapidly."

"How about the holograph providing its own colored background, say, yellow or bright white, and the message be black?"

"Yes, it's doable. But in what language? Off the top of my head, there's at least a hundred significant languages and tens of thousands of aboriginal languages throughout the world!"

"The transponders would have to include autointerpreters to accomplish its purpose, I would imagine," offers Radolfo.

"And what is its purpose, as if I didn't know?"

"What I envision is the capability for, say, a hundred satellites to beam into midair any message you or I desire to communicate all over the world totally simultaneously."

"That is what I thought. Well, can it be done?"

"Given time, sure. But I also suspect you want this capability ready within months, not more than a year or two. Am I right?"

"You are."

"Specifically—"

"Nine or ten months."

"Including the time it will take to create the holograph of your person or additionally?"

"Including both during the same time, and make a holograph or two of yourself as well."

"I'll need to recruit the best laser engineers and scientists in the world—at least a hundred, maybe more, to come even close to meet this schedule."

"Then do it."

As Alex stood up with a perplexed expression revealing he has already begun thinking through details of his most recent assignments, Amid made one more request.

"You might sharpen your once great magician skills, we will need them."

That takes Werner by surprise, but he does not respond, wondering what.

Amid Baker Mohammed now set about his highest priority at the time: Israel's peace. The famine won't last forever, requiring help from Israel. The nations will soon have their own food and water. The existing peace agreement is not near comprehensive enough however. He needs a further reaching and much stronger agreement to keep nations away from Israel. Without it, his own plans would surely be unseated.

With Iraq's huge income surplus from oil, the Antichrist is ready to augment the existing peace agreement with a new strategic deployment: tremendously expanding the peacekeeping military beyond only protecting the temple's completion. The endless oil reserve under Iraq and the riches gained are paying for the accelerated rebuilding of an excessively ornate and splendorous Babylon near Mecca.

He can also acquire thousands of fighter aircraft with accompanying weaponry and ammunition available merely for the taking of them at salvage prices. Source? The USA. How? The Fifth and Sixth Fleets! Not counting what is available from within the US borders. The entire country's administration and military systems are broken down to be nearly negligible—all but depleted. Witnesses who were left after the rapture report that the US infrastructure remains to be in total chaos and disorganization. Millions upon millions of its people are roaming about with short supplies, primarily an extreme shortage of food and safe water. This is a situation no one in America could fathom ever to happen, a country once with millions of shelves filled to capacity of food in grocery stores!

The United States will make a trade: food and water for the aircraft. The sale of warships and planes for food is the only step the United States can take. From all over the world, Mohammed utilized his power to ship thousands upon thousands of tons of food and millions of gallons of water to the United States. With this he was able to create an armada of warships (as a bonus) along with the hundreds of warplanes. Most were dispatched to nearby Lebanon to protect all Israeli borders.

Now, no one would dare break a peace treaty with Israel for fifteen straight years. At least that's what Israel believed. Mohammed had nearly overnight become heralded as the only, true world's peacekeeper. As a result, the world over worshipped and idolized him.

America's politicians had eliminated the US Constitution and all of its power. They had joined in with the EU as coauthors of the World Constitution. While they were sure this step would strengthen their voice in world affairs, they were fully unaware that that step would cause the United States to lose its influence and be unwitting followers on a downward spiral to shame.

In that regard, it declined into a third world country—broke and nondescript, rapidly developing into mere memories, its landmass only important as a place of geography and a fact of history, now inconsequential to the rest of the world. What a waste!

The food and water provided in trade of its aircraft made only a dent in people's lives for a short time, gone within weeks. By cause of a sundry number of diseases from many origins, most financial leaders, politicians, government officials, and dignitaries have died—just as the poor. An amazing number committed suicide, understandably.

Death has not been judicious.

31

AMERINERO'S THINK TANK

The Spider

Eleven of the most forward-thinking scientific researchers in the world had gathered in Mr. Werner's conference room.

"Amid Baker Mohammed has requested we find a way to standardize the world monetary system by creating our own Internet commerce system. The current digital commerce now proliferating all over the entire globe provides us with a template to create a financial platform to replace all others."[1]

"You're referring to the Bitcoin, right?"

"I am."

Many ideas had been prepared and discussed as they had been forewarned of the subject matter. One problem was presented, which gained the most attention. The only way to make this new Internet work is to revamp the technology of the enormous satellite system now in place!

"Can we do that?" some asked.

"Better yet, legally, should we?" voiced another.

Werner responded, "In this room, we have the finest technology experts the world has to offer. If man has devised something, man is able to replicate the existing disciplines to make changes and improvements while doing so. Right? As for the legal issue, I and Amid have the final say now."

All heads nod acknowledgement.

"Four in this room are the finest satellite code writing engineers; so tell me: can reprogramming the satellites be accomplished easily, within reason, and effectively? Or is that impossible?" Werner asked. He looked at Charles Wesson, a former JPL[1] senior code developer. "What's your opinion, Chuck?"

"Mr. Werner, anything can be done with enough time with a surplus of money. Do we have both luxuries? As far as technologically altering the commands and use of data a satellite requires, yes, it can be done. But with one central caution."

"That is?"

"Every one of the thousands of satellites to achieve what they are doing up there have unique, one-of-a-kind elaborate security systems that need to be breached without any detection."

Larry Stull, an electronics engineer who has dedicated his life to satellite control systems speaks up. "I agree we have a very difficult path to follow if we proceed, but I can tell you it isn't as impossible as it seems. Before I can explain that, I need to do a little research to know that what I think will perform as we require can be done. I need three or four days to check it all out."

"We will wait." Werner instructs, "Ten a.m., my office, in five days." They quietly leave as they contemplate the project before them.

At the specified meeting time five days later, Stull looks badly groomed—tired, bloodshot eyes—and attempted to not look a frightful mess, and as though he hadn't eaten a decent meal since they last met. But he was early, eager, and ready for his presentation with reports distributed on chairs surrounding Werner's office conference table. He noticed his appearance caused slight hesitations when each attendee laid eyes on him initially when entering but nodded their appreciation of his dedication.

Before twenty minutes expired, the capable, talented, and resourceful group was convinced of the complexity involved to resolve security issues if they were to trip up the satellites but amazed of the simplicity Dr. Stull described by which they could achieve it. He closed by noting, "I estimate it would require this group with a staff of talented electronic engineers of maybe thirty-five, requiring a maximum of ten fully dedicated months, having a minimum budget of four million dollars—to be successful with our tampering."

"Done! Next week I will have your agenda and timetable for you and the money allocated available," promised Werner. "You have the next five weeks to bring on board the qualified people you need to facilitate our assignment, but begin immediately. You can use my conference room where you will work together one day a week. The balance of time, I expect you to be mobile on secured cloud."

"While you all are creating your tampering technology plan, the organization of our own InterWeb P2P, our replacement for the Internet, will be completed. It will also host our own form of online currency christened as *the Loniancoin* taken from *Babylonian*. This currency system resides in the most secure cryptology ever devised to achieve worldwide access by Dr. Stull. After all, if a small village in Spain[2] back in 2011 were able to create their own reduced version of the wireless Internet, we can certainly create what we need to do to satisfy all of Mohammed's plans."

"Later in the week, they met for an inaugural meeting of the new project in Werner's conference room."

"At some time in the near future," addresses Werner, "Amid will be imposing on all people to wear the number *666* on their foreheads or the back of their right hands. You are to devise a way to do this with an effective and efficient method that's quickly administered. It must be a permanent, indelible technique. Can you do this in eight months?"

Eyes focused on the team leader for an answer.

"Surely. Of course. Having been through the previous project on time and without a serious hitch, we can certainly do this."

The work ahead is accepted by all involved.

Unexpected, the entrance of Amid Baker Mohammed surprises everyone just as a demonstration of the satellite tampering was forthcoming. He sat at the back to observe. A technician stood to introduce the screening.

"In precisely eight minutes, the 'state of the world' address by the secretary general of the UN will begin its satellite broadcast. In preparation, we have inserted one of Mr. Mohammed's more significant speeches to take the place of the secretary general's address. Watch what happens."

The audience of over thirty attending in the small theater is abuzz in anticipation to witness the work achieved by Werner's group.

Right on time, the secretary general's address begins at 11:00 a.m. At 11:07, the image of UN leader abruptly vanishes, being immediately replaced by a speech by Amerinero.

The technician stands to the side of the screen to explain that the entire world is viewing what they are seeing in front of them. "Switching from the secretary general's address to what you are seeing now is accomplished with a mere key click. But what you see is a holograph beamed from a fixed satellite. It is not Amid in person, only a 3-D image is what the world sees."

Amerinero leads the standing ovation and cheering of such a remarkable success. He quickly proceeds to the front with a noticeable excitement.

"Gentlemen and lady, thank you for a job done on time and being so thorough with your assigned projects. It is outstanding work. They will be put to use at their appropriate time and for a very definitive purpose. The fact of the matter is that the whole world should thank all of you."

He continues to stand motionless for a few moments before speaking again.

"You all have one other urgent project to complete also on a tight time frame. Six weeks in fact if it's possible. On campus is a small team of electro-laser advanced specialists who now require a team of scientists to effect this project's completion. Each of you possesses unique knowledge or skills for this purpose. Beginning tomorrow, you will be reassigned. Take the rest of the day and all day tomorrow off and report in two days at your newly assigned laboratory."

A hand is raised and acknowledged. "Must we wait to know to what we'll be reassigned?"

"No, of course not. You will be working on the technology to allow a laser-written message, appearing to be suspended in midair without a visible screen, large and effective enough to be read by thousands upon thousands simultaneously."

In disbelief, everyone exchanged glances, excited to be part of what's coming. The meeting is adjourned; an affectious enthusiasm goes with them.

Werner later began the production of the support programs as instructed:

1. A takeover of existing worldwide satellites
2. The global Loniancoin financial system
3. The omnipresent 666 identification and communications systems
4. The midair laser messaging board to work smoothly and efficiently

The Antichrist, Amid Baker Mohammed, demanded they be ready by the end of the year for worldwide distribution, tested and functioning perfectly—only seven months away.

Werner needed to appoint a qualified technician capable of thoroughly finite satellite tampering by rewriting code to include cyberneurological subliminal control. This person doesn't require to possess neurological knowledge, only how to incorporate it into satellite systems that Trident Technologies will create.

In his search for this project, he comes across the name of a high school student whom the Homeland Security feds were watching. By the time she had graduated from high school, her level of computer code technology exceeded that of highly trained, experienced, and active code/language writers in the world including Dr. Stull, exactly whom Werner is searching.

At the next meeting with Mohammed, Werner makes a request. "I have a favor to ask of you, Amid. We need to have on board a specific, skillful security hacker on board, her name is Alicia Stougard."

"Why Ms. Stougard?" he inquired.

"She has skills so unique, the Homeland Security had to incarcerate her to keep her from hacking into government and finance data that she seems particularly adept of doing."

"What's the problem? Why come to me with this?"

"She's incarcerated in Lexington, under strict surveillance in the US Federal prison to prevent her hacking what was thought impenetrable government and military data, what she's been doing since she was seventeen. By the time of her trial, she was nineteen and tried as an adult, which, because of a very smart attorney, lasted three years. That was a year ago. Her attorney established that she did this only because she could, but without any intention of a treasonable act. She is serving only a ten-year sentence of what is usually a mandatory twenty-year sentence."

"Do what you need to do to free her."

Avril Swenson, Werner's liaison officer, is sent to visit with Alicia Stougard, the code writer.

Lexington Federal Prison for Women

A few days after a notorious riot following the rapture, Avril Swenson in the wee hours of the morning, is escorted with six armed guards with rifles at the ready to a meager conference room. Small piles of cement rubble are lined against the hallway walls, no doubt the aftereffects of both the rapture and the riots.

Alicia is wakened by keys rattling to open her cell door. "You have a visitor, Stougard. Get dressed," demanded the female guard. Alicia quickly does as she's told without taking a moment to look presentable as a woman does. She's led from her cell to a conference room she didn't know existed. A well-dressed male and the warden are seated at the table. The warden indicates for her to sit across from them as the guard posts herself near the closed door. The warden spoke first.

"Placed in front of you is a form you need to sign for your release, Alicia."

"What? For my release? How is this possible? I have almost nine years left."

"By signing the form, you agree to allow the company Mr. Swenson is an employee of to be your legal guardian until you are twenty-five, like parole, of sorts. After that, you're on parole for five years."

"What do I have to do for my early release?" inquired the twenty-two-year-old.

Mr. Swenson answered, "Ms. Stougard, you are an exceptional systems analyst and code writer. It is very simple. We need your skills.

The United States State Department of the government has been handsomely compensated of prosecution costs to allow your early release. We were required to guarantee the prevention of you repeating the activity for which you were incarcerated."

"I can do that. And what about my parents?"

The warden stated, "We're all satisfied with this act taken in your behalf. You should be quite happy about it too. But it includes that you remain under the custody of the supervisor where you will be assigned to work. She is also a systems analyst. Upon signing, you are to go with Mr. Swenson. I remind you that if you become a fugitive and that you're returned here, the time remaining of your sentence will be doubled. Do you understand that? It is one of the conditions of what you'll be signing."

"Yes, I understand." Alicia signed the agreement, accepted her personal belongings in an enclosed cardboard box as she signed for them also, and walked out into the dawning of the new day with Swenson for a new life to begin.

32

ANTICHRIST REVIEWS HIS NEW WORLD SYSTEM

At the announcement by Werner that the three projects are completed and waiting for Mohammed's review, he immediately visited the production sites for presentations.

Walking along a hallway, his gaze is quickly on the image at the end. It is his likeness facing him. When he is but halfway, the image begins to walk toward him. *It's eerie to see myself walking toward me as I is walk to my likeness,* he thought. The image stopped and raised a hand, signaling Amid to also stop; they're just four or five feet away from each other.

"Welcome to our research laboratory where I was created," states the image.

"Thank you," responds Amid.

"I trust I meet your inspection of yourself."

"Looks quite good to me."

"I assume you know you'll have to be satisfied with a visual inspection."

"Why?"

"Because I am only an image. You cannot feel me for I am but a smoke and mirrors image of you. If you try to touch me, your hand will merely penetrate through me. Cool, huh?" This brought laughter from everyone.

Amid steps forward a couple of feet. They're nearly face-to-face. It is difficult for him to distinguish the image is not real. When he thrusts his hand into the image, it is as vapor just as he was told. Not fleshly matter, no resistance, nothing. Behind him is Werner. He turns toward him.

"You and your team have done superbly. Great job! Your work is as how I want it." Not expecting much more, he asked, "How many of the five images are completed?"

"This image is number 6, sir. We have them all ready for your desired placement anywhere in the world. Each, as you requested, has been equipped with total remote control for independent activity. Our own satellites include the controlling of your images. For ease of operation, we have fitted your images with voice control as well as voice articulation from the images your voice will speak. We developed software that induces the tonal quality and attributes of your voice into whosoever voice is utilized for the image to appear talking."

Mohammed nods his acknowledgement and smiles with appreciation.

As the small group walk away in their separate directions, their contented smiles, and proud gaits, they hear a "see ya" from the image. Mild laughter erupts.

"What's next, Mr. Werner?"

"Four other ventures you've requested. They are all in Building D, each in one of the four corner laboratories."

"Why not adjacent to each other?" inquired Radolfo.

"We didn't want the technicians to intermingle too much. They were asked not to. I felt it would be best."

"You're probably right with that."

Ten minutes later, they enter Building D, passing through five autonomous security scanning devices to assure freedom of any contraband.

"What happens in the center of the building?" asked Amid as he notices through a safety glass window an empty large room with a hardwood floor.

"Let's go there first." Werner apparently changes the itinerary.

He opens the door upon their arrival for all to see. It's like an empty gymnasium.

"This is where all of our testing is performed when space is required. Even from each other, all testing is kept hush-hush at the highest level. The equipment and apparatus used for testing is stored in the assigned three-foot-thick hollow walls of this room," he describes as he indicates, "behind the slew of those doors."

"We can discuss any questions you might have later, in my office."

They continue to each of the four locations of the projects.

"First is the Loniancoin system. A room housing what looks to be forty or fifty computer bays where technicians are busy is all that can be seen. It looks as any computer data processing office. But that's not what's happening.

"They're writing lines of data code to have absolute control of the Loniancoin worldwide financial system," explains Werner. "Every Loniancoin is vapor. It is not a coin. Neither is it a currency, at least in the traditional sense. There is a trading, commerce value of the Loniancoin all under our control! We alone will have control over the price and value of the Loniancoin. It will be downloaded here in the Brussels databank where it will be in use when we're ready and you give the word," Werner continues to explain some of the details to Amid.

"Then when Babylon is ready, the Brussels computers will become redundant backup supporting primary data control base that's downloaded from Brussels. All data will then be headquartered in Babylon.

'The Loniancoin is linked to the 666 and our smartwatch. If one refuses to wear the mark, any funds of their bank accounts, credit or debit cards, or any other form of asset will be confiscated electronically and placed into the Babylon account at the current rate of the Loniancoin for random distribution into accounts of those who accept the mark. Those who have accepted the mark, the wearer will retain only their cash assets, recorded in the Babylonian bank trust, and tied to their 666 registration password and smartwatch, which is operated by voice recognition. The mark then functions much like a debit card. There will be no credit system in existence anywhere in the world once the practice of the mark is put into play—no Visa, MasterCard, Discover, American Express, or any other system including the Bitcoin or PayPal will function. They'll all be shut down.

"Prior to the issuance of either the DT-II wristwatcher or the mark, every credit account has been deleted from anyone who had one at that time—that is, if they refuse to accept wearing the 666. On the other hand, with those who accept to wear the mark, we'll create a block of 1,500 credit account applied to their Loniancoin balance. Not that money will mean much. Trading of possessions for food and water might have more meaning."

Still awash with the reality of the mark, they proceed to the next area where two gigantic, swinging doors with sizable windows allow viewing but effectively blocks entrance. Lab equipment of all sizes and strange configurations seem to fill the space beyond what could permit efficient work.

"This is the EMP research lab, but entrance is forbidden without wearing appropriate protective clothing and possessing many levels of security clearances days in advance."

Around the hallway corner, the guests come upon a room filled with work cubicles in the middle surrounded by a continuous workbench around the perimeter where technicians are focusing their attention on various electronic components. "This is the Identity Developmental Lab," he informs them as they enter. Werner expounds what is being built to implement the 666 identity when it becomes mandatory to be inscribed upon everyone. Not far from the door, Werner places his hand on a black box about the size of a small microwave oven, but its designed shape is much like a huge tape dispenser mounted on an overly wide, metal pedestal; a display screen consists the top.

"This machine houses a sophisticated data printer linked to our satellite systems. It contains the bio of everyone to perform three functions. First, by voice input of one's name and a PIN number, in less than five seconds, it will search and find the person's data, assign a registration password like a social security number as shown in the display screen.

"Secondly, within another three seconds, this device will dispense a vinyl-like peel-off tape. The person will then place the tape on either their forehead or the back of their right hand/wrist, press firmly down, and peel off the tape. Instantly impregnated into the skin is dark-blue magnetic ink with a layer of phosphorous that imbeds the person's details in the first numeral of 666 to be worn. The insignia 666 is about three-fourths an inch high. The phosphorous layer is to enable the mark to be seen at a distance in darkness when a light is beamed upon it. We have China to thank for the development of the magnetized ink to create a tattoolike result so easily and quickly managed.

"Third, the subject person will receive a smartwatch that their ID number is ingrained to be continually utilized by the person when buying or selling. As I mentioned before, all existing credit or debit cards are rendered useless, being replaced by the Loniancoin. All other of the world's forms of money are valueless and unrecognized except when exchanged at one half of the value of the Loniancoin's rate that is set for that particular day.

"People will have the choice to wear the *666* or not. Without it, they cannot buy or sell anything, and they will be restricted of having access to any Loniancoin financial benefit, nor are they allowed to trade or barter for any gain of any asset in exchange of any asset they might own. We will know remotely who refuses to wear the mark with communication from the smartwatch. Death could follow immediately when refusing to wear the 666, but not likely. Physical torment is more likely to follow," Werner informs them.

He walks a few feet and places his hand on a second box similar as the other, only it is bright-red-orange and twice the size.

"This machine distributes the physical wrist device, programmed with the wearer's biodata. It's a smartwatch similar to what was introduced in 2012. We call it the DT-II device, named after Dick Tracy, a cartoon character before the 1990s, who sported a crime-display wristwatch. Please walk with me to the windows."

The entourage follows him to the windows with a view of the massive landscaping. Close by, a gardener is tending to a well-groomed rose garden.

"Notice the gardener."

A gardener is on his knees wholly focused upon the bedding of roses. Suddenly he explodes into nothingness, instantly without a trace of previous existence.

"See the messenger walking to her car?"

A young woman appearing to be in her early thirties is walking to her electrically powered car. As she swings her legs in and she shuts the car door, she explodes in a fiery detonation along with the interior of the auto enveloped in flames.

"Both were wearing the DT-II device as experimental testing. Neither of them knew of the detonation capability, and neither knew what hit them."

Werner produces a device for assessment. He describes its function.

"As with the 666 patch, this device will be worn—without choice—by everyone. Refusal could bring immediate torture until submission or outright decapitation if the enforcer loses his patience, who is authorized to do as he wishes when refusal to wear the device occurs.

"This solar-powered device not having batteries requiring to be charged has five functions: First, it is a one-way, uploading, viewing screen which we have full control to make any of our announcements. Second, of course it is an advanced GSP with an accompanying ID number of the wearer, by triangular use of our adjusted multiple satellite systems. Third, the ability to monitor, at will, whether or not the wearer is authorized by wearing the mark to transact business of any buying or selling of anything. Fourth, it transmits the wearer's heart rate. This is to tell us whether or not they're alive or other negative, vital signs. If no signal is received, we merely set off the device to rid of the body into undetectable fragments. And, fifth, we have the control to detonate the same small explosive that causes immediate, sudden obliteration of the wearer, as you just witnessed, for any reason we see fit—mostly for disobedience or failure to yield compliance to us."

"You've accomplished exactly what we need. All of this is ready?"

"Just give the word."

"Splendid."

Werner now could make solid plans for the interference of the satellite system gaining its control for Strident Technologies, and consequently, the world. Chuck Wesson and Larry Stull will be quite pleased to have the young genius girl on their team as intricate code writing is her forte. Certainly, now by her being on board, their job and assignments will be so much easier, with fewer complications, and being completed quicker. All they have to do is to accept the idea of such a youngster—female no less—who can be professionally trusted. To convince them, Werner needed Avril Swenson to talk with them. He had one thing going for him; in this age, even three-year-olds have basic understandings of what a computer can do!

PART IV

TRIBULATION BEGINS

For God has put in their hearts to accomplish his purpose by agreeing to give the beast their power to rule, until God's word is fulfilled.

—Revelation 17:17

33

THE BIG PEACE AGREEMENT

Israel and the Antichrist signed the peace agreement.

Israel is now protected as promised by the Antichrist. They'll be at peace from all nations, the first time since they've become a sovereign nation in 1948. Its borders are cordoned off from attack by another nation with a peace corps assembled through the auspices of the Antichrist, equipped with the latest war technology provided from the US arsenal he had purchased.

In spite of Islam and Arab protests and rioting across the globe, progress on the rebuilding of the Jewish Temple on what was once where the Islamic Mosque stood is steadily noticeable every day of the week due to the rigid 24/5 schedule. Stones from quarries in Italy arrive daily as does cedar lumber from the west and gold bullion donated by the EU. All who see its beauty are left breathless, though it's less than a year from its completion.

Drilling that has been going on for decades to find the Ark of the Covenant under the Temple Mount paid off, finding it where believed. Also discovered is the tunnel that was used to position the Ark in the position it was found, in a tunnel not filled in. That tunnel will be used for its extraction after the temple is built. The Ark's discovery energized the workmen in a highly positive manner.

The Antichrist's satellite network

As Babylon is nearing completion, various developments at the labs of the Antichrist are also nearing their completion. The technologies to convert the existing satellite network control of various other companies and governments are about ready to be deployed. In three separate trials, the switchover worked beautifully and exactly how anticipated.

Alicia Stougard, the youngest employee, not yet twenty-three, had taken the computer specialists along with Wessen and Stull by complete astonishment. She had such skill with superimposing lines of code into existing secure codes no one could disconcert her. Her supervisor insisted that she be run the gamut of testing to establish where she would best be fit into the scheme of things. Alicia excelled. In half the time with the most technically accurate lines of code, she outsmarted the most proficient and skillful code developers on staff.

In addition to being a code writer, she inherited the assignment to make code writing of others to be more efficient. This meant to rewrite code with fewer lines while improving the results. Soon after turning twenty-three, she replaced her supervisor who was promoted when Alicia's leadership skills matched her technical skill. Code writing to provide all the satellites under full control of the Antichrist accelerated with Alicia's leadership.

As with most people in their early twenties, she started to get bored and restless. Though her position kept her mind busy enough, the various sources of challenges seemed to dry up for her. This did not last long.

Alicia Stougard is introduced to Damian Kalenco; control technology meets the new, recently developed cyber manipulation video world. Alicia is energized more than she had ever been.

"Take a look at this resume, Alicia," instructs her boss, "you'll be working alongside him."

She receives the folder and opens it, not so happy she must work with someone shoulder to shoulder. Then she sees the name.

"Glory be! Damian Kalenco? Really?"

"Do you know him? Of course I shouldn't be surprised that you do."

"Haven't met him, but the whole computer world knows his work. How is it that we'll be working together?" For a moment she thought about her question, then "I get it. The satellites we control will also have the ability to possess mind-control behavior of people through a video he provides. Yep. That'll work!"

Within the week, she and Damian are sitting at table with keyboards, looking at a 72" flat-screen mounted on the wall as he controls the video and its images. Whenever she notices where satellite techno lines of code are required, she installs a flashing red dot to identify where control of the complete satellite system will just be a click of a keyboard key.

Their abilities enabled working together completion within the first week when everyone anticipated maybe a month, again a surprising achievement noted by others, regarding Alicia.

In future videos, Damian inserts an undetectable code at precise locations where instructed by Alicia's staff to attach satellite controls. Control of behavior of viewers playing the video games for entertainment will then be maximized. The satellite system becomes the primary source to play downloaded video games created by the latest technology as a diversion during such cruel times.

At twenty-four, Alicia establishes herself as the heroine of the company. She obtained carte blanche of anything she wants to do, except the conditions of her parole. Her 3,400-square-feet apartment is less than a block away from the high-security offices (overhauled by her), elaborately furnished, with all the amenities she requests.

In her package deal, she arranged for her parents to be transported from America. Her father was killed in an auto accident the week before permission to leave the country was granted. Only her mother came, flown from Newark, New Jersey, to Brussels with a company's aircraft.

After their long embrace, Alicia asked, "Ma, who informed you of Papa's accident?"

"The United States State Department. Why?"

"Ma, didn't that seem odd…that the State Department would inform you and not the local police?"

"No. Should it have?"

"Well, yes. It should have made you wonder, at least. Remember, Papa is Russian. I broke into security stuff. Remember how difficult it was to convince them I didn't do it for espionage? Personally I think it was not an accident. I think he was killed—yes by an accident, but it wasn't just an accident. However it happened, it was planned. But it's too late now to do anything about it."

⚜

Infrastructures, by any definition, throughout the world are nearly nonexistent. Social services have been dismantled long ago. Medical facilities have been turned into dormitories, their medical supplies and instruments raided. No police and no fire stations; both are without fuel. For fear of being overtaken by force, most of the oil rigs in the Middle East have been stopped. Mutiny rules; cargoes of the seas are confiscated. Businesses, in a manner of reference in times past, are now only a black market where money is of no value, defined only as what one can trade that sustains survival or increases one's safety.

International diplomacy is dubious at best. Religious animosity is heightened by distrustful volatile tension. Hatred permeates every relationship, business or individually. Where religion barely affects a nation's relationship with another, suspicion of motives infuses an obstruction to work together. Trident Technologies is no exception as even the Antichrist cannot control behavior in his own company.

No one understands why an unruly nation has not yet struck another with a nuclear device. When Mohammed signed the agreement with Israel, the threat of nuclear warfare seemed to wane. But how long can he hold power to prolong the peace? It all comes down to the decision of believing whether or not Amid Baker Mohammed can pull all the diverse elements back together again. Also, can he be trusted? When all is said and done, what is he up to?

Disease control is tenuous at best. There's a great fear that communicable diseases are on the brink of plague status anywhere in the world.

34

ANTICHRIST'S INTERNET TAKEOVER

Headline: United States' ICONN to give up Internet's Control to Foreigners
New York 2016

ICONN, Internet's operational management corporation, relinquishes its responsibilities to a multinational body outside the United States. This newly formed corporation has assured world leaders the Internet will continue to be kept out of the hands of any one country, dictator, company or conglomerate, or other entity for dominate or exclusive use.

It is feared by Internet technologists that if it's all that easy to transfer the workings of the Internet from ICONN to a multinational body, how easy will it be for a bullying takeover by a terrorist organization? After all, it was created by computer specialists; albeit over time, couldn't the codes just as well be rewritten to accomplish clandestine purposes?

Headline: Five Countries Announce Formulation of their own Internet

Prognosticators warned the powers of the old Internet that once it would be given over to any foreign entity, the dissolvent of the Internet as we knew it to be trustworthy will surely happen. That day has arrived; the five country's www is wwwBR (Brazil), wwwRU (Russia), wwwCH (China), wwwIN (India), and wwwCA (Canada). Israel, Iran, Australia, Turkey, and Columbia have theirs in the works, soon to be operational. It doesn't take much imagination to realize how messy and uncontrollable the Internet will soon become. A central administrative authority is no more which once kept the Internet "clean" of derision and governmental self-serving control. That is now lost.

Headline: AMID BAKER MOHAMMED ASSERTS BABYLON BETTER SUITED TO HOST INTERNET
Ernesto Merlinni, May 4

Rome—Amid Baker Mohammed, the known Antichrist, has offered to the world powers who now govern the Internet in a piecemeal fashion that Babylon is better equipped to host the world's Internet than anywhere else. He has made it clear to engage a worldwide conference toward that end.

During the past five months, representatives of Babylon have forcibly proposed to the International Internet Security and Management Association (IISMA) at conferences that the Internet is best served by its primary data and operations center is located in Babylon.

This of course is met with strong disagreement and is interpreted as not more than a subtle threat by Mohammed.

Unanimously all eleven executives who manage the IISMA agree to disallow any Internet administrative or management function by Babylon and/or any entity under the control of Mohammed.

Personally, I consider this decision a wise one. The question is, however: How long will Antichrist tolerate this "put aside" choice of the finest Internet logistic minds in the world?

Headline: MOHAMMED DENIES BABYLON'S INVOLVEMENT WITH THE DEATHS OF INTERNET EXECUTIVES
Ernesto Merlinni, May 12

Rome—Is the Antichrist responsible for the deaths of three IISMA executives who died in accidents over the weekend? "Definitely not," he responded when asked this question. Upon further pressing, Babylon denied the accusation. Two were killed in freak auto accidents; a female executive's remains were identified by dental records after the gas explosion in her apartment (caused by a faulty regulator).

Another IISMA conference with Babylon is scheduled next week, but the eight remaining IISMA executives have already declined to attend. As a matter of fact, they are under security protection 24/7, with continuous alert status.

Headline: INTERNET FRAUGHT WITH MALFUNCTIONS
Ernesto Merlinni, May 29

Rome—The entire world has experienced extensive malfunctions of the Internet, mostly effecting e-mails and e-mail attachments. Google declares that not one transaction or transmission passing through its company has been corrupted. They maintain the faulty communication is in the Internet's own system.

Authorities and Internet technological programmers concur with Google. They all believe the Internet's operational code has been compromised by Babylon as a show of power by the Antichrist. Isaiah Goldstein, IISMA's systems manager, stated there are five separate teams of fifty or more qualified technicians assigned to solve the problems—with that being the only focus.

The authorities also have a strong bias that the world's conflicts outside of the Internet's current status and the Internet are connected to the Antichrist's agenda of controlling the world. Hit hardest by the malfunctions are the Internet systems administered by countries. Their inexperience compounds the overall inoperable effects upon those systems.

Headline: INTERNET PROBLEMS EXPAND EXPONENTIALLY
Ernesto Merlinni, June 14

Rome—Every person involved to return the Internet to its once contamination-free status is convinced the Babylonian computer programmers are tampering with the Internet codes at an accelerated pace greater than can be corrected. For every one step forward, Babylon caused a step backward at the beginning, but now it's three steps backward. The tampering and flooding with viruses has quickened the pace to gain control of the Internet. The feeling it's a waste of time and effort to save the Internet from the Antichrist and Babylon is prevalent. It's predicted that his full control will be gained within two to three months.

Internet traffic is rapidly decreasing for extraordinary fears of rapidly diminishing secure transmissions and transactions. Noticeably however is that anything based from Babylon is consistently "getting through" unhindered unlike all other transmissions.

Headline: INTERNET UNDER CONTROL OF AMID BAKER MOHAMMED
Ernesto Merlinni, August 5

Rome—He did it! The Internet is his! Rather than acquiring the go-ahead by a consensus of the IISMA, he swapped the Internet by sheer imposition to make it his own. All along this course of action a name keeps surfacing: Alicia Stougard, a twenty-three-year-old former hacker of US codes of government data bases and military codes of strategic significance, when she was only seventeen years old.

Babylon brought her onboard for another task, we knew about: To reprogram satellites. Now it is this, obviously.

Along with my peers, I think this could be the last report, unless I'm willing to lose my life by addressing any news that would be derogatory to the Antichrist's actions sure to come. I will say this: He has insidious reasons to possess the Internet under his full control.

Headline: FORMER REPORTER KILLED… LEFT TO ROT IN STREET
August 14

Brussels—Ernesto Merlinni was discovered last evening in an alley where his corpse had been lying for five days, according to forensic observers. Each of his fingers was missing and eyes plucked out; the body stripped of clothing, shoes remaining on his feet. Face crushed in. Dried blood from nose, mouth, and injuries. There is no doubt he had been tortured before the welcome peace of death. Search for Mr. Merlinni had been ongoing over the past four days when he failed, uncharacteristically, to file what was to be his final report.

35

144 THOUSAND FORMED

Magi Reports

One hundred forty-four thousand[1] began their preaching mostly to the Jewish people, convincing them to accept Christ as their Messiah, against the vices of Satan, to accept Christ as savior, and reject the Antichrist. They had a seal, God's sign, placed on their foreheads by an angel, apparently intended to protect them.[2]

This number of people would require two stadiums with a capacity for seventy-two thousand. But somehow God dispersed thirty-two thousand groups of four all over the world. They consist of Jews converted to Believers of Christ, now pleading with others to do the same.

Spider Reports

The Antichrist is appalled and totally beside himself at the sight of not only the gigantic numbers these evangelists amass, but their unheard-of success. Everywhere the evangelists go, thousands are being converted. He continually mutters to himself out of anxiety that these people must be stopped soon. I agree. From his perspective, the world is getting much too aware as people begin to realize the problem these evangelists are causing the Antichrist. Not just regionally, but all over the world. Their success is undermining his being worshipped as he's attempting to garner.

By month after month, he is getting terribly more frustrated with every report of their continual success. Compounding his distress is his failure at various attempts to discourage, dismantle, and disengage their effect on people. Other than to kill them outright, which is not an option, he is at a loss of how to cope with them and stop their winning thousands over to God. He seemed to realize that if he were to mow down a contingency of these evangelists, it would cause people to rally around them even more.

Then, because of the seal of God worn on their forehead, no matter what method is used to squelch them, they could not be harmed. He knew it was God that is shielding them and why their success is renowned everywhere.

To the world's amazement, including me, the Antichrist could do nothing about them for seven whole years. But his hand, somehow, is stopped to harm them!

36

ANTICHRIST'S WORLD
MAKEOVER BEGINS

Spider provides more news

Mohammed is lucky to have Werner as such a loyal associate. He keeps everything on track and ready whenever whatever needs done. They went together from Brussels on a tour through Jerusalem then to the site of Babylon's massive construction. Mr. Dowdson and myself were asked to accompany them. It is two years since the seven-year major peace treaty was signed with Israel.

In Jerusalem, the temple's rebuilding, in all its glory, had been completed three months ago. Its high priest had begun his duties as thousands of Jews worshipped in their new temple every day. We could see the pleasure of pride in the faces of the worshippers; Amid often had told me that he felt a strong ire of regret for having signed the peace agreement with Israel. But for now, he held that irritation in check.

To the Babylon site, as he looked down through the window of his private aircraft, he was filled with enormous pride. "It is beautiful, exactly what I imagined," he declared out loud to anyone who could hear him. When the plane made its landing approach, he observed the progress of the cargo port with equal satisfaction. After more than thirty months, half of the city seemed to be built and one side of the cargo container facility channel is operational. What impressed him the most was the underground, undersea command and finance bunker thinking it being securely unapproachable.

While we were reviewing the twenty massive ship servicing cranes reaching eighty to ninety feet into the air, Mohammad Alysa walked up to the visitors.

"Welcome to the great Babylon," announcing his arrival.

"Oh, Mohammad, thank you. This is marvelous. You've done a great job!" responded Prophet Werner.

He turns to the Antichrist, who at that moment is wondering who this new arrival might be, making an introduction.

"This is Mohammad Alysa. He's my appointed general engineer, responsible for all construction of your city."

"Mr. Werner is right. You have done a terrific job so far," Amid responds. "Tell me what's going on and your schedule."

"Surely," Mohammad replies with noticeable pleasure followed by verbal descriptions. "What you are observing now is the Babylon Port, destined to service forty to fifty-five cargo ships a day including the unloading and loading, staging and the operation of the largest container transfer station of 250 hectares in the world. The other side of the channel is scheduled for completion in three more weeks."

They are all pleased.

"Let's move on, shall we?"

They walk a few hundred feet away from the port toward the city. Mohammed continues, "The core city will be ready for occupancy within three months. We have ramped up the number of workers to assure the completion by that time. The property manager has told me that more than three hundred of the *Fortune 500* companies have committed to conduct business in Babylon. Many are coming from Dubai, Singapore, and Hong Kong—even Shanghai.

"The outlying Babylon, where plush, extraordinary residences are being constructed, is on schedule as related to the entire project, five months before they will be completed. By that time, the landscaping and recreational centers, pavilions, and stadiums will be complete too," he informs them with immense pride.

Maji summarizes the events taking place in the world.

"The reviewed development of the Loniancoin's system has been put into place.

"Israel's peace, the first time in its storied past, is intact. Five more years of peace is expected.

"The temple's reconstruction allows Jews to worshipping in the temple for the first time since its obliteration in AD 47 by the Romans.

"Six hundred sixty-six nautical miles distant from Jerusalem, Babylon is nearing completion with much ado and excitement.

"The big battle's mess as prophesied in Scripture, Gog and Magog, is nearing its final seventh year of cleanup.

"Evangelism of the 144 thousand all over the world is being tremendously successful as also prophesied. The Antichrist cannot seem to stop its success though the world is in such a dire condition everywhere.

"While, apparently, as nations are basically at peace, the terror of individuals inflicting bloodshed on each other without cause is widespread. Such unrest is infiltrating even the sanctuaries. Man's evil hearts cannot be satisfied. Cruelty is accelerating in numbers as well as horrific viciousness in the wake of the four terrifying horsemen.

"The Antichrist is being called upon to settle the madness of the streets, suburbs, farmlands, and forests. So far, despite efforts of many to reorganize the world's systems and infrastructure, Amid Baker Mohammed and his prophet Alex Werner seem to not care except for their own cause and keeping peace with Israel.

"For the two of them to become the world's hope is the world's cry, hoping against hope that something will be enforced to establish safety of individuals."

37

ANTICHRIST'S RULE BEGINS

Maji continues

They're taking advantage of the world's trust in him much as did Adolf Hitler in the late 1930s. The Antichrist is building the world's hope upon his new ideals for all the people. Only this man has an influential man in his prophet, Alex Werner, a man who's developed a persona few can resist. A prophet to target immense attention upon Amid Baker Mohammed, to encourage worshipping him!

Along the way, many signs and wonders are performed by the Prophet. He carries out a number of low-level miracles as would a magician. Everywhere Prophet Werner goes, there are great crowds gathered to see his presentations, speeches, and persuasive mystical exhibitions. Theaters everywhere are filled to standing room only for his free performances conducting engagements in theaters and outdoor arenas.

The Prophet has also perfected a new illusion: an image of the Antichrist by the use of holography. No one knew that what they saw and heard was a simulated form appearing real. Eventually word got out about the image when his likeness was shown when Mohammed was in person only a few miles distant. It didn't seem to matter, the audiences loved it.

I must say he's very eloquent and possesses enormous appeal. Traits of an accomplished speaker are readily recognized. All of these attributes create a magnetic draw to not only hear what he has to say, but compelling to comply with his desire to worship the Antichrist. His points are so succinct it's difficult to find fault.

The world seems to respond to the allurement to follow the Prophet's guidance to worship if not reverence the Antichrist, an evil man, of course, being evil themselves. He has promised eradication of any evidence of God: for every unpleasant act leveled against people, he makes certain that those acts are known to be brought by God.

Somehow I know it to be true when in fact he is the cause for God's wrath simply being the Antichrist.

As a coauthor of the World Constitution, when known as Radolfo Amerinero, the Antichrist had rearranged the world's governments to his liking. As with the Prophet's ability to sway the thinking of the masses, he demonstrated political savvy and powers possessed by the Antichrist! All of this is so much like Satan himself that I know the powers of these two men are bestowed by Satan.

What amazes me however is the continued success of the 144 thousand evangelists crisscrossing over all the earth. There have been numerous attempts upon the lives of any of the 32,000 groups of four, but it's the hand of God that keeps protecting them. Everyone knows that. It must make the Antichrist crazy knowing that time after time, attempts to kill them always proves fruitless. It is only these evangelists and those who heed their call that is not going the Antichrist's way!

To assure that his success continues, I have heard he and his lieutenants have devised a way to have the world worship him. It's really sinister. It's about wearing the number 666 on our foreheads or on the back of our right hand! It didn't surprise me though: Scripture foretold it. Everyone considered it only a rumor, but I knew it was no rumor.

I was certainly bewildered how millions upon millions of people around the world could be tattooed in a matter of a day or two as we were informed. But that was me. Everyone else could only think of the consequences of what was also rumored if one refused to have the tattoo applied. Sure, I was concerned also because I knew I would not wear it. No one knew when this monumental time would take place, where, or how. As each day passed, this topic became continuously more engrained in everyone's thoughts and comments shared. Fear began to permeate the very core of staying alive of what was to come though the present was bad enough.

Many refused to believe such a thing could happen and let it remain as just a rumor. Those who did considered life couldn't get much worse. But let me tell you, it got much worse!

38

WHERE IN *THIS* WORLD IS THE UNITED STATES?

Glen Holtz, the US president's commerce secretary, explains the situation.

"This is a nation who more or less defied God in the last days is reduced to only a great landmass of poor, frenzied, and people turned nomadic going nowhere. Who could have imagined that the United States would not be much more than this? The United States of America is a zero. It became especially true when the Antichrist had overtaken control of the Fifth and Sixth Fleets without firing a shot. This takeover included all of the military bases everywhere in the Middle East and other select locations all over the globe as well. He had used the World Constitution with a technicality which essentially disarmed the US. The Antichrist has shriveled up exporting of any country to anywhere unless through Babylon. His purchase of America's Fifth and Sixth Fleets provide him with the power to enforce the ruling.

"Add to all this, the dollar standard has become replaced by the Loniancoin, now the world's currency.

"As far as America is concerned, only its worn-out, dilapidating infrastructure remains though critically decimated. Except in trade of goods that land at Babylon, importing into the US from any country is denied. And even then, it is not without the distress of censorship at every level.

"Though freeways and alternate highways are somewhat cleaned up from the earlier days after *the Event* took place, goods shipped by trucks is life-risking for the drivers. Trains are a better transportation decision, if the tracks remain to be in place. Many railway tracks have been uprooted to prevent the spread of EMP around major cities and its destruction in case of such an attack.

"Without long-haul trucks bringing smaller cities needed products, there are few short-run delivery trucks operating. FedEx, the US Postal Service, and UPS are out of the question. Their vulnerability is an open season to plunder packages and kill or maim drivers. As a result, stores cannot obtain products to sell. Everything is sold through the black market even when a few trucks get through. A fear of the 666 has all but destroyed any hope of commerce.

"Agriculture has nearly ended. Inhabitants from the cities are as teeming locusts, frenzied to acquire food and water by whatever means possible. Even the corporate, massive farms are constantly ransacked. Most farm buildings are overcome as shelters taken by the desperate, nomadic homeless. Crops in progress are thoughtlessly trampled down by these vagabonds, worse than if a hailstorm had destroyed them. The food chain is completely shattered.

"Grazing livestock is subject to being slaughtered not much differently than the unscrupulous white man who did the same with the Indian's buffalo. These fiendish people killed the animals for a meal or two before leaving the carcass to rot. Ranchers are ruthlessly killed when attempting to save their herds. It didn't matter whether the cattle were dairy cows or range herds, horses or sheep or goats—even dogs and cats.

"Hundreds of thousands died from starvation for their lack of knowing basic survival techniques. It is appalling how many city people, now barely surviving, did not know where food came from, other a can or packaging. When stores' shelves were laid bare, tens of thousands of people panicked from sheer ignorance or the want to get creative to merely survive. Food stamps? They're a laugh. It's been over ten years since they even existed!

"And speaking of the government, every agency existing when *the Event* happened is no more. Gone. Out of business. There are no funds to support any activity of any agency. Programs for the elderly, alone, and in distress, medical attention, the veterans, starving children, and any other social program is…well, no more. Mohammed, the Antichrist of today's world, saw to it that the source of any financial or commercial help must come from and through Babylon first, being approved before any shipment is allowed!

"If anyone travels from one place to another, it's accomplished by walking or bicycling. But bicycles in working order are taken by a stronger person than the one riding, so few ride their bikes. Vehicles driven are for the most part extinct as gasoline and diesel deliveries to service stations has ceased years ago.

"All forms of meanness are discussed on the Antichrist's solitary satellite—are godless, mindless, and evil people committing those acts are shown everywhere all the time. Whether in little towns or larger cities across the USA, it is the same. It has been declared many months ago that the only source of information will be by the Antichrist's satellite system.

"Hunger and being penniless cause havoc for everyone because it's coupled without any form of hope. We have heard of a world commerce system about to be launched by the Antichrist. It will certainly intensify the feelings of hopelessness amid hunger and near hyperventilation. I cannot project how awful it will be when this new financial system is linked with what the Scriptures of the past referred to as the mark of the beast, 666, which I'm informed we must wear if one is to buy and sell. It is tough enough already to buy and sell! And I understand it will be enforced all over the world?"

39

FIRST FOUR SEAL
JUDGMENTS RELEASED

The Four Horsemen of the Apocalypse
Maji Steinman reports his experience

It's been just over three years since the peace treaty of Israel and the Antichrist was signed. It worked well, as a matter of fact, to everyone's welcome surprise. But that didn't mean the world apart from international peace went without enormous suffering of great pain to live in these days offering new survival challenges as each day dawned or that of individuals, for that matter.

Then yet another sorrow startles us all. Four horsemen came out from nowhere, parting the clouds as though coming from the heavens. There were four horsemen on their mount, one after another being disconcerting to everyone. At first we knew nothing of the meaning of their behavior. This had never happened before! How would we have known apart from Scripture? We would soon know.

During our time together, Steven Alexander and I had many discussions of Scripture, a couple of times about the four horsemen appearing.[1]

Being a Jew, I considered the New Testament a belief of faith of the Gentiles, not particularly of interest to us Jews. So I considered especially anything in the Book of Revelation a myth.

So you can imagine my out-and-out shock to see, as others, the sudden appearance in the sky of not just one horse and rider, but four, appearing a week apart! Four—just as Steven had told me. Mythical they were not. They were real. And they were so despicably weird, not ever seen before—both horses and riders. But what they did to us is more than just outright scary. We justly feared for our lives!

They imposed their will upon the people on the earth suddenly and without warning, their appearances upon earth in the same manner from the heavens. They rode the skies from one continent to another during thirty-day spans, for the entire world to see.

First, the white horse[2] displaying a promise of peace and warned us of what soon will happen throughout the world.

Second, the red horse.[3] Its rider removed the peace from the earth and replaced it with such hatred that it caused people to kill each other. Even in my heart, I had the desire to kill for no reason, and I almost did but didn't, happily, while defending myself!

Third, the black horse.[4] This rider allocated upon the earth what people could eat and how much; it amounted to only what was enough to avoid starvation during a famine brought upon the earth by having wheat and barley costing a day's wages. Strange as it was, the famine was not caused by a drought. There was plenty of rain. Only barley and wheat was allowed to grow, or rather, would grow. Trees went dormant of fruit but having bountiful leafage. Vegetables dried up before taking root. Animals that supplied meat and nourishment simply died in their tracks from some unknown disease; death was certain if attempted to make them into edible food.

And fourth, the pale horse, a yellowish green.[5] Its rider made known to all that its name is Death. A persona of Hades followed him. Massive killings then took place by sheer mysterious power to dispense three afflictions: their sword, an imposed famine, and infusion of wild beasts.

The sword of the horseman seemed to kill people merely by pointing, much as though by a laser firearm, though it wasn't.

As the world suffered from the effect of near starvation caused by the third horseman, the fourth horseman inflicted a true famine! Day after day, day by day for thirty days, the continued famine got so acute, nearly a billion died—starved to death.

And the wild beasts! Now that's something else again! Rats.[6] Rats carrying diseases. Diseases as during the bubonic plague in the 1700s in Europe! These rats were huge. Big rats—the size of large adult beavers. The famine of barrenness caused extended starvation for other animals but in which rats can survive, even thrive, from the flesh and blood of recently dead carcasses, of which there is abundance! Just the sight of this awful phenomenon sickened me.

Scientists who track such things estimated that one-fourth of the world's population died as a result of the three events brought upon us by these four horsemen.[7]

Not long after the fourth horseman left his wreckage and carnage behind, God revealed his power. The first of what would be five earthquakes before all is done shook the earth, the whole earth.[8] Not just earthquakes with epicenters. No, *the whole earth shook*. Hard and violent. Historical records show the quakes of yesteryears were not anything so powerful or shook so viciously as these quakes. These quakes reduced everyone's psychic to shriveled confidence. Fear? Yes, indeed. But we were not prepared for what came next. No one could have been.

Nearly simultaneously as the last of five earthquakes, the sun turned black, the moon got bloodred,[9] and the stars in the sky began to fall like fruit from trees.[10] How any person by now could have any belief in themselves would be unthinkable. Speaking of what is unthinkable, two more phenomenal events took place.

First, the sky changed. Amazingly dramatically, like it split in two, creating nothingness between the two sides, like a scroll unraveling.[11] Even Satan could not control the very sky, which he is the prince of.[12]

Then the second phenomenal event occurred. An earth-leveling force, different than an earthquake, took place, causing even the mountains and islands to slip and slide to new locations.[13]

Every class of people, whether the lowly peasant or the rich, government politicians, mighty commanders, or leaders and kings of governments all over the world sought refuge hiding in caves while calling on God to have these massive, destructive incidents to be removed from them![14]

The earth and its inhabitants were never the same since. Though all had cried out to God to end their anguish, as soon as the pestilences ceased, they cursed God for bringing such forces of destruction upon them.

40

SURVIVAL TOUGHENS UP

Steven

It's just plain awful!

All of the chaos around me—everywhere—is caused by uncontrolled lawlessness and guileless individuals, women as much as men. There is no accounting of one's behavior. No laws. No law enforcement. No order of things. Rampage and self-fulfillment is what makes things work. No one is trusted, shouldn't be trusted.

Anyone having any material worth on their person is subject to be targeted to be beaten if not killed outright, forced to relinquish what's desired. This is an everyday norm, not an exception. All through my forty-five years, I've been committed to help people. Here, in this world, I cannot. Within hours, it is reasonable to assume I would be killed by one I tried to help.

This is an earth belonging to Satan. It would have in days gone by so very foreign to me. I was a Goody Two-shoes, and laws and uprightness were my standard bearer. Here I have none of that.

In fact I have become one of those brand of people whom I detested in the world gone by. You know what? I really don't care how terrible I have to be to get what I need to survive either! There are hundreds, thousands, maybe hundreds of thousands of people far, far worse than I who before had never committed a crime and maybe could not harbor such a thing who now think nothing of taking another's life for a piece of bread or a swig of water.

I am what could be called a softy. No military, never got into a fight as a kid. I helped a buddy to safety one time when I put myself at risk. I think the bullies in this world know that for survival, I am ill-equipped. And I couldn't agree more.

To witness the four horsemen is nothing compared to only reading about them. It was indescribably horrifying. There are simply no words to relate the fear these ugly, treacherous riders and horses put into men's souls as they performed their destiny upon mankind in the whole earth! They did kill one-third of everyone living outright without provocation, just as Scripture declared that they would!

I have had enough of this. But there is absolutely nothing I can do about my plight except to lie down and wait for my slayer to come upon me. But that isn't an option. Not yet, anyway.

Talking to others, they've responded the same as me. It isn't easy to talk with anyone. There's too much distrust goin' on. It's right to worry about that. It seems to me a lot of people meet death by trusting who they thought was a friend. No one has a friend here.

As I said, it is difficult. But what does get my admiration is the mothers—the ordeals with their children they have to endure to make it through, but they do. At what price though? That is my question. Or old folks who have such little strength to begin with that meet tormenters seeking what little bread or water they might—or might not—have. Or the physically spent and feeble all around. The heartlessness I see every day has become painless to watch. I have no compunction to do anything about it, unless I want to be beaten to a pulp too. But wanting to help anyone has become nonexistent.

All the living are dependent upon a little food, a little water, enough clothes, and something overhead at night or during foul weather. That's all we ask. However, it is usually not possible without some ingenuity and physical sacrifice. When the rapture occurred, I was a muscular 205 lbs.; now I'm scrawny and probably weigh less than 140 lbs. My body is withering away before my very eyes. I have two firearms, pistols, but no ammo. I keep thinking I might find some ammo someday.

As a feeling of hopelessness engulfed me for more days than I can recall, I had wandered away from frenzied people whom I feared beyond explanation; I came across an almost hidden trail that went into dense woods. It was too enticing to resist.

Not more than fifty feet, it veered to the right, revealing hordes of No Trespassing signs nailed to trees. A few of the signs of warning had the "If you proceed, you could be shot" message. Whoever wrote the crudely scripted sign hadn't realized the threat of being shot had little meaning. Many if not most people coming across these signs would probably welcome death and that if such a message was seriously written, the writer would no doubt have something valuable they were protecting. The signs had no meaning in these times. I cautiously walked ahead.

Overgrown brush and brambles nearly shrouded the trail, altogether making passage difficult. No one I knew had a machete. Or axe. So to forge ahead branches and thick undergrowth stymied progress. That alone discouraged continuing. That is not to say the trail hadn't been traversed recently. It had. Someone had gone on within days before me. I have no idea how long it took before a clearing came into view about two hundred feet across with woods more dense and the trail continuing. I guessed the little meadow was more than a couple of miles from the rural road I had been on.

When casually striding across the field, I noticed a pathway of trampled knee-high grass that gave me proof someone was ahead of me. Was this person discovering this as I am? Or are they returning to what they have claimed to be theirs? Is this the same person who put up the signs? A tough guy or someone like me only trying to survive? A woman? A youth? An elderly? An estimated two, maybe three, miles more beyond the clearing the overgrown trail came to an end.

And so did my trek. Four people stepped out from behind dense thickets, two on both sides, holding rifles at the ready aimed at my head and heart. They were obviously a family: a teenage daughter with her father came from one side, an older teenaged son with the mother came out from the other side. All four had rifles.

They weren't quick to rid of me. While it was tense, I felt no fear as they sized me up. With a reckoning twist of his head, the father signaled for a conference of the four. Discussion. Quiet. I couldn't hear a word. The son kept his rifle trained on me as he listened then nodded agreement with whatever had been decided.

"You're the first person to come here for three weeks. No one seems to notice the entrance of the trail off the roadway. Besides, the county road is seldom used. It's too far out to offer anything. Why are you here?"

Their little confab was whether or not to accommodate me, shoot me, or get me off their property. Their accommodation was beyond being thankful!

"Trying to survive. Got away from the crowd, walked on the county road, and happen to see the trail...couldn't resist knowing where it led."

"You look depraved."

"I am, though I hadn't thought of myself as depraved."

The son spoke, "You are. You look terrible but not threatening. Am I right?"

"You are," I responded maybe too eagerly.

The mother said, "I'm Katy. We just picked a few carrots and potatoes. When's the last time—?"

"Can't remember when."

The daughter of about fourteen entered the simple conversation, "Dad, should I go pick more?"

"Two more. Only two carrots and one potato."

The son had put his rifle down but remained in his arms folded around it. "Dad, I'm going back to watch the trail."

"Follow us to our shack. You have a name?"

"Steven."

"Steven who?" Katy asked.

"Alexander."

The father said, "Somehow I think you're an educated man. Am I right?"

"You are. I was an executive with a master's in business. It didn't and doesn't do me much good in these cruel, perverted days."

"What are 'these days,' Steven?" inquired Katy.

"Are you familiar with the Christian Bible at all?"

"None of us," quipped the father.

We arrived at what he correctly described as the shack. Rickety steps, weak boards for a floor at the porch, a loosely hinged front door that jammed when either opening or closing, few furniture items, freshly cut wood for the antique woodstove, and a small dilapidated table in the tiny kitchen. They all seemed pleased to possess even this. It was inconceivable to me that this family still seemed to care about each other with so much hatred and shamefulness going on in the world. Refreshing did not describe adequately how this family affected me.

Katy continued the chat. "Are we living in the time after the rapture, Steven?"

"We are indeed, Katy. And all of the horrific results."

"I did hear what you're talking about before what you call the rapture happened," declared the father. "Oh, by the way, I'm Calab. Calab Partello. My daughter is Stacey, son is Jack."

We all went silent. Stacey's entrance broke the quiet. "Got 'em. Should I cook?"

"No, it's too early."

My heart sank. I could eat the carrots raw, dirt and all! Calab understood, broke a carrot in half, and gave me one. He nodded permission to eat it. In two bites, it was gone.

"Steven, we cannot put you up for the night. But we will let you hole up in the woodshed out back. But you must do your share of the work to stay."

"What is that? I'm grateful for the hospitality."

"Stand watch of the trail where we intercepted you."

"I can do that. When?"

"Between eleven p.m. and seven a.m. Be sure and get some shut-eye. The woodshed has a darkened corner, good for sleepin'."

For the first time in weeks too many to recall, I actually slept because there was no need to worry about my safety. Jack woke me, "It's ten thirty." I had slept five hours, still tired but feeling good as I hadn't for a very long time.

A tiny dinner of carrots and a baked potato matched that of a five-course dinner of months ago. I age very, very slowly enjoying every munch! Sips of water matched that of the finest of wine I had ever drank. In this terrible world, I was in heaven. Abruptly it ended. Eleven o'clock. "Wake me if anyone, anyone approaches during your watch. You ready?" Calab looked at me with forceful intent.

"Ready," I responded.

This place was so remote and out of the way I couldn't fathom anyone combating the overgrown brush of the trail especially at night. This was true for five consecutive nights. Trouble came during my sixth night watch. It was at 1:35 a.m. I woke Calab by the remote he'd provided. I couldn't see anyone. I heard what I believed more than one intruder by seeing occasional flickers of flashlights through the trees and brush. I knew they could not see me and surely would not see the completely darkened shack blanketed by bushes and trees.

Calab instructed me to stand back, to not interfere with their progress until a few feet beyond the thicket, then quietly follow them. By now I knew there were three stout men in black hoodies and black running pants. This is a planned entrance. No ensemble of three men would come on such a trail in the wee hours of the morning unless on a mission to inflict duress and harm, or worse. I did as Calab told me to do.

They didn't know I had been behind them for at least seventy to eighty feet before I noticed Calab coming slowly and methodically around the corner of the shack from the direction of the woodshed protected from easy sighting by the trees and shrubs.

In a flash of a moment, Calab lay dead. He stepped on a twig, a gunman fired at the sound, I heard Calab drop and struggle with life for a few moments before absolute quiet. I had been able to hide quickly before they looked about for another person. Then I saw Katy come to the door to see what had happened. I couldn't warn her as they shot her too. She died in the doorway, the door ajar.

Fear for Jack and Stacey overcame me. It was the first time I cared for anyone since the rapture. It surprised me. Two of the men went inside while the other went around back.

A few seconds later, I heard scuffling, shouting, crying out in anguish. I could only imagine what was going on! A gunshot rang out as did a death groan. Jack. Another shout of anguish—Stacey. Obviously they were raping her. Another shot rang out.

Moments later, I heard, "There's someone else around here. I checked out the woodshed, and there is reason to believe another person, male, is staked out somewhere. Should we find him?"

"Yes. Find the sucker!"

They were unsuccessful finding me before torching the shack and after throwing the bodies in a heap in the living room, leaving the front door open. I could see their every move. I will never forget the sadistic, wholly sinister expression of satisfaction on their faces as the ignited flames illuminated the room and the murderous assailants. Without pausing, they returned by way of the trail they had come.

My saddened heart could only consider what a waste. Why? Such a love that was so very rare now gone. I could think only that this was possibly the one and only love remaining in this entire, crazy world!

Now what?

The following day, another visitor showed up. He waved a white handkerchief as a peace flag. Yeah, well I had seen this before too as a deception of trust to kill for food! I didn't buy it for quite a few minutes as he explained who he was with Calab's rifle aimed at his face ten feet away.

"My name is Wayne Bradley, a neighbor of Calab's family. I heard gunshots early this morning. Who are you?"

"Steven Alexander. The Partellos allowed me to stay with them. They've been shot, and the shack is burned to the ground with the whole family inside. I swear I did not have anything to do with it."

"I know." He looked down and shuffled some dirt with his shoe as he removed his sunglasses, quietly repeating, "I know."

"How is it that you know I didn't do it?

"Three days ago I happened to be over here visiting with Jack, their son."

"I know who Jack is."

"Sorry. Sure you do." He continued, "Anyway, while we were talking, five strangers came through the brambles with threatening language and pistols drawn. There was no doubt their intent was to burglarize. A shot was fired from behind me and Jack. It was Calab who seldom takes chances when he senses the slightest danger. Being an excellent marksman, he killed one of the trespassers with a clean shot through the heart."

"And then what happened?"

"As we spun around to see where Calab had fired from, we were attacked by the other four guys without warning of any kind. They had a field day hammering us the way they did with their fists and pistol whipping before Calab fired again and killed the second victim with a bullet penetration squarely centered through the forehead. The remaining three suddenly stopped their business with Jack and me and hightailed it into a thicket out of sight."

"They shouted a clear warning to 'watch your back and keep your family always in sight because we guarantee that we will return for vengeance. No one kills our friends without payback!' They scrambled back to the trail out of sight behind the cover of bushes."

Looking toward where the shack once was, he declared, "They apparently did what they said they'd do." That being said, he turned away from me to leave without saying a word.

I stayed in this place for a few weeks that went by without any incidents during the first week. There was a vegetable garden the Partellos planted. Once I found some matches on a ledge in the woodshed, enabling me to build small fires, I did eat well.

Not a moment went by that some memory flooded my mind and filled me with sadness of the Partello family. It was the first and last time I ever remember feeling anything for anyone after the rapture.

As good as it was, I had to leave this four-acre sanctuary. After the first week alone, it became too apparent this place had too much appeal. I could not defend it by myself.

41

TRIBULATION'S FIRST HALF ENDING

Later, Maji in Jerusalem files this report

The world's moving on in spite of the huge success of the thousands of Jewish evangelists all over the earth and the devastation inflicted by the four horsemen.

Most notable is Israel's enjoyment of its new temple. One cannot adequately describe the elation it seems to bring to the temple's worshippers. Tens of thousands are journeying to Jerusalem to worship there. Hundreds of thousands have done so already. It is far and way better than their wildest dreams!

Peace between nations has lasted almost four years since Amid Baker Mohammed signed the peace treaty with Israel.

Babylon is resurrected, beginning to function, as Amerinero visualized (and how prophecy had described).[1] Ships are being unloaded and reloaded with all manner of products.[2] The mariners of the seas are ecstatic. Commerce thrives on schedule.

I have heard that the pleasures of unabated sexual mores, apostasy, and unbounding idolatry have become Babylon's main attractions.[3]

Everyone knows that at a secret, underground concealed location of Babylon are massive computer databanks humming with international data once processed in Brussels, of Interpol, the NSA of the United States, and the Hong Kong Stock Market. It is no secret that it is standing ready for the entire world's communication[4] to go through Babylon, including that of the enormous data center in Utah, USA, thanks to America for its entire collapse of its political, diplomatic, financial, and military influence.

It didn't take much time before we learned that all who worked on the city of Babylon—including architects, engineers, designers, and laborers—were treated to a lavish celebration banquet. Foods from all over the world, all sorts of drinks, and unbounding sexual attractions were provided. But during the next day's nighttime, all were killed and buried somewhere in the desert wastelands. Mohammed, he claimed, wanted no one to know where secret spaces and rooms are located.

Just as Steven had told me of Scripture prophecies of the world's condition,[5] life is valued less by the day. Martyrs are commonplace;[4] they're happening all the time with public beheadings after cruel torture.

It is common knowledge that the Antichrist's research labs in Brussels and some in Babylon are buzzing to finalize various projects feared by us, Jews and Gentiles alike, who are determined to not worship him. There are numerous hints being rumored about that carry ghastly thoughts even when I look around and see what is happening without the Antichrist's inducement. I'm assuming it will get worse.

It is way far beyond my understanding with all the judgments placed on the world for worshipping the Antichrist how anyone could. But they do worship him more than ever! I just don't get it. He's gained a massive following just during the past forty-two months!

PART V

Tribulation's Halftime

42

MAJOR TROUBLES IN
THE TEMPLE

A few days later, Maji gives us a new report

I really thought that maybe after the four horsemen were gone, that there would be some new measure of peace throughout the world. That was not to be!

The temple opens at 6:00 a.m. for worship every day. The Jewish Sabbath begins at sunset on Fridays lasting until sunset Sunday. On this particular Saturday, a militia has surrounded the temple at 5:00 a.m. That is unusual. Werner arrived at 5:55 a.m. among the hundreds of Jewish worshippers who are ready to enter the temple. That also is highly unusual; in fact, it hasn't occurred ever.

As a priest opens the doors, Werner positions his stance at the front with soldiers on either side, blocking entrance of the first worshippers who try to enter. He raises his arm, palm out to cause a halt of the would-be worshippers. The priest attempts to gain audience with Werner but is roughly denied and told to stay inside by a soldier.

Prophet Werner declares an edict: The temple is closed. You have been able to worship freely, without a disturbance of any kind for months. It has been determined that the temple will become an asset of the Antichrist beginning today—now in fact, this moment. Go back to your home, wherever it is.

Unbelieving what the worshippers had just heard, they remain in place, not moving, though talking among themselves, voicing awe of this about-face with the promise of seven years of peace. Only half that time of peace has occurred! The greatest of their understanding taking a hit is that the temple being property of the Jewish nation is taken from them! "The Antichrist promised this temple and peace to be ours, and now he turns on us," they asserted.

"Go home," the military commander called out. As he shouted his command, the soldiers in unison raised their assault rifles to a ready position. Slowly in continued incredulity, the worshippers disband, quietly walking away.

Looking back, I saw the priest being demanded to close the doors, and immediately he does as he's ordered. The temple looks desolate and void as the sunrise of this Saturday morning shines a golden hue upon it.

Every day during the following days, I joined with the crowds of desperate worshippers at the temple's closed doors. And as every day before, we are told the temple is closed and to go away. Armed soldiers remain to surround the temple day and night.

On another Saturday, three weeks later after the temple's closing, I observed four black limos drive to the front of the temple. Amid Baker Mohammed is fittingly attired in Arabic robes as he exits through the limo's door being held open for him. He hesitates to absorb the grandness and splendor of the temple in front of him before ascending the twenty-one steps to the entrance landing. The doors are opened, unwillingly, by the high priest who is accompanied by an armed escort with rifles pointed at him. Amid offers his hand, but the priest makes slight of it, refusing to accommodate a handshake with the man he both despises and now distrusts. The doors had been opened, and I could see everything as could hundreds of others.

The priest, now with the Antichrist at his side, quietly walked through the worship auditorium to the front. As the Antichrist proceeded to walk up the seven steps to the landing in front of the Holy of Holies, the priest quickly positioned his stance to block Mohammed's way at the top to squarely face him. "You are not permitted here. You are a Gentile. Only a Jew, of God's people, is allowed here."

The priest is shoved aside as the Antichrist ignores the remark and continues to the throne. Again the priest rushes ahead of the Antichrist. "You cannot be here," he cries out as his lower lip quivers.

"I can, and will," is the response.

"No!"

Again the priest is shoved aside, this time hard enough to cause him to fall clumsily against the wall. Rather than standing up, he remains on the floor praying, "Please, no," he cries out again. "No, no. Oh, God, no."

"Just then the crowd outside and myself made quite a commotion at the front doors, surging into the temple. We stopped suddenly in our tracks when seeing the Antichrist on the top step of stairs to the throne. We were overcome at the shock of seeing such an atrocity this Gentile seemed to be doing. The Antichrist knew, surely, what he was doing; he had apparently instructed the guards to permit our easy entrance at a precise moment. This is that moment. In front of Jewish witnesses, he sat on the throne reserved for the Messiah! He desecrated our throne, the Holy of Holies, the temple, the basis of our Jewish faith! I convulsed with weeping.

Within hours, the entire Jewish communities knew of this desecration by the Antichrist. He had taken the temple for his own.

He later made an announcement: "I shall now be worshipped. Your god is no longer a god. I am god. From this day forward, you shall worship me."

This is as deplorable as it is devastating. But to me not surprising because of what Steven had told me a few years ago. After all, this man *is* the Antichrist. I knew that this present episode also marked the end of the seven-year peace treaty, merely halfway into the agreement he had made.

If I remember correctly, forty-two months is halfway through the Tribulation when the particular peace treaty with Israel is broken. This halftime is not a time-out from activity, as repose in an athletic game; but the time of indexing the beginning of the next forty-two months of accelerated treachery, violence, deceit, and trickery over the entire world by the Antichrist.

It also denotes the beginning of the worst of wraths of God upon the Antichrist and his followers, the likes of which has never been known on the face of the earth, including the despicable action of the four horsemen and the terribleness they brought upon us!

❧

The city of Babylon

Spider witnessed the following story of the events immediately after the building of the city of Babylon was completed.

Dowdson had to plead for his life when his turn came to face his judgment by the Antichrist's chief prosecutor. He was told he had found favor because of his devotion in past months. The sparing of his life had a caveat however. For the privilege of living, he had to swear continued allegiance to the Antichrist no matter what might befall him in the future. Without concern, he accepted and avoided his brutal slaying. Little did he know the high price he'd have to pay for that decision. Often he would long for the chance to reverse his choice as death would be better.

He did not want to take the path of those who had a hand in the building of Babylon! The day following the banquet of celebration for those who had an integral part of its construction disappeared. The privileged Dowdson later come across a secret file outlaying how the deaths of those people were accomplished. It was a scheme copied from ancient Egypt by Pharaohs: they were taken to the end of a long tunnel they had built and entered an elaborately appointed conference room at the tunnel's end. Unsuspecting as the agent of Mohammed who accompanied them left the room after a short speech of complimentary acknowledgements, they soon realized this room would be their doom when the clank of a heavy, solid lock was heard. There was no way out as they suffocated to death.

Prophet Werner assigned Dowdson to file a report on the activities of Babylon to the Antichrist. A week later, this is the report he filed.

From miles away, as I traveled the thirty-five miles with an associate of Mohammed to

Babylon from Mecca, I could see the monstrous cargo cranes piercing the sky as they unloaded thousands of containers from ships. That was to be the last visual I would have of this city's immense layout as we entered a downward passageway into the bowels of the city. Even here there is evidence of extravagance to demonstrate any pleasurable craving available with use of explicit video screens everywhere.

As we rode an elevator up four levels to Level One, an announcement, obviously a recording by a woman with a sultry tone, is heard: "Welcome to Babylon. Please touch the screen with your forefinger and then your thumb for identification purposes. The results will determine the status of activities to which you're entitled so that your patronage has been a time well spent and you'll always have pleasant memories after your departure." We did as requested by the voice.

From the moment we stepped from the elevator until nine hours later when arriving at the elevator to return home, I for one was treated so completely in a manner that whetted every impulse to do evil, see evil things, and lavishly enjoy sensually satisfying activities. That is for the most part.

I stumbled upon one theater I could not endure to witness all the way through a performance. It was debauchery at its worse. A Bible verse that my mother had read to me a few times before she was taken away came to mind as I watched the horrible scene: "cargos… of bodies and souls of men are brought to this city." I'm wholly convinced that the victims were Christians. What did I watch happen? The methodic hacking away of a victim's body parts by two assailants, who had paid to do the carnality, until death while an audience of people who paid large sums of money per seat cheered as their twisted, perverted sense of wanton pleasure was satisfied! This continued on schedule every hour with a new audience, new victim, and new assailants—twenty-four every day. There was no lack of participants.

He informed me also that from an enclosed glass cage, the future victims were forced to see what is to be their nightmare death, surrounded on three sides of their cage by onlookers who paid to sordidly watch their agony. Many of these onlookers would become part of the audience of the hideous display of killings. My guide told me this was not an exception; it's the norm program in other theaters if that's what one wants in this city.

After I got over that visual ordeal, I witnessed the buying and selling of goods I couldn't have dreamed about by such wealth changing hands that I had never seen! Not only the wealthy either! Known kings and rulers and dictators from all over the world congregated in this city to participate in every kind of sensual immoral act that evil men could contrive.

These sins of the flesh, worse than of Sodom and Gomorrah in historic days, accelerated into diverse acts of depraved perversion for great amounts of money or unrestrained acts of compensation. The decadent acts I saw made me realize how evil Satan has caused this world to be because God withdrew his presence from earth, leaving Satan to do as he wills.

Babylon is in sharp contrast to what is happening all over the world as simple survival is complex, and for many, it is futile to stay alive! The city is such a waste. Tons of money is spent on selfish pleasures of the senses including unlimited drinking and illicit drugs by the wealthy while just the finding of a sliver of bread or sip of water is a treasure trove for all others over the entire world!

Dowdson's report is submitted by Werner; Amid Baker Mohammed read it and smiled as Werner looked on.

Finished reading, he gazed upon his prophet. "It's what I hoped it would be. This city is living up to what I wanted. The important people now have a place to go for untethered pleasure and to purchase or sell whatever goods thy have or want. There isn't anything like providing great pleasure mixed with the ability to create great wealth in a single place to win favor and loyalty. By Babylon, we're doing exactly that with the already wealthy elite, kings, and world political leaders, even to the extent of worshipping me. I could care less about the down-and-out poor across the globe except that they know who to worship—me!"

"Inform Mr. Dowdson he can have anything he desires. I will see that he has it." A messenger is sent who is to tell Dowdson the news, only to find him alone near death from his own hand as a failed suicide attempt, in a near coma condition and unattended in a decrepit alley filled with filth and numerous rotting corpses. A dull knife lay beside him. Torn tissue at both wrists now closed by dried blood revealed his effort to die. Reporting this, Mohammed gave no reply, only a nod of his acknowledgement, except this: "Should Dowdson survive and come to us, make sure he understands he's mine."

43

ANTICHRIST'S NEW TOOL: 666

More from Spider

Amid received a text from Werner:

> *Come to the Main Theater for the planned demonstration. We are ready when you are.*

Werner receives his reply:

> *Will attend @ 2:30*

I received a text along with Dowdson:

> *Join me at 2:30 today in the Main Theater; RA*

This theater is an elaborate video presentation auditorium seating seventy-five. It is filled to capacity. The screen's activity is showing a middle-aged, nondescript male walking about in his search for food, water, and whatever else he might find beneficial.

"We have randomly selected one of the people we know who has declined to side with us. He has been forced to wear the device you see on his left wrist, we call it the DT-II device. A cameraman, at a short distance, is shadowing him the past few days. His name is Thomas Keene.

"You notice that Thomas is frequently scratching his skin near the location of the device and occasionally will try to pull it free. We have purposely caused a slight itching to prompt attempts to remove it. The adhesive is not skin irritant, however. We have done this to assure the adhesive will be durable when we issue the devices to every person whether or not they choose the 666 mark.

"We can communicate with Thomas anytime desired, but unlike this short distance, anywhere in the world through our satellite system."

He demonstrates.

"By the way, all I need to do is key in his ID number to know where he is located. This feature functions everywhere in the entire world with anyone. The device will vibrate and buzz, quite annoyingly to catch his attention. It also transmits his pulse rate. This way we can know if he's alive or not. When not alive, we can cause the device to detonate, thereby eliminating a corpse."

As Werner describes the contact, Thomas looks at the screen of his DT-II device and listens to Werner.

"This is AW. I need you to walk in the northerly direction to the next intersection. There you're to cross the street at your right to walk to the end. You will see an alley on your left. Take it about twenty paces and wait for further instructions."

Thomas continues to the intersection, walks east to the street's end, takes the alley to the north, and walks exactly twenty-five paces before stopping, standing and waiting as told.

"Now, watch this," instructs Werner.

The subject, Thomas, has now stood where told for twenty seconds before exploding into nothingness.

"We have the ability to detonate the device to annihilate anyone we so desire who is wearing it, and remember, whether or not they are wearing the 666 mark, we have total control!"

Amid is held momentarily in amazement of Werner's innovations. He realizes he will acquire total control of every person over the entire globe; maybe too the 144 thousand evangelists who continue to be chalking up amazing success. He remains to believe even they will eventually bow down to worship him

"Once again you have demonstrated why Lucifer has selected you for my prophet and forerunner. We shall indeed do many great things together in the near foreseeable future. Speaking of that, I want to go further into the details of your responsibilities in that regard. How about in three days?"

"Is ten a.m. okay?"

The following day, the Antichrist is busy planning the use of his powers and those of the Prophet at his. Again, as before, the screen of his communication appliance illuminates as Lucifer scrolls another message.

> *You are preparing earth's control for yourself just as I like. At every chance I am empowering you to do as you can to turn people away from God and onto yourself—and me. You and the Prophet are putting the powers of deceit to magnificent use! I comment you of your resurrection that was masterfully done! Sorry you had to go into the abyss before your return to the living.*
>
> *As you can imagine, Radolfo Amerinero, God has gone too far in these times. He's destroying our world. Famines, loss of water, mountains eliminated, the heavenly bodies masked over, earthquakes, hailstorms, wild beasts, and human lives done away with—when does all of this stop?*
>
> *I am paying a visit to heaven to revile against God, his angels, and his saints. I'm bringing a host of my angels with me as I anticipate God will have his ready to combat with Michael the Archangel in command.[1] By defeating them, I will have audience with God![2] I want full control. I do not have that control as long as God remains in power, and I am where I'm at. I aim to change things. I am going there for one purpose: to confront him.[3]*
>
> *Keep up your good work, Radolfo.*

And so it was.

However, Satan[4] and his demonic angels warred against Michael and his angels, the forces of Michael's host of angels were decisive. It was a victory so complete that although Satan had come to have battle with God, he couldn't get past Michael's protection. He and all his evil creatures were tossed out from the presence of heaven, forced to leave in absolute, reprehensibly shamed defeat. Satan returned seething with anger and set on revenge.

His anger is tenfold more intense than when he was first thrown from God's presence for being a rebellious angel before the earth was formed. Rebellion? The world hasn't seen how intense his rebellion will be!

Another message from Lucifer.

> *They in heaven thought me to be terrible before my last encounter with Gabriel?*
>
> *They haven't seen anything yet! My fury upon all those on the face of the earth who will not worship me will pay for this!*
>
> *If I cannot have my way in heaven, I will have my way over the entire earth—beginning right now! So begin what you have devised! You, Amerinero, are to make life totally and precariously dangerous for them who choose God rather than me. They will pay with appalling risks of suffering torturous deaths and discomfort of the kind never known.*
>
> *I bestow upon you and your prophet all of my power to demand and make obedience to me for the entire world to worship me. That is your mission.*

❦

Now the Antichrist is endowed with all the evil powers of demonic deceit of Satan's pent-up hazardous nature. God has provided Satan an open door to do as he wishes, inflict pain, suffering, and death—but with certain boundaries.

A battery of contrivances to affect the world's population is thought of.

Amid Baker Mohammed, the Antichrist, and Alex Werner, the False Prophet, takes immediate action on their two technological fronts that showcase their talent and promotes their cause: satellites and the Internet. Combined, the two technologies will enable worldwide control, instant communication, and other forms of rule in ways yet to be conceived. They set about to achieve their goals quickly. Their premise: whatever man has created or devised, another person or group can alter, improve, replace, or upgrade it—or take it over!

They already possess the finest minds in the world to make it happen.

So they thought.

Israel has been at the forefront of the same technologies since the 1980s. Their expertise in partner with the USA's first ten launchings of satellites produced uncanny successes. Lines of security codes are imbedded as are all satellites jointly written with NASA engineers. Following that they launched their own satellites with improved groups of encrypted codes for security against tampering.

The Prophet's recent launchings and placements of satellites were enabled by funding with the new finances made possible from their oil reserves discovered in recent times. The deep financial trove allowed the implementation of newly developed encryption sets of code written in a computer language not formerly known. If tampering were tried, it would be like attempting to speak to someone who doesn't know a lick of English. Upon detection of an attempt, the line of communication that gained attention thus far is promptly cut off then traced to the offending source.

During the peace agreement, now broken, Israel sensed it would be in their interest to assure their encryption language was not contaminated. They did this by launching a sucker satellite. The language is flawed, that is, in a manner to permit limited tampering to reveal how far into the language an outsider might be.

As it turns out, this precaution was not all that necessary because the new language was far too sophisticated to be broken into in a short time. It trumped all that the Antichrist technologists were able to accomplish. Alicia, the whiz kid programmer, was also baffled by it.

44

VILENESS INCREASES

The Spider reports

On the appointed day, the Antichrist and the False Prophet are in their most significantly prodigious meeting of all time.

"Lucifer has now placed us in absolute, full control of the world," asserts the Antichrist. "We, you and I, have one mission that together we will prevail. I am making clear that in our relationship, you are my prophet and I shall refer to you as Prophet from this day forward. Do you recall a Bible fable about John the Baptist, the storied forerunner of Christ? That's a great idea. You will be my forerunner."

"To what cause," asks the Prophet, "will be my top priority?"

"A life of persuasion based upon the most effective methods and manner of deceit you can contrive! Lucifer has charged us with the great responsibility to capture and enforce the world's attention to worship him," responds the Antichrist.

"That should be easy. There is unrest everywhere ever since the troublesome Believers were taken into the heavens they once alluded to! You, my dear Mohammed, can easily be the world's solution to all its problems."

"There are numerous famines going on, merciless enough for people to starve to death. The masses have no money, and even if they did, money means nothing. Just as Hitler promised relief, so can we. Plus, the world's water supply is at impossible levels for more than eighty-five percent of the world's population. God has seen to that during the past three-and-more years!"

"So do you possess enormous powers, Prophet? You must begin using those powers as you see fit to accomplish your mission. The time has come for you to use the results of the various projects your teams have been working on," the Antichrist clarifies.

"Which do we start implementing first?" Prophet asks.

"Get my likeness to the temple as quickly as possible. Tonight if possible. Put it seated on the throne with full animation control. This will inaugurate the beginning of Lucifer's agenda he has entrusted to us. Can you do that?"

"Sure. Done. What's next?"

"The 666 mark is third on our list. I will tell you about it after telling you what is second on my list. I want that you'll carry out the distribution of the telltale wrist device while the mark is being applied. How soon will you be ready to manage this mandatory exploitation?"

"Within the month, I imagine. It will take two weeks or so for the setup time, and it's thought to take a couple of weeks to get the word out with instructions and designate the reporting locations where this activity is to be achieved."

"That's fine. It fits into Lucifer's scheduling. You can launch worldwide notices tomorrow? Can that be done?"

"Yes, it shall. We have been preparing for this moment during the past three years."

"And the wristwatcher device?"

"It's ready as well."

"Fine. I guess we're ready then!"

The Antichrist hesitates as he looks upon Prophet with concern, tipping the Prophet that there is something else on his mind.

"What about the second item on your agenda?"

"Using your magic, I want you to kill me. Make it look like the real thing. Put me on public display on the next day to let observers think I've been embalmed. Then three days later, I want you to perform a resurrection of me. We are going to copy what Christ did many centuries ago. This should cause an open floodgate of worshippers of me the world over. Don't you agree?"

"So *that's* what you meant a few weeks ago when you suggested that I practice my magic show!"

"Oh, you remember? Yes, it is. Can you pull this off? Remember that the most evil angel of all, Lucifer, has given you unheard-of powers of signs, wonders, and miracles!"[1]

"I can do this…but are you sure about it?"

"I've never been more sure about anything than right now!"

"When is your 'death' to occur?"

"In four days, on the steps of the new temple, I am scheduled to give a talk in Jerusalem. We'll both be dressed in Arabic robes so the audience won't have a clue it is you. From the side you'll rush up to me and slay me there. You'll have our people to take you into custody and me to an ambulance. We'll meet in private afterward. The next day, you will place me on public display with my holograph image."

Antichrist's Death and Copious Resurrection

During the following three days, the Prophet practices his deed with actors. It turns out to be a mistake. One of the actors swaps the collapsing theatrical sword used to fake a stabbing with a look-alike, real sword. Prophet hadn't noticed the switch. The blow to the Antichrist's head bled excessively, shocking Prophet when he realized the blade did not retract. The fake killing became real. He's taken away while the Antichrist receives medical attention by ambulance personnel who pronounce him dead on arrival, a DOA body.

Later, Prophet went to be with the body, but it had disappeared,[2] mysteriously reappearing hours later. As instructed, he puts the body on public display with the head wound clearly visible and obvious that that is what had killed him. "An act gone wrong," authorities said. He waited three days.

With cameras linked to the satellite system for anyone and everyone the world over to see.[3] Prophet moved his arms and hands in a manner of a magician over the Antichrist's still, lifeless body. A large crowd had gathered around to view what was billed as "a theatrical performance above all performances ever accomplished or acclaimed." Slowly the body of the Antichrist began to move, at first, before sitting up. People were stunned at the sight. "But the injury! It was too severe to be faked! He truly had to be resurrected!" they acclaimed. They could see the fatal head wound.[4]

Then the resurrected Antichrist stood, thanked Prophet as though nothing had happened out of the ordinary. Instantly those in attendance went to their knees and worshipped the two of them. Prophet deflected all the attention he received upon the Antichrist.[2] Mission accomplished!

Why not believe in the Antichrist? From that moment on, no one doubted the Antichrist and mesmerized into a complete worship of the man who had been resurrected, just like Christ long ago. Only now they had witnessed it.

45

ANTICHRIST'S NEW WORLD ORDER

Steven informs us of the events taking place

All during the following month with use of the Antichrist's satellite system, announcements are cast on the hour, of a list of regional locations everyone is required to report and when, according to alphabetical last names; lists are relative to the last known addresses. The notices include what to expect.

To have a mark placed on every forehead or the back of the right hand, that without such a mark, buying or selling anything is prohibited; and second, everyone is to wear on their left wrist a device like a wrist iWatch linked to the Antichrist's satellite system. Accompanying the announcements are reminders that death by torture can be expected by anyone who does not report within two days of the assigned date.

I remembered Revelation 19 in detail. Memory served me well as I recalled what was *really* going on. Yes, it is true no one can buy or sell without the 666, but its true meaning is that it also identifies whether one will worship the Antichrist or not! When wearing the 666 tattoo, one is declaring allegiance and endorsement to worship the Antichrist. Another declaration takes place too. Also by choosing to wear the 666, which Scripture calls the mark of the beast, the wrath of God will be brought upon them though the wraths are intended for the Antichrist and Prophet.

Wearing the wrist device on the left wrist is a new idea John the apostle could not have imagined. I can understand why however. It will make the Antichrist's knowledge of everyone person alive easier than any other method. GPS and one-way method of communication to control large masses of people makes this wrist device plausible.

People are counting down their days of their reporting. A mixture of fear and anxiety for many has partially taken away the reality of harshness in the daily struggles to survive.

As for me, I decided I cannot accept the mark. Nope, I can't. I have come to know that what God says he will do exactly what he will do that. I realized that it would be far easier to live without the mark than to bear the agony of God's wrath. Besides, buying and selling is extremely difficult already!

❧

The day for my reporting at 9:30 a.m. arrived.

My assigned reporting station is just two miles away. I have no idea how it could be known where I am because I've been completely nomadic. Because I had already made the decision to not wear the 666, each step toward my reporting equally intensified my fear of what will happen when I refuse to allow the tattoo. My heartbeat rate became dangerous. In fact, if the truth be known, I feared the result of my decision so much I seriously considered changing my mind. But I had to look at the bigger picture.

A long line had developed, but it moved along quite more rapidly than anyone expected. I got at what was called the decision and application spot at 9:10, being told that as long as I was reporting twenty minutes early, I could be processed earlier. That was fine with me. I wanted it to get over as quickly as possible.

After declaring my name into a machine as instructed, one of the three men doing this business informed me the wrist device and the number 666 were impregnated with my name and a special serial number to cause a reliable, mandatory ID. Two men strong-armed me while attaching the iWatch with a sticky substance onto the back of my left hand while asking me where I wanted the 666 placed—on my forehead or the back of my right hand.

"Not at all," I stated. "I have the choice to refuse as so informed in the daily announcements, right? And I say no."

"We have another stupid," one of them announced before commenting to me. "You'll be having that worthless sign on your forehead supposed to be God's protection for Believers. Am I wrong?" He answers his rhetorical question, "No, of course I'm not."

I knew the 144 thousand evangelists had it, but I hadn't looked in a mirror for a long, long time. "Here's another," he shouted toward who I began to know as an enforcer. "Another idiot," he shouted again as he drove his fist into my face hard enough to feel like he broke a cheekbone, causing a profuse nosebleed; then his other fist seemed to tear apart my innards with swift, breath-taking impact.

With that, another enforcer with unnecessary brute force angrily shoved me into a band of people who were being kept quiet by surrounding militia. These people had also refused to wear the mark. They also had the seal from God, a Hebrew inscription that I did not understand except for its meaning. I assumed that the seal would appear the moment a soul accepted Christ as their savior. Some of the captives were attempting to remove the wrist device, but the adhesive the devices were attached tore skin when doing so.

I watched the processing of others before me and who came later. When the subjects indicated where to place the mark, a flexible tape about two inches long and half an inch wide was pressed onto the desired location before peeled away, taking less than five seconds. The numeral 666 remained looking like an indelible branding ink. When thinking about how many reporting stations there must be around the world, millions an hour could be serviced in this manner.

We were kept there in a tight grouping, standing, disallowed to move until 10:00 p.m. They had lighted the location to continue processing into the dark, early night hours. Before 10:00 p.m., enough military-type trucks arrived that we were loaded onto and driven quite a few miles to a large warehouse. Men and women were separated. By midnight the warehouse was crammed full of unkempt, unbathed people, like me, who caused the air to be nearly impossible to breathe with a strong BO. We were quite a sight, what with all of us in scraggly, dirty clothes—the best available in these times. It was surprising to me that the 666 worn by the enforcers actually glowed in the dark with a bluish hue easily seen from as far away as ten feet.

The word went out that the first numeral *6* is magnetic and contains all of a person's bio.

It was then that I realized why other methods, such as microchips or laser zapped IDs, as was thought possible couldn't be used. Whether one wore the 666 or not, it must be readily recognized from a few feet away and is illuminate at night if it is to satisfy the purposes of the Antichrist. This ID's function is much more than the ability to buy or sell, which is merely a side effect of not having the mark. It is to identify exactly whose side one has declared and who they worship: Satan or God. God already knows on whose side one is; he does not need an identifier. The Antichrist requires an ID method to preserve loyalty integrity, although it's forced!

At 6:00 a.m., after the night's long hours, we were all freed. I for one had not had a bite to eat or sip of water during the past thirty hours, and even that, I was lucky! I think we were kept in the warehouse as an example of treatment to expect in the future. Most of us thought we'd all be killed at the edge of a mass grave, but we weren't. Some voiced they would rather die now than to face what was sure to be coming in all of the future days. Already some wished they had accepted to wear the mark of the beast.

I had to walk twelve miles back, feeling very faint; all the way every step was a struggle, including only skimpy protection from the damp, cold morning weather. I had stashed some food and water buried under a tree among its root system, nearby my latest lair. It lair had been ravished during my short absence, as I had expected. But was good that I buried my reserves; fortunately they remained intact.

By memory of reading the Book of Revelation before the rapture, I knew this is the beginning of the worst ever of times the world will be subjected! That is what the Bible had warned all of us about. I wish I had heeded its message when I had the chance!

46

REFUSING THE 666

Steven continues to report after rejection of the mark

Daily the violence of man against another because of the subversion of evilness has escalated exponentially from the moment of the Event.

But now the violence is developing into something more grotesque by the week and more prolific and hideous by the month. Surprisingly, it is fast being turned into the "us versus them" scenario. But I will tell you that torturing those who are not wearing the mark is always imposed, day or night!

I cannot fail to say what is sometimes used to torment people before their welcome of death. Can you imagine the anguish when one is confronted with knowing their flesh is no difficulty when farm implements and dangerous machines of industry are used as instruments to accomplish sadistic acts upon them? It is no longer a matter of being merely bludgeoned to death. Satisfaction has heightened since those days to unspeakable levels of torture! Sometimes the defilement continues after a subject's death, counted upon when resisting torture by assailants.

Finding a place to hide from those whose singular mission seems to be to find us who're not wearing the mark is not only risky but often unlikely. Just the search for food and water, an ongoing pursuit, takes away any chance of peace. The natural instinct of survival is devoid of any serious consideration when simply giving up and dying is a better option. I must admit that I often have that thought.

So I cannot hide. Nor can I be where people have congregated to avoid our continual tormentors. They, as me, are also searching for any little drops of water or garbage-level food for their survival. As with many others, we choose to be alone or maybe team up with one or two others, which trust is now mandatory. A mistake of trusting can mean death too.

Every once in a while, someone more kindly than our prosecutors wearing the 666 could sell us food or water, if they have it, but face the likelihood of themselves being killed for selling to us. Besides, the price for water is exorbitant—a price I do not have any possession to trade, being that money is absolute worthless. Money cannot be drank, eaten, worn, or used as a weapon—the substances needed for survival!

❦

The Antichrist has come up with a new enticement.

It's a wafer. It's promoted everywhere. It is promised that the wafer will reduce the need for the nutritional value of food and will quench thirst. That's quite compelling to me and others in our plight. How to get an unlimited supply of the wafer? Wear the mark of the beast.

It's the side effects of the wafer I heard is a potential killer. Eating the wafer has an effect on the brain in some way that reduces, if not eliminates, the signals of hunger and thirst. Relying on the wafer tricks one to believe they're okay only to have their bodies disintegrate before their very eyes. Before the return to real food and water, it is too late for resuscitation to any form of energy. Even walking is an ordeal. And walking, being ambulatory, is needed for survival whether one is wearing the 666 or not. No walk, no food or water.

In my search for food and water, I have to be ever mindful of the predators who could be observing me. It's like being a rabbit in an open field searching for food while a hawk is hovering above is about to strike to gain his own need for food. Just as quick as the hawk's snatching a rabbit, I could be taken captive unawares without any strength to ward the adversary off me. Because of the lack of body nutrients, my steps are short, I'm in constant pain, and drained of energy. Running to avoid capture is out of the question. Being in my forties and of ill health certainly doesn't help me. There is no being held accountable. I now fully realize how important our penal code and judicial systems were to keep order in our societies back then before the rapture. That's gone now. Done. No more.

In one of the sanctuaries, I met Aaron. He was a former naval mercenary. He gave me a spare dagger with an eight-inch, double-edged, pointed spear blade. Along giving me the dagger, he showed me how to use it by taking advantage of the element of surprise. In that slight moment of hesitation from the surprise, a quick thrust of the blade under the mouth in the soft tissue between the jawbone will kill an assailant. The blade is long enough to reach the brain if I drive the dagger upward to the hilt. I found on four occasions that it works and without requiring much strength—only quickness. Aaron was right about how painful the death is and how disabling it is if death is not immediate. That I witnessed before fleeing any way I could. The dagger is kept in a hastily sewn pocket hidden inside both of the two pieces of garments worn as coats, a concealed weapon.

Worship of the Antichrist—the reverence, respect, and honor contrived by masterful deceit is flourishing, just as God's prophecies had told. The Prophet, a false prophet I might add, has indeed turned out to gain an intense magical draw upon people so strong that I would not believe it if I hadn't seen his forceful sway with my own eyes! He is everywhere—on satellite, in stadiums, conventions, and all sorts of spontaneous gatherings of thousands upon thousands, performing all kinds wonders and miracles. When recalling Scripture, it is no surprise why the Prophet is successful to create Antichrist's accepted appeal so dynamically to bring millions to worship him.

I do not have any regret of the decision I made when I observe the wrath of God upon those who are wearing that idolatrous number, although we who are without the 666 in some way or another are singled out and tortured or constantly abused every day because of it. We know we are a continual target of the Antichrist's hatred and subject to dreadful persecution.

Twice a day the world is shown thirty-minute success videocams of Babylon by the Antichrist's satellite broadcasting studio through the DT-II pad. The city is flourishing on every level.

The port is functioning possibly better than designed to accomplish. Huge container ships are unloaded and reloaded faster than at any such port the world had ever known. An immense water turnaround in the Red Sea is featured to hasten the in-out time of the ships, swung around by highly powered tugboats.

A specific gigantic buoyed marina is marked out to provide ten ships an anchorage to allow their crews to enjoy the vices offered by the city. A video is entertainingly narrated with nasty, erotically suggestive imagery to entice viewers of its abundant immorality of appalling vices. Kings and rulers of the world are often seen in the videos, not just ordinary people. All who enter and participate are wearing the 666.

Another video is shown three times a day revealing to the world Babylon's financial prowess and its world control of the currency. I remembered how many believed that the word *Babylon* meant a code for financial world control. It is true. Also true is the fact that Babylon is the location where financial control of the world now originates rather than Brussels, New York, Hong Kong, or Tokyo. Before the construction of the city of Babylon, when Babylon was a mere code word, is when the details of the Antichrist began the world financial control being put into place away from—but connected to—Brussels.

During between time, videos continually show the vile, nauseating torture inflicted upon those not wearing the mark if not outright public beheadings. These are not quick decapitations with a swift swing of a sword or axe. No. the decapitations shown on these videos are much worse than the slaughtering of an animal, a slow and slicing or sawing severance. The flaunting of these videos causes disgust, nausea, and heightened fear for even the stronghearted.

But it certainly does not require videos to know what happens to those wearing the 666 when God takes action upon them; we witness this all around us at every strike. It is war between God and

Satan with humankind being kicked about as a soccerball with seemingly unbearable painful results.

It is understood that by accepting the mark, one has sealed their destiny to share in the wrath of God because they committed to worship Satan through the Antichrist.

For them life is worse than death itself. Often it is the fear of the pain involved in dying rather than death itself! In these times for these people, there is no difference; there will be pain both in the dying as well their death.

I remember something really significant when God's wrath will be completed. It's to happen now.

And did it ever!

The terror of God's wrath is justified, I concluded as I recalled a Scripture of John's revelation: the opening of the heavenly temple[3] revealing the Ark of the Covenant where the Ten Commandments are put in safekeeping.

Each of the first three commandments—no other gods before me, no graven images before me, and do not take the name of the Lord your god in vain—are being profusely violated by worshipping the Antichrist, the False Prophet, and his imagery.

Maji offered this report

No one seems to know how what I am about to tell you took place. What we do know is that a smoke billowed out of the temple at a time the Antichrist was seated on the temple's throne. We visibly saw him run from whatever it was causing the smoke in the temple and swiftly got into his limo waiting for him. He did not return.[1]

During the months remaining of the Tribulation, I knew from Scripture there were an assortment of curses involving personal ordeals and earth-changing plagues from God to be delivered upon those wearing the mark, those who worship the Antichrist. Steven and I had read this and discussed these events often. As foretold, the scourges came without warning.[2]

Our lives are certainly better than those wearing the 666, what with God's wrath poured out upon them, but we cannot fully escape the torturous acts of the Antichrist. It's as though we're held responsible for the ordeals they're being subjected to. They are blaming God; it stands to reason they blame us too.

The four absolute necessities to live at the very barest are food, water, clothes, and shelter. When push comes to shove, I can live, as now, in unwashed ragged clothes and sleep and suffer without protection. But no one can go long without some sort of food and water. This's what's tough without wearing the mark. The DT-II's tattling doesn't help either, registering our every action, even when relieving ourselves.

As though that isn't frightful enough, I have to always, and I mean always, look over my shoulder to avert being beaten or taken aside to have my head removed. And believe me, worse means *much* worse. Nearly unbearable, so bad in fact I would wish for death to take me away from all of this.

To be killed as a martyr would be intolerably painful to die at the hands of the wicked. How vicious has it become? No one could accurately guess how many different torturous ways, as I said earlier, that have been imposed upon us without the 666 to cause death by those who are wearing the mark of Satan. The brutality recorded in history can compare to the anguish of dying in this time, even when one considers the ways of torture in centuries coming out of the Dark Ages!

During the five months after becoming a Believer, somehow, I made my way six hundred miles west where I happened upon available opportunity in a sanctuary on a one-hundred-acre farm in Wyoming. There were twenty-two people occupying the large farmhouse. Everyone pitched in with the work mostly of raising a small yield of crops. The water is sternly rationed. The crops are hardly adequate. Jim Severson is voted leader; for the past six months, voting occurring each month. A tribunal provides decisions of conflicting viewpoints.

It works amazingly well. Everyone realizes how valuable it is that the sanctuary continues to work well. It turns out that nineteen of the residents have become Believers in recent months. All of us on the farm are not wearing the mark. Gradually I regained most of my strength. I felt more rejuvenated than what I actually was.

Six men stand guard with loaded 12-gauge, double-barreled shotguns 24/7, who are rotated among fourteen men. They have shot and buried nearly twenty intruders during the past year who attempted to muscle onto the farm or rob something.

All this tranquility among the turbulent times of the Tribulation came to an end in October, almost three years after the Antichrist claimed the temple for himself.

I was awakened by what I heard, I think, six almost simultaneous shots. The guards are dead at their posts! As I jumped up and out of the sleeping bag, a dozen militialike soldiers in uniforms I'd never seen before mobbed the farmhouse. Each wore the mark. We all knew why we were being raided.

They were the Antichrist's task force, the Enforcers, who within a few moments took over the farm and threatened to kill us also if we did not leave immediately. We left. That's the way it is. But not all of us could leave. They shot and killed three children "as a warning" they called it. The parents were forced to leave their kids' corpses lying on the floor unattended.

I kept migrating to an unknown location; enduring several malicious beatings for no reason other than not wearing the 666. The dagger saved me another five times.

47

FIFTH AND SIXTH SEAL JUDGMENTS

Maji relates to new events

Up to now it has become an everyday experience to see the killings of those who have refused to wear the mark. Clearly they became martyrs for not worshiping the Antichrist.

Gradually the frequency of killings became notably increased as well as the methods to mete out the hundreds of slaughtering a day as methods became more grotesque. It became just too sickening to take notice. No matter how callused one's heart might be, this is not anything you can get used to! It's especially sickening when children and teens, the feeble, and elderly are the slaughtered—shown live on video—for no reason other than they're not wearing the mark.

Steven responds

Maji's report is about what Scripture says about the *Fifth Seal*. It says that those who have been martyred all through history are pleading with God to end the massacre of Believers and bring judgment on those who have caused their death and responsible for the current deaths occurring. In gracious response, God gave them white robes as an acknowledgement and gave them over to rest and wait for the fullness of time.

The fullness of time would come about when the number of martyrs will be achieved. Only God knew the time or the purpose of this.

I can tell you this. It won't be but a few months more! The wickedness on the earth has turned upon us who are not wearing the 666 with increased brutality by the day. The fear for our lives has heightened far beyond what we once experienced not too long ago. All of us now stand out in a crowd both day and night. There is nothing we can do but try to hide. And hiding anywhere has developed into all but impossible!

At night is the greater problem. Somehow we must sleep. That of course is when we're most vulnerable to be discovered. The trick is to become a silhouette. At least we do not have the lighted hue of a mark to reveal us in the dark. But just as potentially lethal, we do have the DT-II to inform where each of us is located.

We can only hope our ID is not called up by the Antichrist's surveillance team assigned to their assassination task. If so, we will know it all too soon and without any warning whatsoever! We also know we can be blown to bits without any knowledge what hit us. This, however, is not my biggest concern. I would rather be blown to bits than be subjected to the painful ordeals before death that I have informed you!

I constantly pray for God's fulfilling number to come to pass very soon. It is my only hope. And I might be one of them.

The Sixth Seal

*Again, both Maji and Steven describe
the events of the Sixth Seal*

Maji

A lengthy, continuous bone-rattling thunder and frequent sky-laden bolts of lightning lasting for hours announces another show of God's force is on its way producing yet another earthquake. It's my humble observation that through history, God often begins or ends events with earthquakes. And that is precisely what happened!

Steven

Just as Maji experienced, the intense thunder, lightning, and earthquake[1] where he had filed his report, I experienced them here in what used to be the United States; and if I felt them here, so did all the other continents of the world. The heavens surrounding the whole of earth opened up with its ferocious warning for all to experience a snippet of God's power. I too knew the quake was indeed a notice of what's coming next.

Following the earthquake, the sun turned black, the moon became bloodred, the stars began to fall as though a tree shaken of its fruit, and totally unbelievably the sky receded like a scroll as mountains once fixed in position and islands of the sea are removed from their places.[2] What once, just moments before the quake, was reliable now faltered. Darkness of night pervaded daytime. The moon became a scary bloodred, causing the continuously darkened sky. But how can I describe what it's like to see the sky rolled back after a shower of falling stars everywhere?

Everyone who hadn't or isn't following God and have chosen to worship the Antichrist cried out to have the mountains fall on them to take them away from all of this, but to no avail.

The resolve of every human being is tried, regardless of whom they're following: God or the Antichrist. If one is following God a continuing trust, most surely heightened. If the Antichrist, they're shouting and cursing God all the more.

48

THE TWO WITNESSES

The Spider, while told to be in the company of the Antichrist, made these observations of Amid Baker Mohammed's conflict with two old men in clothes of what was worn centuries ago. Rarely did I see the Antichrist in attire other than a dark-blue business suit, a pull-over neck sweater, and a golden chain with a coiled serpent dangling over his chest. Never during the time that I have seen the two old men were they ever separated, always being in the company with each other.

By now, for the Antichrist, it is these two old men who are caus-ing him his most anxiety even after more than three years![1] They are out-and-out pesky disturbances that the public had been listening to after all this time. Mohammed put the word out to kill them with a substantial reward upon proof of their death. Sooner, the better! But try as he might, it has not worked to have them killed. He sent spies into the crowd, where as an example, a shooter was arranged to kill the two preachers. Two shots were fired. The whine of the bullets could be heard, by some, on their way to their target only to boomer-ang, killing the shooter with two fatal wounds into his chest, verified later to be the same bullets he had fired.

The Antichrist could not believe the report by the spies. He repeated the tactic with different weapons. The same result; the assail-ants were killed in the same way they had attempted to kill the two preachers. Usually whenever harm was about to come upon them, fire came from their mouths that devour the apparent assailants. This went on for three months before the Antichrist had had enough.

"I'm done with those guys! Enough is enough," he rhetorically stated to me, "I will send in an army to destroy them."

That was not a good idea either.

All the while, the two continued to tell the Gospel story they had authority to call upon the heavens to do whatever plagues desired and upon whomever they chose. The reason: they were not to be distracted from their mission.

As they were preaching to quite a large number of people who had assembled, one of the old men pointed to soldiers on the road fitted with riot gear advancing double-time toward them more than five hundred yards away. The crowd looked to where he was pointing and separated enough to allow the column of soldiers five wide and ten rows deep to go through. From out of nowhere, a mighty swirl of wind full of grainy dust engulfed all the soldiers but none of the crowd. As the soldiers stopped to cover their eyes from the blinding storm, a crevasse just large enough to cause their falling into opened up beneath them and closed up, swallowing them; the soldiers were no more. This is an example of what went on many times.

"Must I kill those two old men myself?"[5] he asked.

He traveled from Brussels to Jerusalem where the two witnesses, as they were called, are preaching. At the appointed time, after making sure a cameraman was linked to the Antichrist's satellite network for all the world to witness his killing them, he met the two old men on the street. They were preaching their warnings of the Antichrist as they had been doing the previous two-plus years. He wrestled both, in turn, to the ground, stabbing them to death.

The Prophet had set the scene for the entire world to celebrate the killing of these rabble-rousers, including the exchanging of gifts to commemorate this great event. It was enormously successful and celebrated as such. Finally the world needed something to celebrate and got it! These two powerful men had preached condemnation and so much as told the world that everyone will land in hell. So much for those two; now they are dead.

The Prophet also had placed a camera on a pole focused upon the putrefying decomposing bodies lying on the street at the same spot where they were killed for all the world to see. Returned to his office in Babylon, Mohammed made a point to watch the video frequently for a few minutes every day of the two bodies deteriorating worse by the day. Passersby walked far from the bodies to avoid the terrible stench. They only glanced at the ashen forms as no one desired to really look upon the ghastly sight of them.

On the third day, just as the Antichrist began his evening routine of observing the bodies, somehow the despicable bodies commenced to take form, slowly standing up, beginning to breathe, and walked away. Within minutes, they were completely resurrected! Because of satellite video, the entire world observed this happening just as the Antichrist. Everyone is reduced to shock. Within a few moments, people everywhere began fearing God.

Again the world was astounded after seeing the continuation video. The cameraman recorded the sudden disappearance of the two into the heavens.

No other conclusion can be drawn: their mission was as successful as God intended.

49

SEVENTH SEAL: FIRST FIVE TRUMPET JUDGMENTS[1]

Maji continues to describe

It's all so confusing to me when trying to recall everything what Steven told me a few years ago about these times. But I do remember how difficult it was for me to comprehend how the many terrible things could occur. I fear that I'm about to find out.

I had made my way from the mountainous caves to the top of Golan Heights where I could see into the valleys all around—what's left of them anyway.

Suddenly without notice, the sky gushed with what I know no one had never seen: a relentless hailstorm mixed with fire. But what made this unique is that the hail and fire also had blood mixed in. How can I possibly relate to you what it's like to have the heavens spew hail with fire and blood upon the earth? Blood?

At precisely the same time, vegetation caught fire. It seemed impossible the hail could cause fires; though fire was mixed with the hail. There wasn't any indication how the small, falling flames ignited to burn somehow, selectively. Looking in all directions for more than thirty miles, it appeared that a third of any vegetation including trees and grass caught fire spontaneously like torches only burning up completely! For curiosity's sake, I went into a nearby Israeli guard-house to view satellite news reports; fires throughout the world are identically the same!

Then, astonishing everyone, whole mountains near shorelines, ablaze of fire, dislodged and cascaded into the sea. God willed more: Not a second transpired before one-third of the world's surface and aquifer water turned to blood. Not *as* blood or mere blood coloring, real blood killing one-third of life sustained by water to come to an end, which in turn resulted destruction of a third of all vessels of the seas.

Think about it. What with the destruction of one-third of all vegetation, grass, and trees caused another famine difficult to overcome because the effects are still being felt of the peculiar famine caused by the third horseman only four months ago.

Increasing the effect of the famine, a large star became a meteor as it penetrated the sky and smashed, fragmented, into the earth upon rivers and springs of water, causing a bitterness that rendered another one-third of the water unusable. Turning the rivers and springs of water bitter implies that both aquifers and groundwater sources are affected. The bitter water is not just its taste. It is poisonous. Many died. A total of two-thirds of earth's food supply and the ocean's creatures and vegetation is gone![8] The star is so important the heavens named it wormwood.

Then unbelievably another pestilence, the fourth, sent by God came upon the earth: the diminishing of light caused by one-third of the sun, moon, and stars being darkened. Now the remaining one-third of all vegetation upon the face of the earth has minimal chance to grow. Try to imagine the enormous effect of this when added to the compounded existing famine already responsible for countless numbers of death by starvation!

Surprising everyone, a powerful bird, the size of a prehistoric fowl, was given a booming voice. It flew over the earth's continents to warn of the three coming plagues to be ushered upon the earth by angels.

I can recall how preposterous these coming events seemed when Steven pointed them out to me in Revelation during our many discussions. Now, apparently they were to occur. By having read the ninth chapter in Revelation, these far-fetched events are on the horizon! First to arrive are hideous reptilian demons released from an abyss somewhere in the heavens; they came down acting as furious scorpions, being led by Apollyon, an angel demon from the abyss. They're immediately engaged in an unrelenting torment of people for five months with such vengeance, this despair seems like a pent-up anger being released!

Have you ever hit a finger the second time with a heavy hammer when driving a big nail? The pain these demons are inflicting is much, much more painful. No one can escape them because fleeing draws their attention, and they'll swiftly set chase. The sting is excruciatingly painful to the point of wishing to be dead as nerves of a body react with severe convulsions and writhing!

After those five months came to a close, another phenomenon will occur. What is now to appear on all lands over the earth's face has been debated for centuries after John wrote the Book of Revelation.

I remembered Scriptures that foretold what is coming. It stated that four angels who were bound at the River Euphrates, reserved for a specific time—year, month, day, even the hour—would be released to kill one-third of all mankind!

That is the Sixth Trumpet Judgment, next to come. I for one was overjoyed having the seal of the Lord identifying me as one of his. To some degree, I also suffered the inflictions of the plagues affecting vegetation and the water. I certainly do not want any part of what is coming!

Which reminds me. Somehow God in his wisdom has caused us, who chose to not wear the mark, to not endure hunger or extreme thirst as those who are wearing the mark. Many who chose to wear the 666 died from the plagues, causing poisonous water along with a drought of edible plant life.

Author's notations

Because of the Tribulation's time limitations for all of the events needing to take place according to prophecy, it's projected that the Seal Judgments span from the last four weeks of the first half of the Tribulation into the first months of the second half of the Tribulation *before* the first six of the Seven Trumpet Judgments begins. During the course of the second forty-two months of the Tribulation, sixteen separate wraths of God (judgments) occur!

50

SIXTH TRUMPET JUDGMENT

Two Hundred Million Demonic Aliens Released

This is what Steven reports as he witnessed.

Then came the creatures looking so horrible they look as though drawn up by a movie makeup artist hired to create the most terrifying creature ever devised; worse than as though they're from outer space is the best way to describe the *what* that came to inflict their harrowing plagues. By a supernatural power this army of surreal-looking warriors is mounted on steeds of yet another demonlike animal species never seen before. The mouths of the horse-like creatures being ridden belched fire and brimstone, and the tails of these terrifying creatures were like venomous snakes, inflicting injury and death.

There were two hundred million of them according to Scripture I remember reading! They went everywhere over the entire earth. Four angels controlled them, delegating the armies over the four directions of the compass all through the world.

To do this, they didn't merely ride over the mountains and into the plains and valleys, cities and towns, street and highways, they just suddenly appeared out from the heavens! Suddenly with no warning, they overran earth's population inflicting their style of torment of a nature no one had seen!

If they had the energy, people scattered in all directions to avoid them. But most are weak from the intense famine and an extended drought offering little water. Running for cover for any degree of protection is senseless to even consider. Though a demonic force bent on terrifying and killing people, they were apparently controlled to kill one-third of the world's population[8] rather than everyone.

These steed/creatures had equally horrifying creatures riding on them. They went to and fro anywhere, everywhere without any resemblance at all of military formation but as a swarm of insects focused only to dispense torturous death, inflicting injuries on mankind.

But where did these hideous beasts originate? How did the world not know of such unwelcome monsters?

Professor David Verdi, a Bible authority whom Steven studied under while in college, may have the answer to those two questions. He taught as follows:

- Scripture tells us that these troops were held back throughout history and time for a specific month, hour, day, and moment.[10] Even before *the Flood*, they were kept at bay.
- Scripture references strange huge beings that occupied the land where the people of God resided. Against God's instruction for his own to intermingle with these people, they disobeyed. They even intermarried with them![13] This act determined new fate on both peoples. It brought on the flood of which Noah and his family survived, but all of the other inhabitants of the world did not. As for the large beings, they were held off from the earth up to this very time. It is believed these beings are fallen angels or maybe beasts from hell.
- In any event, angels in the four directions of earth held them bound until God spoke, giving orders to release them to the archangel.

51

WHAT NOW?

A Look at the World's Affairs

Jolene Jacobsen makes her report on the current world affairs.

I pulled through a beating suffered when in a moment I got careless by taking chances while pursuing my reporting. I had learned from Steven to not be vulnerable during late evenings or in the night's darkness. Gradually I stayed out later and later before I realized I began to place myself in sure danger. The attack came during one of those dark evenings when blackened rain clouds prematurely brought darkness upon the day.

My overstuffed backpack had obviously been mistaken to have food or water or something of value for survival. It had only necessary personal stuff and reporting technology. I thought I was smart enough to not fight in defense, but that didn't deter the two young assailants. In anger, there was nothing they valued. I was overtaken and beaten with face-slamming to the ground and kicked violently, breaking ribs and causing internal injury. There was no medical care I could turn to. So I had to tough it out.

In the meantime, what Steven had told me and weighing the consequences, when the time came to wear the 666 or not, I refused. While being detained after making that decision, I too became a Believer as Steven had done. The next time after that when looking in a mirror, I saw a Hebrew inscription on my forehead. Somehow I knew it was the seal of God as I had seen it on others. It did not save me from the dangers of those wearing the mark, but it did shield me from the series of wraths by God!

With the takeover of the Antichrist of all the news agencies, I'm now working independently but providing reports to Israel through the same agency who hires the Spider as their mole in the upper sphere of the Antichrist.

At Central State University, before deciding to become a journalist, I had begun preparation to be a history teacher. But before changing majors, I had written a thesis on the failings of powerful regimes and governments and what caused them to be wiped out. I won't go into detail about what I had discovered. My point is that no matter how powerful they once might have been, they didn't last forever!

So now I ask. What about China? Japan? Germany? Russia? How do they fit in with what the Antichrist is doing with the world powers—the kings, rulers, and the dictators who think they can withstand him?

Israel saw to it that I could travel as best I could to answer these questions. They viewed the answers I might find as being vital to their strategies. Here are the results of my investigations:

China

During the years between 1997 and 2011, China's economy increased by the year, reaching gargantuan proportions compared to decades upon decades previously. The world's economy became reduced down to the expression China price.[1] This meant the wholesale prices of every type of product from cell phone bodies to furniture is judged solely on China's price to manufacture products. China prided on making false products by copying toys, shoes, and clothing for instance and exporting them to the world markets. Peasants by the jillions came to the new industrial factories to take them out of poverty—barely. These people needed housing. Housing boomed. They needed services. Services boomed. In fact, from 2001 through 2005, over 40 percent of the world's inventory of building supplies went to China.

Four problems though: (1) shortage of water where the populations are more dense,(2) fuel for heat to the masses and electricity for manufacturing,(3) the supply of manufacturing equipment to make all the sundry of products now demanded by the world's markets, and finally (4) dense unsafe quality of air due to ignoring the environmental effect of misuse of nature!

They built Three Rivers Dam to supply needed water. They neglected to account for the tens of thousands of villages without waste disposal, causing the raw sewage to contaminate the new water supply; heat and electricity has become dependent upon imports of oil and coal from any country—mainly Russia, Iran, and the Middle East. Supply from the United States was stopped by Amid Baker Mohammed to limit America's effect in the world. And finally, the technology and machinery to make products is dependent upon Germany and Japan.

Two years ago, the Antichrist placed an embargo on China for any country to do business with China. All the money in the world, or China, could not alter this embargo. Shipments of machinery stopped, making the closing of factories inevitable. The embargo of oil and coal that provide the capability to the tens of thousands of power plants producing heat and electricity will surely bring their operations to a standstill.

The results are dire, at best. The entire nation of over 3.5 billion, nearly half of entire world's population, is experiencing a collapsed economy, wholly at the demise of the Antichrist. In part because demand for products from any country, any source, in any manner is dependent upon whether or not the 666 is worn, which in turn controls sources of money even for individuals. If products cannot be sold, where is the demand? Even though the infrastructure had not been undermined, China's products would remain in their warehouses.

Out of apparent ignorance and persuasion by the Prophet, the Chinese gave little credence of the 666 one way or the other, so they didn't particularly care whether or not to accept the mark.

God's wrath is felt here in this country just as much as anywhere else over the entire world.

Japan

This nation of under 130 million of which over thirty million reside in Tokyo has long fallen to the Antichrist's regime! They had no oil, no coal, no major rivers to create adequate watts of electricity for the population, and all the manufacturing investments in China had closed and immediately taken over by China. Japanese are deported by the hundreds of thousands. China cannot allow them to remain.

Few in Japan are living above serious poverty levels. Sanitation has dropped to below third world standards. Shelves are bare. Starvation and lack of water is rapidly affecting the population count in cities, towns, and villages. It's an everyday sight of corpses being burned like cordwood. Tokyo is far under the bar of poverty.

As everywhere else, the Antichrist has made his impact by pushing all the eastern religions into exile, threatening torturous death at the hands of his enforcers, for anyone discovered not worshipping him. By wearing the 666, it is proof as to who they're worshipping and obeying without hesitation.

God's wrath is felt here in this country just as much as in China.

Germany

Germany, a country of over eighty-two million has stymied, screeching to nearly a complete halt on every count. Amerinero's embargo upon China nearly did them in. One asset Germany has is its number of scientists in technology and pharmaceuticals. However, it is part of the EU of which the Antichrist is president.

So in essence, the country is wholly at the whim of him. Other than that, there is not a whole lot that can be said except that when the time comes, Germany will be at the front of any skirmish or war upon Israel as the Antichrist might govern.

Russia

It is the most dangerous to the world as an independent nation regardless of its connections to Iran and the Muslims, to the Antichrist as an ally, or as against Israel.

One hundred forty-five million in Russia are governed by the country's financial success in the world. But it's a maverick country, the level of trouble depending upon who might be their czar at the time, being unpredictable. It was Vladimir Putin at the time of the rapture.

What I can report is that Russia is in partnership with a number of other countries. They have placed Israel in their sights as a target to initiate some kind of war. Beginning a few years prior to 2013, Putin has focused on gaining control of money-making enterprises of Russia, folding them into government-owned companies. In that year, he successfully made Tesco Oil, the biggest oil company, a wholly owned government company by buying out British petroleum's interest they had operated in partnership. This acquisition enables Russia to participate in any plot or conquest of which it has a concern or activity that is on their agenda.

He had tested the waters of his authority when he authorized Russia to take over the Ukraine, but backed off. Surprisingly that seemed to work. The very people he overtook voted their approval of Russia's political involvement with the Ukraine!

All this meets with pleasure of the Antichrist as an ally.

52

CAN IT GET WORSE?

The First Five of Seven Bowl Judgments

Maji and Steven witness the next wraths from God though enduring excessive antagonism by Antichrist's worshippers who continue to torment and persecute them.

In spite of the apparent control of the Antichrist over the world, everyone knew it is God who has allowed him and the False Prophet their powers. This implies the world knew God is the one who's actually in control. This is proven by the world's reaction to the pouring out onto the earth his plagues. They curse God rather than repent.

Steven reports

Healthy or sickly, either didn't matter. Those who wore the 666 broke out with hideous sores, as though caused by a flesh-eating virus; the open sores began breaking out over their entire bodies. The pain is so great that even gentle movement of their clothes rubbing their skin intensifies. No one considered whether or not the sores are contagious; they simply did not care even if they were. Medicines and anesthetics no longer exist. Insects begin to find nesting in the sores if left open. Rags, certainly unsanitary, from all sorts of sources are used as bandages, even using the clothes of the deceased, decaying bodies. Removing the dried-blood bandages creates unbearable pain. Day by day for months, people in torment somehow tolerate their ordeal, blaming and blaspheming God for their anguish.

Soon after, the sea, a once reliable source of food, came to an abrupt end. One day it was good. The next day it became like *spoiled blood like from a dead man*, a gooey jell causing all teeming life in it to die. Every living thing of the saltwaters are now inedible. The surface of the sea became crowded with dead sea life as the waters gave up its inhabitants. Its surfaces and shorelines stank horribly!

Then in a related sequence, all of the world's freshwater rivers and springs of water became blood. Not *as* blood, blood. All of the earth's water supply is more than simply contaminated. Everyone realizes that when the springs of water are referred to, it also means the world's aquifers. There is now no water. Not even the springs and streams from the mountains.

Next what happened is as unwelcome as the sores.

On a particular day that is well remembered, the sun seemed to be much closer and at a different angle to the earth than the day before. I, along with the rest of the world, am up and about before the breaking of dawn. We noticed right off the new relationship of the sun to the earth as the sunrise occurred. Astonishing to us was how hot it had become so quickly!

As the temperature rose, I came to realize that because I was wearing the seal of God, the heat became not more than uncomfortable.

For others, who wore the number of the Antichrist, the heat intensified rapidly. By early midmorning, the sun's heat caused sunburn in just a few seconds of exposure suffered by those who chose to remove clothing. By midmorning, the sun's heat penetrated clothing, causing everyone to think they had a dangerous fever. By noon people shed their garments but quickly replaced them because skin began to blister! By early afternoon, clothing had absolutely no effect on shielding the heat that by now is the cause of blistering skin from head to feet. Soon after, the blistering turned to the searing of their skin. Light-skinned people, of fair complexion, seemed to be forerunners of what came to others of darker skin.

Within minutes, the people's skin caught on fire, scorching them, having the effect of searing their skin like cooking meat!

This plague continued for a full day, causing the same events of heat on every continent as the earth completed its rotation.

History kept repeating: no one repented. All the people suffering from this plague cursed the name of God, knowing he caused it. They had no intention to give in and repent, refusing to do so.

I and others who wore the seal of God were somehow protected from all this chaos, plagues, and physical harm caused by these events from God, thanking God for our wisdom of refusing to wear the 666.

I doubt that not many can understand what happens next.

I know that we, who wore the seal of God, gained a reprieve from the awfulness inflicted upon us by the people who wore the 666 for a few days.

They disappeared. I can only repeat what I understand from Scripture to tell you what happened. The Antichrist, the False Prophet, and all their worshippers had somehow disappeared. They had apparently been plunged into the abysmal darkness where they gnawed on their tongues because of the enormous pain of sores over their bodies once again. And they continually cussed God for their travails of pains and sores! Commenting later what it was like, they said though in total darkness, they knew others were all around them experiencing the same thing, but the darkness isolated one from others, which had the effect of intensifying the pain. The experience from wherever they were angered them even more upon their return." To a person, men and women alike, who endured this darkness could only curse God more violently for bringing this upon them. Still, they refused to repent.

I noticed they talked with a slur caused by their tongues being gnawed raw. It must have been painful for them to speak even afterward.

53

SANCTUARY TROUBLES

More from Steven

As many things, the sanctuary concept took root for all the good reasons, mostly safety from the outside world going on. It was good while it lasted. A sanctuary that worked was always made up on those who had refused to wear the mark, and usually everyone in a sanctuary had the seal of God on their forehead.

But sooner or later, the sanctuaries had problems that began taking their toll on its residents. First disharmony and turbulent behavior was caused by the simplest reasons. A whole lot of "he said, she said" disagreements. Then came more serious accusations too numerous for any tribunal to resolve, followed by the treachery and malice among residents. "Fair share" crop attending and work dropped off. Thievery of food became more commonplace, whether on the vine or stored, breaking established rationing agreements.

It didn't take long for water to become an attraction too difficult to curtail the temptations to horde or plain out steal. Unreasonable and feverish behavior seemed to be the new norm, especially when children are involved, parents protecting their children from the constant dangers inside or out of the sanctuaries.

Infighting became constant; day and night, it went on and on. The evilness became front and center in daily life. Anyone weak or feeble was overrun being robbed of their food and water. This became the final undoing of sanctuaries. Behavior became identical to what is going on outside the sanctuaries, thereby negating their reason for them, safety of an individual.

By their own accord, sanctuaries were abandoned one by one to become only a memory in these times. Such is the case over the entire world. Human nature thrives equally no matter where people live.

54

SIXTH BOWL JUDGMENT

First Part

Maji, in complete awe, relates the Sixth Bowl Judgment as an unbelievable action witnessed on the Antichrist's satellite video station. The world no doubt too viewed what transpired.

A whole new variety of three events occurred.

First, what is believed to be an angel from heaven came upon the head waters of the now Great River Euphrates. The angel gestured and spoke. Instantly the water of the river dried up from Turkey through towns and villages lining the shores to continue southward to the Gulf, where only a tiny stream barely moved. It evaporated into nothingness.

No one at the time knew why, except that Scripture says it was for the purpose to make the way for kings of the east to make war upon Israel!

The shock of what took place upon the Euphrates River nearly immobilized the entire region. This, much to the demise of Amid Baker Mohammed, adds to his frustration the success of the 144 thousand Jewish evangelists, a vital concern required for his continued dominance over the world.

It is ludicrous and a waste of time for his array of the finest minds in the world at his beckoning to contemplate how it happened. That the river no longer has water flowing between its embankments is cause enough to now deal with what to do about it. They must face the reality before a solution can begin with incomprehensible resolve.

In all the combined wisdom of the Antichrist and his Prophet, they recognized all their key thirty-five lieutenants had to be called in from their respective locations for an imperative, emergency conference convening the next day. All were notified directly. All knew the importance.

A world audience knew about the goings-on at the Euphrates River and wondered what the Antichrist would do about it. How would he respond? Werner, the Prophet, coordinated with Dowdson for the conference to be shown on the satellite-fed "air screen" for the world to view, knowing with full confidence that a display of power by Mohammed and himself would surely unfold. He wanted the world to see firsthand this demonstration of supremacy.

A whole twelve minutes before the appointed time for the conference to begin all who were told to attend were seated at the huge horseshoe-shaped table. On time, the two dictators sat at the two chairs behind an elaborately detailed display placed at the front facing the larger table.

On the wall at the back of the conference room, the video display revealed what the world is watching. They glanced at it, all seeing themselves seated at the monstrous conference table.

For a full fifteen minutes or more, attendees were reminded how prevalent and powerfully dominant the Antichrist had become throughout the world. He included mentioning how that though many plagues and troubles that God had placed upon them, they are still stronger than ever! A standing ovation confirmed his proclamation.

As the clapping continued, their leader rose to give homage to their worship-like support. After an extended time of applause, he sat down and exchanged the pleasure of the moment with his Prophet. The two nodded, having a smile of accomplishment shared between them.

Surprising both of them, the applause continued, much as a curtain call of a great performance by actors or musicians. Mohammed stood again, and with prompting, he included Werner, who also stood to share in this honor. So there they both stood, the world watching them.

And then…

All mankind became wholly stupefied by what they witnessed next, as cameras focused in disbelief upon the Antichrist and the False Prophet.[3]

Suddenly, without forewarning, a loathsome reptilian dragon-like creature appeared out of the mouth of Werner! It was out-and-out bloodcurdling to see this happening. Most who saw this thought it was by advanced technology trickery or his magician showmanship to create such shocking special effects as a science-fiction movie! But it was too lifelike to be that.

This creature writhed and contorted with oversized fangs gnashing at the air and eyes ablaze of what looked like red-hot cinders, trying to be completely free of the body that is bearing his arrival.

Amid jumped away in disbelief as his adrenaline took command and, in astonishment, stared at Werner, his Prophet, with his mouth wide open, wider than humanly possible, bearing this dreadful snake! But that was just the beginning!

Then out of the mouth of the writhing dragon came three demonic spirits appearing as obnoxious slick frogs from the grotesque bowels of hell itself.

Yes. Like frogs!

The thought occurred to me that it's appropriate for Satan to appear as a serpent at this precise time, similar in style as he had appeared to Adam and Eve long ago. But the frogs were not so understandable.

Caught on camera was the bizarre flaunting of the power of the frogs performing a series of amazing signs and phenomenal feats on display before their departure from everyone's presence. In a moment's flash after their performances, they flew as birds to destinations unknown. For now unknown.

It looked like the Antichrist and the False Prophet were men in astonishment at what had taken place, taken by complete, unadulterated surprise. Werner, especially!

We heard from all the corners of the globe that the demonic beings went all over the earth visiting leaders of the world—kings, rulers, premiers, and presidents. Frogs that speak? And do signs? And wonders? Miracles too? Yes, they actually did those things.[14]

It was then I also remembered what the evil spirits were up to.

Their objective being fulfilled, that is, the mission to unite as many armies as possible for a battle on the great day of God Almighty. Their success became quite evident of legendary scale because a few weeks later, kings and their armies began gathering to a valley called Armageddon, the forming of a significant battle. To orchestrate the destruction of Israel and anything or anybody with God's name attached, Jews and Gentiles alike, it had become the occupation of the world's powers in a collective cohesion. Even the Euphrates River has cooperated!

I realize it is right here that I had overlooked a Scripture because it seemed so out of place in this location! It's about clothes, being naked, and shamefully exposed. I didn't catch its meaning—not at all, even when Steven tried to explain it to me. When I read that short warning, how was I to know what it meant? It seemed to have nothing to do with being in the middle of the description of the Armageddon battle.

But now I think I know what it meant…maybe. It is telling us to not be caught in God's wrath upon the world without a relationship with Christ of worshipping him, which are the robes of salvation.

I should be fearful. But I am not. He's kept me to this day. Why doubt now? I'm sure Steven Alexander feels the same way.

55

TRIBULATION IS
NEARING ITS END

144 Thousand Return

Steven and Maji report

Maji

No matter where the groups of eight comprising the 144 thousand evangelists preach, they are enormously successful. Their greatest success is with us Jews. This acceptance is in spite of known life-endangered risks that could be inflicted by the absence of the mark. But then again, they had their own mark, the seal of God to protect them! Not one of the 144 thousand perished.

I am one of their successes, realizing Jesus is the Messiah that we have waited for all these centuries!

Here in the Holy Land, Israel, there are many thousands of Gentiles being swayed too by the same power as I was to accept what they are urging. A count of two thousand groups of four evangelists is threading their way all over the Israel countryside though it's such a tiny geographical space on the globe.

I've heard another thirty thousand are all over Asia, Europe, Africa, and the other continents as well and just as successful.

They're derided continually without any letup by known agents of the Antichrist. I suppose it's just the same anywhere else. They're being personally assaulted. But strange as it may seem, they never suffer physical harm, being protected by some kind of invisible shield by God.

I've heard there's three or four thousand of the evangelists roaming about in New York City. That's good strategy. It's where the largest gathering of Jews is in the world, and millions of Gentiles also, needing reprieve from the Antichrist's rule.

It's obvious their success is having a ripple effect with the resolve of the Antichrist to make those who aren't worshipping him, and not wearing the mark, more torturous. Also obvious is that the violence of God's wrath upon those who wear the mark is more brutal by the day. The awful stuff from God upon them is causing greater anger, which is meted out in retaliation upon those not wearing the mark.

Steven

We've never seen anything like it! As like busy ants, there are thousands of little groups of four converging all over the United States, mostly in fifty of the largest cities, still in forms of chaos. They're taking every opportunity to preach salvation through Christ in spite of tremendous persecution and attempts upon their lives.

What I cannot understand is that no matter the vile an attempt to inflict injury or even kill them, it's like a shroud of some kind protects them. They don't even have to be huddled together. They can be standing or sitting alone with the same result! Surely it is God's promised protection.

I remember from my studying Scripture that a colossal number of evangelists would cover the entire world to preach as they are now. If I correctly recall Scripture, they're Jewish preachers who are converted to Christ. I guess that's why they seemed to target New York more than anywhere else in the United States.

Proportionately, large audiences are drawn to these people even though there are a lot of beatings going on to keep audiences from forming. But even at that, crowds form anyway.

And oh yeah, many of the non-Jewish people who wore the 666 when coming into the attendance of such a crowd and upon accepting Christ as the preachers invited, somehow the 666 immediately faded and fell away. Not even a trace could be detected.

Another observation of the evangelists is that they don't look dehydrated or undernourished. Yet I have never seen them eat or drink. Their energy is unbounding, as they rotate the speaking function between them.

It took them over a year before they showed up where I now call home, for a few weeks more. Their message carried a fascination and curiosity enough for me to brave against the risk of harm to be in their audience. Four times in fact. Each time was more compelling than the last one attended.

Of the four times I attended their presentation, I was beaten with a club thrice, so were others.

The first group left after a week or so. A second group came to the town three weeks later. During week number two, I attended four times again, twice on two different days. Nine days in a row, I endured severe beatings by thugs when I was already feeling sickly from the lack of eating or drinking. Relief came a day later.

I now had renewed hope. It was thirty months after the second half of the Tribulation began. I could die, now, with the hope of seeing my family again. But I thought life was tough up till now? I dreaded what was still to come!

Their work is finished. Every last one of the evangelists is accounted for.[1] Through all of the earth's chilling torments and chaos caused by God's wrath and the Antichrist's relentless persecution, and their continuous threat of death, each of the 144 thousand return safely. God had protected them, as they had a number given by the angels placed on their forehead[3] to guarantee their protection.

The world had never witnessed such a resounding success of what the evangelists had accomplished.[4] Jews and Gentiles alike,[5] converts chose to side with the evangelists ministry, in spite of taking great risks of death by brutality and beheadings. God miraculously snubbed out the 666 when one chooses Christ, readily signifying who they have given allegiance, willing to pay the price, whatever it may be.

Steven recalls Scripture

Up to now, the number of martyrs during these times cannot be known. When those who suffered terrible deaths at the hands of the Antichrist's followers are added to the numbers who were killed following the efforts of the 144 thousand, the number has to be in hundreds of thousands.

One fact remains. Those who had been killed for their allegiance to God were now in the protection of God under the skirts of the altar of God, waiting for the final judgment, wearing white robes of valor.

56

ARMAGEDDON

Sixth Bowl Judgment

Second Part

Maji reports from his lookout at the highest peak in the Golan Heights of the West Bank in the Holy Land.

The six demonic spirits as frogs that came from the two serpents' mouths a few weeks previous have completed their mission. Their performing outlandish signs and wonders before the kings and rulers over the entire world have compelled those leaders of nations to destroy God and Israel at Armageddon. They are told this will be a holy war: evil against good, Satan against God, the world against Israel. Evidently that was all they needed to hear along with the fact the joining together of many other nations. So they came, in great numbers they came!

It is a sight to watch. Armies have assembled just north of Baghdad, coming from everywhere, mostly the east! The Euphrates River is empty of any waterflow, making the armies' trek to the battlefield easy. They're led by scores of kings, rulers, dictators, and generals. They are on horseback and with teams of warhorses with all sorts of warfare vehicles, modern and primitive. It seemed like millions of personnel to me, but it's actually more like hundreds of thousands. It is truly a spectacle in the making!

The assembly of the enormously huge army is slowly taking place in the Valley of Jezreel, which is also known as the Plains of Megiddo, below me stretching eighty miles long and two miles or more wide. I remember from history books that many significant battles were fought here because of its perfect battlefield attributes.

It is more than obvious the troops have only one objective: to destroy my country, Israel. To lay it bare. To kill every man, woman, and child who are Israeli—to annihilate it.

My heart is racing as I watch the forming of a battle of such a large number by the enemy; I cannot, by any stretch of my imagination, understand how Israel has a chance, even with God's help. I'm sorry, but I dare not to have faith enough to believe Israel can pull through this one. I know the Old Testament stories—miracles upon miracles from Noah to Joshua, from Moses to Jericho, from Elijah to Jeremiah, and Jonah. I know them all to be God's intervening. But this? There is no way!

Commanders are busy organizing the regiments into numerous attack formations and giving precise orders to company leaders.

Horses are becoming impatient as they quiver in anticipation to engage what they have been trained to do. The troops are just as anxious. The war machines equipped and ready. Even the generals are obviously restless as the final details of engagement are prepared and made ready.

All await the command to battle. But the waiting is happily interrupted. Unexpected by all, the Antichrist—adorned in festive Arabian robes and a symbolic war band around his head—joins in with the leading commanders as moral support.

After focusing on the surprise visit by Amerinero, I trained my powerful telescope on other numerous locations where my people are preparing for the onrush of the assembling troops. I see only a few horses, mostly war machinery, assault vehicles, and a wide array of weaponry.

There is dismay among the Israeli soldiers, even confusion. The anticipation of the coming onslaught of the enemy so massive in numbers is overwhelming. It's obvious there is great fear among the soldiers made up of young men and women. But they're ready to engage in the coming war of resistance and defense, ready to die for the saving of their country.

Now with the arrival of the Antichrist, I could sense, even though I was more than two miles away, the engagement will begin in a few minutes. Postures have become stalwart and ready for the conflict on both sides. The front line of Israel is only two to three hundred yards away from the front line of the enemy, now both slowly marching in step toward each other. I watched, mesmerized by the great odds against Israel. The complete army of Israel is almost the number of soldiers of the first wave of the combined army coming upon them!

As the Israeli frontline soldiers are easily killed, the enemy's legion of soldiers make their way to Jerusalem, sixty miles away, killing anyone who dares to impede their way. An occasional explosion from Israeli-fired armament causes the killing of a small number of enemy troops. Three or four such outbreaks in an average time of ten minutes fail to thwart the onslaught of the invading army. Israel has determined the use of hard war machines such as tanks would be futile with so great a number of advancing troops. They wouldn't so much as make a dent.

The marching militia soon overtakes Jerusalem, the city. The capturing of the city causes a great number of nonmilitary Israeli people to flee their country and hide in the caverns and crevasses in Edom, near the rocks of Petra. I remember those that flee, God refers to them as Israel's remnant.

After capturing Jerusalem, the battle becomes an all-out war expanding from the Valley of Megiddo where the army of foreigners assembled throughout Israel. Apparently trumpets are used to communicate directives and orders of engagement. The trumpet sounds are terrorizing to the victims as the enemy is with swords drawn, scourging all the people.

But then God steps in. The result is the splashing of the invader's blood so violent that it reaches symbolically to the height of horses' bridles in measurable amounts. The enormous effect of gushing blood is so severe it causes the water to turn red miles away in all the streams threading through southern Israel. The decimated number of slaughtered enemy soldiers is far too great a number to count. They're buried in mass graves.

The intended slaughter by the enemy of Israelis and its taking of spoils of war from Israel never materialized.

57

SEVENTH BOWL JUDGMENT

The Final Earthquake

Jolene describes this earthquake

From a vantage on the beach of Long Island, I watched New York being leveled. There was an atmospheric, all-encompassing eerie quiet calm of about a day before the lightning of horror proportions began.

Flashings of lightning more prolific than man had ever seen were accompanied by loud rumbling peals of deafening, brain-rattling thunder that covered the world day and night for seven days. It was as though a warning from heaven of something more terrible is to come. Soon we would know it.

Of all the furies deposited on the earth so far, none of them compared to what is to come next. Man has never experienced such woefully traumatic turbulence of the earth, I guarantee! This earthquake was like no other. The earth surface did not just move as though underlying rocks shifted. This was different. It felt like the earth was being tossed about. As though it's being roughhoused. It wobbled!

Like God had taken the scruff of its neck and jerked the earth about, causing the rocks to twist and break apart, not just shift! The landscape of earth was leveled as mountains were tossed into the sea.

You might recall what cities look like after a tornado or hurricane flattens them? Take your thoughts to another, more-intense next level. This is what an *entire* city of New York—all of it—looked like. Satellite videos told the same massive destruction happened in Dubai, Singapore, Shanghai, Montreal, Sydney, Beijing, Moscow, London—all of them leveled; jagged steel frames were poking out of the rubble. But they were nothing compared to mountains being dislodged!

Oh. There's Jerusalem built on solid rock. It too came down, broken into three parts.

Then the hailstones. Big stones of ice! How can one explain how hailstones could weigh a hundred pounds? These giant hailstones came out of the sky causing violent, irreparable damage on anything that endured the earthquake.

If, as unlikely it might be, whatever remained standing after the earthquake or anything or any properties of value, they were pummeled into oblivion by the indescribable end result of 100-pound hailstones!

Only Babylon, mysteriously how, survived marginally unscathed, obviously saved by God for its own demise.

A day after she had written and dated this report, Jolene was found dead. Her throat slashed crossways, the signature of the Antichrist's Enforcers, she was left lying on a street lined with twenty or more others who met with the same terror. She had become a martyr. Another not wearing the mark found the above report inside her coat and dispatched it through the Spider's network.

58

WOE IS BABYLON!

The Mighty City's Destruction

Emile Dowdson survived the earthquake by being in Babylon. Cameras all over the world reported the following world's destruction on video and reporting the results of the earthquake all around Babylon, Mecca's towers as well as all other towers in Muslim mosques and in cities.

I am overwhelmed that Babylon withstood the last earthquake. Not a single building significantly damaged. Not a single life taken. No break in the walls of the city or sides of the canal. All continued as though the earthquake all around the city hadn't taken place. Yet there were those video scenes from across the globe and nearby regions of the out-and-out destruction everywhere. Everywhere, that is, except Babylon. I noticed that even the cities and villages along the canal were destroyed. How could that happen without damage to the canal? Amerinero was totally elated.

Were the videos duped? Made up? I knew that Amerinero was clever enough! But no, he assured me there was no tampering. I came to the conclusion that only God could so effectively isolate damage that was devastating in one location from another so near without a scratch!

I got plenty scared in spite of his attempt to calm my nerves.

Emile reports his observation before his own death occurs:

> A day or two later, I had taken flight in a smaller craft of Amerinero's private jet fleet from Babylon Airport to have a look-see. During take-off, there wasn't anything unusual going on.

Only a few minutes later, he suggested I look out the starboard window because he had observed smoke rising from the city.

Sure enough! As I looked through the window, I grabbed the videocam and recorded the scene. There were indeed many thick flumes of dark smoke caused by ground-level fires throughout the city; I cannot believe what I'm witnessing!

Amongst the rapidly ruinous, spreading fires, people are scurrying about in no distinct direction. Merchants are busy trying their best to protect their wares to no avail. Smaller water craft are being put underway from their moorings. Scantily dressed men and women obviously caught while engaging in their vices are outside dashing about to seek refuge where none can be found. Mariners are running to swiftly board their ships. The loading cranes have stopped operating. Hundreds of container lifts have halted midroute as operators join the throngs heading nowhere fast. Traffic from highways leading into Babylon is stopped by police barricades, and traffic leading outward is jammed by fleeing masses.

Apparently the air's temperature is increasing as I can feel it rising fast, even affecting the plane's air conditioning. Life on the ground is aghast of the torturous heat. The animals are dropping as they pant for air. Some, both human and animal, are becoming scorched—literally. Death is rapidly becoming rampant.

In the aircraft, the heat is overtaking the output of the AC. What little cooling there is, it keeps me alive. If it were not for that, I know my own death would be certain. I pray the AC doesn't stop operating.

I can see that the smoldering heat is beginning to slowly disintegrate the city's walls and structures as flumes of black smoke have turned whitish-blue, filling the air above the city that darkens the sky. According to the plane's exterior thermometer, the atmospheric heat is 127 degrees, which means at ground level, it's approaching 160 degrees.

By zooming in the lens, I can detect blistering on exposed skin of the people. They're about to give up the fight for their lives.

The walls of the seaport are being affected too; bit by bit, chunks are slipping into the sea. South of Babylon, larger ships navigating in either direction have turned to 180 degrees. Crews have abandoned ships, determined to make it to the safety of the nearby hills.[1] Those with only a single layer of clothing don't make it. They're scorched alive as by now, the ground temperature is over 175 degrees.

I can only hope Mohammed will have the chance to see this video recording.

The aircraft's various systems were beginning to malfunction as the heat caused a fire in the pilot's cabin. I quickly placed the video into a fire/water proof metal case having a pulsating beeping buzzer, hoping it could be found quickly. I knew my life will soon meet its end.

A moment later, fire engulfed the aircraft before exploding into tiny fragments. The metal case was propelled far away from the wreckage, found days later. That afternoon, messengers[1] wearing firefighting garb rapped loudly on the door where Amid Baker Mohammed is in agony reviewing what had been video tapings of special interests to him. Quickly and without much ado, they hand him a video within a metal case, still beeping.

He instinctively knew it was bad news…very bad; worse than the earthquake just experienced. Hastily he opened the case that stopped beeping when the seal was broken, then loaded the video into the computer.

He is stunned by what he sees as Dowdson's aircraft circles about Babylon with an intense heat that the video recorded. His city is in flames, then utter chaos, and now in ruins.

At 11:12 a.m., the pilot had informed the passengers the sky was clear and nothing out of the ordinary to report. Then at 11:17 a.m., only five minutes later, he said there was identifiable numerous huge flumes of black smoke rising from all parts of the city. Five minutes! How can this much damage occur in five minutes! Preposterous! Unless of course there was an earthquake like as all around the city a couple of days ago. But none was reported. A fire? How could it spread so fast and so thorough? And all those corpses lying all over the place!

It is then he remembered God had warned him!

All the Antichrist could do was to watch his Babylon being destroyed as Dowdson's aircraft circled over what will soon become *was* his city! Just under one hour has now taken place, and it already appears the city will be totally, wholly demolished; already it's nearly flattened with the streets littered with piles upon pile of rubble and a collection of thousands of corpses in the streets.

Suddenly as a final stroke of wreckage, without warning, a continuous series of blasts ignited that lasted more than three hours, disintegrating every piece of rock, plaster, construction materials, gardens and landscaping, and street paving into unidentifiable fragments so thorough there is no evidence any city was ever there!

The inoperable ships too are damaged beyond salvageable condition, fast being covered over by the suddenly formed high-velocity, wind-blown sands of the desert plains.

Maji reports

With the destruction of Babylon came the end of all that the city controlled: worldwide banking and finance, the Internet, satellites, and both land and water commerce. Including the pleasures of sensual obscenities, the city had become known throughout the entire world. Every living being within its walls are dead, not an indication that they were ever there can be seen.

Thousands of merchants, mariners, and kings and rulers cried from the surrounding hills as their livelihood of commerce has disappeared before their very eyes as they watched.

All that the Antichrist and his technological geniuses had put together over the past ten or more years has disappeared from the global scene within one day! The city and the canal, his masterpieces, are laid so bare none of their former existence can be seen. With the satellite becoming a worthless mechanism of the near past, the DT-II ceased to function. Its screen is black. All of his worldwide communication devices are no more or also have ceased to function.

A very angry Antichrist is now overcome with a resolve of revenge by what has taken place. Amerinero and Werner promise brutal retaliation upon all people wearing the seal of God and not the 666.

I know that God has other plans during the next seventy-five days.

Standing on a rise of the desert, Maji had written the above report in the company of another wearing the seal of God, Amond, who fled from an attempt on their lives.

Maji didn't make it. They caught him and, after inflicting pointless torture, beheaded him with an unexpected swing of a sword. Later Amond returned to bury what was left of Maji's body. He too sought the Spider to tell the story of Babylon's utter destruction, dedicated in the memory of Maji.

PART VII

THE TRIBULATION'S OVER!

59

THE SEVENTY-FIVE-DAY TRANSITION

First Event: Christ's Return!

Steven

I had found favor with the Spider because of my reports, assisting with the details and travel coordination not easily achieved in these days of getting to the Holy Land. It simply could not have been possible except by way of the intricate Israeli network. It was a two-week complex time of clandestine lies and cover-up of adventurous intrigue I never knew existed, though my life had been full of the similar experiences during the past recent years. But I arrived safely with only two close calls being discovered. I immediately began reporting what I witnessed upon arriving.

I was standing outside Jerusalem not far from the temple, behind a thick clump of olive trees in full bloom.

What I saw happening and what had happened with the temple is just plain disgusting! Though I am not Jewish, my heart is crushed by what the Antichrist had done to it.

The Mount of Olives is across the valley to the east. As I gaze upon the godless activities going on at, around, and in the temple, an ear-splitting thunderbolt of lightning at very close range announced the spectacular way the sky literally opened up,[2] the likes of which the world had never before seen. Suddenly the sun darkened as though to set the final stage of an appearance of what caused my feeling the power of heaven to shake the earth!

Everyone who heard the thunder and seeing the lightning then experiencing this darkened world became terrified, knowing to seek protection was futile just as before. We had seen quite enough of these rumblings and strikes of lightning during the past seven years! "What now?" in dismay we all wondered.

Then magically there was no mistaking. Jesus Christ, just as he said he would in the New Testament, broke through the parting clouds and opening sky in his great glory and a clear, bright white light surrounding him. A light of a sort no one could have realized existed. He did return to the same exact place as he had ascended multiple of centuries ago, the Mount of Olives!

Those with the 666 took flight for any sort of cover they could find, knowing instantly their doom has come in the person of Jesus. They were right about that.

His magnificence was so pronounced we didn't take notice right off that Christ did not arrive on earth alone. There was a host of heavenly angels and others behind him. He didn't arrive on earth as a pleased king either, he is a conquering king.

Immediately I knew I now had nothing—absolutely nothing—to fear. I am wearing the seal of God on my forehead that now identifies I am one of his, not that I needed it. He knew that already.

Mystically, just his presence caused the DT-II on my left wrist to drop off. Any connection to the Antichrist in any form is now no more! Gone. God saw to that.

More importantly it was so obvious Christ came to reign! It was plain he didn't come as the savior, but to make sweeping changes of this chaotic place!

Soon after, I made my way not too far from the Mediterranean Sea. It was raging. The tide had come in, risen unusually high, and acting violently, acting weird. Quite honestly?

I was surprised and at the same time elated by what I saw next. Not so were millions of others wearing the 666, which now marked them for Christ's vengeance. It was then I watched their demise of desperate anguish to attempt to strip the mark of the beast off; the ID could not be removed. Some were even willing to disfigure their foreheads or wrists with chemicals, if they could find such substances, to escape the ire of Christ soon to judge them. They failed to grasp the fact that Christ already knew they had betrayed him to worship the Antichrist. What a waste!

At that moment, I knew I was ready and will soon meet Christ face-to-face. With full comprehension, I also understood all the danger of torment and suffering I had gone through by the hand of Antichrist's people and the power over me had ceased. I no longer needed to fear them or the power of the Antichrist and his false prophet.

In fact they had become totally harried in their attempt to avoid their horrific end they knew quite well was coming!

Second Event: The Beasts Are Disposed

Amid Baker Mohammed, "the Antichrist,"
and Ales Werner, "the False Prophet"

Christ returned all right!

He did not come back with open arms with a welcome with a gracious smile. No! He came riding on a white horse wearing a bloody robe with a sword in his hand, eyes aglow with inordinate anger, and his concentration bent on eradicating his enemies. He had a banner on his back that read, "King of Kings and Lord of Lords."

If I were wearing the 666, I would now be trembling with fear and go into hiding, not that hiding would do any good; and as many of them tried, to rid the ID if I could, he found them all quick enough.

On the left hand and on the right hand, he slew enormous numbers who had converged upon Israel's land. They suddenly came to know their fate with Christ. Though they could clearly see the demise of their forbearers, they charged full force to fight, and those who thought could defeat him met with their death.

Amond

But where are the Antichrist and Prophet? Where did they go?

Spider found where they had gone days afterward and what they were up to.

They're preparing to make war against the Christ, who was rumored, at the time, to be returning within hours after the destruction of Babylon! Don't they ever learn? I guess not, as Satan has so thoroughly deceived even the Antichrist and the False Prophet they will believe whatever is told them by the Master Deceiver, including preparing for a victory against Christ.

And make war they did—with devastating results!

A short time later, Christ turned his focus on two of Satan's men, the Antichrist, the Beast, and the False Prophet. Though the two could do all sorts of signs of wonders and miracles, but now they had become wholly powerless with the Christ. Wisely but futilely, they tried to escape. Christ caught them and bound them as would an officer with a perpetrator. Then what seemed out of nowhere, God provided an abyss that Christ flung the two captives into. From the yellowish red glow of the abyss' opening, I concluded the flames are of fire and burning sulfur.

Their screams of anguish haunted me for days. But what little I know of Scripture, they would be there for eternity. Not in my wildest imagination can I comprehend what that would be like! More about this later. The remaining soldiers of their army are killed by the sword of the one riding on a white horse, Christ. The bodies of the slain army lay where they were mercilessly killed and are picked clean to the bone by birds as though on cue—swarmed all around, on a feasting frenzy, as is prophesied.

Third Event: The Jewish Remnant Returns

After the conquest of Jerusalem by the foreign troops and God's earthquake that split the city into three parts, the remnant of the Jewish nation hiding in the rocks near Petra began returning. The city is in partial rubble that with some cleanup, it too can be restored along with the temple.

Fourth Event: The Temple Is Restored

The Jewish Nation is thankful for the vacating of the Antichrist of their temple, no matter how it occurred. The rights to the temple are now once again in their possession, making possible its restoration in full earnest. The Jordanian monarch gave up on the ownership of the Temple Ground, too much turmoil.

This restoration is what the Old Testament foretold.

Now the Messiah had come. It is being made ready for him to sit on its throne to complete God's prophecies. All the enemies of God's chosen people are vanquished in these truly last of God's days before his reign of a thousand years.

EPILOGUE

Millennium

Steven

It is beyond my comprehension what the world will be become in a short time from now...for a thousand years. But with what I have been through over the past eleven years, one thing is clear: it's very welcome change beyond comprehension! But first a war that's prophesied must take place: a second Gog and Magog war. But the name of this war is a reference to the first one because of its severity.

⚜

It is, by far and away, the best experience of my life at the beginning of the one thousand years of peace with Christ's glory and power being in full sway. For a little more than eleven years, I constantly had to look over my shoulder as both my well-being and my life were at jeopardy. That was getting old fast! It is all over, a thing of the past.

Peace has taken over. The world's peoples have never known such a condition. At least not since Adam and Eve were in the Garden of Eden before succumbing to their temptation. Is this what it was like for them then?

An overwhelming peace shrouded over me because of the glory of Christ! That glory that shines all over is simply not describable. It more than lights the earth, it is the power of the earth's whole existence. His presence is in everything—the people, plants, animals, every little thing!

Other than the peace, the first observation is that there's no longer the 666 or the seal of God so engrained into life's existence before now! The second thing that struck me is that I can look people in the eye. That was just plain dumb to do before; it made one vulnerable, the sure way to invite being attacked, maybe killed.

Then I recognized everyone—if they had accepted Christ—whom I had known before even though from the distant past. Conversely, I remembered others I had known who were not to be found—apparently they had not accepted Christ.

Out of nowhere, I realized a powerful absence of what I considered important; before the rapture, I honestly wondered whether animals, golf courses, athletic events, or pleasures such as fishing and hunting would exist in the presence of Christ—heaven, for instance. You know what? I don't care! His presence is so much more adequate that no one wants anything else!

While I was wondering whatever happened to Maji, we crossed paths. What a reunion that turned out to be! For a long time, we shared stories of our experiences over the past more than ten years. Most of all, neither of us had conceded to wear the 666. Right up toward the end of the Tribulation, Maji managed to stay alive. For weeks after our reunion, we remained in close contact.

Not long afterward, I was in an orange grove slobbering on the juiciest, best-tasting orange ever. Jolene happened to be wandering between the same rows of orange trees. She saw me first and called out my name; I was dumbstruck but overjoyed.

We too shared our stories of the past as Maji and I had done. She told me of her death. To my complete surprise, she asked, "Have you seen Maji?"

"How did you know Maji?" I inquired.

"I never knew him. But the Spider told me about him."

"Oh yeah, the Spider. What do you know about him?"

"I often reported to him, as did Maji. We got to know each other quite well, but Maji and I never crossed paths. The Spider was watched too closely toward the end before Babylon was destroyed."

"How he became a successful double agent and working so close to both the False Prophet and the Antichrist, we'll never know. I'm sure he saved many Jewish lives with his warnings of planned troubles upon Israel before an Enforcer killed him.

"Back to Maji," I reminded her, "I know where he hangs out."

"Let's go then," she replied with anticipation. He was exactly where Steven had expected him—not far from the temple under construction where Jesus is destined to soon sit on the throne.

Maji was among a group of Bible scholars discussing what this life during the millennium is like compared to what was told about it. He soon took notice I had come close to where he was sitting. A moment later, I introduced Jolene to him. They instantly seemed to know each other through their dealings with the Spider. She informed them she knew he had been beheaded.

"Steven," Jolene asked, "acknowledging you're the one more versed in Scripture and prophecy, what's expected to happen next?"

"Jolene, that's a good leading question. This superwonderful peacetime lasts one thousand years. A time of peace Christ has provided for himself and those who chose to worship him rather than Satan and his angels.[1] Then as for the second part of your question, this time is a kind of cleansing of the earth absent of Satan's power of deceit.[2] Plus, there are some prophecies that need to be fulfilled on the earth before heaven."

"We'll be here in this incredible, extraordinary world for a thousand years?" Maji asked, shaking his head with a measure of inconceivable contemplation. "A thousand years."

"Yes, it's true," reassured Steven.

"The prophecies are what?" inquired Jolene.

"For one, the final—the fourth—temple[3] must be built in which the throne for Christ to rule the earth will be established. And that has to happen in Jerusalem.[4] He will decisively ascertain his rightful place as the Messiah of your people, Maji."[5]

"I understand that's happening now."

"It is."

"What other prophecy?" continued Jolene.

"The permanency of the Jewish nation, without threat, must occur,[6] and that has not ever happened other than the three-plus years of a false peace not long ago."

Over time, the three would visit numerous times, but Maji and Jolene mostly.

❦

Ruling justice

"I recall what I read before the rapture," Steven informs, "and now that Scripture has become reality."

❦

After a many months, they married and became parents of three children, one a maverick—a wayward daughter[7]—and two who followed their parents into salvation with Christ, the older son and the younger girl. Concerned for the troublesome daughter, they asked Steven to talk with her. They listened in.

"Denise, you must stop acting as though you have no need for God in your life. You have such great examples all around you, so I know you know better. We all are not judging you. We are simply recognizing that your behavior is not of God. It isn't of Satan either because his influence is bound up and not in this world. You are living the way you are because your soul is broken.

"Honey, your brother and sister have fixed their soul by accepting Jesus and worshipping him. This is the only way to fix the sin nature you were born with, and quite honestly, it is silly to do nothing about it.

"Let me remind you of something. It is more difficult to live a reckless life than it is to live a righteous life. And there's a reward too, Denise. Because your heart will be at peace, so will all aspects of your life be happy.

"You're really lucky. Do you know that?"

"Yeah? Why?"

"Because you don't have to wrestle with Satan to make the decision you know you should make! Right?"

"Maybe."

"Come now, Denise. Not maybe. Just say yes. Okay?"

"I'll think about it."

Steven sensed it was time to stop. He took her at her word that she'd think about it. Maji and Jolene weren't as confident at first before realizing their daughter had time, but she was wasting her life away on unrest and unhappiness that in a flash could easily be changed.

Fortunately she had a glimmer of sweetness as her mother's.

Many weeks later, Denise ran home and breathlessly tried to get the words out that she had accepted Christ and at his feet had worshipped him.

"How? What happened? Where?" Her parents couldn't get the details fast enough because of the joyfulness they all felt.

"Just outside the city, I was walking in an olive grove and had stopped at the well near the center of the grove. Then I saw him. He was walking in my direction. When he was only about ten feet or so away from where I was sitting, he put out his hand as though to say, 'Come.' At the very moment I stood to respond to his gentleness, an indescribable peace and calm came over me. I knew he knew my thoughts. I couldn't help but to fall on my knees to worship him."

"And then?" Jolene asked.

"He told me to tell others who were like me before he gave me peace. So that is what I am going to do. I know lots of kids like me."

Maji encouraged her, "It's about time. You're twenty years old, my angel." His heart felt excited as the three embraced.

Gog and Magog: The Final Battle

Steven

We knew the thousand years of world peace—true world peace—was about over! Thousands who knew Scripture from the past as well as we had been told by being in Christ's presence understood what signifies the millennium's end.

Gog and Magog

I have to trust that God knows what he's doing! For the thousand years Satan was bound up to deprive him from deceiving mankind, and now God is going to release him! Why? All that I know is that Scripture says he must be loosed.

Further, it tells us that he, the Beast, will gather together all the world's kings and governments in one place to once and for all destroy God in a final battle. This I can understand. He's got to be angry more than he ever has toward God. He had to be at the top of his anguish as an example he experienced of what will come for an eternity, but now released from the binding chains, now released. That pent-up anger is fully directed at the one who had bound him.

So into all the world, by every means available to him, he set out to assemble the greatest, largest, and most dedicated force of armies he can muster to join in concert in battle against God. Actually I can see that assembling such an array of combat-ready troops would be fairly easy for him. By this time, hordes of masses of people are boiling over with a deep-seated hatred of God.

Obviously, Satan, after all this time, still has not realized God is god, ruler over all.

Once again Satan is overthrown, and all his army of hundreds of thousands, in a matter of moments by fire from the heavens! It's as though all of God's attention and resources were deployed to focus on this one affair. Though apparently Satan knew he would win, God turned the table over on Satan, leaving him in shambles. Demoralized. Outdone. Finished.

Satan survived but not by much.

In the same moment after the devouring of all his armies, he survived alone to be thrown into a lake of burning sulfur, joining with the Beast of Babylon and the False Prophet! Never will they know of each other.

The place where they were thrown into is dark, very dark. Even the glow of the flames and burning sulfur does not pierce the darkness, and darkness intensifies the mental anguish of pain. Additionally is the difficulty of quenching thirst and breathing! Burning sulfur sucks in oxygen, proportionately enormous amounts of oxygen for it to burn; the hotter, the more oxygen. However, that is not the worst of sulfur: breathing sulfur chemically chars the lungs even in normal times; this is certainly not a normal time. Then, after a short time, people died from choking and coughing as a result. Now the pain is intensified; breathing in this inescapable prison of utter darkness is a perpetual difficulty. The hot, moistless air provides little satisfaction, amplified by continual thirst for water not to happen. Plus, the stench of *burning* sulfur causes vomiting, and the odor of scorching human flesh is enough to drive one to insanity with the knowledge that escaping is impossible!

All of this—on top of all this—is the departure of any hope. The single most important emotion of being human is hope. Here, it's gone. No hope exists—none, zilch. In all the torment and pain and darkness and putrid air and extreme thirst and intolerable near suffocation is the realization that there is never to be any relief. Ever? Yes, forever!

Steven informs us of an additional couple of notes:

> I must tell you Christ had said that he came into the world not to be a judge, but a savior of the world. That was then; this is now. He became the judge when the Book of Life was opened. If one's name was not found there of having accepted Christ as their savior, they joined Satan, the Beast of Babylon, and their Prophet, in the lake burning of sulfur with flames lasting forever. *Forever* the same as for the three creatures of which this hell was created.
>
> Further, for those who say, "If I go to hell, I'll have plenty of company," they fail to realize that no one will see or be in the company of any other; they'll only hear the shouts and cries of the pain and anguish being experienced the same as they in darkness so black the bluish hue of brimstone cannot penetrate!

UX10: Earth's Cleansing with Fire

I have wondered many times how the cleansing of the earth as we know it will be made new, Steven relates to us his thoughts of this event as to the how of it.

It is a given that the upholding of this present earth must give way to a total remake into a new earth. That is what God promised. That is now what is to happen. [1] It is, of course, quite easy to understand why. All evidence of sin, evil, its carnage, and deceptive powers that caused man's separation from God has to be wiped out without a trace. Even during the days of the thousand-year reign with God, there was sin.

But why a new heaven remains unanswered. I'll leave it at that.

Back to the cleansing of earth by fire.

Though I admit the preposterousness of how an astronomical event is taking place might fit into the theory how God will cleanse the earth, I've a few questions about what is coming next. It might be a little on the outrageous side.

Astrophysicists are attempting to explain their recent discovery during the past few months: a gaseous planet twice the size of earth has obviously left its normal gravitational path of its universe three galaxies removed is considered a rogue. Its erratic course has been documented and charted, of ID as UX10, of east-northeast skies, consisting of fifteen identified planets, the UX10. According to those tracing its course, it escaped out of its own galaxy over a year ago!

Dr. Ebinigh Holger, the astrophysicist team leader assigned to observe UX10, says that such a phenomenon cannot be explained why or how one planet can break out of orbit from its own galaxy. He actually said, "An act of God" is the only way to explain it.

Being twice the size of earth, this will not be just an asteroid gone awry. I recall the verse of Scripture Colossians 1:17, which says, "In Him all things hold together." Maybe the doctor is right.

Another discovery Dr. Holger made is that this planet isn't of rock, volcanic lava, or any other hard surface. It is gaseous without much of any solid matter except by what metal may have been caused by the intense heat fused together with another substance, but that is highly unlikely. It's more likely that its composure is like the sun; hydrogen nuclei fusing into helium resulting in convective energy within a magnetic force field that holds its various elements together.

Only recently has the UX10 been seen to the naked eye as a star much different than other stars; it has more of a glow, a red-orange color having a yellowish band at its extremity. Because it can be seen, although without much detail, it denotes that it has successfully passed through neighboring galaxies without a mishap. According to Holger, there is cause to believe that a real danger is possible if it travels through our galaxy.

Lately I've noticed the UX10 star is brighter, though scarcely detectible month to month, I think that it is possible to be destined to be pulled into earth's magnetic field. Dr. Holger claims that its temperature is far too hot to be dissolved by the earth's atmosphere should that happen. Is this God's way to bring earth to its fiery end? God's way to eradicate what's not wanted has been the use of fire (except the one-time flood).

Ever since the discovery of the hydrogen bomb and nuclear fission, it's been speculated by ardent scholars of Scriptural prophecy that a nuclear blast would be the apparatus God will use to destroy earth. I really don't think this theory is true now, with the knowledge of UX10.

Here's why. First: We know UX10 has limited gravitational force being gaseous, made up of heat that's two-thirds of our sun's, 7,150 degrees at its surface. Colliding into earth will instantly scorch, as quickly as the *phwoof* when igniting gasoline on a burn-pile. It's as Scripture precisely describes. Before impact however, vegetation and every wooden structure will first smolder before igniting into flames. The oceans will begin to be minimized; rivers, lakes, snowcaps melted, and all sources of water, reservoirs and aqueducts, will reach near-boiling temperatures before being vaporized immediately upon impact. All vegetation is no more. Buildings of all types flamed and wiped out. Remember the towers on 9/11? The metal superstructure melted at 1,700 degrees from the jet fuel igniting! The UX10's heat is 6.5 times hotter.

I'm convinced God is not only continuing to hold the entire universe together, he is directing UX10's path to collide with earth.

I mean why not?

It is all his own creation in the first place. He has the right, the authority, to do whatever he wants to do with it as he pleases.

The first earth will be done away with[2] by a great fire and laid bare melting Earth's elements in the heat.[3] This is the first stage. The second stage is God's provision of the New Earth as foretold. The first earth has to go before God can dwell on earth as told that he will.[4]

God has already made a new earth! John saw the New Earth in a "forelook", which came down from heaven. God has also made a new heaven, a new Jerusalem.[5]

We can depend on that because it is described by God to us!

The End

1. "EMP is one of a small number of threats that can hold our society at risk of catastrophic consequences. EMP is triggered by the detonation of a nuclear weapon at a high altitude over the earth. As a result of this detonation, an electromagnetic field radiates down to the earth creating powerful electrical currents."

   "These fields cause widespread damage to electrical systems—the lifeblood of a modern society like the U.S. In turn, the damaged electrical systems can cause a cascade of failures throughout the broader infrastructure because the electrical power grid will simply become non-existent thereby blanking out the banking systems, energy systems, transportations systems, food production and delivery systems, water systems, emergency services, and...perhaps most damaging...cyberspace—the internet and all communication apparatus, wired and wireless phones."

   "Effectively, the U.S. would be thrown back to the pre-industrial age following a widespread EMP attack." "The United States is unprepared for an EMP attack."

   According to Baker Spring, a recognized authority on EMP preparedness, "This report was augmented in 2008 with a follow-up commissioned report. It clearly stated the fact that the U.S. has done nothing, except militarily, about EMP and no doubt will continue to do nothing about it in the future due to congressional neglect of providing adequate attention and funding."

2. The scenario of the EMP in the story of "The Beast of Babylon" plays a significant role as a tool to be used by the Antichrist and the False Prophet to keep people throughout the entire world under his control. Further, the Antichrist utilizes satellite technology as the launching site, placing them in space to detonate nuclear devices to cause EMP blasts at his will. This is in addition to current emphasis upon earth launchings and focusing on timely destruction of an enemy's EMP rocket launchings during liftoff before being airborne.

3. Of special note, God does not require or need man to assist him in his wrath of the Six Seals, Six Trumpets, and Seven Bowl Judgments with nuclear explosions or modern warfare or technology. God is god and the creator. Satan on the other hand does require man's help. Any evil machinery and apparatus he can get his hands on, so much the better for him. Satan is not the creator; he is only the imitator and master of deceit. He will use technology, psychology, and neurological manipulation further than anyone thought possible or can even, today, imagine!

11   1   "A city built on seven hills." Can this be Rome? The author thinks not. Many prophecy scholars consider the *seven hills* to represent seven kings that "the woman" controls (Scripture says "is her residence" or "residing in"). Verse 10 implies terms of power: "Five have already fallen, one is, and another is to follow."

2   Rev. 17 and 18. This Scripture reveals numerous characteristics of Babylon that must precede its ruin before it can be destroyed. Its commerce and its maritime trade become a significant world player, and its reputation for sensual pleasures requires certain elements, features, and enticements for any city to be as influential as these passages indicate. Reading closely, a tremendous amount of infrastructure must exist to substantiate such a city. The more one reads these verses, the more many things are understood about this.

2   Rev. 18:17–19. Babylon will be the commerce center of the world with an enormous maritime volume of trade. Today's topography of the Euphrates River makes such maritime navigation impossible between Babylon and the Gulf. It is imagined that during the construction of the new Babylon City, the canal will also be built by the Antichrist's design and leadership.

3   Conjecture.   Speed is of the essence for Babylon's prophecy to be fulfilled because there is only four to six years for an entire city to be functional starting from scratch. Therefore, the height of structures is limited to forty-five

feet because one-third of the height of any must be under-ground to provide a safe foundation. There simply is not enough time to go down before building upward.

4   Rev. 18:11. A point often overlooked. The Scripture says "merchants *of the world*" weep and mourn because their cargoes cannot be sold. It does not say "*merchants of Babylon.*" Verse 11 can only be interpreted exactly as what it says. The entire earth's business suffers with the loss of Babylon. So it must first possess lavish wealth, control, and prosperity before a loss of this magnitude as described can occur!

13   1   CIA International Factbook Report 2012
23   1   1

24   1   Ezekiel 38 and 39
     2   Psalms 83
     3   Ezekiel 39:2
     4   Ezekiel 39:9–10
     5   Ezekiel 39:2
     6   Ezekiel 39:18
     7   Ezekiel 38:9, 16
     8   Ezekiel 38:19
     9   Ezekiel 38:20, 21
    10   Ezekiel 38:22
    11   Ezekiel 38:22
    12   Ezekiel 39:17–22
    13   Ezekiel 39:4

31   1

34   1   Rev. 7:4
     2   Rev. 7:4

38   1   Rev. 6:1
     2   Rev. 6:2
     3   Rev. 6:3

4   Rev. 6:5

5   Rev. 6:7

6   Conjecture: It is highly possible the "wild beasts" with nearly three billion people being killed and the severe famine throughout the world, rats are most likely to infest the world, carrying diseases as in the 1700s bubonic plague. In a famine so severe that food must be rationed to levels of starvation, animals cannot survive. However, rats can obtain the liquid and meat they need from the blood and flesh of a recently dead human. The results of the fourth horseman are not a pretty picture.

7   Rev. 6:7. Twenty-five percent of the earth are killed; an estimated 2 billion, 750 million (refer to World's Population chart); consider the repulsive stench and the awful logistics of being among 2 *billion, 750 million* corpses rotting before being burned or buried in mass graves!

8   Rev. 6:12

9   Rev. 6:12

10   Rev. 6:13

11   Rev. 6:14

12   Eph. 2:2

13   Jer. 4:24

14   Rev. 6:15, 16

40   1

     2

     3

43   1

     2

     3

     4

46   1   Revelation 7:12

     2   Revelation 7:12–14

     3   Revelation 7:16

ALPHABETICAL LIST OF REFERENCES

Title	Author	Publisher	Year
23 Minutes in Hell	Bill Wiese	Charisma House	2006
40 Days through Revelation	Ron Rhodes	Harvest House	2011
A to Z Guide to Biblical Prophecy	Hays, Duvall, Pate	Zondervan	2007
All Things New: A Study of Revelation	Arthur E. Bloomfield	Bethany Fellowship	1959
Book of Revelation (Bible Book Set)	William R. Newell	Moody Press	1935
China, Inc. (Challenges to the World and USA)	Ted C. Fishman	Scribner	2006
Countdown (of the World's Population)	Alan Weisman	Little, Brown, Co.	2013
Financial Armageddon	John Hagee	Front Line	1987
Game Plan	Kevin D. Freeman	Regnery Publishing	2014
Heaven	Randy Alcorn	Tyndale House	2004
Hidden Persuaders	Vance Packard	Ig Publishing	2007
How to Make a Zombie	Frank Swain	One World Publications	2011
Iran / Israel	Mark Hitchcock	Harvest House	2013
Jesus Is Coming Middle East	William Blackstone	Kregel Publications	1989
NT Commentary: Revelation	John McArthur	Moody Press	1999

One Nation, Under Attack	Grant R. Jeffery	Waterbrook Press	2012
The Coming Financial Armageddon	David Jeremiah	FaithWords	2010
The End	Mark Hitchcock	Tyndale House	2012
The End Times in Chronological Order	Ron Rhodes	Harvest House	2012
The Israel Lobby and US Foreign Policy	Mearsheimer & Walt	Farrar, Straus, Giroux	2007
The Manipulated Mind	Denise Winn	Malor Books	2000
Unlocking the Last Days	Jeff Lasseigne	Baker Publishing	2011
War Play	Corey Mead	HMH Publishing	2013
What Every American Should Know about Population Growth	Melissa Rossi	Plume Books	2008
What in the World Is Going On?	David Jeremiah	Thomas Nelson	2008
Who Is the Antichrist?	Mark Hitchcock	Harvest House	2011

NOTE: All Scripture references and quotations are NIV (New International Version), unless specifically referred to otherwise. KJV is the King James Version.

ABOUT THE AUTHOR

The author is a lifelong evangelical Christian, who at sixty-five years old began an ardent study of the Book of Revelation. Understanding of Revelation was a result of prayerful guidance by the Holy Spirit during his study, only to conclude that there is a lot of wiggle room for interpretations of how the prophecies will be fulfilled, while being precise as to what and the chronology they will take place! The author is merely an active layperson whom God called to write and provided the gift of this ability late in his life, making no claim to be an authority on the Book of Revelation.

He lives in Deming, Washington, with his wife on a pristine sixty-acre farm shared by six Percheron draft horses.

CPSIA information can be obtained
at www.ICGtesting.com
Printed in the USA
LVHW051613040322
712646LV00007B/369

9 781098 003081